PAYBACK

PAYBACK

A DI Charley Mann Novel

R.C. Bridgestock

THE
DOME
PRESS

Published by The Dome Press, 2020
Copyright © R.C. Bridgestock 2020
The moral right of RC Bridgestock to be recognised as the author
of this work has been asserted in accordance with the
Copyright, Designs and Patents Act 1988.

This is a work of fiction. All characters, organisations and events portrayed in
this novel are either products of the author's imagination or are used
fictitiously.

A CIP catalogue record for this book is available from the British Library

ISBN: 9781912534173

The Dome Press
23 Cecil Court
London WC2N 4EZ

www.thedomepress.com

Printed and bound in Great Britain by Clays Ltd, Elcograf S.p.A.

Typeset in Garamond by Elaine Sharples

To our family, who lived with us through the
real crime and support us in fiction.

For law-enforcement officers – the true heroes –
who strive for justice for victims and their families.

CHAPTER 1

Charley knew almost nothing about the woman who had married her childhood sweetheart so soon after Charley's departure, except what she had seen on Facebook. When the woman's pictures started constantly showing sunnier climes, Charley guessed that the happy couple had emigrated to start a new life. She was relieved – especially when she heard the news that she was going to be transferred home.

What was odd, though, was that Charley's ex was conspicuous by his absence on social media. It was especially puzzling given that his line of work normally required its considerable use.

She couldn't remember ever not having trusted Danny. Older than her, and living on the neighbouring farm, he had taught her to climb trees and hurdle walls. He had soothed her when she tumbled. It was Danny who'd shielded her eyes when his father drowned the injured farm cat who was about to have kittens; Danny who'd wiped her tears when lambs were stillborn; Danny who disposed of the bodies of the dead animals they came across in the woods with respect and decency, always noting the place with a handmade wooden cross, sometimes made from lollipop sticks. They'd tickled trout together in the river and he'd shown her how to gut the fish so they could be cooked and eaten on a fire he built. Living alone with his dad on the farm after his mother left had taught him self-sufficiency at a very young age.

Danny had never failed her while she was growing up. One day he had appeared out of nowhere like an avenging angel to deal with Colin Jenkins, who had lured the unsuspecting Charley behind the bike shed. She'd watched in awe as Danny dragged the would-be Casanova to his feet and beat the much larger boy until he ran off snivelling. Danny Ray had been her safe pair of hands. He'd played the tough guy at school, but to her he was a protector. He had an innate ability to soothe her, assuring her he would always be there – and he always was…

When Danny had got a paper round, he'd saved for a whole year to buy her a season ticket for his beloved Town so she could go with him. She went as often as she could – she did love football, after all – but Sunday was also the only day she could see her best friend Kristine and ride the horses, the other love of her life, so she could never make all the games. Danny didn't seem to mind, at first, but when the girls entered local horse championships, and visits to the games got fewer, he started to seem less happy about it. Sometimes even angry…

As they got older, Charley became quite capable of looking after herself. She conspired with Kristine to apply to join the police force, like Kristine's father, and they applied together. Charley had always been interested in the police. She wanted to work with people and do one of the things she loved best: help those who were less fortunate than herself. She loved her home town, but even she could see that in many ways it was declining. She wanted to help stop that. Something – she wasn't sure what – made her hold back from telling Danny about her plans.

When she and Kristine had both been accepted, Charley had been surprised by the strength of Danny's reaction. He'd yelled and accused her of going behind his back. He didn't want her to go away for training. He seemed jealous of her new prospects and resentful that she didn't need him any more. Then, when she backed away, he professed undying love, hoping to persuade her to change her mind.

'Anyway,' he had said smugly a few days later. 'You can't be a copper because you're a thief!'

Charley had looked at him, puzzled.

'Don't you remember we stole that bar of chocolate that you wanted so much?'

'I was nine years old,' she replied. 'And I didn't steal it, you did!'

'Ah, but you were with me when I stole it for you, and that makes you an accomplice to the crime.'

Charley protested. 'I was under the age of criminal responsibility.'

When his argument was lost, he didn't leave it there.

'Who else would have lied for you just so that you could pursue your dream?'

Charley rolled her eyes. 'Not that old nugget.'

'I never told a single soul that you were with me the night I stole a police car… Well, not yet anyhow.'

'What on earth are you talking about?' she'd asked, horrified.

He grinned, though it was more of a grimace.

'Since when did you stop being able to take a joke? I'll be a reporter and isn't it every reporter's dream to have a cop as a girlfriend?'

Still, Charley was puzzled, finding it hard to follow his train of thought. 'Why?'

His smile was wide. 'Well. For one thing, you could give me the low down on all those juicy crimes.'

She'd been prepared to miss Danny when she was told she had to move to London on her promotion to detective sergeant. Nothing could prepare her for his behavior, though, when she tried to say goodbye. London was a big, lonely, frightening, intimidating place to Charley the country bumpkin and her loneliness was made worse by the horrible break with Danny.

At first Charley had just wanted to forget what had happened. She couldn't understand it and she couldn't deal with it. The only way she'd found to cope at all was to let the whole relationship die, because Danny's actions that night had led Charley to believe she had never known the real Danny Ray at all.

Four years had passed since then and Charley was now seated at a table by the bay window of the village bistro, a finger vase of flowers arranged in a drooping bouquet upon the red-and-white checked tablecloth. She was staring into space, drumming on the tabletop with graceful fingers, excited to be meeting her best friend again and hungry to hear the local news.

'Just like old times,' said Kristine sweetly, placing a hand gently on her shoulder.

Coming out of her deep reverie with a jolt, Charley looked at Kristine and breathed in the coveted smell of horses that emanated from her; she had obviously come straight from the stables. The palm of Charley's hand tingled at the memory of the muzzle of a horse seeking the Polo mint she held in her pocket between finger and thumb. Instantly the smile fell from her face. 'Except in the old days you weren't in a wheelchair and Eddie was here…' Instinctively, her hand went to the golden horseshoe hanging from a chain around her turtle neck jumper. It felt warm and reassuring to her touch.

Kristine's face turned momentarily glum. 'Touché!'

The pair chatted for a while and sipped coffee; the waiter brought them muffins. 'I wouldn't chuck him out of bed for burping out the wrong end,' said Kristine, nodding her head in the retreating waiter's direction.

Charley giggled. 'I'm glad to see you haven't changed.'

Kristine peeled the baking case from her muffin. She took a big bite and chewed while she talked. 'Tell me, how do you feel about seeing Danny Ray again?' she asked.

Charley froze. 'Why? Is he visiting his dad?'

Kristine took another bite and washed down the mouthful of muffin with a swig of coffee. 'Visiting? Didn't you hear the news? He and his wife separated not long after their marriage. She emigrated.'

'So, he's still living *here*?'

Kristine saw the look of panic on Charley's face.

Charley lowered her eyes and shrugged her shoulders. She took a deep breath. 'Last night I dreamt you and I were on parade, in uniform, at the Palace ... I was riding Eddie...' Her eyes prickled with tears and she closed them to keep from crying, 'and you, Wilson.'

It was obvious to Kristine how shaken her best friend had been by her horse's death.

'I'm just as unhappy as you are, though I don't let everyone see it.' Kristine reached out for Charley's hand and squeezed it tightly, hoping to reassure her. 'There was nothing to be gained by coming home at the time, but there is something you can do now you're back. Help me find the person responsible for his death and bring them to justice. Come to the stables – soon.'

Charley nodded her head. 'I will, I promise.'

Kristine called the waiter over and ordered a bottle of wine. The waiter returned with an ice-filled bucket, two glasses and a towel-wrapped bottle. He showed the label to Kristine and she questioned Charley's approval with a tilt of her head.

Kristine raised her eyebrows. Her lips curled up at the corners. 'How long have you been back? Two days? You don't waste much time, do you!'

'I've been eating here while I arrange my little life, that's all,' Charley said, with a deep sigh.

A grin spread across Kristine's face, brightening up the whole room. 'Yeah, I believe you, thousands wouldn't!' Her big green eyes were teasing. 'Remember I've known you since I was knee-high to a grasshopper. I've got you sussed, mi'lady.'

'That saves me time explaining then...' said Charley.

Kristine was curious at the flush that appeared on Charley's cheeks. She chuckled and held her arms wide. 'Come here, give us a hug. I'm so glad to have you back, Charley Mann. Boy, I've missed you.'

Charley's eyes suddenly lit up and when a warm feeling flushed through her veins, tears threatened. 'And I've missed you, too, and the horses ... It was all very well being promoted, but to be seconded immediately to a big city, apparently to help further my career, was definitely life-changing!'

Again, Kristine was curious. 'Why?'

'The clubs and bars – let's say they are a bit different from those we're used to round here.'

'What, you mean no bingo and meat raffles on a Sunday afternoon like in The Mechanics?'

It was Charley's turn to chuckle. 'No, it was cocktails and as much champagne as I could decently neck on my weekends off. And the characters I met…' Charley cocked an eyebrow. 'I've certainly had my eyes opened, let me tell you.'

Kristine looked sad. 'You sound like you enjoyed yourself too much. Tell me you're not going back?'

Charley shook her head. 'Not if I can help it. There's no place like home. There were days when, if I could've put on my ruby slippers, clicked my heels three times and been back here where my heart is, I would have, in a flash.'

'I could tell from your messages that it wasn't all sweetness and light, even though you got the perfect job in the mounted section. But it can't have been that bad. As much champagne as you could neck? You'd have to get married up here to sample the good stuff.' Kristine's tone became conspiratorial. 'I'd love to hear all about what you got up to. You've no idea what it's like being stuck in this chair, having to rely on my friends for entertainment. Come on, Charley, do tell. And don't spare the details, especially the juicy ones! I think my ticker can take it.'

Charley's toes were icy. Her feet, still damp from the shower, were bare as she crossed the bathroom's worn wooden floorboards. She wondered briefly if it was true what people said, that time was a healer; it didn't appear to be changing the way she felt. But what she did know to be true was that what didn't kill you made you stronger. At the sink, she turned on the tap, and while she waited for the water to run hot, she stared at her reflection in the mirror. Her fingertips gently stroked her lips, which still held faint traces of scarlet lipstick.

Monday morning. She was tired, and with good reason. It had been one hell of a weekend revisiting her old haunts and sampling new drinking holes – and she'd drunk too much. The Bar Amsterdam didn't call last orders. Instead, when most sensible drinkers would be heading back to their beds, Charley had been delighted to see the lights dimming for the first of several 'acts'. Dressed to the nines, Charley had blended in with the hookers and scammers, and knew she would never be recognised. She liked the anonymity this gave her, especially here, back in her home town.

Brought back to the present by the slamming of a door, Charley looked around her bedroom. She shivered and peered for a moment through the window into the yard of the terraced houses opposite. With one puffy eye on the wardrobe mirror she tugged at the roots of her wet hair with a fine-toothed comb. With gel applied, the colour appeared several shades darker than her natural blonde, and it pleased her. She leaned forward to get a closer look and stroked her widow's peak with one finger. She heard the voice of her late mother in her ear.

'A dominant trait that my girl!'

In her mind's eye, her late father, Jack, raised his brow. 'And I wonder where she gets that from, Ada?' A mischievous twinkle was never far from his eyes.

Charley could see him now, as though he were sitting before her at the kitchen table, peering at her over his half-rimmed glasses.

'I'd watch out if I were you, Jack.' Her mother scowled, and growled the words out of the corner of her mouth. 'They say us with a widow's peak are destined for early widowhood.'

Charley and her father chuckled at her mother, always the serious one of the three.

Charley lowered her eyes to the floor, clenched her teeth and curled her toes into the soft, shag pile carpet as she scraped her locks back into a tight bun that sat at the base of her neck – a habit born from her uniform days. One thing was certain, there would be no early widowhood for Charley, because she had no intention of ever tying the knot.

Her mind wandered back to the weekend as she dressed. After four years away, she realised, her return brought about as much excitement as it did trepidation. The closing of shops on the high street, which she had been dismayed to see when she had briefly returned for her mother's, and then her father's, funerals, had resulted in its reinvention, the being knocked down simply an invitation to get up and stand taller. And that, she now acknowledged, could be said for the town's entire history. Looking down the main street, eating options were so varied it was impossible, it seemed, for the locals to make recommendations. The same could be said for the pubs and the clubs. Nowhere in the UK, she had been proud to read, had reinvented itself so successfully as Huddersfield. She had found the Bar Amsterdam entertaining: as the party atmosphere had grown louder and more brash, there had been no dash to the bar for the last drink, or prolonged arguments for the next half hour – as in an ordinary pub – as the landlord tried to prise drinks from the customers' hands with a 'have you no bloody homes to go to?' Instead there had been a rush of activity to down the last drinks and return the glasses as quickly as possible, for as soon as the bar and security staff gave the nod that all the glasses had been cleared from the tables, the lights dimmed, a huge cheer went up from the crowd and a theatre spotlight illuminated the place into which stepped the first act.

Ruby was light-skinned, with a rounded, firm arse and small breasts – if you could call them that when they were actually the result of domed foam inserts. She had a cute nose and her naturally long, dark eyelashes framed the most striking green eyes, which roved up and down Charley's frame as she walked elegantly down the precarious wooden steps in six-inch, bejewelled heels. When she slipped, Charley had been quick-witted enough to catch her at the bottom.

'*Mon ange,*' Ruby said, a short while later, with a hand held over her heart. 'I don't wish to be mean…' she pursed her perfectly painted, full Cupid's bow lips at Charley as she was offered a glass of water that was quickly replaced by a brandy Alexander from an admirer, for which she proffered a 'see you later, darling' and a wink, '…but if you want to make serious money, you're gonna have to do better than that, sweetheart.' Ruby could easily have passed for a woman. Her voice sounded chemical-burned and raspy in Charley's ear.

''Scuse me?' Charley said, with attitude. Charley smoothed her knee-length, red-velvet dress with the flattened palm of her hand down her right hip and looked down at her black, seven-denier-stockinged toes that she had carefully slid into kitten-heeled, patent shoes earlier. Seeing jealousy flash across Ruby's face, a tingle travelled up Charley's spine.

'If you want the boys to notice you, you need to show a bit of flesh, loosen up,' Ruby said, with a swaying of her shoulders and provocative roll of the hips. Her eyes sparkled, though her smile was tight from the chemicals used to paralyse the muscles that were pulling down her jaw. She wore a tight skirt and an off-the-shoulder blouse to complement the serious heels. Her make-up was applied with skill and it looked good.

'Tell me, how much do you make?' Charley was genuinely interested. What type of weirdos picked up transgender prostitutes?

Ruby paused and then a mischievous look lit her eyes. 'Well, now. That depends. On average about five hundred a night. You?' She took a dainty sip of her exquisite cocktail, without taking her eyes off Charley.

Charley cleared her throat, hoping the shock on her face wouldn't register with her new-found friend.

'Hey look, I don't fuck half of the men who pick me up and, hell, most of the time I get my dick sucked,' she said, throwing her head back and the remainder of the cocktail down her neck.

Charley didn't know why it shocked her to hear Ruby say she had a dick, but it did.

'So, straight men actually set out to pick up …? I mean, the stories of transgender women picking up unsuspecting straight guys and surprising them when they get intimate have become urban legends.'

It was Ruby's turn to scoff. She put her hand to her face, threw her head back once more and this time laughed out loud. 'Baby, they absolutely love us! We get more business than you could ever dream of.' She nudged Charley playfully with a bony elbow. 'You ought to come out equipped with a dick,' she said, with half a wink. 'I'll show you a good time.'

Charley tried to hide her shock once again. 'Do you have a pimp?' she asked, spurred on by a genuine interest and a liking for Ruby.

'Some do. Not many, though. We regulate ourselves on the whole. I mean, do I look like the type that'd give half my hard-earned cash away?'

Charley shook her head. 'I figured as much. Females have pimps for a variety of reasons, but mostly for protection, I guess.'

'Exactly! Oh, and by the way – just for the record – those of us who are of sound mind would never pull a stunt the way legend would have you believe.' She drew a pointed, vivid pink, painted nail across her throat. 'I'd be dead by now. It's a fact.'

'You ever get arrested?' Charley asked.

Ruby frowned. 'You sound like a cop and I should know. My dad was one.' She looked over her shoulder at a good-looking, suited, dark-haired man who was walking towards them with a wide smile.

'Now, that's what I call eye-candy. He's a salesman if ever I saw one, and he's all yours,' said Ruby, before being swept off by another. Her presence was required: payback for the cocktail.

When they'd moved from the farm, the house Charley's parents had bought and which she had subsequently inherited was a Victorian terrace. At the back, yards formed a grid. Her bedroom looked across the street towards a small playground, the view so familiar, yet the emptiness surreal. She sighed as she watched a hooded youth race around the corner and launch himself over a wall into next door's small front garden. A uniformed police officer, his helmet discarded, suddenly appeared, the scene reminiscent of a cop chase from the silent movies of a bygone age. Scratching his head, the officer stood in the middle of the road, looking and listening. Crouched and unmoving, the absconder peered through the hedge. Charley looked up to the sky as she heard a helicopter, low overhead, searching.

'This is Detective Inspector Charley Mann.' She spoke into her mobile phone, her eyes fixed on the runaway. 'The person you're looking for is hiding in the front garden of number 22, Beatrice Avenue.' Her voice was monotone. Information dispatched, she laced her black leather brogues, picked up her satchel and descended the stairs. There was no need, or indeed desire, to put on any make-up for work. Charley knew who she was. She was confident in both herself and her ability in what, she was aware, was still deemed by some to be a man's world.

When she opened the front door, she was greeted by a raucous frenzy. The hooded prisoner shouted abuse at his captor. Handcuffed, he kicked out whilst being unceremoniously frog-marched to the marked police car. The driver acknowledged Charley with a nod of his head and the prisoner promptly spat at her feet. She calmly stepped sideways. She didn't want to fight. She didn't need to prove anything to him or to anyone else. Charley Mann knew that she could kill him with a punch if she wanted to.

The sun was peeping over distant hills, creeping slowly into a pale blue sky as she travelled down from the well-defined terrace in the hillside. A freezing mist hovered and hung like a low cloud above the lowlands, before slowly evaporating to reveal the bow-shaped village basin of Marsden. It was early January, yet they hadn't seen snow this year.

'It's too cold to snow,' she'd heard the elders of the village say. Perhaps they were right, but winter was far from over according to the weather forecasters.

Slowly and carefully, she traversed the steep, narrow road, hugged by dry-stone walls, to the west of the mill and terminating in the main street. The view changed with the seasons and never ceased to take her breath away. She'd dreamed often of this mesmerising landscape – her childhood playground.

Once on the road that ran through the village, it felt a coat warmer. She opened her car window and breathed deeply, allowing the crisp, fresh air to fill her lungs. Charley caught a glimpse of her ice-blue eyes in her rear-view mirror. Spread out on the back seat was her riding gear. The pain the sight generated was as acute now as it had been when Kristine had rung to inform her of her police horse's death.

'The operator of the drone flying in restricted airspace hasn't yet come forward. CCTV footage shows Eddie looking spooked in the paddock,' Kristine had said. 'He vaulted over a fence and collided with a wooden post. There was nothing anyone could do...'

Tears clouded Charley's vision at the memory. If only she hadn't gone away... Would Eddie still be waiting for her this morning when she got to work? Would the outcome of the investigation have been different? She frowned. What still puzzled her about the incident was that Eddie was used to the police helicopter taking off and landing nearby and had been trained to cope with loud noises. The incident had eventually been written off as an accident and, although drone parts had been found nearby days later, it didn't take them much further. Nor had the police appeals brought about a satisfying result. Over the years Charley had been away, nothing had happened to change her view: always trust animals more than people.

The view ahead was blocked by a truck waiting its turn to go under the railway bridge. It brought her back to the present. She was transfixed by the muddy waters pouring from the hillside and running, as if with a purpose, into the blackened mouth of the tunnel below. People walked past as the traffic waited. A hot and bothered woman with a child stopped on the pavement edge. The little girl, whose hand the woman held tightly, jumped mischievously off the kerb and instantly the woman swung her back by her scrawny arm. Her eyes were crinkled up with humour. She gave Charley a cheeky smile and poked out her tongue. Charley chuckled to herself, noting her buttons didn't match with the buttonholes on her coat and her bobble hat was about to pop off her head. She waved them across in front of her car with a sweep of her hand and they disappeared under the wooden entrance to the church which, it was rumoured, had been carved by one of her ancestors.

This place ... Nothing changed. That could have been her twenty years ago ... Memories of her childhood flooded back: the sepia pictures on Granny's mantel; Grandpa standing at that very spot on the Green, at the opposite side of the road. She smiled and looked around for the telegraph pole she knew to be next to the church, where he had rested an elbow, such was the height of the snow drifts that year. Her eyes sought the memorial garden where his team had leant on the shafts of several large axes, shirt sleeves rolled up, tin mugs in dirty hands, a break from chopping away at the icicles hung from ceiling to railway track, the steam train stationary, waiting patiently for them to clear its path.

'Tha's n'er seen *proper* snow, lass,' he'd say, year upon year, as he sat her down on his chair by the fire to pull off her Wellington boots. On their return from herding the cattle she'd snuggle into a rainbow-coloured crocheted blanket made from unpicked, damaged or outgrown woollen garments, which her granny had warmed by the coal fire. Instinctively she yawned, as she recalled the comforting feeling that had flowed through her body.

The spell was broken by the roar of the engine belonging to the vehicle in front. Charley adjusted her sitting position and shifted her gear stick. Her ancestors hadn't been quitters and neither was she – they'd made sure of that in her upbringing.

Harsh as the weather had been in winter on the farm, she had fond childhood memories of building snowmen and making igloos, and having snowball fights with Danny from the neighbouring farm, rolling around in the snow until her clothes were soaking wet. Grandpa was right, she hadn't experienced the depth of snow he had, nor did she want to. She preferred the warmth of the summer sun. Short as the season could be in the North, it was one that turned the moorland she knew into a wonderful welcoming terrain for picnicking, tree swings, jumping the stones on the waterfall in the hillside and swimming in the brooks.

From the railway bridge, her twenty-minute journey took her past the old pasture fields and the wilder moorland, grazed by sheep, cattle and horses, and into the town of Huddersfield, where Peel Street police station headquarters was located, some seven miles from Marsden.

It was seven thirty a.m. when Charley arrived at Peel Street – the twenty-nine-year old's first day as head of CID.

She took a moment to stand before the great glass doors and look above them to the Force crest. She took a deep breath, drew her shoulders back and stepped forward. The action prompted the doors to glide silently open and, before she knew it, she was presenting herself at the front desk. Her smile was wide.

'How's it going, Marty, my old fruitcake?' she asked the front desk sergeant who appeared as if by magic from behind the screen.

'By 'eck lass,' he said, showing a parade of uneven, yellowing teeth. 'It seems like only yesterday you were stood right there in yer T-shirt and shorts after a nine-mile run and a kick-boxing class, to start yer first shift here as a rookie.' He raised an eyebrow and gave a slight nod of his head. 'Got tongues wagging that did, all right.' His bright eyes clouded over. 'And then, o' course, you had to go and upset a few of 'em upstairs, according to the rumour squad. Where've yer bin? I heard on the grapevine you were seconded on a secret squirrel job; police corruption jobby, weren't it?'

'Aye, they sent me down to the big smoke, but like Dad always told me, there's always a positive. I learnt a lot in the city and now I'm back; older and a lot wiser, that's for sure.'

Marty's face took on a serious expression and he beckoned her closer. 'Do something for old Marty, will yer?' he whispered in her ear. 'Keep yer head down, yer mouth shut and watch yer back this time, eh?'

Charley winked at the old-timer. 'I'm not here to be liked; I'm here to do a job. And no matter what it takes, I'm going to do it.'

Marty shook his head and gave a little sigh. 'Well, I've gotta say, lass, the place hasn't been the same without you. I, for one, am glad to have you back, and I know our Winnie will be, too. You'll be pleased to see we've a new custody suite. If I recall rightly, when I worked in the cells there was never an empty one on Charley Mann's shift.'

At the press of a button, Marty Webb automatically unlocked the internal door. Charley slapped the steel plate with the flat of her hand when the buzzer sounded its unlocking. The adrenalin rush that soared through her body as she stepped over the threshold was huge, though it soon turned to apprehension as the door banged shut behind her with some finality; she was now officially on duty.

'She might look like a petite blonde, but I wouldn't want to be on the end of her right hook.' Marty nodded knowingly at his civilian colleague as he stepped into the back office. At the sound of his voice the young woman swivelled her chair to face him and he stepped over her feet to sit down at his desk. 'Her dad, Jack, he could have been a professional boxer if he hadn't been needed to run the family farm. He wanted a boy. Sad really.' He stopped and appeared thoughtful. A whimsical smile crossed his lips. 'By gum...' he paused for effect. 'I pulled him out o' many a scrap in my time – a bit of a lad was our Jack in his younger days.' His smile turned to a more serious look. 'Taught the lass everything he knew about the boxing, though.'

Marie-France looked amused.

Marty guffawed, tilting his head. 'Born weighing nigh on twelve pounds! Charley went straight into our little 'un's hand-me-downs and our Kristine were six months old at the time. Inseparable them two were, growing up. What with them having the horses in common, they're still best o' friends to this day.' Marty reached for his coffee cup and put it to his lips, but instead of taking a drink he sat back in his chair and cradled it in his hands as it rested on his round stomach. 'Charley worked as a bouncer in the pubs and clubs in Huddersfield before she joined up.'

'She's always worked around 'ere then?' asked Marie-France, her accent slipping into her adopted Yorkshire tongue.

'Kirklees, Calderdale as a detective constable. When she was promoted to detective sergeant, they shipped her off to work on an enquiry into police corruption in another county.'

Marie-France smiled and offered Marty a ginger biscuit. 'Bet she's glad to be back.'

He took a bite. 'Aye, especially as it's on promotion.' Marty dunked the remainder of his biscuit into his cup and chewed thoughtfully, pushing back his chair. 'It won't be easy for her, coming home.' He frowned. 'There were things going on around the time she left that we weren't privy to, but I heard she was in a bad way.'

'And she's not been back since?'

'Briefly, for her dad's funeral. Then Ada, her mum, died suddenly – of a broken heart, they said.'

'Do you think people really do die from a broken heart?'

'Dunno. I guess they must. Or maybe it's the shock that kills 'em. I think our Kristine thought she'd come home when Eddie died. But maybe she couldn't...'

Marie-France's eyes were wide open. '*Mince alors, pas son frère, aussi?*'

'No, her horse … Eddie was her police horse. Our Kristine was looking after him at the time. Spooked to death, they say he was.' A huge sigh escaped from his lips as he rose from his chair to go to the aid of the person ringing the front-counter bell.

'I guess she needs to face all the bad stuff, before she can move on,' Marty shuddered, involuntarily. 'Poor kid.'

Charley skipped up the steps, two at a time. She stood on the first landing for several seconds, gawking at the amazing view beyond the historic town buildings immediately in front of her, to the green rolling hills and valleys beyond. Suddenly, she remembered why she was there and her heart leapt with pure joy. This was the best feeling; to be chosen as the top detective in the place of her birth.

'Thank you, God,' she said, looking up at the bright blue sky through the long, high window. The winter sun passed through, and its warmth on her face felt like a welcome. She took a moment to survey her domain through the glass pane. As her eyes scanned the rooftops, the roads and the countryside, she recalled numerous traumatic scenes. There were people out there who wore extreme violence on their sleeves, but she had no desire to do any other job and she was ready for the challenge. Every day she'd worked in the city, she'd vowed to learn something new, something that would help her police her own town more efficiently and effectively. Now, as the senior investigating officer, she was at the cutting edge of major enquiries. All her life, Charley had pushed boundaries to their limit. If someone said she couldn't, it was like throwing down a gauntlet, a red rag to a bull, making her even more determined to succeed, especially where others had failed.

'Always try to look for the positive in everything,' had been her dad's words when she left, and she had continued to live by those words, hard as it had been at times. Last time she'd stood here she had been a broken woman – but now she was changed, her strength regained, and she was ready to face whatever lay ahead.

As she walked through the windowless corridors where the management resided, she noticed very quickly that there had been little change at Peel Street police station in her absence. The same names were on the locked doors. The smaller office housed the Divisional Commander's secretary, Becky, her old friend, who was deep in conversation on the telephone, in the cubbyhole. Approximately fifteen-feet long, six-feet high and about six-feet wide, the cubbyhole was in the centre of the arched room. It had been used as a stationery cupboard before becoming an office for a blind typist, Ruth Hollingshead. Her Labrador, Flora – no more than a youngster when Charley had left – lay by Ruth's side, surveying the newcomer at the door who had very obviously not been forgotten, judging by the vigorous wagging of her tail.

Walking through the CID office as the boss felt surreal. A couple of uniformed officers were standing at the water dispenser, so deep in conversation that they didn't turn their heads or even acknowledge her presence. She felt slightly disappointed that no one was there to greet her. Sure-footed, she continued across the large open space, marvelling at the new desks with their chairs neatly stored underneath, and with only upright computer screens on top, just waiting for the command to bring them to life. Their owners, however, were nowhere to be seen and Charley could only deduce that they were out interviewing, or – as good detectives should be – catching criminals; or were they merely avoiding the new boss?

She followed the ultra-modern storage cabinets that extended beyond the desks and lined the wall to her office. Then a large red arrow on the wall caught her eye. It pointed to the sign saying 'NIGHT REPORT', where details of the night's activities were left for the day team by uniform patrol.

'*Man in cells*,' she read. '*Lock-up by traffic patrols overnight. Driver arrested on suspicion of theft of a black Mercedes saloon. Car seized and presently situated in the back yard.*'

Even though the digital age had arrived, the handwritten report was still more practical.

The 'Detective Inspector' signage was in bold letters on a plaque in the middle of her half-glass door, under the window. The window had a tatty, homemade blind on the inside of the door. She stopped for a moment and stood with her hand on the cold metal door handle, reading the names of her staff and their duties that were written on the dry-wipe board. A couple of names on it were new to her, but most were as well known to her as the paintwork. Before opening the door, she peered into the dark abyss. A blast of warm, stale air hit her as she flung the door open and stepped inside. The room appeared just as unimpressive as her greeting had been. It was deceptively small – smaller than she remembered – and it hadn't been upgraded in the same way as the outer office. She looked at the large, black, leather executive chair that lorded it behind the solid wooden desk and the worn, red, cloth visitor's chair in front – the one she had sat on when she'd visited the already old, kindly then-SIO. When she'd told him she saw herself sitting behind his desk in the future, he hadn't discouraged her. 'Never assume,' he'd told her. 'That's the trick to solving a crime.'

Charley slid behind her desk and pushed the button to boot up the computer. The PC grumbled into action, announcing the home screen, but its brightness soon turned to dark as it cut out, her passwords yet to be verified by HQ. Immediately she picked up the phone and dialled the technical support extension number. When there was no answer, she looked up at the clock above the cork board and rolled her eyes. Technical support would be better called at a later hour perhaps ...

Impatiently, and with nothing else she could do in the office until she had resolved the computer issue, she splayed her hands on the desk and slid from behind it. The newspaper clippings pinned to the cork board on the opposite wall drew her towards them, turning her thoughts to the controversy regarding the police station's new custody suite Marty had spoken about. The cells, which had been recently upgraded to meet with health and safety regulation demands, were reported to have cost a mint and it appeared that the locals weren't best pleased, according to the headlines in the local press. She understood it was hard for anyone to accept the lack of police officers on the streets, and to see the huge amount of money spent on refurbishing a facility to make it more comfortable for the wrong-doer, but she was well aware that the money allocated had never been in the manpower budget in the first place. Damn it, it was hard enough for her to accept the fact that funds were unavailable for extra personnel. It would leave her no option but to ask her staff to work for the love of the job, or for time off in the future, just to get necessary work done. Her sigh was audible. How could anyone put a price on catching a murderer? Charley would never be able to get her head around that.

Heading towards the custody suite she knew she would let curiosity get the better of her, forcing her to take a look at the person her officers would be speaking to after his overnight arrest. In a way, it was a shame that the cells had been upgraded, she pondered, as her feet tap-tapped down the tiled steps. Those very cells had seen many a 'cough' to her from a criminal; simply because they didn't want to spend a minute longer than they had to in the damp, stark, stone confinement. She pressed the button on the lower corridor wall, to the left of the custody suite door and, with only a moment's delay, entry was permitted at the showing of her ID to the CCTV camera.

On the sounding of a buzzer and the melodramatic clunk of the lock Charley was able to slide the cool, metal handle of the inner-sanctum gate to allow her to step over the threshold into an empty open space, where thick, foetid air met her. She smacked her lips together and screwed up her face and wafted her hand in front of it, to help dissipate the gasses as she walked towards the signposted custody suite. The smell was all but forgotten at the sound of murmuring voices that very quickly morphed into shouting, banging and laughing. Walking as if on a mission down the windowless corridor, she passed two empty interview rooms to her right, shoulder-barged a door and, this time, was met by a warren of cells. The banging came from within one, and the shouting from a drunken detainee at the end of the corridor, who appeared to have just head-butted the custody sergeant's desk. The smell, it seemed, had emanated from his subsequent projectile vomit and, as she then became aware, the fact that he was defecating on the floor.

Charley stopped in her tracks and stood at the partially open door of the small kitchenette from where she discovered the laughter was coming. A police constable, partially hidden inside, was talking on his mobile phone, presumably to a colleague. From here, Charley could see directly above the stocky custody sergeant's head a large whiteboard with a list of cell numbers and the names of the prisoners who temporarily resided there. There was also space for any detainee's medical issues, officers' safety concerns and the reason the suspect had been arrested. The board was full of angular letters, blurred edits and multiple red warning marks. Many, she saw, had some kind of drink or drugs related medical condition; some were known to be violent. Beside cell M2 there were no warnings, just a name: Taylor Thomas. With the duty staff all otherwise occupied, Charley lifted the cell door hatch that housed the overnight arrest, took one look, and then a second, before letting the hatch slam shut with a bang.

Loud enough to wake the dead, the noise ricocheted off the chewing-gum white, shiny walls. With her heart threatening to beat out of her chest, Charley stood in the quietness of the corridor for a moment, her back to the wall, allowing the solid, cold structure to hold her upright.

It couldn't be? Was her mind playing tricks?

No, there was no denying it. On Saturday night, she had been in bed with the prisoner. 'A salesman,' Ruby had said, 'from London.'

'My arse,' she muttered, gasping for air.

Slipping as quietly as she could out of the cell area, she sneaked into the adjacent toilet. She grabbed hold of the sink, her knuckles white. The porcelain felt icy cold to her sweating palms.

A brief encounter; no commitment, was what he'd said, and what she'd wanted. 'Sex with no strings. Is that too much to frigging ask?' she questioned her reflection in the mirror.

She breathed in through her nose and slowly out through her mouth. Counting to ten with her eyes closed she threw back her head, looking to the ceiling. But hey, she thought, finally allowing her reflection a faint half-smile, he would never recognise the painted woman he'd slept with as the one looking back at her now in the mirror. Her pale, thin lips forming a straight line, she frowned: would he?

She shook her head. Nah!

But it wasn't worth the risk – she'd just have to make sure he didn't see her.

Walking back along the corridor with her shoulders back and head held high, she pondered her dad's advice always to look for the positive. 'Well, at least he was good in the sack…'

The little old lady, duster in hand, who stood aside for Charley to pass at the bottom of the stairs, looked at her questioningly. They smiled at each other pleasantly and the older woman declared loudly, 'Well, Charley Mann as I live and breathe. What a sight for sore eyes you are, my girl!'

Charley's appearance out of uniform was unusual to her and caused Winnie to scrutinise her closely with cloudy, narrowed, cataract-ridden eyes. She touched her arm affectionately and Charley bent down and hugged the buxom woman.

'Good God, Winnie! When the hell are you going to retire?'

Winnie's eyes were tearful. 'You know me. Part of the furniture. No doubt they'll carry me out of here in a box.'

Charley eyed her sceptically.

'Well, someone's got to look after you lot, haven't they?' Winnie's thick white brows knitted together and she grabbed Charley by the arm with an arthritic hand. 'I've been waiting for you.'

CHAPTER 2

Men have one-night stands without a second thought, Charley thought to herself, so why couldn't women do the same without being judged? She knew her professional credibility would be ruined if her secret was outed on the first day in her new role.

Now she sat at her office desk with a little apprehension as she awaited her scheduled 'welcome to the division' appointment with the Chief Superintendent. Maybe, just maybe, she should go back down to the cells and ask the prisoner what the fuck he thought he was doing, tell him who she was and watch his arse drop out? The thought caused her to smile, albeit briefly.

Absent-mindedly, Charley slid open her drawer to see someone had been diligent in supplying her with stationery. Taking a pen and a piece of paper, she drew a central line from top to bottom of the A4 sheet and began to scribble. On the left, she wrote the positives in the situation: the man in the cells didn't know her real name, or her occupation – she hadn't told him; the name she'd seen recorded on the night report hadn't rung any bells – so he hadn't told her his real name, either.

Her pen hovered over the opposite side of the line, now for the negatives ... But, instead of putting pen to paper, Charley put her head in her hands. She heard a loud moan and realised it had come from her. 'Oh, Jesus...'

Taking a deep breath she leaned back in her chair and cracked her knuckles, a habit she had inherited from her dad. She wheeled her chair away from her desk with the push of one foot, then decided against leaving and wheeled herself back in. If she confronted the prisoner, the team would be suspicious of the attention she was paying him, given the senior post she held; gone were the days when an officer could visit a prisoner without it being recorded on the detention sheet. Charley slammed the palm of her hand on the desk. 'For fuck's sake!' She hadn't intended to see him again – no further contact, no exchange of numbers, nothing; that was the point of one-night stands. It was easy to be invisible in London, but back here this had probably been bound to happen one day. The first day back on promotion, though? Jeez ... the timing could not have been more perfect for those who would love to watch her demise – and there were a few, as Marty had said; especially those who thought the job of detective inspector should have been theirs, and certainly not a woman's...

She watched her staff walk into the CID office from where she sat.

Detective Sergeant Mike Blake's team were the early shift, comprising old-timer Detective Constable Wilkie Connor, DC Ricky-Lee Lewis and, new to the division and to CID, Annie Glover, recently relocated from the south of England. The team were now all present, and with their heads down they appeared to Charley to be busy. They'd clocked her, that was a certainty, but no one had yet set foot over the threshold of her office. Charley took a deep breath and eased herself out of her chair. Propping her hand against the doorjamb, she leaned forward into the outer office.

'There's one still in the traps from overnight, Sergeant Blake: black Merc, back yard. Let's see if we can sort it and get rid asap.'

'DC Connor, can you deal? I've got to get these to court in...' Mike lifted his right arm to read the time on his watch. In his left hand he lifted from the top of his desk a collection of brown paper bags, with elongated windows through which showed exhibits '...five minutes. I'll catch you when I get back, ma'am,' he said, as he hurried towards the door, his free hand held high in a wave. 'Nice to have you back where you belong.'

Charley felt a glow of warmth spreading through her. It was nice to be back.

Wilkie Connor was sitting, reading the night report. 'Name doesn't ring a bell,' he said nonchalantly, turning up his nose at the banal task his supervisor had bestowed upon him.

'I don't mind dealing, ma'am,' Annie said, pushing aside her thick, blonde fringe with a jaunty smile. At six feet, Annie was the tallest of the group. Attractive, but gangly, with long, slim arms and legs, she wasn't model-perfect – she attempted to disguise her English pear shape by wearing a tunic over her trousers – but she had a finely chiselled face that was interesting rather than beautiful.

Charley shrugged a shoulder. 'I don't care who executes the action. Glean what you can about him and tell me when he's gone.'

'No probs. I'm on it.' Annie walked towards Charley and, leaning forward, looked left and right to make sure the others weren't listening. 'Like the eyebrow ring. It's cool.'

'I think the Chief Super might have something to say about it, though, don't you?' Charley said. The women exchanged a knowing look. 'They're not quite as accepting of things here as they are in the city.'

'Since when did it bother you what the hierarchy thinks?' Wilkie was as round as he was tall. His large, mischievous, brown eyes met hers. He undid the top button of his shirt, loosened his tie and plopped down on a chair behind the desk that Charley presumed was his, as he promptly opened the drawer and fumbled around inside. He smiled when he found what he was looking for – in what was, in fact, his colleague's desk – took out a tin and fiddled with its combination lock. When he opened it, his eyes widened to see the treasure within, which he promptly popped into his mouth. As he busied himself collecting crumbs from the container, it was snatched away and Charley became aware of a middle-aged woman, Ellen Tate – Tattie to her friends – who now stood in front of the desk she had claimed, next to the window, where she could place her beloved green plants on the windowsill. She had lipstick on her buck teeth and a nest of frizzy, sandy-coloured hair, pulled back from a remarkably wrinkle-free forehead, smooth mostly because of the tight hairdo.

Wilkie wriggled out of the chair. Mouth still full of cookie, he grinned a wide, toothy, chocolate grin at the normally quiet and inoffensive administrator who, having seen what he had done, looked at him with disbelief. In the moments that followed, his expression softened, sharply in contrast to the anger displayed on Ms Tate's face. If steam could come out of people's ears, Charley was sure it would have happened there and then.

'One day ... one day you'll get what's coming to you, just you wait and see,' Ms Tate hissed, grabbing the tin and clutching it to her chest.

'Hey, you know what they say, Wilkie. The quiet ones are the most dangerous,' said Annie. 'You'd better watch your step.'

'I'll get my own back. You see if I don't!' Ms Tate said.

Charley looked on, comfortable with the banter.

'At least you can tell when she's mad, which is more than you can say about you,' Wilkie said, nodding his head towards Annie.

Annie was clearly not intimidated. 'I've had Botox,' she whispered to Charley conspiratorially. 'I know this woman who does it cheap if you ever fancy a dabble.'

Charley frowned as she scrutinised Annie's facial features. 'Where?' Cheap Botox didn't sound good.

'Hebden Bridge.'

'No, she means where on your face, imbecile!' said Wilkie.

Annie giggled and pointed to the gap between her eyebrows and her crow's feet. She attempted a frown, but her eyebrows didn't move and it only left her looking angry. 'He's right,' she said with an attempt at a wink. 'My face gives nothing away these days. You should try it.' Annie prodded Wilkie Connor in the shoulder. 'And I suggest you mind your own!'

The administrator turned on her heels, slightly appeased by the reprimand Wilkie had been given, and headed towards the door of the kitchenette.

'When you standing us a drink to celebrate the promotion then, boss?' asked Ricky-Lee.

'Railway Inn still open for business?' Charley asked.

'Yeah, but there's no sawdust on the floor, or black pudding on the bar these days,' said Wilkie.

Charley pulled a face. 'Shame.'

The office phone rang and Annie picked up. Her grimace told Charley that Annie hadn't had Botox in her lips and lower jaw.

'Apparently, Roper the groper is ready for you,' she said, replacing the phone slowly.

Charley raised her eyebrows. 'See if you can behave in my absence, will you?' she said over her shoulder when she reached the door.

'Be careful. He's not changed while you've been gone,' Wilkie called after her. 'He's still a twat.'

Charley had reached the third floor when she heard someone calling her name. She stopped.

'Boss, we've got a body.'

The words that the senior investigating officer often heard in her sleep sent her into automatic pilot.

'What do we know so far, Annie?'

'The body – it's hanging from a tree.'

'And it's not thought to be a suicide?'

'Uniform think not, no. And there's something else you should know. It's not any old tree, it's the Bramley Elm.'

On duty for less than two hours and she'd already been called to take charge of what was deemed a suspicious death. She spun round to look directly into the eyes of her younger colleague. Adrenalin-laced hunger stared back. Those loitering on the landing looked at the pair with some curiosity as they turned and began to retrace their steps posthaste.

Annie followed her boss down the steps in double-quick time. Such was their haste those who passed by turned their heads to look after them asking the unspoken question, what's the rush?

'The English Elm tree, located at the north-west corner of the parish church graveyard.' Charley quoted the statistics verbatim. 'It stands thirty-three metres, fifty-two centimetres tall and has a diameter of one metre, forty-two centimetres. Named after James Benjamin Bramley, the local hangman who, according to local folklore, hanged many a villain for relatively minor offences, lawfully, from it.'

'What – in the church grounds?' Annie held open the door for her boss.

Charley forced a smile. 'Not exactly; just over the dry-stone wall.'

The door swung closed in their wake and Annie eagerly continued asking questions. 'What sort of crimes would the guilty hang for back then, do you think?' The corridor wider here, she was able to walk alongside Charley, matching step for step.

'You're presuming that they only hanged the guilty?' Charley's face showed a wry smile as she pulled open the door to the next corridor. The CID office was now in sight. 'During the eighteenth century, the death sentence could have been passed for picking pockets or stealing food.'

As they entered the CID office, there was already a palpable sense of urgency. Some staff hurried around with papers in hand, others were standing at the printers eagerly awaiting the information they spewed out, and the rest were either inputting data or on the phone. Each person in the room had a focus, a purpose, otherwise they wouldn't have been there.

The two women walked directly to the conference table from where Charley would soon be addressing the team. Charley sat and instinctively sought the return from court of her sergeant, as the evidence she would require for the briefing was brought to her.

'Mmm … How very clever of them,' Annie said thoughtfully as she also sat down, next to Charley.

'Who?'

'Those in charge of hanging people, of course.'

'Clever, how do you mean?' Charley said. 'Thankfully, we've moved on a long way in how we deal with prisoners.' Charley shuffled papers into a pile and tapped them on the desk to even them out. She suppressed a smile, took a deep breath and called for the others to join them at once. This was what being an SIO was all about, getting a job and running with it – grateful for the well-oiled cogs in the incident room wheel.

Annie went on, 'Yeah, but just think. The body of the guilty person could be shoved straight into a prepared grave if we still hanged 'em nearby. I say it's a pity we don't still do the same today. Save us a hell of a lot of time and money,' Annie said. 'No undertakers, no service, no wake…'

'In t'olden days the likes of you, Annie Glover, would've been classed as a scold,' said Wilkie, who had obviously been listening in to the conversation and now swivelled his chair round to join them.

'Who rattled your bloody cage?' Annie snapped back.

'A troublesome and angry woman, who by brawling and wrangling amongst her colleagues, breaks the public peace, increases discord and would be at the end of a ducking stool if it had anything to do with me.'

'God loves a trier … Why don't you fuck off!' retorted Annie, showing him a middle finger.

Wilkie chuckled. 'It'd be a foolproof way of establishing whether you really are a witch,' he said, through slitted eyes.

When Charley was a child, the hilltop church could be seen from afar at night, its illuminated cross a beacon shining down to protect the town below. Now, it was nothing more than a derelict shell: Nearer My God to Thee, being the reason Charley had considered in her youth. She'd latterly conceded it was more likely that the hilltops were difficult to till and thus less promising as farmland than the bottom land near the rivers and the creeks. As the land would originally have been donated by a landowner, a hilltop parcel would have been more expendable than valuable farmland.

She knew the old graveyard well. Once a meeting place for her and Danny in their youth, a stomping ground where they frightened each other almost to death with ghost stories and where he'd hide his treasure – a penknife, matches, rope and a scarf he said smelt like his mother. When Charley had needed a project for her history thesis it had been the place she'd chosen to research. Beyond its partly tumbledown, dry-stone walls, an overgrown and extended field was surrounded by moorland – it was still an enchanting place.

Paperwork held high in one hand, she banged the table with the other, stood and called for silence in the room, grateful to see Mike Blake appear just in time for the address – fully briefed, she hoped. If those present couldn't see her from where they sat, they moved, or stood. The sound of chairs being pulled nearer to the centre island, in order that their occupiers could hear what Charley was about to say, made a cringeworthy sound on the floor. When all was still, she began.

'OK, OK, anyone got anything else for me before we begin?' she asked. She looked around her. No reply, paperwork, or information was forthcoming. Heads were all turned in one direction, their focus solely on Charley. All was still. She turned to the sergeant. 'Mike?' she said. Mike nodded and stood. Charley sat and looked up at him, as eager as the others to hear what he knew.

'A woman was found dead this morning by a local farmer, Peter Stead, when he was out walking his dog,' he said, referring to his notes. 'He was the one to ring three nines from his mobile phone. At this time, he was also able to describe to the operator the scene he had come across.'

'Do we know what time that was?' said Charley.

'Around seven-thirty, ma'am. Uniform patrol is now on site as the first responder and they're requesting CID attendance.'

Pen in hand Charley scribbled notes on her writing pad.

'Life pronounced extinct by?'

'Paramedics.'

'Have they cut the body down?'

'No, they didn't want to disturb the scene. Apparently, it was quite obvious to them that the woman was dead, and the circumstances of her death had to be suspicious.'

A thousand thoughts fought for supremacy in Charley's mind as she stood up to conclude the briefing with instructions. Just minutes later she watched the fingers of her team dance instinctively across the keyboards, their eyes focused on their computers, flicking through various screens, ticking boxes, updating data – doing what they were trained to do. Ricky-Lee's hands, however, were raised over his mobile phone as he looked up to see her looking in his direction. He raised his eyebrows expectantly when their eyes met. She walked towards him

'I want you to deal with the one in the cells, instead of Annie,' she said. 'Quick as you can. I need you at the scene ASAP.'

Charley pointed to Mike and Wilkie as she walked towards her office. 'I want you two to take the firm's car and I'll see you at the scene pronto.' Murmurings grew in volume, in her wake, with an intensity that ran around the office.

'Ring the Commander's secretary and make my apologies will you please?' she called over her shoulder to Tattie. Her request was met with a nod of the head. 'As much as I was looking forward to the welcome back,' she mumbled out of the corner of her mouth as she passed Annie's chair.

Annie rolled her eyes and smiled knowingly. The younger woman looked up at Charley, her eyes brimming with excitement. 'I've never been to a murder scene,' she whispered. 'If that's what it is ... murder.'

It was Charley's turn to be surprised. 'Want to see how it's done?' she asked.

Annie nodded eagerly.

'You're with me,' Charley said with a wink of one eye.

Annie's eyes lit up still further. 'O.M.G! Thank you,' she mouthed.

There was a collective banging of drawers shut, rustling of paper, the printer spewing out yet more, a shout of 'Who had the firm's car keys last?' and a flinging of a pen across a desk to an awaiting Wilkie, who had beckoned it from Tattie.

Charley stopped briefly at her office door and turned to see the retreating figure of her second in command. 'Mike,' she called. Mike spun around on his heel and looked at her expectantly. 'Will you get hold of the scenes of crime supervisor, ask them to join us and tell them to bring a crime scene investigator?' DS Blake acknowledged her request with the raise of a hand.

The Commander might not be best pleased that she was postponing his invitation to meet and greet, or at the likelihood of there being a suspicious death on his patch to take up his limited resources, Charley thought as she entered her office, but he couldn't blame her, as much as he might want to lay a budget overspend at someone else's feet.

'OK, let's get this show on the road,' Charley shouted with an energy she'd got out of the habit of using. Her door was wide open and as she prepared to go to the scene she continued to shout out instructions, as thoughts for further immediate enquiries popped into her head. 'Annie, check intelligence to see if we have any females reported missing.' Charley put her pen to her lips and took it away immediately the next instruction sprang to mind. 'And you might care to check over the borders too – just in case: Derbyshire, Greater Manchester, Lancashire, North Yorkshire and South Yorkshire.' She checked the five counties off on her fingers.

An experienced copper, Charley Mann had worked on many murder enquiries, but that didn't mean that the hairs on the back of her neck hadn't risen, adrenaline wasn't pumping wildly through her veins, or that her heartbeat hadn't quickened at the thought of what lay ahead of her. She was no stranger to crime scenes – in her relatively short service she had dealt with a large variety of man's inhumanity to man and her approach had become somewhat routine – but Annie's announcement that she had never been to a murder scene before had set a multitude of thoughts and emotions reeling through her brain. Never complacent, she had kept abreast of forensic breakthroughs – one thing the police were good at was training their officers and she would ensure her staff would get the training they needed. She was more than aware that no two crime scenes were ever the same and that there were lessons to be learnt at each and every one. As they travelled to the scene, Charley contemplated what the crime scene would teach her, as much as what it would teach her younger passenger. A thousand questions, and instructions to give the personnel under her command at the scene, did somersaults in Charley's head. Annie was respectfully silent.

Just short of their destination, Charley swung the car down an unmarked and almost invisible unmade road. The vehicle bounced and rattled, suspension creaking, as it lurched along the track. Bouncing off the verge, the car came to a halt, two tyres in the dirt and brambles. Annie looked around her. There were no other vehicles to be seen.

'Where are we?' asked Annie.

'It's quicker this way when approaching by car, trust me.'

Taking Charley's lead, Annie got out of the car. Shivering, she looked on with angst as her boss stepped into her Wellington boots and pulled on her hat and gloves before shuffling into her weatherproof overcoat. Finally, she wrapped a woollen scarf around her neck and pulled it up over her nose and mouth before slamming the boot shut. Charley turned to Annie, her face set, on a mission. Immediately she stopped and looked from the girl's grey, pinched face to her stockingless feet and flat plimsolls at the end of her long, black cotton trouser-clad legs. She groaned, opened the back door of her car, pulled out her riding boots and offered them to the girl along with her riding jacket.

'Lesson one,' Charley said. 'Always be prepared with sufficient warm clothing and footwear; or be prepared for your clothes to be ruined and to be the butt of the others' jokes, like I was.'

She recalled her first body on the moors. By the time she had returned to the office, her smart, heeled shoes had been completely ruined and her size six feet were killing her. However, she'd taken some solace in the fact that she'd had the presence of mind to roll up her trouser legs and therefore her one and only suit at that time wasn't ruined too.

Annie nodded gratefully, the icy cold creeping all through her body. Surprisingly, the smell of horses didn't make her baulk as she'd imagined it might when she'd first put the jacket on, but when she closed her eyes against the elements she imagined freshly cut pastures and a tractor spluttering somewhere up ahead – not the dead body hanging from a tree she was about to encounter. The pleasant thoughts gave her great comfort to forge ahead into the unknown as she followed her boss.

Accustomed to walking over rough terrain, Charley knew that the best footing was in the middle of the trail. 'Don't try to pick your way, or pussyfoot around the puddles,' she advised. 'It'll only result in mud all over and you'll end up falling over.' She checked on Annie struggling a few yards behind her, like a baby fawn learning to walk. Once or twice she stopped and waited for her to catch up.

'You'll have guessed by now that I'm a townie,' Annie said, breathlessly.

Charley didn't seem to hear. Instead of responding, she nodded her head towards the rendezvous point. 'Just follow me, you'll be fine,' she said. The air was sharp and wet, but she felt invigorated by it. The ancient plot was in two open fields divided by a dry-stone wall that was, she saw, badly in need of repair. As they approached the five-bar gate, she paused, feeling slightly disorientated by its newness. She tilted her face into the wind as if listening for some direction Annie was unable to hear. The younger of the two struggled behind, finding it harder and harder to breathe and to keep up. With increasing ferocity, the harsh northerly wind circling the three steep-sided Pennine valleys made a howling sound, not unlike a wounded animal. Annie wondered if she could possibly be dreaming: her apprehension grew until the tight band around her heart was as much from anxiety, as from the cold. Were the dilapidated remains of the old burial ground getting any nearer? It didn't appear so to her.

Charley turned and threw her arms wide at the top of a mound while she waited for Annie once more.

'Hundreds of people died in Marsden during the Industrial Revolution.' She looked down at her feet and the uneven ground. 'I'm reliably informed most of them are buried here. That said, many more died before then from sheer lack of food or basic resources. I guess they'll be here too, buried by their families in unmarked graves, as near to the sacred ground as they could without having to pay for it.' Charley waited for Annie to catch her breath and then carried on walking.

'The Luddites used to hold secret meetings at the Old Moor Cock, at the top of Mount Road,' Charley shouted over her shoulder. 'You'll be seeing a lot of that place, I imagine, if you stick around.' Her words were carried surprisingly clearly on the breath of the wind.

Charley stopped abruptly, bent low beneath the knotted overhang of branches of a tall, broad oak tree and, as Annie stumbled beside her, she pointed a finger at a small group of uniformed police officers, hopping from foot to foot in an attempt to keep warm, no doubt. 'There!' she pointed, with some satisfaction.

The graveyard that lay before them was like the ruins of an overgrown garden. Headstones were toppled and strewn across the ground. Where flowers and shrubs had once flowered, now there were only masses of brown stems and low, sweeping, misshapen trees.

Apart from securing the scene with outer and inner cordons of blue and white crime scene tape, which danced happily in the wind, uniform could do nothing more than wait for the SIO to arrive – and God help them if they hadn't secured the crime scene properly for Charley Mann. Training would have made them aware, or experience shown them, that they had only one chance to preserve a crime scene.

'Neal Rylatt is CSI supervisor, ma'am, and he's on his way,' stated a uniformed police officer. Annie watched Charley scan the area surrounding them with an expert eye, collating the information she would later rely on to make important decisions. There was the odd mumble of officers exchanging words; a radio bleep; instructions; requests being made over the airways. The ground beneath them, strewn with leaf litter and dead vegetation, smelled of pungent decay.

'I expect the first on the scene to ensure it's kept sterile and protected from the elements, as well as from people, no matter who they are. Do you understand?' Charley asked Annie.

Annie nodded emphatically, instinctively putting her hands deep into her pockets. Only then did she find a woollen scarf in the coat Charley had lent her – and the odd Polo mint or two, covered in fluff.

Annie's puzzled look at the mint in her hand was met with a knowing smile. 'The horses love them,' Charley said.

Whilst the SIO spoke to a uniformed officer, Annie wrapped the scarf around her head where a hat would have been, if she'd had one. She followed Charley's lead and also looked about her — not sure what she was looking for other than anything out of the ordinary. A crisp frost remained in the sheltered areas and although the sun was up, the wind chill reminded her in no uncertain terms that it was still winter, and winter in the North was at least 'a coat colder' than in the south of England.

Those who knew Charley were aware that she would not tolerate any idleness, laziness or lack of professionalism from her team. Her time away had taught her that law enforcement in the city centre was very different to rural policing. Here she was reminded she had limited resources to call upon. However, the feather in the cap for the rural police was that the vehicle fleet included two Land Rovers, which enabled the officers to reach outlying areas of the challenging terrain that covered their patch, and she knew she was going to need them here.

'Have you been on your off-road training yet?' she asked Annie, as they waited for the CSI.

'No, I've only been at Peel Street for a month and I don't think my sergeant was very impressed,' she grimaced. 'He seconded me straight into CID as soon as the vacancy arose.'

'Well, we'll have to remedy that as soon as possible. It'll help you gain confidence; it did me.'

'Really? I'd love it. What does it entail?'

'Going over the top of steep, muddy banks, when all you can see over the bonnet of the Landy is the sky as the vehicle plunges over the summit.' Remembering that scene still triggered a cold sweat in Charley. However, Annie looked ecstatic.

'I'd been so sure that I would nosedive into the mud. And how highly amused the instructors would have been,' Charley continued. 'Ex-Army. I'm sure they tried to frighten me to death, but being a thrill-seeker, once I'd done it, I wanted to repeat the process over and over again, much to their surprise.'

'Where will I do the training?'

'In a worked and excavated quarry, consisting of steep inclines, a mixture of shallow and deep water troughs, slippery sided slopes and serious axle twisters, as well as a mesmerising blast howling through the trees. And the highlight for me – but the nightmare for others, apparently – is the bridge.'

'So, the murderer could have driven on this rough terrain if they had the ability and the vehicle to drive off-road?'

'Absolutely!'

'What's the Holme Valley Mountain Rescue Team doing here?' Annie queried, slightly surprised.

'To rescue me, I hope! Rural policing comes with its advantages. It's a team effort, from many different sources and types of organisation. We rely on the goodwill and professionalism of local volunteers who know the area and the community well. Refreshingly, once they know that they can rely on you to make decisions, you'll be accepted and respected, whatever your gender.'

Annie looked puzzled. 'But why wouldn't we all know we can trust you? After all, you've been chosen to head crime in the division.'

'Sadly, common sense does not always come with a title, or rank. You'll learn m'girl.'

Fortunately, near to where the body was hanging was a narrow stone opening, which meant that those in attendance didn't have to clamber over the ancient dry-stone wall. The crime scene supervisor, Neal Rylatt, arrived with a scenes of crime officer. Already suited and booted, along with three others, they could be seen walking sheep-like towards them, in the opposite direction from where Charley and Annie had come, but on a direct route from the main road. Their approach had obviously been thought out by their leader.

Neal could be seen turning around periodically. 'DON'T wander off the given path,' Charley heard him say. 'We need to preserve what evidence we can, while we can.' His attention was also on the skies above them and on the distant landscape.

Now suited and booted herself, Charley halted a couple of feet from the corpse. The magnificent, centuries-old tree was strengthened by man-made supports. Her eyes locked in on the dangling body, which was hanging from a low, sturdy branch. The dead person was almost white except for the lower extremities which were red with blood. Charley turned towards Annie.

'Does it remind you of anything?' she questioned, thoughtfully.

'An upside-down red-hot poker plant?'

'My thoughts exactly,' said Charley.

'Well, it can't be suicide, hung by the feet,' said Annie.

'Do you think we are looking for a murderer who is big and strong enough to get the body into that position then?'

'No, not necessarily.' Annie considered the question for a moment. 'Not if you throw a rope over the branch to enable the weight of the body to be hoisted over. The other end of the rope could then be secured to a lower branch.' She excitedly pointed to the rope secured on a lower, shorter stump she found at the back of the tree.

'From a practical point of view, I think it'll be easier for us to lower the body once we're ready, rather than fetching ladders and cutting the rope,' Charley said, voicing her thoughts as she studied the scene.

All those gathered in the outer cordon were deathly quiet, waiting for Charley's instructions and hanging on to her every word. She turned her head and lowered her ear to a faint tapping noise. Silencing those around her with the raising of her hand, she listened intently and when it came again, her eyes sought its source, spotting drops of blood periodically hitting the plastic sheet beneath the body.

'Confirmation for me, and you Annie, that this is not the scene of the murder, but a dump site,' she said. 'My experience tells me that if this person had been killed on site by slitting the throat, there would be much more blood present.'

Charley's trained eyes scanned the head. As much as the eyes bulged, so the tongue protruded. She shook her head and pointed to the tree netting that covered the trunk of the body, trussing it up like a Christmas tree. Her eyes asked the question.

'Easier for transporting, I guess,' said Annie.

'I think it's very obvious that someone has given this scene a great deal of thought, don't you? What I want to know now is when was it put here, how and why?'

Annie grimaced. 'The body reminds me of an animal hanging in a slaughter house.'

'Me too. And the reason the animal is hung is so that the blood drains. But the blood hasn't run from the body here because it's already drained somewhere else.'

'It almost feels sacrificial.'

'Maybe it is. A golden rule I learnt a long time ago, Annie, is always keep an open mind. As investigators, we must never assume anything.'

As the experienced scenes of crime officers busied themselves taking photographs and videoing the scene, Charley explained to Annie why it was absolutely essential to document a crime scene.

'Why do you think her boots are on the wrong feet?' asked Annie.

'I don't know,' replied Charley. 'Do you think it's relevant? They might have fallen off, or been taken off at some point. It might be nothing more than someone rushing to put them back on.'

'But why would you bother putting boots back on the dead body?' said Annie.

'Why, indeed?' Charley said, thoughtfully.

Through the netting it could be seen that the dead person was wearing a fluffy white jumper and a short leather skirt.

'Shelter and protection of the scene is imperative,' said Charley. She looked up to the darkening skies. 'And I think immediate action needs to be taken, don't you?'

'Really?'

'The biggest enemies of the CSI are extreme temperatures, wind, humidity and precipitation. Once Neal is satisfied the inner scene has been protected, we can lower the body into a body bag. Would you have them untie the rope around her ankles here?' Charley added.

Annie looked puzzled. 'Why wouldn't I?'

'Because you could potentially lose evidence. Perhaps a fingerprint of the killer could be secured from inside that knot. Or, maybe they cut themselves and bled, or shed a hair or two. We might be lucky enough to get DNA, so no, we remove the rope at the mortuary where we have the best chance of securing any evidence present.'

'The private ambulance is on its way,' came the message over the airways.

Annie studied Charley. 'How come you're so calm? You didn't rush me over the moor, even though I know I held you back, and now you're taking your time explaining it all to me. Surely there is something more pressing?'

'I would smile, but there's probably a zoom camera about somewhere by now, filming us.'

Annie looked from right to left and all around. 'You're having a laugh?'

'Not at all. My advice to you is never let your guard down. As innocent as it may appear, there is always someone ready to trash the enquiry and sadly, in my experience, a would-be friend might be a foe. Truth is, as the SIO there is no point in killing yourself to get to a murder scene. The body is going nowhere. The most important thing for you, as the person in charge, is to make sure that the scene is kept sterile. Once that's done, it can be unwrapped slowly, ensuring no minor detail is overlooked. Evidence should be gathered at every stage of the enquiry, if possible, and that evidence will hopefully connect the killer to the scene and to the body, in time. A bit of luck plays its part in the capture of a murderer, or so people say. But I don't think it's about luck; it's about being thorough, seizing what the scene yields and dismissing nothing as inconsequential. For that small something could become a crucial, relevant bit of evidence at a later stage. I don't know if you're aware, but we are also obliged, owing to data protection regs, to record, retain and reveal to any future defence team everything we seize at the scene, whether it is used as part of the enquiry or not. The relevance will be up to a defence team to decide, not the prosecution. We, the police, are duty bound to give total disclosure. The defence, however, are not legally obliged to do likewise. And whilst disclosing the evidence might be a long time in the future, the process has to start from the outset of the enquiry: day one and all the data recorded. Got it?'

Charley stooped down to look more closely at the clenched right hand of the deceased.

'You think she might be holding something, don't you?' said Annie.

'Rigor mortis has set in. I'm not going to try and force the fingers apart,' said Charley.

'Probably have to break them, to open them up,' said Neal, overhearing the conversation. 'Do you want me to do it for you?'

Charley showed him the palm of her hand. 'I think the mortuary would be the right place to do that, don't you?' The old-timer smiled knowingly.

Neal took plastic bags from his pocket and secured them around the dead body's hands, tying them at the wrist.

Charley nodded her approval.

'The last thing we want is for anything to be lost in transit, isn't it?' Neal said.

CHAPTER 3

The sight of a corpse had never scared Charley; instinctively, she was aware the soul had gone. Perhaps it was the legacy of growing up on a working farm and spending time with her father at the slaughter house, which had certainly prepared her for post-mortems: the dead body a shell, another tool for the investigation.

'Say goodbye, Charley.' Jack had made her kiss the dead's hands at family funerals; he always kissed them goodbye. 'It's the last chance you'll get on earth to physically touch them,' he said. When he saw Charley's mother turn her nose up in disgust, he would have an argument ready for the more religious of the two. 'Mary lovingly held her son's body in her arms when he was returned to her from the cross.'

Funerals were the only other time Charley wore red lipstick, and when her beloved grandpa had died, she'd kissed his head and left an imprint of her lipstick on his silver hair. Mother said she was brave. Truth was, she was a realist.

It had been two hours since the macabre discovery. Charley stood beside Annie. The pair looked down at the body that had now been lowered to the ground.

'D'ya know, I don't think I want to be cremated when I die,' said

Annie, wrinkling her nose. Her eyes found Charley's. 'Tell me, who the hell in their right mind would choose to end up as a pile of ashes amongst the scraps of bone the fire doesn't burn, eh? Nah, tell 'em to let the worms eat me up.'

Charley looked from Annie back to the body and considered the younger woman's words.

'But there'll be blowflies laying their eggs in you before the maggots get their turn.'

Annie pulled a face. 'Maggots before the worms?'

Charley's eyes narrowed. 'Yep, and stage-three maggots travel en masse – they'd have a good old attempt at eating you up before the worms even got a look in.'

Annie's eyes were wide. 'Really?'

'And maggots generate a lot of heat, so they move around quite a lot to keep cool – in between eating you up that is.'

Annie swallowed hard. 'Why's that then?'

Charley was momentarily distracted as her eyes sought, beyond the upland solitude of the blanket peat expanse, the warmth of the red-roofed village that had been her home. She became transfixed by the ridge upon ridge of purple heather stretching as far as her eyes could see over moorland which held the deep, secret valleys she'd explored since her childhood. From experience, however, she was more than aware that all that glistened here was not gold and that, in just a heartbeat, this area of outstanding beauty, peace and tranquillity could morph into an unforgiving, wet, wild and dangerous place, even for those who knew it well. She turned to Annie.

'Well, it's a double-edged sword for a hungry maggot. If they stay on the edge, they're more likely to get eaten by a bird, but if they're in the centre of the decaying body too long, they might get cooked.'

Charley slowly turned towards her colleague as she spoke, to see Annie shaking her head as if dismissing the gruesome image that had just popped in. The younger woman lowered her head slightly. 'I'll bear it in mind when I do my final bidding.'

'In the meantime, he's gonna need some assistance,' said Charley, pointing a gloved finger in the direction of the driver of the private ambulance, who was failing dramatically in his attempt to reverse the vehicle onto the moorland.

Annie scowled. 'He's got no chance, has he?'

Charley raised her eyebrows and slowly shook her head before tilting it to indicate that Annie should head over there.

Annie's eyes were wide. 'What, you want me to go help the grim reaper?'

'Give the chap a break. That vehicle isn't capable of driving over this terrain.' Charley stuck the toecap of her boot into the rutted grass at her feet to illustrate the point.

Mr Grundy, dressed in a dark suit, a tie and a white shirt, got out of the vehicle and slammed the driver's door shut. He held his head high and proceeded to stagger on the uneven path to the rear of the vehicle. He placed his soft hat upon his head. A shard of sunlight caught the highly polished black paint when he flung the back door open with purpose. As he walked towards them, Annie appeared to become transfixed with the little man. He had a large head and very short legs, which trotted him up onto the grass peaks, through ever-increasing levels of thick mud and over hidden sump holes; as he proceeded slowly over to them. He was holding a black carrier. It bumped against his legs, obviously too heavy for him.

Annie rolled her eyes at Charley. 'Does he always walk like he's got a broom handle stuck up his arse?' Her facial expression became one of dislike as she took in the loud grumbling and groaning of the man trying to negotiate his way, clad in unsuitable footwear and shin-deep in the heather, over an unidentifiable path studded with rocks only too keen to trip him up.

Charley could see the dents appear at the sides of her mouth as Annie attempted to suppress a smile. 'Just make sure he takes the feet,' Charley whispered in Annie's ear, pointing towards the dead body.

Her warning was met with a puzzled expression.

'Sweet Jesus, please tell me it's not messy,' Mr Grundy said, followed by a huff and a puff. He stooped down to pick up the shoe from which his foot had become separated in the peat bog at the entrance to the inner scene. He raised the back of his hand to his round, red face, his forehead streaming with perspiration.

A loud shout alerted them to the arrival of two Operational Support vans, which now joined the static convoy and the private ambulance.

'Saved by the cavalry!' declared Annie, with a nod towards the suited and booted officers that quickly disembarked.

'Indeed!' Charley watched as, within minutes, the body was lifted from the scene, with the due care, attention and respect that a deceased person deserved.

Those accustomed to carrying people over rough terrain, whether dead or alive, trod the moorland with the minimum of effort, such was their fitness, ability and level of training. Mr Grundy tottered on in their wake, somewhat relieved and extremely grateful for their assistance. Arriving at the open door of the private ambulance, the transporters of the dead carefully slid the bagged body on its stretcher into one of the four airtight compartments.

'Feet first,' said Mr Grundy. 'The dead must always travel feet first.'

'Why feet first?' whispered Annie to Charley.

'It's more practical. Dead bodies are liable to leak fluid out of the nose and the mouth. Believe me, if you've not experienced it yet, it's not very nice. Keeping the head higher than the torso prevents it.'

Annie pulled a face. 'So, if we're carrying a body down steps, it's always feet first?'

'Most definitely.'

Annie looked puzzled. 'So why has nobody ever told me that before?'

A moment later, Charley knew from Annie's change of expression that the proverbial penny had dropped.

Neal laughed. 'Because, they'd be quite happy for you to take the shit...'

'Ah...' Annie said, rather slowly, her eyes lifting skywards. Charley knew she didn't need to explain that her more experienced colleagues would have found the situation highly comical.

'Thanks for that. I'll bear it in mind when I'm asked to help move a corpse.'

Wilkie Connor and Ricky-Lee joined them.

'What you got to smile about?' asked Ricky-Lee.

'That I'm not in her shoes,' said Annie, jerking her thumb over her shoulder in the direction of the private ambulance, its doors still ajar.

Since the ambulance was mainly used for transporting corpses, its interior was plain, with steel ribbing forming the shell. The container shell itself had a rusty primer coat of paint.

'Who's going with the body?' asked Annie, with about as much enthusiasm as she would have if she had been asked to suck eggs – she detested eggs.

'Well, we'll need someone to go with it for continuity purposes,' said Charley.

Annie blanched, appearing to hold her breath, expectant. There was a pause.

'But not you,' Charley concluded. 'I need you with me.'

Annie exhaled, her relief obvious. 'Of course you do,' she said, throwing a smile in Ricky-Lee's direction.

'Is that a yellow streak I see down your back, cowardy custard?' Ricky-Lee chided. 'Wilkie and I'll go, ma'am,' he said, raising his voice for all to hear. 'I've an appointment in town at twelve.'

'Is that with a sunbed or your face-lifter?' Annie snapped.

Ricky-Lee flicked her a middle finger.

Raising her hand to subdue them, but enjoying their banter, Charley turned her back on the fractious pair. Disrespectful at a crime scene? Charley knew that if you didn't 'remove' yourself from the macabre job in hand, you'd never cope.

The search team, that had gathered in groups discussing the job in whispers, silently awaited her instruction, eager to begin. With pointed finger and raised voice, Charley began to speak.

'Ladies and gents, the immediate area where the body was is the inner scene, the outer being the graveyard extending into the two fields beyond. Use the natural boundary of the wall and hedgerow as the perimeter.'

The sergeant in charge of the POLSA team, Sergeant Richard Kay, was reassuring as he watched his officers go about their work. 'If there's evidence to find, we'll find it for you, ma'am.' His fluorescent coat ballooned behind him. The wind strength was such that most of the ongoing noise was stifled. He looked skywards at the low gathering of the clouds as CSI Naomi Clarke joined them. 'Some clouds look like fluffy cotton balls, some warn us of approaching storms and others bring rain. I think we need to proceed as a matter of urgency,' she said.

'Remind me to get the pathologist to take nasal swabs for traces of pollen.' Charley wrinkled her nose and spoke to no one in particular.

Naomi frowned. 'Pollen's unlikely at this time of year.'

Charley cocked her head at the CSI. 'What is likely, is that we won't be leaving anything to chance, will we?' Charley's eyes glinted like steel.

'No. No, of course we won't,' Naomi replied.

Charley lifted her face skyward. Eyes closed, she felt a spot of rain on her cheek, then another.

'Give me a fucking break, will you?' she pleaded with the Hobgoblin.

The blanket of dingy white clouds rapidly thickened to the gloomiest shade of grey, peaking here and there in ominous, black thunderclouds. They drifted menacingly from the west, rapidly turning the moorland dark and dismal. The team worked frantically, hoping to secure what evidence they could.

It became hard to see where the distant hills ended and the sky began, except where an orange glow betrayed a house or two in the valley below. Then the rain came, softly at first, pattering gently onto the land. There was so much to do at the scene and so little time to protect the gifts of evidence they had been given by both the victim and the perpetrator.

'Shit!' Charley bellowed as, involuntarily, she ducked at the clap of thunder which made all in her sight line cower towards the ground. 'What did I do to upset you, Hobgoblin?'

As if to mock her, the sky lit up with a zig-zag flash. There was a precarious half-walk, half-run back to the vehicle, before the rain turned to hard, rippling sheets.

Charley and Annie sat side by side in her car, both soaked through, but Annie definitely the wetter of the two. She shivered.

'Are there any aerial photos of the area on the database, Annie?' Charley queried, raising her voice to be heard over the noise of the rain on the roof.

Water, trickling from her hair, running down her face and dripping from the end of her nose didn't deter Annie from her focus as she plucked her mobile phone from her pocket.

'If not, I want the helicopter up to get us some, as soon as this damn weather allows,' Charley said, looking upwards through the driver's seat window. She shivered, suddenly chilled. She had forgotten how easily the cold could seep into her bones and sap her energy. The younger woman now appeared totally unaffected by the cold, the noise of the rain on the roof or the lightning that hit the ground directly in front of them, so intent was she on the job in hand.

While Annie spoke to Force Control, Charley sat looking out into the bleakness, listening to Annie's cajoling and gentle persuasion. It was more than apparent that the things she was requesting would be sent directly. Charley considered the situation and began to feel that, actually, luck was on her side. Neal's three-hundred-and-sixty degree filming of the scene, along with digital stills, had been secured – invaluable to her and the investigation. These would be used to brief not only the team members yet to be drafted on to the enquiry, but also the Home Office pathologist.

'Done!' Annie's mobile phone was raised shoulder high in triumph. Her face was glowing. 'What d'you want me to get on with next?'

Charley smiled. 'I'll liaise with the Coroner's Office; hopefully the post-mortem will be done today. Next, we need to get the incident room established.'

The rain finally ceased and Charley wound down her window. Mist had engulfed the inside of the windscreen. A myriad of thoughts raced through her head as she recalled each police procedure she must adhere to. She rhythmically ticked off every stage one by one with a tap of a finger on her steering wheel while she waited. And waited. Her impatience showed when she took her handbrake off long before the windscreen was clear. Automatically she clicked onto full beam. Looking in her rear-view mirror, she saw nothing but a dark moorland abyss. She put her foot on the accelerator and had travelled only a few metres forward when a dark figure suddenly appeared in front of the bonnet. Charley shouted and immediately slammed her foot on the brakes.

'What the fuck?' Annie squealed.

CHAPTER 4

Charley's heart missed a beat as she waited for the inevitable thud, but none came. Instead she heard a man's deep voice as he came alongside. Deep heat ran though her veins. Her eyes began to sting and as her heartbeat grew in intensity she was taken to another time, another place. She knew those eyes; they had penetrated her soul in past times and she felt them searching now from the mask he'd worn then and still maintained now. She wound down her window.

'Welcome home, Charley,' he said, in a smooth, broad Yorkshire accent.

'Why, Dan! Top man! What the hell!' Annie was first and foremost relieved – and then surprised. 'Are you trying to see us off?' She put her hand to her heart. He acknowledged the younger woman with a dip of his head and the slow removal of his flat cap. It shocked Charley to see curly white hair framing his face down from his temples to his well-kept jawline. He wasn't old. His facial hair was jet black, matching his dark, seemingly empty eyes.

Danny Ray was the local newspaper reporter. Now a lot chunkier than she recalled, she noticed he still wore a charismatic smile – and obviously hadn't lost his way with the ladies.

'Now, I ask myself, what would a girl like you be doing in a place like this, on a day like today?'

He looked over his shoulder and then around him, as if checking to see if anyone else was listening – which they weren't, because few people knew about this spot and what had happened here, and he knew that as well as she did. He got down on his haunches.

'Unless ... it's murder?' he said, in a whisper that was carried away on the breeze. Charley could smell stale cigarettes and it made her recoil.

It was as though the rain had washed Charley's features away; her face had become blank and pale, as if she had seen a ghost.

'Can you spare me a minute?' asked Danny Ray. He stood up straight and his hand found the handle of Charley's door. 'Don't worry, it's stopped raining,' he said, misreading her reluctance to leave the car. He opened the door wide and courteously held his hand out for her to take. 'I've got some nice pictures of the countryside, including that tent of yours, and what I need now is some narrative to go with it. Can't think of much worse than a murder happening on your first day back. Can you?'

'Oh, I don't know...' Charley's eye's narrowed. 'Anyway, how do you know it's my tent?' she asked as she stepped out of the car, brushing away his outstretched hand.

Danny tapped his nose on the side. 'I make it my job to know ... you know me.'

Her eyes spoke volumes: I thought I knew you, but turned out I didn't ... they said.

Annie leapt out of the car and the spell was broken. 'I've just done the media course,' she enthused. 'Can I do this?' she pleaded.

Charley shrugged her shoulders. 'Go for it,' she said in a monotone.

Annie ran around the car bonnet and stood directly in front of Danny, her womanly frame making his six-foot-six physique look all the broader ... and more masculine.

'He'll only print what he wants either way,' said Charley, shrugging off the hand that had found her elbow. She noticed his clothing was dry. And that he wore a wedding band.

'That's not fair,' he said quietly.

With her hands firmly thrust into her coat pockets, Charley turned away and walked the few steps over to the dry-stone wall, cold, gritty and slimy to her touch. She gazed across the valley, remembering the last time she'd seen him. A shudder ran down her spine. Trust had been at the root of their friendship. In her mind's eye she saw them, as they once were, running amongst the boulders hand in hand, him picking her up when she fell, her hands forming a foothold so he could climb a tree, him hoisting her up to swing from the branches, squealing and enjoying themselves immensely, her parents' admonitions to be careful long ignored, not in a defiant way but in a carefree, childlike way.

Brought back to the present by Annie's girly laugh, Charley's stomach suddenly felt as if she'd swallowed a handful of nails. How dare he act now as if nothing had happened between them?

Annie was studious when she looked in his direction. 'OK, so how's this sound Danny? Police are treating the discovery of a body, found hanging from a tree in the graveyard this morning, as suspicious. They think it's a dump site. An investigation is underway, led by Detective Inspector Charley Mann.'

Danny Ray's eyebrows rose and he pushed his bottom lip out in a boyish way. 'Is that right?' he drawled, his eyes found Charley's, the police mask she wore unreadable to him.

Charley remained silent, all-consumed, watching his interaction with the younger woman, the younger woman from whom he wanted something. Putting one foot in front of the other she found herself being drawn towards them, magnetically. In an almost maternal role, she would not – could not – let him use that tool to coax her into his world. She might have trusted Danny once, loved him even, but he had betrayed that trust by trying to control her. She hadn't noticed it happening at the start. The psychological games were subtle and insidious. But when the control became more physical – and when it had all finally come to a head on that fateful night before her departure for London – he had shown a side of himself that she had been glad to run away from. Maybe she had spent a long time denying what had happened, but faced with his manipulative charms again, she realised she would never stand back while he tried them on another woman.

A change of tone in Annie's voice broke Charley's reverie.

'This was a gruesome find. The enquiry is in its infancy and the body has been recovered to the mortuary.' She looked thoughtful and continued. 'The scene remains sealed by uniformed officers and a Home Office pathologist will carry out a post-mortem as soon as possible, after which we will obviously understand more. We are unaware of the deceased's identity at this moment in time. Hence we are appealing for anyone who has a female family member or friend who has recently gone missing, to contact us.'

'Body 'bin there long, do you reckon?' Danny asked Charley.

'How long's a piece of string? As DC Glover said, we'll know more once a post-mortem has been carried out. And now, if you don't mind, we need to crack on.'

'Of course.' Danny stepped to one side and allowed her to pass.

She spoke to Annie. 'And now, of course, we're going to have to ring the press office.'

'Because otherwise we'll be accused of favouritism,' Annie said in a sing-song voice, giving Danny her best wink.

'I'm very grateful to you,' he said, his words aimed at Charley. Charley took her seat behind the steering-wheel and his eyes found Annie's over the roof of the car. His boyish smile had returned. 'Just give us a five-minute head start, will you?'

Sitting perfectly still, hands on the steering-wheel, Charley brought her focus to the best way back to the main road as she waited for Annie to get in the car. The pain was still so sharp it took her breath away. 'The clock's ticking,' she said flatly, looking down at the watch on her left wrist. Charley's parting tight-lipped smile at Danny Ray disappeared as quickly as if she had been doused with a bucket of water. As she drove off, there was purposefully no backward glance. Out of the corner of her eye she could see Annie's lips moving, but she heard none of her chit-chat.

'Give me a minute,' she said, as they reached the junction. Her hand shot to her temples. 'I need to think.' There were too many thoughts crowding her head. Annie obediently sat in silence for the rest of the journey, aware of Charley's need for quiet, but unaware of the reason for it.

Charley had an overwhelming feeling of distaste at Danny's reaction to seeing her. Never in all the time she'd investigated serious crime had it occurred to her that one day she would be a victim.

Hands-free, she spoke to the press office as they neared the station, repeating what Annie had told Danny Ray. Necessary, but also as an excuse not to have to make idle chatter. She needed to remain focused.

The HOLMES team were in the process of getting an incident room up and running at Peel Street when Charley and Annie arrived. The team was a mixture of well-versed and well-rehearsed personnel, with a very broad spectrum of experience. It was organised hustle and bustle, using established police procedures. They were a godsend to the SIO, and it was a comfort for Charley to see them all getting on with it.

Five burning questions fought for supremacy: who was the corpse? From where had she come? How had she been murdered and when? And, finally, why?

'Professor Matthew Whitehead is the on-call,' Ellen Tate said stiffly, blinking habitually, her sandy lashes drooping over pale eyes of indeterminate shade.

'He's presently in Sheffield, but traffic permitting, ETA is five o'clock.' She sat down, opened her perfectly arranged drawer and took from it a new notepad and pen.

'Dick and Liddy are here,' called Annie from the kitchenette where she was making a cup of tea. 'They want to know where you want the furniture putting, Tattie?'

Reluctantly the office manager moved out of her chair and scurried across the floor in order to organise them, chuntering to herself all the way about Dick and Liddy having no common sense.

'I remember when we had to make use of whatever space we had in the old station. Them were the days ... All this palaver; sheer waste o' money if you ask me,' said Dick, taking off his flat cap and looking distastefully at the pile of furniture yet to be put in place. He turned his cap over and looked at the lining; it was a very old hat. Still counting under his breath, he spun the cap around in his hand and brushed some dust from the brim. 'I suppose we'd better get on.'

Annie saw an opportunity and, to Dick's surprise, she snatched the hat from him, swapping it for a mug of tea. She placed the cap on her head and pulled a face. He looked at her and shook his head.

'Eeh,' she said, nodding her head sympathetically. 'No more smoke-filled rooms wi' t'matchboard stained brown, plastered with e-fits and paper files all over t'shop. And t'index filing system that meant t'incident room floor had to be reinforced to cope with t'weight … Ey, them were't days.'

Dick chuckled and took a sip of tea. 'You can mock me young 'un, but it was difficult to keep track of the number of potential suspects we might have in a murder enquiry back then. What with the limited technology we had, let alone the hoax calls and thousands of time wasters who clogged up the system. You don't know you're born nowadays. Everything had to be handwritten in my day and then put on a manual card system. It was a slow process and difficult to keep up with at times.'

'And I guess there were the drunken callers ringing in claiming they knew who the culprit was?'

'That there were,' he said, with a nod of his head.

'Now't's changed there then,' Ricky-Lee piped up as he walked past them and out of the office, papers in hand.

'Aye, the buggers were only out for the reward money. And, of course, every crime would be in the local paper, back then, even a bit of pilfering. Papers were printed every day; everybody read 'em…' Dick sighed. 'Sadly, too much of the information we got vanished in the backlog. It's a wonder we solved anything when I were a detective. Good old-fashioned common-sense policing in them days, it was. That's what we had to have in our time, an abundance of common sense.'

Tattie's eyes were disbelieving. 'Really?'

He met her eyes and cracked a smile. 'Better crack on,' Dick said.

Annie watched the men at work. 'Thank God for the likes of Dick and Liddy,' she said to Charley, tossing her head casually in the direction of the huffing and puffing pair, putting Ellen Tate's orders into practice.

'Making optimum use of space is critical for running a productive and efficient workplace.' Tattie's words were reiterated more than once and, too often, fell on deaf ears.

'Just as important as manners and tea,' said Annie, a forced smile upon her face, too busy mimicking Tattie to notice DC Ricky-Lee Lewis walking back into the room.

'Ricky-Lee!' called Charley. 'I want you at the post-mortem as Exhibits Officer.' Annie turned and took the briefest moment of satisfaction from seeing DC Lewis's skin pale significantly under his recently acquired sunbed glow.

'Mike, you're my deputy,' she informed Detective Sergeant Blake.

Charley's mind was busy establishing the foundations for the investigation as DC Wilkie Connor passed by her. 'How did you fare with the guy with the Merc? I noticed it gone from the yard.'

'Bailed.'

'What do we know about him?'

'Seems straightforward enough. Runs a successful computer solutions business in Manchester. Mercedes dealership confirmed this morning that he bought the car from them, *et cetera, et cetera*.' Wilkie shrugged his shoulders. 'Still no idea why the car was flagged up in the first place – may just have been a computer glitch.'

Charley gave a half-hearted laugh. 'A bit ironic considering his line of work. Why was he arrested in the first place?'

'For some unknown reason, he gave a false date of birth and address at the roadside.'

'I bet he wasn't best pleased to have to spend the night in the cells, then.'

'His wife was even less suited. He'd told her he was three hundred miles away in London.'

Charley's eyebrows rose. 'Just out of interest, what did you say he was called?'

Wilkie looked puzzled. 'I don't believe I did.'

Charley waited expectantly, her face pinched.

'Ripley. Robert Ripley,' said Wilkie.

Charley's eyes dilated. 'The Robert Ripley from the Believe It Or Not! empire's success might be owed to the fact that he mixed lies that couldn't be verified with an enormous dose of audacity. Our Robert Ripley might find combining lying with risk-taking leads to his downfall.'

Wilkie looked bemused, but still he nodded his head in agreement.

Charley hastily turned and walked in the direction of her office. Colliding with the door frame, she stumbled into the room. She turned to see Annie's mouth open wide; her mouth a perfect circle.

'Close your mouth, Glover, before you catch a fly! And fetch me a large map of the area where the body was found, together with the corpse's photograph, so that we've got something visual for the team to see pinned up in the incident room.'

'Yes, ma'am,' Annie gave her a mock salute and hurried away, a bladder of a face looking fit for bursting.

Charley felt a tug of a smile on her lips. Her secret was safe.

News of the major incident was outed; both in-house communication and the media saw to that. The Chinese whispers ensued and the story soon became distorted, the most popular variant being that the woman who'd been found was a celebrity. The sooner an official press release was put out, the better, thought Charley.

The setting up of the incident room began to breathe life into the investigation. Computer terminals lit up one by one and display boards were wheeled into place. Visual aids were exhibited – all to the sound of tapping on keyboards, akin to the noise hungry woodpeckers make in search of insects in the trunk of a tree.

Inside the incident room, Sergeant Mike Blake was being given a demonstration of Ellen Tate's organisational skills; ensuring that the investigation hit the ground running was paramount at this stage. His face was ashen and he looked a little shell-shocked, but his immature features were contradicted by the intelligence of his vivid chestnut eyes, which gazed at Tattie with disturbing fixity, giving the impression that he was reserving judgement until she had concluded. Charley spoke to them briefly, then left them to it. Mike was obviously a man with a purpose: not to be distracted from the task given to him, nor to be dominated by Tattie.

As Charley left the room, she collided with Divisional Commander Brian Roper, almost knocking the officer, senior both in age and rank, to the ground. The muscular, ruddy complexioned six-footer was not the image of the man she had carried with her for the past four years. Roper's greying hairline had receded dramatically. He had grown a beard which was speckled with copious amounts of white hair, and it severely aged him. To her astonishment she saw he had taken to wearing large, round, thick, dark-framed glasses. Upon seeing her, the fine lines that wrinkled at his eye corners sank almost immediately into a rigid, drawn expression: the police officer's mask Charley knew so well.

At first, he appeared forgiving of Charley's blunder, but not with the grace that she would have expected from someone she had known for such a long time. She was immediately aware that the natural prowess he had possessed had deserted him since their last encounter. What she saw before her now was a shadow of the man who'd, at one time, been her mentor: the man she would have expected to help her when she needed guidance, not to add to her angst. So, the rumour squad had been correct. His selfish, self-serving lifestyle had got the better of him, and taken its toll on both his body and mind. Roper's brash disposition dropped from his face at her knowing stare, and his yellowing eyes smiled at her somewhat patronisingly.

That was more like it.

'Girl found dead in a graveyard, Inspector?' he said with a raised eyebrow. 'Bet you envisaged an easy life when you were promoted back here from the city, didn't you? You've got me to thank for that, by the way.'

'Thank?' she murmured, with a frown and a tilt of the head.

He gave a little nod, and a smirk, and lowered his voice as if conspiring, as the tap, tap of heels could be heard coming down the stairs towards them. 'But you do realise that won't be the case, don't you?' Roper glared at her over the top of his spectacles. 'I got your message. But don't worry, I'll catch up with you for a little chat sooner or later.' With the flap of a dismissive hand in front of Charley's face, he spoke out of the corner of his mouth. 'Put this one to bed quickly, there's a good girl. Murder enquiries are such a drain on resources. For God's sake, even if you do solve it, let's face it, it's only one crime for the stats.'

Charley felt herself seething inside as she watched him disappear down the corridor, trailing behind him the simpering young woman who appeared to hang on to his every word. He was a disgrace to the uniform; a weak-willed man who liked nothing more than getting his own way, feeding his addiction by using the easiest trick in the book: an abundance of arse-kissing of the hierarchy, even if it involved putting a colleague's career – or wellbeing – on the line.

She berated herself for her youthful errors, when she'd mistakenly believed he'd been someone to look up to, to confide in: the big man he'd wanted her to think he was. In truth, he was nothing more than a dinosaur, a philanderer, a womaniser, a skirt-chaser, a bully, a liar and a cheat. He had no integrity and certainly deserved no respect; neither from her nor anyone else.

In fact, Charley saw that there was something to be pitied about Roper's continual craving for attention and approval. She recalled his loutishness, which she now saw retrospectively as arrogance. It had been aimed at the officers under his command back then, in his bid for control. She narrowed her eyes. How could she have been so naïve as to trust him?

She remembered the way the officers back then would wrangle over a contested, timely result, just to gain his support for promotion. Of course she knew now that he was no hero, simply the lout grown older, albeit somewhat tamed by necessity owing to the increasing diversity in the police regime and the shifting nature of police work, which ensured that such anomalies would be eradicated for ever. Police leaders had to reflect the changing needs of society within their own jurisdiction; and by God she would help make that happen here if it was the last thing she did. She would not be silenced. Ethics, integrity, discretion and the social work elements of policing would be met and taught and implemented in every area of policing under her. There would be no more nepotism, whether that was by familial relations or any other group or society, secret or not. She would do her absolute utmost to ensure positive changes came about, no matter what the cost.

Charley could see the colossal power that his rank gave him, which he obviously enjoyed, but wondered whether over time this had somehow manifested into a self-adoration where he clearly considered himself to be better than anyone else; a demi-god, no less. She had suffered dreadfully at the hands of people like him. Performance target syndrome had drastically altered the way policing was delivered, but, for Charley, the crime of murder was still the ultimate test for a detective. She was aware more than most of just how much it impacted not only the victim's family and friends, but also the community as a whole. It might be 'only one crime' to add to the performance figures for the chief, but it was much more than that for her.

She was faced with a jigsaw with no picture to work from, no corner pieces and no straight edges – and with a massive amount of plain blue sky. It was a puzzle that she vowed she would solve.

With no cause of death yet confirmed, Charley refused the press conference requested by the Force press office. 'But we could use the information for the evening news broadcast,' pleaded Connie, the young press officer.

'We don't know the exact cause of death; we don't know the identity of the deceased and the search of the scene is still ongoing.'

She saw Connie's face fall.

'Look, once the post-mortem has taken place I might have a better understanding of what we're dealing with and then I'll be more than happy to do the press conference.'

'OK. Ten o'clock tomorrow morning? The media can use the lunch-time news to release the story if they wish.'

Charley quickly responded to her sweet smile. 'Ten o'clock tomorrow morning it is.'

Using the breathing space she'd been afforded, Charley immediately picked up the phone. The Force HQ Logistics department agreed to second three detective sergeants and nine detectives to the enquiry to complement the contingent of DS Mike Blake, DC Wilkie Connor, DC Annie Glover and DC Ricky-Lee Lewis already under her command.

Charley yawned. She looked up at the clock on the wall above the office door before heading out. She had precisely three quarters of an hour to get to the mortuary before the post-mortem began. The journey was less than eight miles, but, in rush-hour traffic through the town, she was more than aware of the possibility of delays.

She had a blue flashing light on her car dashboard and was in no doubt that if she was stopped, a traffic cop would tell her she was in contravention of the Road Vehicles Lighting Regulations 1989 and take great delight in quoting the relevant section of the Road Traffic act to her verbatim. She patted the forbidden object affectionately.

'Sometimes you just have to be practical,' she said, her eyes brightening and a rebellious smile spreading across her lips.

CHAPTER 5

The mortuary building had an abandoned look about it, as though reflecting the empty vessels kept within. There were weather cracks in the doors, weeds growing out of unattended gutters and patches of peeling paint in the corridors. It was as cold and uninviting inside as it was out.

The mortuary assistant was brewing up. Knitting needles were firmly lodged under her arm from which soft, baby pink wool bulged. Eerily, there was the tinkling of a music box, with soothing lullabies playing in the background.

'You must think me mad,' Margery said with the briefest of smiles at Charley, 'but at least it's something I can do for the wee bairns; I can't bear to see a baby buried naked.' She shuddered suddenly. 'Ooh, my old mama would have said a goose had walked over my grave.'

Charley smiled back as she took a pot of tea from Margery's aged hands. 'And mine too.'

There was a tin on the side marked 'Tea Fund'. Charley dug deep into her pockets and pulled out a few pound coins. She dropped them in the box. Ricky-Lee saw what she did and came to stand beside her. She saw him gingerly checking his wallet as she moved away. There was no noise to suggest any money had been put in the tin by her detective, and she felt a little ashamed.

'Marge...' Ricky-Lee gushed instead. 'You're looking very lovely today. Could it be a new hairstyle?'

Charley sat down facing the pair and watched him putting heaps of sugar into his mug, and then accepting a home-made ginger biscuit. Catching Margery's eye, she shook her head, her lips forming a tight line. Marge smiled at her, a twinkle in her eye as she put the biscuit tub back into the mortuary fridge with the 'samples'.

Charley allowed herself the briefest of chuckles.

Shortly before five, Charley's nominated officers were sitting by her side awaiting the arrival of Professor Matthew Whitehead. The pathologist was a tall, slim man with thick, white, wiry hair and wearing half-moon, rimless glasses. He was a smart individual, infamous for his colourful bow ties and white, lace-up pumps. He spoke quietly and precisely; clearly and with great authority.

Charley showed the Professor the photographs of the body *in situ*, and informed him of the details of its discovery. They discussed the lack of identification and the police appeal to find a name for the deceased.

Having drained their mugs, it was time for those joining the pathologist and the dead body to put on their protective coveralls. Charley familiarised herself with the mortuary whilst she waited. A quick peek inside pleased her; it had been brought into the twenty-first century since her last visit. In her estimation, for too long the focus of funds had been on the experience of illness and dying rather than what happened after death. Margery followed Charley's eyes as they wandered towards the new refrigerators. 'Health and safety a priority, I guess,' said Charley.

Margery was standing at the sink. She nodded in agreement and proceeded to dry her hands with a paper towel.

'And the rest of the building?'

'The rest is listed; phase two.' The smile left her lips and she looked to the ceiling. 'Only him upstairs knows when that'll be though.'

Charley retreated to the viewing room with its all-seeing window, seating and speaker system which would allow the SIO to interact with the Professor as he carried out his role. It was the first time she had witnessed a post-mortem this way. No more did she have to stand at the pathologist's side. 'Have those mortuary tables got bigger?' she asked no one in particular.

'I think they have,' said Wilkie. 'Probably something to do with the growing obesity epidemic.'

Charley nodded silently.

The body lay rigid on the slab. The forensic pathologist had adopted the sombre air of the dissecting room. His actions and spoken words would be recorded as he worked; the information to be formulated into his report at a later stage. The exhibits officer Ricky-Lee and the CSI Neal Rylatt, also hovered around the dead body till they found suitable places to stand. All became still and all eyes were on the Professor as he stood quietly and observed. There wasn't a word said, or an apparent breath taken, during those few seconds.

'Well, Inspector,' Professor Whitehead said, eventually. The boom of his voice echoed around the viewing room and for a moment the loudness startled Charley. The Professor's eyes peered over his face mask and his eyes found hers. 'Please tell me there is no Santa inside the Christmas tree netting.' There was humour in his tone and, at once, the atmosphere began to feel more relaxed. Very slowly, he moved around the table and, as he did, narrated aloud precisely what he was seeing for the voice recorder.

Charley was immediately impressed by his thorough, cautious approach, not unlike her own at a crime scene.

'The body has been hung by its feet; the rope is still attached at the ankles. There is, as described by the police, netting covering the torso, very similar to that used for tree transportation. The deceased's eyes are bulging and tongue protruding. I can see an injury to the right side of the head. There's a bulge in the mouth, which may well be swelling, and we appear to have an inch-wide strip of her hair cut cleanly from her head. In addition, I can see that the boots appear to be on the wrong feet...'

Professor Whitehead stopped, his body appearing to stiffen. When he looked up at Charley, his eyebrows were raised, his eyes wide. His stare made her feel uneasy. He hesitated, his face serious. 'Inspector, this is not the body of a woman. It's a male.'

Click! Click! Click!

She was guessing that Neal Rylatt, as experienced a CSI officer as he was, was as surprised as the rest of those round the table at the discovery of the gender of the corpse, but always the consummate professional, he carried on snapping away regardless.

With gloved hands, the Professor proceeded to remove the netting from the torso, rolling it down as carefully as he could towards the feet. Charley took a moment to breathe, to ground herself, transfixed as she was. She remained standing, touching the window in front of her with tentative fingertips, and steeled herself for what was yet to come. She realised that she found it far easier being at the table instead of up here as a voyeur. As much as the viewing room experience was likened to being in the room by those who didn't want to be up close and personal with the corpse and its dissection, it was far from the same for her. At least in this viewing place she was removed from the odour by the distance, walls and windows; the recollection of the smell associated with a post-mortem still made her gag.

'The male is wearing calf-length boots. A black, possibly leather, skirt and a would-be-white woollen top.'

The Professor continued with his rendition of the facts. Charley watched intently as he took tapings from the exposed flesh and clothing before he started to remove the cadaver's garments.

'There is severe bruising around the neck and a deep ear-to-ear laceration.'

The Professor's gaze drifted away from the corpse to find Charley's face and, when their eyes met, he continued, 'I think our man has been strangled, Inspector, and his throat cut whilst he was suspended. Certainly, this was done after death,' he said, pointing towards the wound. His hand moved slightly to a head wound. 'And this injury most probably fractured the skull. We'll know for sure when we open him up. Someone was either making perfectly sure this poor fella was dead,' he continued, 'or they were testing my ability to find the cause of death. He could have died from a number of his injuries. Now we just have to identify which one killed him.'

The boots were the first items to be removed. Unhurriedly, they were handed one at a time to the exhibits officer to bag and label. The second boot appeared to cause concern. It was shown to the Professor. Gingerly he put his hand inside and retrieved a fifty-pound note, which was also placed in an exhibits envelope. The next item to be removed was the skirt. Charley's lip curled up at its corner at the revelation of what was beneath.

'There's nothing cute or sexy about having a permanent wedgie,'

Annie whispered, noting the position of the neutral-coloured thong, which held the penis and testicles tucked up tightly.

'Oh, I don't know about that,' said Wilkie. 'That little itsy-bitsy strip of fabric running right up a tranny's arse is bound to turn some queer bastard on.'

Charley turned her head quickly. 'I beg your pardon!' she snapped. Her eyes narrowed and Wilkie Connor found the SIO staring down hard at him. 'That dead man on the mortuary table is a person, and unless you can be respectful, then get the fuck out of here!'

Startled by her tone, he was instantly quietened. For the first time in a long while, fury threatened to overtake Charley. With difficulty, she forced herself to turn away, angered but not distracted.

Sex worker? The thought lingered for a moment or two as she turned back to the window. But, as she had learnt from her mentor, assumptions were not to be relied upon.

Now that the body was naked, swabbing continued: penile and anal. Then more tapings and more hair samples, this time plucked from the pubic hair, of which there was very little.

Moving swiftly up the body the Professor checked the mouth where he found the cause of the bulge he'd mentioned previously. A pair of tweezers aided the extraction of a tightly rolled pair of red lace knickers stuffed inside his cheek – hadn't she an identical pair in her linen drawer? Charley shuddered.

Desensitised to some extent, this wasn't as shocking a revelation as it might have been at another post-mortem that hadn't produced so many surprises already. Matthew Whitehead's concentration moved back to the scalp. 'A lock of hair horizontally cut from the head is not in keeping with the style.' He cut the same from just above and passed it to Ricky-Lee for retention. His hand hovered over a concave injury to the side.

'I can't quite think what type of instrument would have caused this injury. I have never seen anything like it before. It would have been a heavy object, something akin to a club, but the pattern the cosh has left is not round, or square, as I would expect. I suggest it was done by some home-made, macabre, heavy, club-like weapon.'

His hand left the head and travelled over the bruising around the nose and left eye. Having taken nasal swabs, he moved on to the dead man's hands. The left hand was the first to be removed from its plastic bag. The bag was passed to the exhibits officer.

The Professor took swabs, obtained nail scrapings and then, following procedure, collected nail clippings. The right hand was harder to deal with and nothing could have prepared Charley for the impact the audible snap at the forced opening of the dead man's clenched fist had on her. Those around the table flinched. Annie gasped, but the Professor carried on regardless, taking nail scrapings and clippings as before – if she had forgotten for a moment, it came to her now that breaking bones was all in a day's work for the pathologist.

The opened hand offered them two green leaves.

'I believe them to be leaves from a plant. Could be cannabis?' the Professor said, as he held them out to Ricky-Lee on a gloved palm.

Charley could see the collective nodding of heads as all present around the table appeared to agree. Later examination by Forensics would confirm it.

The body was turned over and Professor Whitehead repeated the procedure he had carried out on the front of the body.

'The scuff marks to the back of the legs and upper torso, I suggest, were probably caused in the moving of the body from where this person was killed, to where he was found,' he said. Pointing to a small wound at the centre of the shoulder blades, he turned and accepted a ruler the mortuary assistant offered him. He measured the narrow oval shape. It measured one centimetre.

'Now, if I was a gambling man, I'd say that whatever made this hole also went straight into his heart and, when we open him up, I anticipate that we will find a mass of blood in the body cavity – hence why we have no evidence of external bleeding.' The Professor noted that there were no obvious marks or holes in the fabric of the bra, or the jumper.

'I think we can deduce that the garments were not on the person at the time of death, or that the clothing items mentioned were pulled up above the wound before impact.'

The mortuary assistant produced a long, thin metal probe and handed it to the Professor. Carefully, he inserted it into the hole, where it was accepted by the body without obstruction. When the full depth was reached, it was measured. The Professor made notes before turning the body back so the dead man faced him once more.

He stood back to give the mortuary assistant who carried the saw enough space to do her job. 'OK, once the skullcap is removed,' he said, whilst watching the attendant flip the skullcap off with the help of a metal lever, 'we'll be able to see the internal damage that the head injuries have caused.'

Professor Whitehead stepped forward and his assistant stood to the side. The cap removed, he went about cutting through tissue and bone to detach the brain. Scooping the brain out he joggled the soft, squishy organ in the palm of his hand.

'So that's what brain matter looks like,' said Annie, rising from her chair to stand with Charley.

'All three pounds of it,' Charley said, echoing the announcement that the Professor had just made, when he'd weighed it on the scales.

'I've often wondered what a mass of tens of billions of neurons looked like.'

'Now you know,' said Charley.

Samples of brain tissue were taken. The rest would be placed in the chest cavity so that the body would be intact when given to his family for burial – once they'd been found.

There was an obvious fracture to the skull, but the Professor was satisfied, on seeing its severity, that strangulation had been the cause of death.

'I can see now that the blow to the head was more than likely just used to disable the victim initially.'

Whilst post-mortems were not very pleasant, Charley knew just how important they were for ascertaining the cause of death and explaining the mechanics of the killing. There was always hope that it might also reveal some clues as to the identity of the killer.

On opening up the torso it was clear that Professor Whitehead's theory was correct: the heart had been pierced from the rear and they could see that the body cavity was swimming in blood, which Whitehead scooped out with a plastic jug in order to reach and examine the other internal organs.

The heart and lungs were weighed and showed that these were quite normal in size and weight and free from disease. Blood samples were taken for DNA and toxicology reports, along with a urine sample from the bladder and the stomach contents for the examination of undigested food.

Two and a half hours later the examination was concluded. At the revelation that the organs posed 'no cause for concern', they were put in a plastic bag and returned to the body cavity, which was ready to be sewn up with large blanket stitches, not unlike a mailbag, by the mortuary attendant.

Professor Whitehead's summary concluded that the cause of death had been strangulation. The single stab wound to the back that had punctured the heart was believed to have been done post-mortem, and the fractured skull consistent with a blow to the head with a heavy object akin to a prehistoric club. The bruising to the nose and the eye was consistent with a punch and grazing on the body compatible with being dragged across the floor, pulled over a stone wall, or both. The interference with the knickers, and the cut hair, suggested the likelihood that the attacker was a sex offender with a fetish.

'The killer definitely knew how to despatch a victim effectively; either he's killed before or is an accomplished hunter of animals. It's not easy to use a knife to end someone's life, but the man's body shows no signs of clumsy failed attempts or violent anger. Those wounds were done intentionally and extremely efficiently.'

The Professor walked back to the office with Charley. 'Did you notice the beautifully manicured nails?'

Charley nodded. 'He obviously took great care of himself.'

'A lifestyle that might have contributed to his death maybe?' He shook his head. 'Sorry, that's your domain.'

'No, you're right, go on, I'm grateful for any suggestions or thoughts you might like to share with me.'

'Well, in my view, the murderer has been very methodical in the killing and unusually specific with regard to the injuries he has caused; and when – as though it was carefully planned. Like I said in the post-mortem, whether that intention is to confuse the cause and time of death, or confuse you in catching the killer, who knows? The public displaying of the victim for all to see, after death, is quite mediaeval to my thinking ... Making a public spectacle of a person by hanging was abolished in 1868.'

'Five thousand...' said Charley.

'Five thousand?'

'Yes. Five thousand people suffered death by hanging in Britain between 1800 and 1964 when it was finally abolished. And the number of attacks on lesbian, gay and bisexual people in the UK has soared by nearly eighty per cent in the past four years. It's worrying data.'

'You find facts and figures interesting, Inspector?'

'I find these facts and figures abhorrent, Professor, don't you?'

'I am not here to judge.'

'I'm glad to hear it.'

Professor Whitehead continued to discuss the case with the team, in a professional manner, in the office at the mortuary, 'I would estimate that our John Doe is in his late twenties. There was no sign of any jewellery being worn long-term, and there was no jewellery found on the body, but it could have been stolen, of course. The weapon that caused the wound to his back, I would say, was a thin blade, no more than three inches in length. The cut to his throat, perhaps a hunting knife?'

Charley thanked him and, making her exit quickly, she and the rest of the team headed back to the Peel Street incident room. Had the killer left his hallmark for them? Only time would tell ... For now her focus was on identifying the victim. Somewhere out there was someone missing a son, partner, dad, boyfriend, friend, work colleague ... She wanted to hear from them and she wanted to hear from them badly.

Her press release would pull no punches, she would tell it straight; the man who had been murdered had been brutally killed and the body hung in a graveyard for public viewing. She would share with the public the fact that he had been dressed as a woman but was, in fact, a man. Whether that would help her in finding out who he was or not was a problem for the future. She would empathise and reassure people that anyone coming forward with information would be treated in the strictest of confidence, and she meant it.

Charley clutched a picture of the deceased taken from the side of the head that hadn't been damaged. She was cautious of giving it directly to the media but, as a last resort, if nothing was forthcoming from her appeals, she would have no choice. The first conference scheduled for the next morning would be Charley's debut, before the cameras, as the head of CID. She was more than aware that the killer could be watching.

The killing had the hallmark of someone who was calm and confident, as confirmed by the pathologist. She was in no doubt that the murder had been planned. How else would the murderer have felt comfortable enough to spend time causing the victim further injuries after death, and truss him up in such a fanciful way in a public place, without fear of being seen? Maybe the danger added to the excitement. Or maybe the killer had wanted to be caught. Perhaps the cutting of the hair gave the killer their trophy. What concerned Charley was how prolific the fetish and traits appeared to be ... might they possibly be the work of more than one person? As Matthew Whitehead had suggested, was the killer merely attempting to test the ability of the pathologist? Or could it simply be that the murderer was new to the game and dabbling in a bit of every fetish they knew or had read about?

The only thing she was sure about was that whoever had committed this heinous crime needed to be caught, and fast.

'No reports of a male missing, either in the area or over the border, that fit the description of our deceased,' said Wilkie Connor, avoiding eye contact. He stood in front of her desk, head down, his thick, greasy hair smoothed across his forehead.

Charley couldn't bear to look at him. Her focus returned to her computer screen.

Nervously, he continued. 'I've created an enquiry for the intelligence unit, to liaise with the National Crime Agency to check their database for any previous bodies found with the footwear on the wrong feet, or for anyone with a known hair fetish.'

She nodded, still not looking up. Wilkie turned and walked towards the doorway with trepidation, waiting for the bollocking he knew was inevitable.

'Keep me posted,' was as much as she could manage, for now. She knew it was best to wait until she had thought through how she was going to deal with his homophobic outburst.

Her first day's work was now in its thirteenth hour and a full debrief was over. Tomorrow the investigation would move forward at pace, she'd told the assembled personnel. Most of them exited quickly, some in need of a decent meal having snacked throughout the shift without a break, others desperately in need of their beds. Charley gave a wry smile upon hearing the slight tap at the door, and the owner of squeaky shoes heading her way. She wasn't surprised to see Wilkie at the other side of her desk when she lifted her head.

'I'm off now,' he said.

Charley nodded.

He waited. After a moment or two he turned and walked towards the door. With his hand on the doorjamb he looked over his shoulder, 'Unless there's anything else?' he said.

There was a commotion in the hallway and moments later Annie bounded into Charley's office.

'See you in the morning, bright eyed and bushy tailed!' she said to Wilkie's retreating figure. 'What's up with Smiler?' she asked Charley, as Connor walked across the CID office, his rounded shoulders telling the story that he was in no mood for the younger woman's jovial banter. Annie's wan face showed a slightly tight-lipped smile and she began to giggle as soon as Wilkie was out of earshot. 'When I was a child, my grandmother would always say, "They squeak because they aren't paid for." I always assumed the Ones and Twos she'd be talking about had been stolen, but I think in his case it means he bought them from the bargain basement, don't you?'

When Charley didn't reply, she carried on. 'Where do you think it came from, that phrase?'

Charley lifted her head, put down her pen and sat back in her chair, muffling a yawn. 'Contrary to your generation's belief, there weren't always credit cards or holes-in-the-wall.'

'No?' Annie's shocked expression, fake or otherwise, drew a smile from Charley.

'No,' she said seriously. 'My parents bought most of our stuff on the tick. Dad had tabs at the pub and the bookies, and Mum paid her shop tab off when either the farm, or dad's fights, brought in some money.' Charley slammed her policy book shut. 'Now I don't know about you, but I'm all in.'

CHAPTER 6

When Charley arrived at work the next morning, she found the incident room empty: the lights dimmed, computer screens blank and telephones silent. It was six a.m. The rostered twelve-hour shift for the investigative team typically began at eight, though the working hours of an incident room were guided by the need to be proactive and effective. The downside to working in CID, especially on a major enquiry, was that the life/work balance was 'neither good for man nor beast'.

With butterflies of anticipation in her stomach she slid behind her desk and switched on her computer. Immediately, the machine sprang into action, the screen seeming extra-bright in the darkened room. She heard the melody-cue, a programme starting. A few clicks, a pause, her jaw set, Charley urged herself to be patient. Another screen, another click, a whirr and the distinctive sound of the police database as it fired up. Enthusiastically she flicked through the screens, willing information that would assist with the identification of the body to have come to light overnight.

Charley jumped when her office door clicked open, so deep was her concentration. She saw searching fingers fumbling around the doorjamb. She suppressed a chuckle. Once they found the sought-after switch, the lights juddered into action and Winnie, polish and duster in hand, stumbled into the office. She stared at Charley with a surprised look on her face. 'Wet the bed 'ave you young 'un?' she asked, handing her the newspaper that was under her arm.

Charley gave her a fixed smile and took the newspaper from her. She laid it on her desk and pointed to the front page. 'All this media attention, and yet no one has come forward to report a friend or relative missing? Why do you think that is?'

Winnie's expression turned guarded as she ran her cloth along the top of the filing cabinet with its piles of files stacked in precarious-looking towers. 'I don't get paid enough to think…' she said, busying herself. Charley's coat was strewn carelessly over the floor on top of her handbag. With a tut, Winnie hung it on the back of the door. She turned to face Charley with a look of renewed interest on her face. 'Maybe because it was the nearest and dearest who did it?'

'Hmm … Maybe,' said Charley cautiously. She drummed her fingers on her desk.

Winnie stood by her side and nudged her affectionately. Charley raised an eyebrow at the old lady.

'Can't you go and make yourself a brew or summat while I finish off in 'ere,' Winnie said, running her finger over the top of her computer to show Charley the dust on it. 'Instead of getting under my feet?'

Taking her empty cup from the desktop, Charley dragged herself from her chair and walked through the CID office. She switched on the kettle in the kitchenette and, waiting for it to boil, stared out of the window that overlooked the car park. Immediately she was distracted by the giant security gates closing. Two prisoners were led from the rear of a police van, their hands cuffed behind their backs, heads down. The kettle boiled and automatically clicked off, breaking her reverie. Turning back to the job in hand, she ladled several spoonfuls of coffee into the cup and, pouring the boiling water over, watched as the clear liquid turned dark brown. The infusion kicked up an intense aroma and she closed her eyes and breathed in deeply. To Charley that smell was possibly the best in the world. Her thoughts were instantly transported to another time, another place: her granny's farmhouse kitchen had been the sanctuary she sought when her life had spiralled into a deep, dark pit of depression. Changes that were beyond her control had threatened the world as she knew it. At work, she'd grown tired of fighting the hierarchy, the nepotism and the secret groups who influenced decisions. For why else, she'd asked her gran, having challenged Roper's actions, would she have been promoted at the next boards only to be seconded hundreds of miles away to help solve 'problems' in another force? They'd obviously sent her away to teach her a lesson and, as a result, she'd decided that, in the future, she would keep her thoughts to herself. In her private life she'd been sick of struggling to be the person her father wanted her to be – that hadn't helped when it came to committing to any kind of relationship: she was fucked up, and she knew it.

Granny had always been a woman of few words, and although life had been far less complicated then, in some ways, bringing up a family in a house with no electricity, no gas, no running water and a dug-out for a toilet had been just as hard. Instead of lecturing Charley, she'd filled three pans with water and placed them on the stove to warm. Charley was intrigued. In the first she placed a carrot; in the second she lowered an egg on a spoon; the third pan of water was left to boil. After a while she turned the gas out under the pans and carefully took out the carrot and egg, placing them on a side plate. From the third pan she poured boiling water into her percolator pot in which, it became obvious from the aroma, there were already coffee grains.

Granny placed a cup of black coffee and the plate in front of Charley and slid onto a chair opposite at the old, worn kitchen table. 'Which one are you?' she asked, rubbing her hands on her apron.

'Me?' replied Charley, bemused.

Grandma smiled. 'Go on.' She nodded in the direction of the carrot. 'Touch it.' Unquestioningly Charley did so and noted it was soft. 'Now, try to break the egg.'

Charley frowned. 'It's hard boiled?'

Granny's eyes glistened. Her mouth tugged at its corners. 'Peel it.'

After removing the shell Charley observed the egg. Finally, the old lady asked her to smell the coffee. Its rich aroma brought a smile to Charley's face.

'But what's that to do with anything?' Charley asked.

'Well,' said Granny. 'The carrot, the egg and the coffee beans have all faced the same adversity – boiling water. However, each one reacted differently. The carrot went in hard, strong and unrelenting, but in the boiling water it became soft and weak. The egg was fragile, with a thin outer shell protecting the liquid inside until it was put in the boiling water. Then the inside of the egg became hard. However, the ground coffee beans are unique. After being exposed to the boiling water, they changed the water and created something new. So, again, I'm asking you, when adversity knocks at your door, how will you respond? Are you a carrot, an egg or a coffee bean?'

When Charley returned to her office, Winnie was gone. She sat down and sipped her coffee thoughtfully. Before her lay street maps and aerial photographs of Marsden Moor and the surrounding Force area. She gripped the picture of the deceased between her finger and thumb. Who are you? The question repeated itself over and over in her mind, shouting louder and louder to the rhythm of the ticking of the clock from somewhere miles away and yet in the core of her being, like the voices one hears when going under anaesthetic. Who the hell are you?

The morning briefing was scheduled for eight a.m. and its duration was expected to be approximately forty minutes, to allow her time to focus on the press conference. Although the plan of action was formed in Charley's mind, the officers drafted in and new to the investigation needed to be familiarised with the scene location and what the original team members already knew. In Charley's experience, photographs and video footage couldn't substitute for standing at a crime scene and soaking up what it had to offer. Therefore, they would all visit the scene as soon as it was physically possible. Aware that there was a lot of information to get through at this initial meeting, Charley would also fire the warning shot across their bows: 'If anyone brings the investigation into disrepute, or takes the media attention away from catching the murderer, they will be removed from the enquiry, the CID and possibly the police service with immediate effect. Do you understand?' A murder investigation was no place for slackers. Workloads were constantly monitored and it was the SIO's job to ensure that everyone pulled their weight. Charley would not carry passengers and, with that thought in mind, she started the briefing in full, to a silent room of personnel, outlining what had been discovered about the scene and the victim so far.

She was momentarily distracted by DC Wilkie Connor, slumped in his front-row seat. His smirk and the way he was leaning towards Annie Glover, whispering out of the corner of his mouth, infuriated her.

Annie choking back her shock sharpened Charley's wits.

'Something you'd like to share, DC Connor?'

Wilkie mumbled something under his breath.

'Sorry, I didn't quite catch that,' said Charley loudly.

The tension turned the atmosphere uneasy. Holding his gaze, Charley let the pressure build, wanting Wilkie to be painfully uncomfortable. It worked. He sat up straight and looked down at the floor space between his splayed legs.

'It was nothing; just a joke,' he said, shaking his head and refusing to look up for a moment or two.

Charley's voice cracked. 'But if you found something I said amusing, we could all do with a laugh, couldn't we?' Charley's eyes passed over the sea of solemn faces before her.

Wilkie shifted uncomfortably in his chair, rubbing the back of his neck. 'No, no it's OK.'

Charley said nothing, waiting for him to carry on. When he didn't, she turned her attention to Annie. 'Maybe you'd like to tell us what DC Connor said, DC Glover?'

Sensing his young colleague's embarrassment, Wilkie eventually found his voice. 'I just said we should concentrate on those who knew ... slept with him.' He waited, expecting a wave of nods and mumbled agreement from those surrounding him. When that didn't come, he swallowed hard. 'Look,' he said chummily, giving a little laugh and turning to search his colleagues' faces for reassurance and support. When it wasn't forthcoming, he slapped his thigh. His voice rose. 'Oh, for Christ's sake come on! Be honest. If you were about to sleep with someone and found out they weren't the sex you'd thought, you'd want to murder 'em. Am I wrong?'

Annie turned to him, her eyes narrowing. 'That's such a ridiculous thing to say.' She looked from Wilkie to Charley. 'He really, really doesn't mean it, of course; he's just showing off.'

It was the worst possible thing that Annie could have said. Wilkie was obviously furious with her for taking up the cudgel for him. He spoke up.

'I most certainly *do* mean it. I couldn't deal with it.' He grew visibly agitated. 'In my mind, I'd be *gay* then!'

The room felt electrically charged.

'So, you truly believe a person who doesn't disclose to their partner that they were born the opposite sex should warrant an immediate, final payback?' said Annie. She allowed her words to hang before adding. 'Really?'

'There should be some kind of repercussion,' Wilkie continued to dig himself deeper, 'and until there is I'll be taking matters into my own hands … if that ever happens to me, which it won't, because I'm not that stupid.'

Charley tried to wipe the look of hatred off her face, but her jaw jutted out furiously, despite her efforts. She made a desperate effort to gain control and speak in impassive tones as she addressed the team. 'Our deceased may have chosen to live as a woman, or simply dress as a woman. We may find out once we have identified them: I say "them" purely because he was born a man. We will not judge our victim for his gender identity. He was brutally murdered by a sadistic killer and I expect you to remain professional at all times. Do I make myself clear?'

Wilkie's eyes shied away from Charley's icy stare which threatened him with unfinished business: this was not the time or place. At that moment, Connie Seabourne the press officer entered the room in her usual cheerful way. Charley instinctively checked her watch, saw it was almost time for the press conference and promptly ended the meeting. Red mist still swirled around her thoughts. Was Wilkie Connor homophobic and transphobic? Not if he wanted to be on her team, he wasn't! Following Connie into her office she could see him talking to Annie, in what looked like a heated exchange.

'Everything OK?' asked Connie, the moment they stepped through the door. Involuntarily, she shivered as she sat down and faced Charley who walked round to ensconce herself behind her desk. 'I mean, it was decidedly chilly out there.'

'Nothing I can't handle,' Charley replied curtly. 'Just a narrow-minded detective who speaks before he engages his brain.'

Connie put her hand in her overlarge handbag which rested on her knee and removed a notepad and pen. 'Well, the media are out in force. So take a deep breath and try forgetting everything except the press conference,' she said with a calm, reassuring smile. What Charley couldn't see was her own ashen face which appeared stone-like to her colleague. Connie gave Charley a questioning look.

'Don't look at me like that. I'll sort it!' said Charley, tucking a stray tendril of hair behind her ear.

Connie rolled her eyes, 'I don't doubt that.'

The look on Charley's face silenced her for a moment and the women held each other's stare. Connie was the first to look away and raise her hands to show Charley her palms.

'OK, OK, if you're not going to spill…' She put her handbag down on the floor at her feet and pulled up her chair. 'Like I said, there's a lot of media interest.' Connie bit her lip, looked to the ceiling and scowled. 'I hope we can get them all in the conference room...' She pulled a comical face when her eyes found Charley's again. 'I'm anticipating a bit of a squeeze.'

Charley's face softened and she smiled. 'I'm sure it'll be fine.'

There were ten minutes to go. The noise from within the conference room drifted down the corridor. Charley had her back to the open door of her office. She was rummaging through her filing cabinet when a call came up to the incident room. A man by the name of Scott Tyler had walked into the front desk at Holmfirth Police Station and reported a missing person. With her head cocked to one side and an ear to the CID office she listened to what was being said by those within earshot.

'Two days ago, Mr Tyler's partner went out to meet friends, apparently, and never returned,' said Annie, half-reading, half-memorising the words she'd written to relay to the SIO. 'The officer taking the initial verbal report has a description of the clothing she was wearing and it appears to match the dead person.' Her face was grave.

Mike Blake came to stand behind Annie.

'I can't get out of this press conference,' Charley said, as she moved from her office doorway to join them. She looked from Annie's face to Mike's. 'You and Annie go. See what the state of play is with this guy will you?'

'You might like to know that Scott Tyler has a police caution for drugs and a couple of previous convictions for Public Order. He's known to us. A bit of a gobshite if truth be known,' said Mike.

'But that doesn't make him a murderer, does it?' said Charley, putting a hand to her head to smooth her hair. She went back into her office and plucked her jacket from the back of her chair. She put her hand into one sleeve and shuffled into the garment saying, 'Keep me posted, and if it's sounding like the missing person is our victim, bring Tyler in. We're going to need a detailed statement and to arrange for a going-over by CSI of the home address and any vehicles they own. Let's not forget we haven't found the crime scene yet, just the dump site.'

Annie left and Charley turned to check her hair in the mirror. In the mirror she saw Mike turn and hesitate.

'Yes?' said Charley, feeling his stare upon her back.

'Talking of gobshites…'

She looked over her shoulder at her DS. 'I didn't know we were, but go on…'

'Wilkie isn't a bad 'un, you know. He's all talk. He just can't help himself sometimes. We all know he doesn't mean it.'

'Has he ever knowingly met a transgender person?' asked Charley.

'I've no idea.' The question appeared to shock him. 'Anyway, what I'm trying to say is, you don't need to fret. I've had a word,' he said, tapping the side of his nose reassuringly, as a father to a child. 'He won't do it again.'

Charley's eyes widened. 'Since when? Because, earlier, I overheard him telling someone on the phone that he's on the faggot murder,' she said. 'He wants to think himself lucky the press are waiting for me.' Her eyes narrowed under a furrowed brow. 'I'll be having more than a word with him, DS Blake.'

Sensing her mood, Mike grimaced, turned and left.

A packed room full of journalists awaited the SIO. Charley sat on a lone chair behind the solid oak conference table where microphones appeared to have taken on snake-like lives of their own, wiggling and writhing in front of her, each begging for supremacy. When the camera's flashing lights ebbed, she found herself furiously blinking to rid her eyeballs of their legacy. Fast and furious images of the dead person flashed at her and took her breath away: the purple tongue protruding from the mouth; the bulging eyes pleading with her to find the killer; the body laid out on the grass in the body bag, then naked on the mortuary table; the mutilated body being sewn up like a mailbag. Her heart raced. All eyes were upon her. Then the room dropped suddenly into silence.

Charley was nervous, but she knew that was a good thing. The SIO was confident in her knowledge of the incident. After all, she was the only person who knew the full circumstances of the discovery of the body and the findings of the post-mortem. Slowly and concisely, she imparted the information that she thought may help to identify the deceased. She appealed for witnesses who might have been in the area at the time, or who might know of a person who had gone missing. She focused on an appeal to employers. 'Have any of your employees not turned up for work?'

Excusing herself from the one-to-one interviews afterwards, the ladies' toilets were her haven. She threw cold water on her face and meeting her own eyes in the mirror, made a solemn vow.

'I will put this killer behind bars.'

CHAPTER 7

It had been five days since the macabre discovery of the body hanging from the tree in the church graveyard. The cogs of the incident room had kept turning, both proactively and reactively. Charley had been grateful for the early identification of the victim which in itself had opened up new leads, but so far four teams had turned up nothing further.

It was eight thirty a.m. and Charley had been at her desk in the incident room for two hours. It was true that she had gone to bed and closed her eyes, but her brain had remained on autopilot. As the days passed with no signs of a breakthrough, sleep was becoming increasingly hard to come by.

The office set-up of the incident room meant team members worked opposite each other in pairs. Charley sat at the head, which enabled them all to keep her in their line of sight throughout the morning briefing. She had a team specifically looking at background information.

'The victimology study will help us ascertain Kylie Rogers' lifestyle and daily routine. This, in turn, will hopefully give us some idea as to the killer's motivational process, leading to the victimisation and the decisive role of the process of selection. Basically, we're looking at those close to her first, putting them in or out of the enquiry, and we will continue to work outwards until we ultimately catch our killer; it's what I like to call the ripple effect. Kylie's lifestyle may well have played a crucial role in why she became a victim, but then again, it may not. I appreciate it would be very easy to wear blinkers on this investigation, but I want you to remain at all times open to any information that comes your way and consider every possibility to gain intelligence. It must have taken a great deal of courage for Carl Rogers, a manual worker by trade, to take the necessary steps to change his life forever by coming out. We know by his actions that he didn't take his decision lightly. He planned, he saved, he waited. He travelled and he paid to have plastic surgery at a private clinic in London to feminise his appearance, including work on his eyes, nose, brows, chin, hairline and Adam's apple reduction. He also had laser treatment for hair removal and undertook voice coaching lessons. That, according to his diary, was only the start of the surgical procedures and techniques in his long-term plan for gender reassignment from male to female.'

'No wonder we couldn't tell which team he was batting for,' said Wilkie.

Charley felt her jaw clench. Her voice rose as she surveyed those in front of her then, making her case to Wilkie Connor, continued, 'We don't do finger pointing. We rely on irrefutable evidence. Now,' she said, scanning the sea of faces before her. 'Where's everyone at?'

Detective Sergeant Blake glanced to his left. Nothing short of disgust showed upon his face, reddened with anger towards the detective at his side. 'We are liaising with management and staff of the obvious bars and pubs in the area, ma'am, that we know Kylie frequented, and her workplace too,' he said.

'Good. We need to concentrate on securing a timeline of Kylie's final movements. I want to know who spoke to her last and where.' Charley's face took on a puzzled expression. 'Besides murdering Kylie, what do you think could possibly have been going through the killer's mind when he cut her hair in such a specific way, put her footwear on the wrong feet and staged the dump site scene?'

'The time it must have taken the killer to stage the dump site tells me they weren't in fear of being apprehended, or maybe they had a lookout?' said Mike.

Wilkie raised an eyebrow. 'Or they wanted to be caught.'

'Maybe it wasn't the killer who staged the dump site. Maybe there was more than one person in on it: the murderer and an accomplice,' said Annie.

'Killers are cunning. Some make purposeful mistakes to throw an investigation,' said Wilkie.

Annie frowned at him.

'One thing's for sure, this murder was definitely premeditated,' said Mike.

'And that's good news?' said Annie.

'It's good news for the boss, because there's less chance that the CPS will try to reduce the charge to manslaughter,' said Mike.

Annie narrowed her eyes. 'Of course! Do you think the murderer is trying to taunt us?'

Wilkie's eyes followed Charley as she stood and walked to the dry-wipe board where photographs of the deceased, the scene and other important information appeared. She turned her back to the group. Her office phone rang and, with her back to her audience, she looked to her left, but decided to ignore it. Instead, she tapped a picture on the board with her pen. She lingered for a moment.

Wilkie leaned over the table towards Annie, a cocky look in his eye. 'Or maybe the murderer is just taunting you, ma'am...' he whispered menacingly.

Annie kicked him under the table. Wilkie stopped and glared at her. She glared back. Charley turned back to them.

'The netting...' she said, pointing to a photograph of the deceased laid out on the mortuary slab, '...used here to wrap and transport the body, is an obvious positive line of enquiry. I want someone to visit all the local garden centres and nurseries. I want to know if any of the establishments use or sell this type of netting. I am keen to know its origin.' There was a twinkle in Charley's eye. 'What the killer may not have realised, is that the more they tampered with the body, the more they gave us opportunities to find evidence against them.'

Wilkie slouched back in his chair. 'That's easy. How many different horticultural netting outlets can there be, for Christ's sake?'

With a swipe of her finger on her mobile phone Annie looked directly at Wilkie and promptly said, 'Fifteen pages on Google.'

'There you go DC Connor! What are you waiting for?' Charley's expression was challenging.

The office phone rang on the desk in front of DS Blake. He picked the receiver up and listened gravely. After a few seconds, he glanced over at Charley. His frozen expression immediately told her there was something wrong. He offered her the receiver and she walked over towards him and took it from his hand. The control room inspector was direct. 'Two young boys, aged nine, on their way to school at the Fairways have discovered the body of a male, lying face down at Four Fields.'

'Do we have anyone at the scene?'

'PCSO Richard Adams, boss.'

'Who's pronounced life extinct?'

'Paramedics. They suggested it was suspicious. Further uniform personnel are en route to secure the scene and to deal with the kids who found him and rang three nines.'

'Well done, lads!' Charley grabbed her coat, picked up her bag and headed through the CID office at pace, slowing down as she reached the door and fixing on her detective's mask. At the entrance, Ricky-Lee shedding his coat blocked her path. 'Don't bother,' she said. 'We've another body. CSI are en route; you're with me.'

DC Lewis did an about turn and quickened his pace to keep up with Charley, who marched across the car park in front of him. 'It was quiet around here before you arrived,' he said. 'Not that I'm complaining. I could do always do with the overtime.' He heard the beep of her car alarm. Her opening of the door was swift. The engine was already running when he slid into the passenger seat next to her. He looked across at her, raising his eyes in a question, but before she could answer, Ricky-Lee's impatience got the better of him.

'So, what 'ave we got?' he asked.

Charley was pleased to see that the area was already cordoned off with crime scene tape and that a six-foot screen had been erected around the body to shield the scene from prying eyes and allow passers-by to concentrate on their footing as they traversed the uneven, boggy terrain. Uniform personnel had a visible presence standing guard. Charley took a protective suit from the boot of her car. She nodded towards Neal Rylatt's CSI van that was parked nearby, and it was from the back of that that Ricky-Lee found one for himself, along with a pair of Wellington boots. Charley couldn't help but smile to herself. 'You're a lucky bastard,' she said to a wide-eyed Ricky-Lee.

'What?' he said, with a twinkle in his eye as he slid them on his size ten feet as easily as if they were his own.

'You know what. Back in the day, if I had rocked up to the office late, sporting a newly acquired spray tan, and attended the crime scene with my boss without the proper attire, I'd have been rolling in that mud by now. You're on borrowed time, son. Be warned.'

Such was the saturation of the grass that Charley's own Wellington boots sank an inch with each squelchy step she took; the going was very tough. Protectively, Ricky-Lee reached out and touched her elbow once or twice when she stumbled, and to her annoyance, she found she was glad he was there.

It was hard to put a timescale on how long the six-foot, black male who lay in the clearing amidst the long grass and moss-covered boulders had been dead. He was face down, with legs apart, arms outstretched and palms to the ground.

Unshaven, the deceased sported a gold-coloured stud earring in his left earlobe. A camouflage baseball cap, obviously too small for him, sat atop his scruffy head. His faded denim jeans, too big for his waist, were tied with a cheap cloth belt of a darker shade. A washed-out grey hoodie was pulled up to his shoulder blades, and on his feet he wore training shoes that had not only seen better days, but were a size or two too big. Under his right hand lay a syringe which appeared to be empty. On the ground nearby lay a used condom and several scattered cans of lager surrounded him.

When the body was turned, it revealed beneath it another condom, this time still in its Durex wrapper. There was swelling around the cadaver's neck. Neal Rylatt pulled back his sleeves and when the CSI's eyes met Charley's they told her that she was not the only one who was wrong to have anticipated needle marks.

'It's not uncommon to inject elsewhere,' he said, flatly. 'We will be looking for more evidence of drug abuse at the mortuary.'

Charley was deep in thought. She looked about her, taking in the scene that she had been presented with. Close by, a horse and its rider galloped away across an adjoining field. Seeing the rider's long dark hair blowing wildly behind her, for a moment she envied them both their freedom. Cattle nibbled on luscious grass and sheep grazed on the surrounding hillside. At the side of the dead man's head a tumbling stream hurried towards an unseen source beyond, where field met dark woods. Charley stopped and listened. 'Did you die here?' she said in a whisper.

A high-pitched screech startled her. 'What the hell?' she said, and, as if in answer, a pale barn owl came flying silently towards her, carrying a mouse proudly in its beak.

Ricky-Lee looked concerned for the creature. 'She must be starving and struggling to catch enough food at night,' he said, following the onward flight of the bird. 'Mice are more likely to come out during the day in winter,' he said by way of explanation for the owl's appearance during daylight hours.

'How do you know it's a she?' Charley questioned, surprised.

'Females often have darker brown feathers around the rim of the facial disc, as well as darker bars on the tail and small black spots on the chest and underside of the wings,' he said, as if everyone should know that.

Charley was taken aback. Ricky-Lee observed the scene closely. 'If sex had taken place here, you'd expect the ground to be disturbed, wouldn't you?' His eyes lingered on the worn dirt path, searching for clues.

'And his clothing isn't in disarray, which suggests to me that he's been killed elsewhere,' said Charley.

There was an unspoken agreement and a shared feeling of anticipation between Charley and the CSI as he placed the used condom in an evidence bag for further examination. 'It may contain DNA that will connect someone to the deceased,' Neal said.

Nodding her approval at his asking, Ricky-Lee searched the dead man's pockets. 'Nothing,' he said. His mobile phone rang, and he stood up to take the call, shaking his head at Charley as he hung up. 'No one of a similar description has been reported missing.'

Charley raised her eyebrows and sighed. 'Looks like we've no option but to trust that DNA and fingerprints can give us a clue as to who he is.'

A number of things about the dead body and the locality didn't sit right with Charley, but there was no doubt in her mind that the scene was a dump site. The corpse would be transported to the mortuary where the post-mortem could confirm this and, she hoped, tell her more about where the victim had come from and how long he had been dead.

The next port of call was to the school to interview the boys that had found the body. Ricky-Lee slouched in the passenger seat of Charley's car, sensitive to her need for quiet as she drove away from the scene. They completed the short journey in silence, past farm land bordered by dry-stone walls. Charley surveyed the surrounding fields, thinking how they were unlit during the hours of darkness and open to the public at all times.

Ricky-Lee waited for a cue from his boss to talk. As they approached a woman on horseback, Charley looked in her mirror, the vehicles behind her slowed down and the drivers tooted. She smiled and passed the horse wide and slow. The rider thanked her by way of a wave and a nod.

'Do you know her?'

Charley turned to Ricky-Lee as she indicated and turned left through the school gates. The way to the car park was well signposted.

'No. What makes you ask that?' she said, driving cautiously past several Portakabins, evidently being used as extra classroom space.

He shrugged his shoulders. 'Dunno, I just thought, maybe...'

'Horse riders just happen to be the most courteous of road users. Didn't you know that?'

Ricky-Lee scoffed. 'I come from the inner city, ma'am. We don't have much to do with horses, unless they're policing a footy match.'

Charley parked her vehicle inside the wire perimeter fence over which tumbled an abundance of thick ivy of various shades. As the two detectives got out of the car, they were immediately reminded of the activity at the crime scene. The POLSA search was taking place in a field below, the officers were on their knees using their fingertips to search. Their elevated position gave the detectives a good overview of the dump site and its surrounding area from where they stood, side by side, for a moment or two. Charley broke the silence.

'Why the mass planting of trees down there, do you think?' she asked, pointing towards the area of the little stream at the bottom of the hill. She was thoughtful and her eyes didn't stray from the focal point. 'To help reduce flooding maybe?' she uttered in answer to her own question.

It was obvious to Ricky-Lee that she didn't expect an answer from him. He studied the scene for a moment or two. 'Well, that's what they say. However, the benefits of creating natural flood defences by planting trees and creating water meadows may have been slightly overstated.'

Charley frowned. Taking her eyes off the scene for a moment, she turned to him. 'You think? You seem to know a bit about nature and the countryside, for a Towny that is.'

He nodded and smiled. She noticed he had a nice, reassuring smile.

'I studied Geography and Criminology for my Masters. Autumn's a good time to plant saplings and that's when I think those were dug in.'

Ricky-Lee's eyes met Charley's gaze. For some unknown reason he was pleased to see she appeared impressed.

Fifteen minutes later, the detectives were ushered into the principal's study, where a tray with a pot of tea, a jug of milk and a sugar bowl stood alongside a plate of chocolate digestives. Ricky-Lee's eyes lit up.

'In my experience, a person who stumbles across a body is as likely to need support as the family of a murder victim. Shock takes on many forms. For some the horror lasts for a few seconds, others are haunted for life,' Charley said to him.

The two boys entered the principal's warm, stuffy study, soft-footed. They stood, heads bowed, the smaller of the two with his hands clasped together in front of his tiny frame. The other, the taller and broader of the two, gripped his left forearm with his right hand. They both looked scared.

Charley immediately praised the youngsters for their actions and they relaxed a little, even raising their heads enough to look Charley directly in the eye when she introduced herself and Ricky-Lee to them.

'Tell me, David, Kenny, how did you know it was a dead body and not a mannequin?' she asked.

The smaller of the two studied the detectives, deciding they looked trustworthy and sympathetic, for police officers at least. Slowly he unclenched his hands and pointed to the ground with his index finger, hesitantly, as if recalling the act. 'I touched it. It was freezing cold,' David said. He stepped back and closed his eyes to the horror. A shudder ran through his little body and when he opened his eyes he continued to stare at the carpet. 'The birds were singing after days of rain…'

Kenny, the taller of the two and the more brusque, cocked his head and dramatically jabbed the air with an imaginary weapon. 'I prodded it with a stick, just like that. It didn't move. I'm not daft. That's what happened when my grandad's dog croaked.'

'In your own words, can you tell us what happened this morning?' said Charley.

David was pale and looked unsteady on his feet. Ricky-Lee offered him his seat. The little boy took it with a sideways glance at the officer that told him he was grateful. Kenny took the lead. 'We were walking to school, kicking a football between us, weren't we, Davy?' He looked down to his friend for confirmation. David nodded. 'The football rolled off the path and down the hill and it stopped by what I first thought was a pile of clothes. I wondered if it was a human being, but a hat covered the head. When I poked it, I knew we'd found a dead body.'

David put his head in his hands, rested his elbows on his thighs and groaned. Holding his stomach, he retched and promptly threw up on the carpet.

It was ten o'clock when the detectives arrived back at the incident room. DS Blake was studying intelligence reports, his shirt sleeves rolled up, one elbow on the table and his knuckles supporting his head. He didn't look up at their entry, but, pen in hand, continued flicking through the pile of papers, page after page, scanning the information and making notes.

'Mike, I need you to keep a watchful eye over the Kylie murder enquiry. Just while we find out the cause of death for this latest body. My gut instinct tells me we've another runner,' Charley said.

He looked across at her, his eyes bloodshot. 'Yeah, will do.'

'Anything?' she said, as she walked the few extra yards to stand by his chair.

'No, nothing.' He covered his mouth with the back of his hand. Arching his back, he stretched and yawned, slipping a pile of papers with names on across the desk in her direction. 'Nothing but a list of those we've spoken to.'

'And?'

'Some were sincere, meant well,' he said with forced cheerfulness. 'But most were clearly either barking mad, looking for someone to talk to or out to get a bit of notoriety.'

'We're still listening to anyone who has anything to say though, right?'

'For sure. I've got officers out visiting a medium who contacted us this morning to say she thinks she might be able to help.'

Wilkie Connor was slouched back in his chair. He swivelled round to face the pair, rolled his eyes and tutted as he shook his head in disdain. His phone bleeped. 'They should be charged with wasting police time,' he said, before swivelling his chair back to his desk to continue his text conversation.

Charley's eyes met Mike's. 'Great! I for one couldn't care less who the information comes from, alive or dead, as long as it can be substantiated,' she said.

Mike forced a smile.

Charley bent forward and ran her blunt-tipped finger down the list of names on the papers Mike had shared with her. Her expression was one of disbelief. 'We've seen all those and still nothing?'

'Nope,' he shook his head. 'Not one person has given us anything we can use.' Mike reached out for a blue cardboard file at the far corner of his desk, grabbed it and handed it to her. 'Here, we've also got a list of criminal behaviour for the purpose of identifying our killer.'

Her eyes lit up and she raised her eyebrows.

'Don't get too excited. The behaviourist isn't telling us anything we don't already know.'

'Well, at least we've ticked the boxes, eh?' she said with a little sigh.

Charley followed Mike's gaze as it wandered to the corner of the incident room where a group of four sat quietly at tables of two, opposite each other, attention focused on their computer screens. 'Intelligence are trawling through recent releases and anyone that has recently come to our attention where a victim has been hanged, where there's a sexual motive or the victim's sexuality and/or gender identity is in question.'

DC Wilkie Connor scoffed and turned his attention from his mobile back to the two of them. 'Glad I've not picked up that action,' he said, his eyes glowing, but before either had a chance to question his remark, his eyes dulled. 'On second thoughts,' he said, a happy look slipping back into his eyes, 'How's the overtime budget looking, boss?' he said, with a wink.

Charley positioned herself near the window in her office next to the cast-iron radiator, sipping her lukewarm coffee, waiting for the right time. Someone coming through her door would never guess at the annoyance that simmered beneath the surface of the Senior

Investigative Officer. Her face wore its normal aloof look, her blonde hair was in its usual tidy bun, her white, long-sleeved shirt was fastened to the neck, her suit as impeccable as ever. But Wilkie Connor had pushed her restraint to the limit, and clearly found it quite amusing, the way he tried to goad her and the taunting in his voice. His time was up. The low heat of the radiator was delicious against her legs, almost sensual, she thought, as she watched the detective stomp through the office in Annie's direction, gurning.

'Grin, grimace, tongue out, squint; that's the secret to a good gurn,' he said.

'Yeah? Well, I'd be careful, because if the wind changes, you'll stay like that,' Annie said.

Undaunted, Wilkie sat down beside Annie, put his arm about her shoulders and gave her an unwelcome squeeze.

Annie screwed up her face, attempting to pull away. 'Gerroff!'

'Tell me the latest murder isn't another tranny?' he said, collapsing back in his chair with a low moan.

'Detective Constable Wilkie Connor. My office,' Charley shouted, in a deep, rasping voice which she hardly recognised herself.

The ex-crime squad officer raised his eyebrows at Annie, got up from his chair and strolled over to the office. He tapped at the SIO's door gently with his fist and stood in the doorway. It was raining heavily outside, and he noticed the shutter blind on the window to the back yard was closed. Funny how different it made the office feel.

'You called?' he said.

Charley stood with her back to him, steadying a pile of old news reports she'd retrieved, and which were now piled on top of the filing cabinet. 'Close the door. Sit down,' she said.

Wilkie walked over to her desk but remained standing. He turned to her. 'Can we make this quick,' he asked, jiggling the change in his trouser pocket. 'I've got places to go, people to see…'

Charley slammed the drawer of the cabinet shut, turned and smiled sweetly at him. 'Of course,' she said. As she walked past the door that he'd left wide open, she kicked it shut with her heel before walking slowly towards him. He looked down at his watch.

'Sorry, this won't take long…' She held out her hand and he looked at her strangely. As she reached him, she touched his elbow. He froze and in an instant found himself pinned against the wall, the SIO's long fingers around his neck, her knee to his groin.

'What the hell are you doing?' he said, in a strange, gargling whisper.

'One more negative comment about transgender people and I'll break your fucking nose. Do I make myself clear, DC Connor?' Charley's teeth were clenched. Her nose to his, warm spittle flew into his face. His body weakened in her grasp and he shook uncontrollably. 'I'm sorry…' he managed to squeal.

'Sorry what?' she hissed.

'Sorry, boss.'

Charley cocked her head to one side. 'If you want a fight, just say,' she hissed. 'If you want to walk the streets, I can arrange it. Do you understand?'

Wilkie nodded his head in little jerky movements as her hands moved to his jaw bone. She tilted his head back further and held it for a moment or two, stretching him up to his tiptoes before releasing her grip. He slid down the wall back on to the balls of his feet. Her voice became more normal. 'I want you on board, DC Connor, but if you're not going to pull your weight – and if you can't think before you speak – then say so now and I'll arrange for you to go back on the beat with immediate effect.'

'No, no ... I promise. It won't happen again.'

Charley calmly walked the few steps around her desk to the chair and, straightening her jacket, she sat. 'You're lucky, DS Blake speaks highly of you. I want an example setting to the younger end. Do you think you could do that?'

Wilkie ran a hand through his hair and slumped into the chair opposite her. He looked puzzled. 'Yes, I'm sure I could ... Why?'

'Good, because you're going to be doing some mentoring for me.'

'Really? You – you want *me* to be a mentor?'

'You're qualified, aren't you?'

'Yes, I have been for years. But the others, they've never given me the chance. Thank you,' he said, with a note of sincerity in his voice.

'So, from now on, do we have an understanding? I don't want to fight with you, and you don't want to go back to walking the beat, do you?'

Wilkie nodded his head subserviently. 'I don't mean any of it, y'know, boss, it's all bravado.'

'Off you go, then, to whatever you were late for. And remember, next time there'll be no warning, I'll smack yer one and thereafter you'll be wearing a uniform.'

Wilkie Connor jumped up and hurried to the door. He opened it to see a few inquisitive faces looking up at him. He stood tall, straightened his tie and walked to his desk. 'I'm going to be a mentor,' he said to Annie.

Charley looked at herself in the mirror. 'You're a bully, Charley Mann,' she said. 'But sometimes you just have to communicate with them in the only way they understand.'

The concave line at the side of the skull told the pathologist that the young man had been hit with something heavy.

'Something like a piece of lead piping. Approximately one and a half inches in width, or about four centimetres, I would suggest. But, deadly as the wound looks, it didn't kill him,' said Old Man Butterworth, concluding the three-and-a-half hour post-mortem examination. 'He's been strangled. And, I'm sorry to say, you have another murder, DI Mann. Back in the seventies,' said the wiry old man with the trademark side whiskers he called mutton chops, as he walked back to the office with Charley, '...long before you were a twinkle in your parents' eyes, I and the senior police officer would be going down the pub about now and getting pissed. It was a bit of a tradition. But we're supposed to be more professional these days, aren't we – more's the pity – and we have to appear impartial,' he said. Playful wrinkles appeared around his grey-blue eyes and she likened the look to Marty at the front desk, who often reverted to a mischievous mood in her presence.

Charley frowned. 'How impartial can we be when we both want to see the guilty get locked up and the innocent go free?'

'I think I'll drink to that,' he said.

'And I think I'll join you!' she replied.

A couple of thoughts ran through Charley's mind. Was this the work of the same killer? Or could it be that there were two killers using the same method to attack their victims, at the same time, on her patch? It seemed highly unlikely. She had nothing to connect the two killings at this stage other than a hunch that the murder scenes were both dump sites and both victims had been strangled. She spoke on her hands-free whilst moving her car, and updated Mike Blake.

A large glass of red wine, as calm as a mill pond, stood on the highly polished, dark wooden counter of the dimly lit wine bar and Old Man Butterworth was accepting a large glass of brandy from the big, blonde, high-coloured, high-bosomed bar person in exchange for a twenty pound note when Charley arrived. She hesitated in the doorway for a moment or two to let her eyes adjust to the light before weaving in between the leather sofas, round-topped tables and stools towards them. It was apparent the old man hadn't seen her because when she arrived to stand at his side, his face brightened in a sudden smile. 'I was just telling Helga about our little drinky poos. Mind you, we wouldn't be drinking these in THE day,' he said, to Helga, nodding towards the glasses on the bar. 'It'd 'ave been pints of Tetley's then, for her and me. And none of those…' He looked slightly aghast at the tiny bowls of peanuts, pretzels and olives dotted around. 'The landlords knew how to treat us back then. There'd be piles of thick dripping bread to greet us, on huge platters, with an abundance of salt atop. And black pudding too,' he said, in a softer tone.

Charley chuckled. 'Were they trying to kill you off, d'you think?'

'Well, it never did me any harm.' He held his glass up to her and she raised hers to his. 'Cheers,' he said. 'And good luck with the enquiries.'

Charley slid onto the bar stool beside him. 'Waiting for the lab results is a ball ache for us,' she said.

Butterworth gave her a questioning look. 'Seriously?'

She looked down and stroked the rim of her glass. 'Seriously. Waiting for forensic to enable us to move on can feel like waiting for God at times.'

He took a sip of brandy. 'Well, he's never let me down yet,' he said, patting her arm. 'We've done all we can for now. The victim's DNA and fingerprints have been taken. Swabs, and...' he pulled a face. 'Well, I don't have to tell you...'

'There was no evidence whatsoever to suggest to you that the guy had been involved in any sexual activity, was there?' asked Charley.

Butterworth shook his head. 'No, would be my answer.'

'I've just spoken to the team. The condom containing the sample found at the scene is at the lab and it's being forwarded for DNA comparison.'

'And I would have thought the origin of the condom packet found beneath the corpse will be the subject of a priority enquiry, along with the syringe too?'

Charley's eyebrows went up in momentary surprise. 'You should have been a detective.'

Butterworth sucked on his false teeth. 'My pater told me that by choosing a job I enjoyed I'd never work a day in my life and, being a lazy bugger, I did as he said; about the only time I ever did,' he chuckled. 'And, now, I can say I am living proof that having an interest in a subject makes learning easier.' He paused in thought for a moment, then leaned forward. 'Where will you begin, when trying to find out where a particular condom packet might have been purchased from, Inspector?' he said, in a whisper.

Charley briefly raised her shoulders in a shrug. 'The usual, shops, pubs, clubs...'

Suddenly, the double doors swung open and a group of people came bursting into the bar, laughing and jostling one another. The noise caused Butterworth to turn up his nose. His eyes scanned the room for Helga. 'Where is the wench when you need her to show a bit of authority?' he said with a freezing stare as he spotted her on the other side of the room. Helga, struck between the shoulder blades by that concentrated stare, turned suddenly about, and discovered Butterworth, his arm in the air to get her attention, as if she needed to be flagged down to know that the noise would be unacceptable to him, a regular.

Charley instantly recognised some of the growing crowd as local press. She jumped off her stool, drank the rest of her wine in one gulp and forced a smile towards her companion. The wine warmed her as it went down. 'Thank you for the drink, but right now I think I had better make tracks,' she said, with a throw of her head towards the noisy corner. 'The press office needs an update.'

Butterworth nodded understanding. She picked up her bag, threw her coat over her arm and, before he could say Jack Flash, she was out of the door.

'Is it true you've another body?' She heard the dulcet tones of Danny Ray the instant she stepped outside into the cold night air. She turned to her left and saw him standing against the building, one foot to the wall, the other in the gutter. He took a long drag of the cigarette that was pinched between his finger and thumb.

'I'm pleased to hear the native drums still work,' she said as she passed. He lurched forward, threw his tab end away and proceeded to follow her across the car park.

'It's my job,' he said. 'Come on, short quote for an old friend?'

With shaking hands, she pressed the button on her key fob that deactivated her car alarm. The beep appeared louder than normal to her ears. She berated herself for parking so far away, under the trees and out of sight of the main road. The warm feeling in her stomach gone, it left a void for the butterflies now doing somersaults. As she neared her car, she heard the quickening crunch of Danny's shoes meeting the asphalt behind her. Reaching the door, she hurriedly opened it and, swinging her bag before her, jumped into the driver's seat, reaching out to pull the door towards her. As she did so, Danny lunged forward and caught the door handle, gripping it tightly. Charley's heart beat ferociously against her chest. She looked up at him. 'Didn't you get the message last time we were here?'

Danny's eyes remained unblinking.

'Have you forgotten I had you on your fucking knees, right here in this car park, and I swear,' she said through gritted teeth. 'I swear, I'll do it again.' Charley put her keys in the ignition and started the engine. She tugged at the car door. 'Let me go,' she spat at him.

'How could I forget? I tried to explain ... You wouldn't listen.'

She caught her breath.

His eyes softened. 'OK, OK. I admit, I was jealous ... But you shouldn't have lied to me.'

Her nostrils flared. 'I lied because I knew how you'd react ... and you shouldn't have followed me.'

'I acted like any other red-blooded male would if he thought his girlfriend was cheating on him.'

'Cheating? You knew I was going to a colleague's leaving do ... I should have known when I caught you looking at my phone that night, and then, conveniently, my purse went missing and you'd no cash you could lend me.'

Danny scoffed. 'He was trying to get into your knickers. I'm a bloke – I know these things.'

'Richard was my partner and he's married, for Christ's sake. Grow up! Now, if you want your precious quote, I suggest you speak to the press office. I'm busy.'

'I could always make something up...'

His reply almost made her laugh out loud. 'Oh, you're good at doing that Danny, I'll give you that.' Her eyes were like steel. 'Tell you what, why don't you do your damnedest. I'm past caring,' she said and, catching him off guard, she gave one almighty tug on the door and the wet handle slipped from his cold fingers. He stumbled backwards. Shifting the gearstick into first, Charley slammed her foot down on the accelerator and concentrated on negotiating her exit. At the mouth of the car park she stopped and slammed the door shut. She glimpsed him in her rear mirror, sitting where he'd fallen. It brought a smile to her face.

CHAPTER 8

Charley walked into the makeshift incident room with the air of a woman who had something on her mind. Ellen Tate lingered by the doorway, pulling at her sandy-coloured hair as she silently watched the computer experts diligently rigging up extra computer terminals.

A whistling Dick the handyman delivered a cart-load of office equipment and Tattie searched with fevered eyes for a place for him to unload it. The room was cramped, with old, wooden stacking desks and chairs taking up most of the floor space, and no cupboards or shelving to speak of. There were only two telephones, but Charley knew most detectives used mobiles. Her mind wandered as she waited for the rest of her team to join her.

Annie carried two mugs of tea into the room, bearing her usual sunny aura. 'About time,' Charley said in a quiet voice as she took the hot drink from her.

'The sooner the HOLMES team are established the better,' she continued, her voice rising as she moved over towards the window where the boards already being put to use for the enquiry were propped up neatly against the wall. 'On the positive, turning the conference room into a second, temporary incident room means that both investigations are under the same roof which makes it easier for me to maintain an overview.'

Both detectives were silent as they perused the bulletins and photographs. Next to the map of the area was a large sheet of paper with a description of the victim, the location, date and time of discovery of the body, along with the contact details of those dealing with CSI, forensic and suchlike.

Fingerprints identified the latest victim as Stewart Johnson, aged nineteen years. Local intelligence told them that he had recently been checked out after having been seen sleeping rough in the town. He'd had the wisdom to seek out warm air vents, Charley was told. 'Apparently, he told our officers that he had only recently arrived in West Yorkshire from Birmingham,' said the intelligence officer.

Annie took a gulp of her tea. The photographs of the close-up shot of the victim's face made her feel slightly queasy and the lukewarm, milky drink did nothing to help. The dead man's opaque eyes bulging from the sockets were dotted with red spots; his swollen tongue protruded between grimacing lips and bared teeth. Blood ran down his chin where he had partially bitten off his tongue when he'd been strangled and some teeth could be seen hanging loosely from his mouth.

'So, no needle marks on the body,' Charley pointed out, 'and we have a negative result from swabs taken from the syringe.'

There was an excess of saliva in Annie's mouth, and she swallowed hard several times. 'You'd hoped for a trace of drugs in the syringe?'

'It would've been nice to get another action to follow up. But it is what it is and we'll just have to go ahead with what we have.'

Annie turned away from the photograph. 'It just doesn't make sense. The killer is messing with the scene again in an attempt to confuse us … he must be.'

Charley shrugged her shoulders. 'Only time will tell. And who's to say it's a he?' She looked at her young colleague's blanched face. 'You OK?' she asked.

Annie nodded her head. 'I bit my tongue when I was little, playing with my cousin on a seesaw ... It wasn't her fault, or mine ... I had to have it sewn partly back on. It's something you never forget.'

Charley grimaced just as her phone rang. 'I bet,' she said before taking the call.

'Forensics have established a DNA profile from the used condom,' she told the team at the debrief a little later. The collective faces looked hopeful. 'However, there's no match on the national database.' Charley moved on quickly. 'Anyone got an update for me on potential locations for purchasing the condom packet?' The faces grew longer and more morose.

DC Ricky-Lee Lewis took the lead. 'It appears the type of Durex condoms we found beneath the body are typically sold in most of the clubs, pubs, restaurants, supermarkets and chemists in this area, ma'am.'

'OK. I guessed as much. Anything else?'

'Marks lifted from the fifty-pound note from Kylie's boot have been checked, but the only one identified at this time is hers, apparently,' said Ricky-Lee.

The room was deathly quiet. Charley waited for the anticipated throwaway comment from Wilkie Connor and for a moment or two they eyeballed each other. Instead, he respectfully raised his hand. Charley encouraged him to speak with a nod of her head.

'A local couple from the nearby Dirker estate in Marsden are putting a vast amount of information on social media. Their Facebook page is pretty much dedicated to the death of the young black male.'

'Is the information in the public domain?'

'As far as I know. However, what concerns me is that they have taken video footage at the scene and are insinuating it was a racist attack.'

Wilkie went on to brief the assembled teams about the couple, Grant and Tracy Shields, who lived in a two-bed council flat and were well known to the local PCSO as people who got themselves involved in anything and everything bad. Both overweight and extremely loud-mouthed, they were regularly seen hanging around town and were regulars at the betting office and on the fruit machines in the pubs. They craved attention, and appearing on the local news to make comment would be a highlight on their calendar.

'Who's quoting them, and putting them in front of the camera?' queried Charley.

'Who do you think?' said Annie, walking over to hand Charley the newspaper she held in her hand. 'Dan the man. You're not going to like it,' she said, pointing to the headline: 'LATEST MURDER, A RACIST ATTACK?' Police baffled after two killings in a week.

Being thanked for imparting the worst news that anyone could wish to hear always baffled Charley. But even though she knew the truth would hurt, it was important that people knew they could rely on her honesty and her dogged determination to find the person responsible.

Stewart's parents had travelled north and liaised with the Coroner's office before they had been introduced to the officer in charge of their son's murder enquiry. Charley knew their lives would never be the same again when she took them to view the body and they confirmed his identification as their son.

Mrs Johnson confided in Charley about her son's sexuality. 'It was never a problem for me,' she said, staring down at the handkerchief nestling in her hand which she periodically used to stem the tears that washed over her cheeks. 'He was a sensitive child, always wanted to please. We loved him deeply.' She clutched her husband's hand. 'The last time I spoke to him he told me he felt such guilt that there would be no grandchildren for me.' Her voice wobbled. 'He was our only child you see.'

'He told me he was going to stay with friends in Leeds,' said Mr Johnson. He drew in a deep breath and a sigh followed. 'He's never done anything that has caused me to doubt him before, so why the hell wouldn't I believe him?'

Mrs Johnson began pounding at her thigh with a balled fist. She turned her head towards her husband and spoke through clenched teeth. 'I knew something wasn't right. I'd never heard him mention friends in Leeds before, had you?' Her voice was low, her tone accusing as she stared at her husband. She turned away, looking defeated, after she was met with silence. She shrugged her shoulders at Charley. 'Or, did he choose Leeds because he thought he could get lost in the crowd and be himself?'

'He was nineteen years of age, Jane. We couldn't actually lock him in his bedroom.'

Mrs Johnson shook her bowed head. 'I know, I know. I just can't bear to think of my son sleeping in a doorway as if he was alone in the world.' She lifted her head. Her eyes were hooded. 'Because he wasn't, Inspector. He had a perfectly good home.'

Mr Johnson was growing short of patience with his wife. 'Why do you feel the need to justify our family's lifestyle? What I want to know is what you are doing to try and catch his murderer, Inspector?'

Charley was sympathetic, but firm. 'First of all, it may help you to know how Stewart's body was discovered and how he died. I will be designating an officer to you – your family liaison officer, or FLO as we call them – who'll be your link with the investigation. However, I will personally keep you abreast of developments. One thing I want to warn you about from the outset is that you mustn't believe everything you read in the newspapers. If you have a question, and you want an honest answer, then please either ask your FLO, or me. We will always be straight with you, even if the answer might not be the one you want to hear.'

Charley led the Johnsons out of the police station. When they'd gone, she leant against the door of the front office and looked up at the fluorescent lights. Her blurred vision made them appear brighter. Emotionally drained, she walked back to the incident room, made herself a coffee in the kitchenette and, with the local paper under her arm, carried it back to her desk. She moved the visitors' chairs back to their rightful places and sat down in her chair. A bitter taste of anger rose in her throat, at seeing Grant and Tracy Shield on the front of the paper again, with the headline: 'LOCAL COUPLE SAY THEIR COMMUNITY IS LIVING IN FEAR Drugs prevalent in the area. Story by Danny Ray.'

So focused was the bartender on his colleague, who was blatantly flirting with a dark-haired, handsome, suited gentleman customer, that he caught his toe in the corner of the carpet as he entered the bar with a tray of clean glasses. The glasses slid in a tinkling avalanche to the floor as Charley walked in.

Despite the commotion, instinctively noting the signs saying there were security cameras in the establishment, Charley glanced around the room and found their location. She took a seat. Young Josh the barman glanced irritably over his shoulder, remarked that the newbie's days were numbered and, with a face like thunder, he left the customer to help clean up the pile of broken glass. The suited gentleman grimaced at Charley and winked; she smiled across at him. He slid off his bar stool and walked towards her.

'You on your own?' he asked amiably.

Charley nodded her head.

'I'm Edward. May I join you?' he asked, proffering his hand.

'And I'm the Queen of Sheba,' Charley said, leaning forward. She took a wooden cocktail stick and stabbed an olive in the dish that resided on the bar. She offered the olive to Edward. He raised his eyebrows, a knowing smile crossing his lips.

'So, what's your real name?'

She stabbed another olive and, holding the fruit momentarily between her teeth, smiled, sucked the succulent dressing from its skin and turned to see Josh wiping his hands on his apron as he walked towards them. 'I told you: the Queen of Sheba.'

Josh's smile was forced. He asked politely if they'd like a drink.

'Whatever the lady wants and I'll have a Jack Daniels and Coke,' said Edward. His mobile phone rang and he grappled in his pocket to find it. His screen flashed insistently. 'It's the missus.' Hurriedly, he silenced it. 'I'll have to take this,' he said, flustered. He stepped away from the bar and spoke to the caller in whispered tones. 'I've just this minute got out of the meeting.' He rolled his eyes at Charley. 'No. I've got to see another client tomorrow. Don't you listen?' There was a pause. He turned and looked away. 'You know I do,' he whispered. 'Yes, I promise. I'll be home as soon as I can.'

Charley shook her head at Josh and stabbed another olive.

'May I say, you're looking very lovely tonight.' Josh's eyes were smiling at Charley when Edward returned to his seat. 'Lime green suits you. It doesn't suit everyone,' Josh continued, pushing a slice of lime onto the rim of her glass, 'but it suits you.'

'How's he making out?' she asked, nodding her head towards the new bartender who was stacking glasses at the far side of the bar area. 'He looks very young…'

'Well, apparently, according to the boss, he's a better shag than a bartender, so it looks like he's here to stay,' said Josh, rolling his eyes to the ceiling.

'Josh and I were discussing the Marmite of fruit earlier,' said Edward.

'I loathe olives,' Josh said. 'In fact, I probably didn't go within a hundred yards of an olive until I started working in bars.'

'In my country, the olives have grown for more than nineteen thousand years,' Edward said. 'I was raised on them.' He watched Charley stab another olive and grinned. 'It appears we have things in common.'

Charley turned her head to face Edward and frowned. 'We do?'

'Well, we both like olives, and it looks like I'm in town for the night, so perhaps you'd like to join me for dinner?'

Charley ate a hearty, five-course dinner and helped Edward to finish the third bottle of Champagne he purchased, a Dom Pérignon 2009 vintage.

When he excused himself to go to the men's room, Josh cleared the table. 'Do you think he's trying to get you drunk?' he said to Charley with a laugh, as he collected the corks in the palm of his hand. 'Not that I'm complaining; my pay check is going up by the minute. Brandy Alexander?'

Charley nodded her head eagerly and chuckled to herself. If only Edward had known he didn't need to ply Charley with drink, and that her nickname 'Champagne Charley' had been long in the making: she'd often drunk even the most hardened of detectives under the table.

It would have seemed rude not to take up his offer to stay the night; she knew that in the morning she would be in a better frame of mind to make her decision about merging the murder enquiries ... afterwards.

It was Charley's custom to leave the hotel before breakfast was served. She was at her desk by seven a.m., her face completely devoid of last night's make-up, her long, blonde locks tucked-up in a bun. While she waited for the login screen as her computer booted up, she sipped a cup of coffee and nibbled a slice of toast and jam – cold, just as she liked it. Winnie, with dusters, rags and polish sticking out of her apron pocket, flittered around her. 'Why can't you be like the other buggers and have a lie-in sometimes so I can give the place a good clean?' she grumbled.

Ignoring Winnie, Charley grabbed another piece of toast from the plate, ripped it in half and stuffed it into her mouth. Whilst chewing, she opened the brown envelope containing the toxicology report for Stewart Johnson and feasted her eyes on the contents to the sound of the vacuum cleaner. 'All clear,' she read out, in a loud voice. At that very moment Ricky-Lee opened her office door wide and stood to the side to let Winnie hobble out with her trolley.

'I imagine that will come as some relief to Mr and Mrs Johnson,' he said.

'He's still dead,' Charley replied.

'True, but at least they now know for sure he hadn't indulged.'

'More to the point for the investigation, there are no traces of drugs in the syringe either.'

Ricky-Lee still wore his outdoor coat. He sat down and tucked his bag between his feet, resting his hands on his thighs. "Another deliberate taunting by the murderer, do you suspect?'

Charley felt even more determined to secure the evidence to nail the murderer. She knew they'd reached the darkest point of the investigation and it seemed a new depth to her anguish. Both murders seemed so pointless, so random, so inexplicable. 'I've decided to link the enquiries,' she announced.

'What's your reasoning?'

'The cause of death ... Both Kylie and Stewart were manually strangled, and in both cases I feel that the murderer is trying to mislead us at the scene.' She leaned in towards Ricky-Lee. 'Now, if Stewart had been sleeping on the streets, we should have sightings of him on CCTV.'

'Which may lead us to those he had contact with,' Ricky-Lee said thoughtfully.

'We've got a DNA sample from the condom, but there's no trace of the individual on the National database.'

'That's interesting; a plant by the murderer do you think?'

'Possibly. I think we're looking for someone with crime scene experience.'

'Someone with a knowledge of killers and their fetishes?'

'Exactly! I think the murderer is getting off on creating the scene at the dump site to try to confuse us.'

'And they are able to satisfy themselves through reading about it in the media.' He was thoughtful. 'But we need the public's help, and that means we have to use the media. It's a catch twenty-two situation.'

Charley nodded. Her expression was grave. 'It is...'

There was a quick knock at the door and Annie burst into the office. Charley sat upright in her chair, a questioning look on her face. Ricky-Lee turned to face her and see what the urgency was.

'Did you hear the Shields on the local radio this morning?' Annie said. Neither detective spoke as Annie continued. 'I've liaised with uniform. Recent intelligence tells us that as well as previous for receiving stolen goods they are suspected of cultivating cannabis in their flat. Do you think we should give them an early morning visit?'

Charley allowed herself a little smile at the young woman's outburst. Annie reminded Charley of her younger self in so many ways, especially with her unbounded enthusiasm.

'I don't think for one minute they're involved in the murders, but they are a distraction ... and we could do with them out of the way.' Charley scowled. 'Who's working this morning?' Charley turned to the computer screen, tapped a few keys and focused her eyes on the duties of the officers that were readily displayed. 'Sergeant Percy Shaw is on six-two shift. Let me speak to him.' Charley picked up her phone.

'Leave it to me,' he said, and Charley knew from old that she could take Percy Shaw's words as gospel. If there was one person she wouldn't want to cross, it was the ex-Army commander.

The officers examining the CCTV footage focused on a piece they'd found showing Stewart Johnson sitting on a bench in the town centre. He got up and wandered around, but didn't go far as, within a few seconds, he was back sitting on the same bench. The clarity of the footage was good enough to pick out the bow front of the solicitors' offices, the brown bark of the chestnut tree and the sign for the old timber yard, but not the faces of the two individuals who stopped for a moment to speak to him, appearing to hand him something before walking away. The clock showed the time as being twenty-four hours prior to his body being found.

On receiving this news, Charley was hopeful it could be a major step forward – could it be the killers, she wondered, or were they just Good Samaritans? – until she saw for herself the quality of the footage. 'What can be done to enhance it?'

'I don't know, boss,' answered Mike.

'Well, find out. Push the boundaries.'

An hour later he came back to her. 'The quality of the film can't be enhanced in this country.'

'Does that mean it can be in another?' When she put the telephone down, she stood and looked out of the window, suddenly feeling the need to escape. She grabbed her coat and headed out of the door. She needed time to think, and a place to think things through – her brain felt scrambled. 'Why have CCTV if the quality is shite!' she grumbled as she left the building, yearning to get away from the confines of the bricks and mortar.

Charley hopped in her car. She found herself driving over the moors before she realised she had gone further than she had planned. At Hell Fire crossroads she glanced over her shoulder: a decision needed to be made as to her direction. She saw her riding gear on the back seat and was instantly drawn towards Willowfield Stables. She missed riding, hungered to be around horses, but still couldn't find it in her heart to visit the police mounted section when she knew Eddie wouldn't be there to greet her. Kristine hadn't been able to ride since she'd had her back operation, but Wilson, her ex-police horse, needed exercising and Kristine had given her an open invitation to ride him. The decision was a no-brainer. Just being around horses for a while would be enough, for now.

Charley had helped transform Wilson, a reluctant, girthy horse, into a happy, willing partner. He was excited to see her and as ready as she was to get out into the open moorland.

'Still no trace on the drone user?' said Kristine, hopefully, from where she sat in her wheelchair at the stable door, a manure fork held precariously in her hand. 'I won't let it lie. As soon as I get back to work, I'll have the bastard who killed him.'

Charley shook her head sadly. 'I think everyone is of the same mind – Eddie was one of us – but I guess it's hard for other police officers who've never had an animal as a partner to understand the bond.'

Kristine looked downcast. 'As time rolls on, I feel less reassured that we'll find the culprit, don't you?' Suddenly, she was distracted by the actions of a young stable hand. 'Hey, you! Don't you ever give water to an overheated horse you bloody moron!' she shouted. Wilson goggled at his mistress. Did she mean him? Kristine sensed his angst, slowly put the fork down and manoeuvred her wheelchair towards the horse. He wasn't troubled in the slightest by the motorised chair.

Charley spoke to him in soothing tones as Kristine reached out to touch his upper leg, first making contact with her fingertips. She rubbed his chest when Charley threw the saddle upon his back and he put his head down to nuzzle Kristine's head. Charley tightened his girth with a confident pull on the straps. Wilson swished his tail and gave a deep, satisfied sigh when Charley mounted him. Heels down, head up, she sat deep, interlocking her feet under his body for balance.

The women's eyes locked before Charley and Wilson departed, no thanks from either party necessary.

Charley felt good to be alive, to taste the fresh air, to feel the cold wind against her face. She raced the fluffy white clouds. Where they would take her, she did not know, did not care. Together, horse and rider trotted, cantered and galloped across the moorland as one. She gritted her teeth, her own sweat ran into her eyes almost blinding her, but she wasn't perturbed. Her trust was in Wilson and his in her. They galloped on, pounding the moorland where the darkness grew grizzlier, the windchill sharper.

At the top of Carter's Hill, Wilson suddenly stopped and would go no further. They stood for a while. Charley could see the police mounted section livery yard from their viewpoint. The track that led to the stables was around the next bend, through a hundred yards of ruts and potholes. Charley's heart raced and for a moment or two she struggled to catch her breath. She was sweating, her shirt sticking to her back, her face red, her fringe in her eyes. She turned Wilson back and gave him a long rein. The horse shivered, stretching his neck and snorting clouds of hot steam, just as she heard the unmistakable sound of a drone. Charley leant forward and patted Wilson's neck encouragingly. When she lifted her head back up, she was sure she smelled tobacco. Charley smiled. 'I know what's up with you, old man. But Old Peggy is long gone…'

News buzzed around the incident room. A distributor had provided Wilkie with two local sources who supplied the specific type of netting used to truss up Kylie's body.

'One is Gibson Horticultural, just off the Bradford Road, and the other a tree nursery in Meltham. The latter is presently being run by

Gerry Driver and her partner. Apparently, she bought a cottage with a few acres of land when she retired from the police, and started the place as a donkey sanctuary, but it needed something else to keep it viable and the horticultural business grew organically.'

Charley was shocked. 'Geraldine Driver? Big, butch, fiery, ex-detective Gerry Driver? She's retired? No way!'

Wilkie nodded. 'She lamped Roper in a meeting and immediately threw in her ticket before they had a chance to sack her. She'd done her thirty.'

'Who's she with now?'

'Ex-scenes of crime, Hilary Sharpe from Lancs.'

Charley shook her head and frowned. 'I don't think I've come across Hilary.' Her subsequent smile reached her eyes. 'But I'm really, really looking forward to catching up with Gerry.'

Gibson Horticultural, as grand as it sounded, was nothing more than a potting shed converted into a shop, with half a dozen polytunnels hidden from sight by a huge pile of wood shavings and top soil that had been dumped either side of the entrance. A visit by car was only achievable via a single dirt track, which meant negotiating the dips, bumps and potholes so as not to cause serious damage to the vehicle. Serendipitously, Charley had spotted the old wooden signpost, crooked and weathered, the colour of bones, located at the top of the track leading to the livery yard on her ride with Wilson.

'I want research and background checks on both premises before any visits are made.'

'Hear that, Wilkie?' said Annie. 'The boss doesn't want you jumping straight in with yer size tens.'

Wilkie Connor raised his chin in the air. 'I'm actually a size twelve – and you know what they say about men with big feet.'

Chapter 9

Within forty-eight hours of Charley's request for Sergeant Percy Shaw to 'take a look' at the Shields, they were in custody for cultivating cannabis. Arc lighting and thirty cannabis plants had been recovered.

'People in glass houses, an' all that,' Percy said to Charley with a wink. 'We'll update the press once we've charged 'em, and that will very quickly take the credence out of their previous comments as far as the readers are concerned.'

'I'll make sure they're spoken to by someone from the murder investigation team to eliminate them from the enquiries and get their DNA taken and checked as a matter of routine,' Charley said.

'Kylie had what we thought might be cannabis leaves in her hand, didn't she?' Annie reminded her.

The research on the two premises identified as being suppliers of the tree netting found that they were two small businesses who relied on the goodwill of others and on ad hoc seasonal staff. Although information on the system on Geraldine and Hilary was plentiful, owing to their link with the police force, Mr Gibson, the elderly owner of the horticultural premises and his sole, full-time apprentice gardener, Solomon Myers, did not show up on any of the searches. What did come to light was an altercation where the police had been called to the premises to deal with a dispute between a disgruntled customer and Mr Gibson in which force had been used by Solomon Myers.

Charley came smiling into the office, rubbing her hands. Mike looked downcast. 'What's up Sarge?' she asked.

'Just contemplating the review,' he sighed.

Charley stood by his desk. Her eyebrows knitted together. 'We've done all we can, haven't we?'

'Yes, but it's still ... Roper told me, he hates the idea of a review,' Mike grimaced. 'He collared me on the stairs this morning. "Pull your finger out, won't you? There's a good chap!"' Mike's mimicking of Divisional Commander Roper made Charley chuckle.

'And the rest, I bet ... I know you well enough to know you're far too polite to tell me what he said about me behind my back.'

Mike looked sheepish. When his eyes found her face again, he looked sad. 'But the truth is, we are no nearer to catching the murderer now than when the investigation broke.'

Charley frowned. 'I think you need to get a grip.' She lifted her hand, counting off each point with her fingers. 'First of all, I don't care what the fuck Groper says. Remember, I'm your immediate supervisor, not him, and I think we're doing just fine. Secondly, I have no problem with anyone coming in to review a case of mine. In fact, I appreciate any help I can get and so should he. This isn't about me, or Roper, it's about solving a murder and getting some sort of closure – if that's what they want to call it – for the victims and their families. And thirdly, as long as we are all working our bollocks off, we know we can't do any more.'

Mike looked at her strangely. She smiled briefly. 'Well, you know what I mean ... I'd work my bollocks off if I had any.'

His eyes were unblinking. He appeared to be processing a new way of thinking that Charley had given him.

'Aren't we following up every lead?'

Mike nodded.

'Aren't we being proactive, as well as reactive, with the resources we have?'

Mike nodded.

'Then I have every faith that we will catch our killer and, more importantly, so should Roper. As Percy Shaw would say, if we don't catch 'em on the swings, we'll catch 'em on the roundabout. Now I don't know about you, but I fancy a trip out. We need to obtain a sample of the netting from the premises identified. A bit of fresh air will blow away the cobwebs.' She raised her eyebrows. 'Fancy a ride?'

His mood appeared to lighten instantly.

'Which place do you want to visit first?' she asked.

Mike put his hand in his trouser pocket. 'I'll flip a coin, shall I?'

'And I'll shout you dinner!'

Charley and Mike ate their warm meat pies in the car outside the little sandwich shop under the Marsden Railway signage. There was no break in the clouds, but the rain had stopped and the cold, blustery east wind howling through the tunnel was right at their backs.

'An ex-detective and an ex-scenes of crime officer. They would certainly know their way around a crime scene and, let's face it, Geraldine no doubt hates the way she was treated,' said Mike.

Charley looked thoughtful. 'They're animal lovers, caring people, served the public for most of their lives – do you honestly think they'd commit murder, and go to the extremes the killer has done to boot, merely to watch us tussle with a complex crime scene? I guess we both know that we should never assume, but I think I know Gerry well enough to realise there's no way she'd do something like this. For one thing, she probably hasn't the time: a crime of passion maybe, but not a premeditated sacrificial killing.'

The animal sanctuary and tree nursery had large, black, iron gates at its entrance. A painted sign requested that they be kept closed at all times. Both overall-clad, Geraldine and Hilary were in a field standing on top of a heap of freshly turned earth.

'Thank goodness we don't have identity parades any more,' said Mike, aghast. 'Could you imagine trying to pick one of those two out of a line-up?'

The similarity between the two – from hairstyle to colouring, stature and chunky knitted jumpers – was truly remarkable.

Charley seized Mike by the arm, and the two detectives strode towards the ladies in an amiable way. En route Mike noted a patch of earth that had been raised and untidily replaced and made Charley aware of it by way of a tug at her sleeve and a nod of his head in the appropriate direction.

As they neared the pair, Geraldine stepped forward with an outstretched hand. 'Well, to what do we owe this pleasure?' she said. 'And you only just returned to the bosom of the police family, Charley Mann.' Without waiting for a reply Geraldine introduced Hilary, put her arm around Charley and patted her on the back.

'Not much gets past you, does it, Gerry?' said Charley.

'Come on in,' she said, turning her in the direction of the house. 'I'll put the kettle on and you can tell me what's happened since I abandoned ship.'

Mike and Hilary followed in silence.

'I must say, you're both looking extremely well. Retirement obviously suits you,' said Charley as she sat down on the comfy farmhouse chairs at the round pine kitchen table. Home-made cookies, lemon drizzle cake and Yorkshire parkin were placed on little cake platters, and tea and coffee quickly served. Charley was surprised by Gerry's domesticity.

'What you looking at me like that for, young Charley? You shocked I've got a domestic side?' Gerry chuckled. 'You're not the only one who thinks I'm odd. We're not bothered, it means the locals give us a wide berth,' Gerry chuckled. All of a sudden, her face took on a sadness. 'Tell me, did they ever get the bastard who flew the drone that frightened your poor Eddie to his death?'

Charley shook her head sadly. 'No, but I spoke with Kristine the other day and together we vowed that we'd never stop looking, even if the investigation is officially over.' Charley's eyes gave away her sadness. 'Anyway, enough of the doom and gloom. I hear I missed your dramatic exit?'

'Ah well, I wasn't going to let Groper get the better of me.' Gerry pulled a face. 'I was just missing that knock-out blow you have.' Her eyes blazed. 'The red mist came down. I kid you not; I could have killed him that day. Better I leave and keep my pension intact, I decided, so I chucked in my notice before he could report me for insubordination. Although he didn't, because he's a wimp, and if they'd asked why I lamped him, I would have told them. All them years I suffered his prejudicial abuse.' Gerry threw her arms up in the air. 'I'm gay! Hurray!' she hollered. Her voice lowered to almost a whisper. 'Big deal. Did I tell *him* who he could shag? Him a married man an' all.' She took a deep breath. 'Now, I'm waiting for the Karma ... I believe in Karma.'

'Me too. And Hobgoblins. I noticed your jug by the door.' Charley winked at Gerry.

Mike smiled, tutted and shook his head. He looked more relaxed than Charley had seen him yet, and years younger when his smile was genuine.

'You might well mock, my lad, but she knows,' Gerry said, pointing to Charley. 'She knows the power the little people have.' Gerry gave Charley a knowing look and a wink. 'Brought up like I was, she were.' She leaned forward as if to share a secret. 'They were the good old days … on the farm.' Hilary tapped Gerry's hand that sat idly on the table between them, encouraging her to help her clear the table with a tilt of her head towards the sink. There were mumblings of thanks and a clatter of crockery as Gerry stacked the cups and removed the empty side plates to the draining board to wash later. When she had finished, she sat back down, put her elbows on the table and ran her fingers though her short, cropped hair before looking at Charley. 'Enough chit-chat,' she said, giving her a perfunctory smile. 'What can we do for you?'

Charley fingered the netting in her pocket, took it out and handed it to her. Hilary peered over the table and Gerry passed it on.

'Do you use this type?' said Charley.

'Yes, yes we do,' Hilary said, reaching for her glasses that were hanging around her neck on a chain, and placing them on the end of her nose. 'It's not cheap. You wouldn't get your big retail DIY places stocking this. Us old-timers, we're savvy enough to know the cheapest is not usually the best.'

'It's in the barn outside. Feel free to take samples of what we've got, no doubt you'll want a snippet or two, for the file,' Gerry said.

Hilary stood and headed towards the door. Charley beckoned Mike to follow.

'Do you want to know what Roper said to me that made me want to hit him?' said Gerry, when they were alone.

Charley nodded.

'I'd been to a fatal, on the unlit road at the bottom of Peggy-in-the-Woods. I'd taken the dying declaration in front of the paramedics. He wanted to know the 'ins and outs' because he wanted to do the media stuff. I asked him to give me a minute to compose myself and he said, 'I once had a dog like you, Driver. No matter what kind of enticement you offered it, or punishment you gave it, that bitch would not come to heel. I had no option but to shoot it in the end. What does that tell you about you and me?'

Charley was quiet on the onward journey.

'You OK?' Mike asked.

She took a deep breath. 'Just thinking about man's inhumanity to man not always being physical,' she said. 'Any further thoughts about the ladies being involved in the murders now?'

'I'll bare my arse on the town hall steps if they've anything to do with it,' he said.

She laughed. 'I've heard a few people say that and rue the day.'

'Before CCTV?' Mike's smile was broad.

'Of course. You won't catch me tempting fate.'

'Shame,' he said.

Peggy-in-the-Woods was the name given to the road that cut through Gibson's folly, a legendary haunted patch of woodland. A signpost peeking out between the overgrown trees that lined the entrance from the main road announced Gibson Horticultural to the officers. At right angles to the old road, now a footpath into the woods, the unmade road opened up to a single dirt track that they found to be made as much of pot-holes filled with hardcore, as grit and soil.

The car rocked. Back and forth it went and side to side like a cradle. Intermittently, they passed piles of logs, branches, bark mulch, soil and bricks. There were a couple of small copses of trees that cleverly screened the dilapidated, ivy-clad old buildings. The saturated, roughly made car park was no more than a large clearing full of muddy puddles of all shapes, sizes and depths. The remnants of Old Peggy's hut caught Charley's attention and she pulled up beside a cluster of ferns at its entrance. A couple of rusty cups could be seen still hanging on the ivy that swamped what was left of the structure. In silence they got out of the car. All was still, deathly quiet.

Charley looked up to the sky through the trees and screwed up her eyes against the brightness of the winter sun. The sunlight filtering through the branches cast shadows which was quite beautiful, she thought. There was a great sense of peace.

'Where are the birds? Why aren't they singing?' said Mike.

'Depends which legend you care to believe,' she said, matter-of-factly, as she jumped over the tree roots that threatened to foul her.

Every crackle of leaf, snap of twig and scattering of debris brought them a step nearer to several buildings of all shapes and sizes: a small outbuilding, that would once have been a buttery maybe to the farm building, and a coal 'ole, as well as sheds and polytunnels. Wading through the little stream made walking more difficult for Mike's feet; he slipped and slithered in his smart dress shoes.

The first polytunnel was open at both ends and once they stepped in front of the entrance they were immediately blasted by an icy cold wind. Charley put her hands in her pockets. Mike pulled his collar up and tried to wrap himself more tightly in his jacket. Through the polytunnel they could see the huge expanse of fields and trees beyond. The shelter itself was empty of anything either green or living.

At the second wooden and aluminium structure, someone could be seen stooping over hedging plants, as he bundled them together ready for sale. He wore a sack coat and a soft felt hat; his attire could have been from the nineteenth century.

'Hello!' Charley called softly. Her voice and her footsteps echoed. She took her ID from inside her jacket pocket as she approached the man slowly and softly, not wanting to startle him. When he didn't reply to her calling, she called again. This time her voice was raised. 'Detective Inspector Charley Mann, Yorkshire Police. And this is Detective Sergeant Mike Blake.' It was obvious to her that the old man hadn't heard her voice until she was close. He staggered a little as he straightened his short, stick-like legs like a figure pulled on a string.

'There's no need to shout. I might be old, but I'm not bleedin' deaf.' He hobbled a few steps to greet them. 'What d'ya want?'

'Mister?'

'Gibson!'

'Mr Gibson.'

Mr Gibson's watery eyes had a peculiar, hard, glazed look. Charley met his gaze with a harsh glare.

'We're here on police business.'

There was a silence, a stillness. Mr Gibson gave her a questioning look, but he did not speak.

'We are investigating two recent local murders and wondered if you could help us.'

Mr Gibson's face was devoid of emotion.

Charley continued, 'You may have read about the murders in the newspapers, or seen an appeal on TV?'

Mr Gibson screwed up his nose. 'No, I don't read the newspapers, load of shite if you ask me. And I never bothered getting the telly repaired after the wife died.'

'Do you live here?' Charley cocked her head in the direction of the old stone farm building.

Mr Gibson's face broke out in a half-toothless smile. 'It might feel like it sometimes, but no, the wife was superstitious you see ... and that place over yonder, it's not fit for man nor beast these days.'

Charley seized on this amiable spirit and explained about the murders and the use of the netting, which was the reason for their visit. She showed him samples, as she had done Gerry and Hilary. Mike stood to the side and observed Mr Gibson's reactions.

'There have been a lot of young trees planted at Four Fields. Would you know anything about that?' she asked, nodding in the direction of the rows of saplings he was tending.

'Yes, yes I would,' he said, surprise in his voice. 'We won a contract with the Council for a hundred to be planted. It kept young Solomon busy for a while,' he tittered.

'And the netting, Mr Gibson,' Charley said. 'Do you use that particular type of netting?'

'Aye, we do. It's kept in the woodshed, with the tree baler. I suppose you'll be wanting to see it?'

Charley nodded her head. 'Yes, we'll need a sample for comparison purposes.'

The three walked at Mr Gibson's pace. 'You know a bit about Old Peggy then?' he said in conversation.

'Aye,' said Charley. 'I spent quite a few hours on my grandpa's knee listening to old Yorkshire folklore when I was a nipper. And subsequently I went to more accidents on the Bradford Road when I was in uniform than I care to recall.'

'And do you believe any of it? I thought you lot only dealt in facts.' Mr Gibson appeared genuinely interested.

'Well, I was riding out here yesterday and my horse stopped at Dry Arch. I must admit to having smiled to myself, because my grandpa used to say…'

'…if Peggy asked the carters to fetch her shopping and they forgot, their horses would stop altogether on their way back and refuse to move. Or something would go wrong for the carters.'

Charley smiled and nodded her head. 'You heard that one too…'

The three reached the tunnel and they stopped for a moment for Mr Gibson to catch his breath.

'Aye, well I wasn't going to tempt fate,' she said with a wink of an eye. 'So Wilson and I turned around and went back to the stables.'

Mike scowled. 'You don't really believe in that old rubbish, do you?' he whispered in Charley's ear. Charley raised her eyebrows at him. 'I'll believe in anything if it helps us catch a killer. And so should you.'

Mr Gibson looked around inside the shed, pushed his hat to the back of his head and ran a hand across his forehead. 'Well, I'll go t' foot of our stairs! I could have sworn it was here afore. Solomon must 'ave moved it; he's allus cleaning up. Gets excited when I give him the jet wash and a yard brush.'

'What does Solomon do?' Mike asked.

'Solomon? He's a big, gormless sod: my lackey. I know this might be hard to believe looking at me, but I'm not as agile as I once was.' Mr Gibson chortled. 'A mate of mine persuaded me to get some help after the wife passed away. Solomon is built like a brick shithouse and as strong as an ox. He's as daft as a brush too, but I've found him to be a godsend. He works hard. In fact, I don't know what I'd do wi'out him now, but don't tell him that, he'll want a rise.'

'Is Solomon here now?' Charley looked about her.

'Tuesday's his college day, I told him when I took him on that he had to do it proper, which means schooling. He's not the brightest bulb in the box, but he does as he's told, and although he doesn't find the three Rs – as the wife used to call it – easy, it's a credit to him that he's never missed a day at college.' Mr Gibson raised his eyebrows. 'Well, as far as I'm aware.'

As they neared the machinery, Mr Gibson pointed with an outstretched finger to a large funnel, through which the tree would be forced to compress the branches tightly to the trunk and into the netting.

'There it is. That's our tree baler. It's a simple machine that can be operated manually, requiring one person to push the tree through the funnel and another to wrap it.'

The netting was still attached, the area around the machine pristine. As Mr Gibson had predicted, in the corner stood the much-coveted jet wash and the yard brush.

'Boys and their toys, eh? He loves his toys. Better cleaning up than playing with them there computerised gadgets he appears to waste his life on.' Mr Gibson reached over and pulled some netting from the machine with his gloved hand. 'Will that do? That bit's neither use nor ornament to me.'

'Perfect, thank you,' said Charley, accepting the net from his arthritic hand.

'Tell me. Do you own a vehicle?' asked Mike, as they headed back towards the car park. 'I didn't notice one when we drove into the yard.'

'Aye, two. My car is in the garage at home and Solomon uses the works truck.'

'Has Solomon ever been involved with the police, do you know?' asked Mike.

Mr Gibson stopped, turned and wrinkled his brow at the detective sergeant. 'Solomon?' He looked quickly from one officer to the other. 'No, he hasn't! And he knows beyond doubt he'd be out on his ear if he ever was.'

Charley put her foot forward and the three continued to walk to the car. 'If it's OK, we need to get some personal details from you and we'll call back tomorrow to see Solomon.'

'That's not a problem,' he said, his tone calmer, but still a little chilly. 'You'll find me here seven days a week.'

CHAPTER 10

A statement and DNA had been taken from Mr Gibson. Charley was eager to leave him on a friendly note, so as the three stood by the car, she asked him about the ferns. 'It's the only place they grow in this wood, on the site where Old Peggy's hut once stood, I read somewhere,' she said.

'So they say.'

'Who is this Peggy?' asked Mike.

A big smile crumpled Mr Gibson's face.

Charley nodded her head towards the cups hanging on the ivy. 'Put there to catch rain water for drinking, or a spare copper or two from her allies. Nobody was meant to know she was here. She lived in this smoke-dried hut and stayed hidden from the gentry for forty years after being chucked out of the gamekeeper's cottage when her husband died.'

'A hundred she was when she popped her clogs, so the church records say,' said Mr Gibson.

'Or,' added Charley, looking up at the high brick tower, 'you could believe she was a young girl kept in the tower without any food and water and starved to death. It's her ghost that supposedly haunts these woods now, anyhow, wandering out on to the unlit road in the dark to cause accidents.'

Mr Gibson looked surprised but pleased at her local knowledge. The old man turned to Charley with kindly eyes. 'It warms an old man's heart to see another generation taking an interest in our local folklore.'

'Aye, like I say, my grandpa told me the stories that had been passed down from generation to generation. She smoked a clay pipe, Peggy, didn't she?'

Mr Gibson nodded. 'And they say an admirer of hers put tobacco in her coffin, as it was to her taste.'

'I heard that too. Rumour has it that when she died the sub-bailiff tried to burn the hut down and he reported that he saw Peggy fly out of the chimney on her broomstick.'

Mr Gibson chuckled. 'That story was relayed to my wife as a child. Frightened the life out of her. Hence why we never lived on site. She did have a sensitive nature, bless her soul.'

'You two are having me on,' said Mike with a scoff.

Their look told him otherwise.

'Aye, well if you value your time, don't get Solomon on the subject, he's taken it upon himself to be an authority on the era and the old girl since he's been here.'

It felt good to climb back inside the car and feel some warmth. Charley started the engine, angling the rear-view mirror so that she had a better view of Mr Gibson waving them off.

'Actually, you can mock all you like, but I for one am open-minded about these things, in fact about most things. If it makes people happy, and it's doing no one any harm, then who are we to criticise?' Charley turned to face her colleague. 'And explain to me why the birds in the woods can't sing and the road through Peggy-in-the-Woods has gained notoriety even amongst Traffic as a dangerous place to drive after dark. It's not uncommon for locals to refuse to pass through the woods once the sun has set.'

'Really?'

'Really.'

Sergeant Percy Shaw was waiting for Charley in the incident room when she arrived at the station the next morning. He followed her into her office. 'The Council has given Tracy and Grant Shields notice and the pair are seeking to be rehoused.'

'And that's of interest to me because?' she said, sliding into her chair behind her desk and firing up her computer. She didn't notice the hopeful, anticipatory look on his face.

'Because with any luck, ma'am, they will be moving onto someone else's patch pretty darn sharpish if they want a roof over their heads.'

She stretched her back and sat upright, looking crisp and fresh as she gave him a tight-lipped smile. 'Excellent,' she said with some finality. Then, having a second thought, 'Make sure we know a forwarding address.' Eyes down she reached out to pick up a stack of files that had been placed on the corner of her desk in her absence. She bent to put them on the floor at her feet, then picked up the stack of papers on her blotter, tapped the bottom of them against her desk and shuffled the edges until the stack was neat and tidy. She looked up to find him staring at her. He looked uncomfortable in a should-he-go-or-should-he-stay sort of way.

'Have you given the intel to the press office?' she asked.

'Yes, along with the future court date for the pair, but nothing appears to be in the local paper.'

'Local crime reporter?'

'Danny Ray.'

"Nuff said.'

His eyes followed hers as she looked beyond him and into the main office.

Divisional Commander Roper stood in the incident room with his hand on Annie's shoulder. Annie looked up at him warily. He smiled down at her.

Charley ushered Percy to the door. Her presence in the incident room didn't go unnoticed by Roper who removed his hand from the young officer's shoulder as if it was on fire, nodded his head at Sergeant Shaw as he passed, and stepped forward towards Charley. Arms crossed, Charley blocked her office doorway. Annie inhaled deeply.

'To what do we owe the pleasure?' Charley queried, raising her eyebrows at the Divisional Commander, her tone mocking.

'I've a meeting at headquarters and I wondered if there was any update I could impart.' Roper's arrogant tone grated on her nerves.

'Well,' she said slowly, 'you could tell them that the team are working flat out to trace those responsible, sir.' There was silence in the room, apart from the printer that carried on churning out data. A telephone rang somewhere close to her, but she wasn't to be distracted. However, Roper looked at Wilkie as he reached into his trouser pocket and withdrew a mobile phone. Hesitantly, Wilkie took the call. Momentarily Roper closed his eyes in despair.

'Oh, come on, Detective Inspector, you must be able to do better than that? Two murder enquiries and there aren't one or two leads that I can share, to show them you're on top of it?'

'We've had lots of positive lines of enquiry sir, if that's what you want to hear? But none so far have proved to be fruitful. The killer, or killers, are still out there enjoying themselves.'

'So, arrests aren't imminent?' Roper sneered at her with a condescending look upon his face as he looked around at the faces turned in his direction.

'Correct. Best I can do is get the HOLMES team to print off some data to show how many people we've interviewed, how many statements we've taken, how many exhibits we're working through, et cetera, if you think that may be beneficial?'

'No, no need, I don't want to overload them with pages of figures and statistics,' he said, looking uncharacteristically flustered. He flapped his hand. 'Just get on with it. The sooner the murders are solved the better, then normality can resume.'

He turned his back to leave. Charley walked towards Annie, who had her back to the door.

'The difficult we do immediately. The impossible takes a little longer...' she heard Annie say and she saw she was reading from the front of her notebook.

'How true...' she said in a lowered voice.

Roper stood with his hand on the door handle and looked back over his shoulder at them. 'Better get off, I don't want to get stuck in traffic and miss the buffet. It's usually a good spread at these sorts of meetings.' The Divisional Commander opened the door, rushed out and let it slam in his wake.

Charley released her grip, realising only then that her nails had been digging into the palms of her hands, leaving red marks.

'Could that man be any more patronising if he tried?' said Annie, through clenched teeth.

Mike tapped his pen on his desk. 'Yeah, you enjoy your waitress-served grub in your ivory tower while we go out to the sandwich shop, seeing as how you've closed all our canteens down. I hope discussing how things should be done, and could be done, and that work on paper so should work in real life, gives you indigestion. Tosser!'

Charley looked across at Sergeant Blake, aware that she ought to berate him for insubordinate behaviour, but she didn't. How could she when she felt the same? Instead, she suggested they look at the positives. 'At least he came into the incident room ... Now how many bosses have you seen in an incident room?'

Mike Blake had to agree.

'And that's a good thing because?' said Annie.

'Because it's in everybody's best interest that he knows what's going on.'

Mike looked up at Charley. 'I'm going to see Solomon Myers. Do you want to come with me, or shall I take Wilkie?'

'No, you two get off. I've got to sign off some enquiries as a matter of urgency. Have a nosey around the vehicle he uses, will you, and get me the reg number.'

Mike pushed his chair back, stood and shuffled into his coat in quick time. 'We'll run it past ANPR on our way back, and see if that tells us anything,' he said, grabbing his mobile phone from his desk.

Charley threw him the CID car keys. 'Find out if Myers has access to the site at all hours, will you?'

'Can you smell tobacco?' asked Wilkie when he got out of the car in Gibson's Horticultural car park.

Mike rolled his eyes. 'Don't you bloody start,' he said.

'What?' Wilkie's eyes were confused.

Mike shook the hand of Mr Gibson, who introduced him to Myers. Solomon looked like a navvy. He wore a flat cap, corduroy pants, heavy-duty boots and a hoody underneath his donkey jacket.

When he saw the officers, he put down the shrubs he was carrying and closed the penknife he had been using. He threw back his hood and took off his cap to reveal a bald head. When the officers introduced themselves to him and explained the reason for their visit, he replied in a broad Yorkshire accent.

'I didn't do it,' he said. 'I never go anywhere, do I Mister Gibson? I'm 'appy as a pig in pig muck 'ere. Tell 'em, Mr Gibson.'

'They're not saying you did it, yer big gormless sod.'

'We just need to eliminate you from our enquiries,' furthered Mike.

'All we need to do is take a statement from you, get your fingerprints and DNA, and then we'll leave you to get on with it,' said Wilkie, nodding in the direction of a pile of saplings.

The officers saw something that looked like panic flash across Solomon's eyes, and Mr Gibson saw it too. It quickly became apparent that his agitation might not be due to the officer's request, but to his not comprehending what was required of him. Mr Gibson reached out and put a hand on his arm.

'Hey, there's no need to fret. They took my fingerprints and DNA yesterday and I'm still living. It didn't hurt, yer big soft lump.'

'But I've done now't.' Solomon looked confused.

'They're not saying you've done anything wrong. Come on. Let's just get this over and done with, shall we?'

Solomon Myers stepped back one pace, then another. 'No,' he said. With shaking fingers, he pulled his hood up. 'I have to go to work. Bye,' he said. He put his head down, turned sharply and without a backward glance walked away.

Mr Gibson raised his eyebrows, took a deep breath and suggested that the officers give him some time to talk to Solomon. 'Could you come back later?'

Mike offered Mr Gibson his business card. 'When you've spoken to him, give us a call. We'll try to pop back later today, or it may be tomorrow.'

Wilkie recorded the number of the Navara pick-up truck in his pocket book. His whistle was long and low. 'What I'd give to have one of these,' he said.

As Mike drove the car out of the car park, Wilkie frowned. 'Sarge, am I missing something? Didn't you say that Mr Myers goes to college and that he drives that monster?'

Mike looked left and right before driving out onto the main road – and then again to be doubly sure: the tales and subsequent accidents might just be folklore, but he wasn't taking any chances. He nodded without taking his eyes off the road. 'Yes.'

'So, the guy can pass exams and he's capable of gaining a full driving licence? I think someone might be playing a lot dumber than he actually is, don't you?'

'Do you think that's because he doesn't want to give us his fingerprints or DNA?'

'I don't know, but whatever the reason, I think playing the imbecile is a perfect character to pick out of the hat when he wants to. And there's no doubt in my mind he is strong enough to strangle someone – and to carry a dead body.'

CHAPTER 11

The team had secured a collection of CCTV footage at the time of the discovery of each of the bodies, and it remained in the property store, bagged and tagged. The seized items were a useless tool, the viewing a wasted exercise until they knew who, or what, they were looking for. Maybe the time had now come to revisit the CCTV.

'Nothing concrete from Forensics yet?' Charley asked at the morning briefing. A shaking of heads was her answer. 'Frustrating as it is at this moment in time not to be able to connect anyone to the murder scenes other than the victims, we must carry on playing the cards in the hand we've been dealt and try to remain patient. The break *will* come,' she assured the team. 'I'm going to see Solomon Myers today and Wilkie,' she said, fixing her eyes on his face, 'you've already met him so I want you to come with me; but before you do I'd like you to revisit the CCTV footage of Stewart Johnson in the town. Solomon may well be the recluse he portrays, but now you've met him it would give us something to talk to him about if, by any chance, he appears on the footage.'

Wilkie nodded.

Charley turned to Mike. 'You're taking the netting over to Forensics?'

'Yes, I'm going to hand it in personally and reiterate the urgency.'

'Another gift is the DNA we got from the used condom at the scene of the Stewart Johnson murder, and although the user isn't known to us yet, I feel confident that one day they will appear on the national database. We know this is not a Durex, like the other found at the scene. A question for you: why do you think two types of condoms would be at the scene of a murder?'

'The perpetrator uses whatever is available for them to buy at the time?' suggested Mike.

'Or maybe it depends what's on offer?' said Annie.

'They've been nicked?' said Wilkie.

Charley was thoughtful. 'Or maybe they were supplied free at the local clinic. Can you check out that line of enquiry, Annie?'

There was no mistaking the sound of the Divisional Commander's metal-capped shoes against the cement paving outside in the car park. The two detectives walked on, but Roper reached the external door before they did and opened it. He was in his shirt sleeves; they were wrapped up for the weather, as it had been raining earlier. Roper held the door open and allowed Wilkie to pass. However, his next step put him directly in Charley's path. She stopped and stepped to the side to let him through, her back to the wall. His eyes narrowed as he leaned in ominously to speak to her. 'How's it feel to know the pressure's on?'

She gave him a questioning look.

The smirk he'd fashioned on his loathsome face faltered, but he understood and nodded his head in return. 'Remember. All eyes at HQ are upon you...' he said.

'I have nothing to offer but blood, toil, tears and sweat,' she declared in response to his retreating figure. Brian Roper stopped and turned. For a moment, he appeared speechless.

Charley walked outside. She was shaking. The door slammed

behind them. Chuckling, Wilkie had to run to catch up with her, so long and determined were her strides.

'That was a belter. His face!'

Charley raised an eyebrow at him, on an otherwise deadpan face.

He frowned. 'I mean, that was very profound, boss ... what you said, was...' He slumped down into the passenger seat of her car.

Key in the ignition, Charley's concentration was on starting the engine. At the exit of the police compound she turned and gave Wilkie a half-smile and indicated left. 'It's Winston Churchill's words quoted on the back of the five-pound note.'

'By gum. They say you learn something every day, so that's my lesson for today.' His face became serious. 'You'd better watch your back, though. If the look on Roper's face was anything to go by, he's got it in for you.'

'I'm long past caring,' she said with a shrug. 'He'll do what he wants, when he wants, for as long as it benefits him. You know that, I know that, everyone who knows him knows that.'

Wilkie was unusually quiet, for a change.

'Penny for them?'

He turned towards her. 'I feel like I owe you an explanation.'

'For what?'

'I've never felt the need to tell anyone about this before, but I want you to know I'm not the heartless bastard you think I am.'

'Really?' Charley scoffed. 'This I gotta hear!'

Wilkie forced a smile. 'Really. It's just that men dressing up as women and women dressing up as men sort of creeps me out.' The detective's admission surprised her.

'I imagine that that is magnified in the case of people who actually change their bodies with surgery?'

'I know it sounds ridiculous … Like I said, I've never felt the need to tell anyone before. I know how bad it would have made me look.'

The sound of sirens could be heard in the distance. They got louder and louder and it was apparent they were travelling from where Charley and Wilkie had just come. Wilkie checked his wing mirror, Charley her rear-view. Flashing blue lights and horns alerted Charley to pull the car into the kerbside. The police vehicles passed by and, before she could move on, a paramedic car and two ambulances followed.

Wilkie frowned. 'Wonder what's happening,' he said, turning up the police radio.

It appeared that, for reasons yet to be established, a vehicle had hit a tree on the A62 Bradford Road … at Peggy-in-the-Woods.

It was a freezing cold morning, the wind chill spoiling the heat from the sun when it peeked periodically from behind small, fluffy white clouds. But as far as the accident went, there was no immediate concern that the weather had been a factor.

'That's the eighth fatal car crash on that part of the road in the past decade. All but one of which remain unexplained. That's if what Gerry Driver was telling me is true.'

'Unexplained and with no evidence to show that there was any other vehicle involved, or that the vehicle was going at speed,' said Wilkie.

The voice of the traffic inspector came over the radio. 'It looks like the driver negotiated a right-hand bend, then for some reason yet to be established, left the road, rolled over several times and collided with a tree.'

Pre-warned about road closures, and with her local knowledge, Charley managed to drive to Gibson's Horticultural car park without any undue delay. It appeared that Mr Gibson had been waiting for them. He was wrapped up warmly, with his cap pulled on his head and a woollen scarf round his neck, hands dug deep in his pockets.

'No work for the wicked today?' asked Charley as she alighted from the car.

'I'm actually waiting for Solomon.' He hesitated. 'God knows where he's got to.'

'I have the same problem keeping tabs on 'im,' Charley said, jerking her head in Wilkie's direction.

'Maybe you should lock him up. At least you know where they are when they're in the cells.'

'Don't tempt me, Mr Gibson. I must say, in my experience, locking them up is a great leveller.'

'I bet it is. Ah, talk of the devil,' he said, pointing to the entrance of the polytunnel where a pale-faced Solomon had suddenly appeared. The three walked towards him in silence, concern on their faces. His breathing was heavy and, as they got close enough to the sleeveless T-shirted man to see, they realised he was sweating profusely, his hair slicked back from his ruddy face. His muscular, left upper arm was bloody and scratched, as if he had been clawed by an animal.

'What on earth...?' said Mr Gibson.

Solomon lolloped to the water butt, bent over and reached in with both hands. He swilled his face before coming up for air, cocked a brow and twisted his neck to look at his shoulder. 'Oh, that must have been the branches. I've been lopping trees over yonder.'

'You have?' said Mr Gibson.

Wilkie took Solomon's fingerprints from hands that were like huge shovels. His fingernails were long and grimy, a breeding ground for germs.

'Does Mr Myers have his own keys?' Charley asked Mr Gibson, whilst Wilkie took swabs from Solomon's mouth.

'He does,' said Mr Gibson.

'You must trust this young man implicitly?'

Mr Gibson nodded. 'Yes, I do.' Which caused an undeniable smile on the face of Solomon.

'Can I go back to work now?' Solomon asked.

Charley smiled. 'Yes, and thank you for your co-operation, Mr Myers. It's much appreciated.'

Mr Gibson shook his head. 'What am I going to do wi' you, lad. It won't hurt to be courteous. The police officers are only doing their job. And put some ointment on them cuts and wear your overalls in future,' he shouted to Solomon's retreating back.

'I heard your lot down on the main road just before you arrived,' said Mr Gibson as they walked back to the car.

'Looks like it might prove another fatal one, too,' said Charley, a flash of sadness crossing her face as she put her hand to her police radio.

Mr Gibson shook his head, sighing heavily. 'That's going to upset mi' laddo. He's a lot more sensitive than he lets on. He wasn't the same for weeks the last time there was a fatal down there, absolutely devastated…'

'Do you remember the Honey Monster in them breakfast cereal adverts?' asked Wilkie as they drove back to the station.

Charley nodded and her smile widened. 'Massive shoulders, not too bright. Solomon reminds you of him?'

Wilkie nodded his head. 'He's an oddball, that's for sure.'

'It's his eyes. My grandpa used to choose his racing pigeons by their eyes. He always said he could tell by their eyes whether they were rogues or not. Maybe we should adopt that theory for humans too?'

'Do you think he could be involved?'

Charley shrugged her shoulders. 'He's certainly a person of interest to me, but I just don't get the feeling he'd have the nous to display the bodies, or the intelligence or capability to add the red herrings into the mix.' Charley's eyebrows were raised. 'But the golden rule is…?'

'Never assume. We might be underestimating him.' Wilkie grabbed the evidence bags that sat in the footwell. 'Hey, at least we did what we set out to do and got his samples.'

'And there's one thing for sure. If he was on any of the CCTV footage, he would stand out in the crowd.'

Back in the incident room, the samples taken from Solomon Myers were handed to the exhibits officer, who diligently recorded them.

'Data protection means…?' said Wilkie, pointing directly at Annie.

'Record, retain and reveal to any future defence team,' said Annie. 'I'm not that green.'

'Humour me. I'm practising for when I get my aide.' He waved his hand in an encouraging gesture. 'What happens then?'

Annie rolled her eyes at Tattie, her voice monotone. 'Once recorded, the DNA sample has to be signed out, timed and dated, before it goes to Forensics. When it's returned, it must be signed back in. Every exhibit item's movements must be chronologically recorded and whoever is removing the said item from the store where it is booked in must sign for it.'

There were two urgent messages waiting for Charley on her return. One made her heart skip a beat. She hastily dialled the number of the forensic science laboratory.

'Simon?' she said, her voice full of anticipation.

'Inspector!' The upbeat tone in his voice gave her hope of good news. 'I've been working on the soil samples from the churchyard scene and the victim's clothing. There was blood on both, however, the soil from beneath where the body had been hung, and what was on the clothing, is completely different. Now, I'm not going to bore you with the details. Safe to say the cemetery sample is much as I expected, the soil having similar fertility to a sports field and urban sprawl lawns. However, the soil on the clothing is dark, peaty and full of organic matter – bits of leaves and plants et cetera. In short, the soil on the clothing is consistent with that found in a well-cared-for garden.'

'So, you're confirming the churchyard as a dump site, right?'

'I don't think that was ever in dispute, do you? But that's not all; I've saved the best till last. The soil sample on the clothing of the deceased at the cemetery is of the same composition as that taken from the deceased at Four Fields.'

Charley's lips parted in shock. 'You're actually telling me that you can prove both bodies have been in the same location before being dumped elsewhere?'

'I can tell you it's highly likely, yes. I've authorised more tests to be done on the composite soil sample to identify other ingredients that might help you to pinpoint an exact location.'

Charley Mann could hardly believe she had heard Simon correctly. This revelation brought more questions, but the emergence of proof required for court purposes meant that pieces of the jigsaw puzzle were slotting together.

Though needing to discuss the breaking news with the team, she made the decision to return the call to the press office.

'Connie Seabourne,' announced the jolly voice at the end of the line.

CHAPTER 12

'DRUGS NOT AN ISSUE According to murder squad detective investigating recent killings ...' was the headline in the local paper.

'Have you spoken to anyone without my knowledge?' asked Connie.

Charley frowned. 'No. The last time I spoke to Danny Ray I told him to liaise with you.' Charley raised her eyes to the ceiling as she slumped back in her chair. 'That article must have been after he spoke to me...'

Connie nodded her head. 'He's persistent, you've got to give him that.'

Charley put her hand to her forehead and covered her eyes. 'Hold on,' she said. 'If my memory serves me right, he said at the time that, if I didn't give him something, he'd write the piece anyway and insinuated he wouldn't do me any favours. I guess this article is payback.'

'Well, he didn't get anything from me,' said Connie. 'But he has got pictures of the inner scenes somehow and, surprisingly enough, he's managed to come up with a fair yarn.'

'What can I say? I've not spoken to him and if he's hoping for a response, he's going to be very disappointed.'

'You don't think anyone else on the team has spoken to him?'

Charley shook her head. 'No, they wouldn't, not without my approval.' Would they, she wondered? 'Look, once I have something I can share with the media, I'll do so via the correct channels. I'm calling a meeting now. You might want to be there.' There was a smile in her voice.

'Why is that?' Connie said, coyly.

Charley put the phone down…

A whoop went up in the incident room when Charley announced the information the forensic officer had imparted earlier.

'It appears that we are looking for just one killer lurking in our community,' she told them.

A few moments later Annie Glover burst into the incident room, a slip of paper in her hand. 'Solomon Myers' DNA sample is an exact match for the sample found in the condom at the side of the body of Stewart Johnson.'

Charley gestured to those assembled to be silent. All eyes were upon the SIO. 'OK. So, we've linked him to the murder scene, but remember, that doesn't make him a killer.'

A strategy meeting to discuss the arrest of Solomon Myers and the availability of adequate POLSA search teams was called, and as she talked to those involved she counted off the actions that needed to be a priority on her fingers. 'Number one, his home address. Number two, the buildings at Gibson's Horticultural and the vehicles he has use of, will all need searching. We will be working outwards, which will also include the area we all know as Peggy-in-the-Woods. This is going to require a number of officers, but it's necessary for us to do this thoroughly and as quickly as possible. Think response, arrest and detention; vulnerability, potential for violence, fitness for detention, fitness for interview, custody record.'

'I wonder if he'll come quietly,' said Wilkie.

'Who knows, but we need to look at the possibility that he may be violent, the risks involved and how we deal with an injury to the prisoner – self-inflicted or otherwise – and, of course, to our officers. I want him arrested on suspicion of murder and, that done, taken to Huddersfield Custody Suite. Once he's in custody, the searches can begin.' She looked at her watch. 'We've got approximately sixteen hours to prepare. Seven o'clock tomorrow morning I want him cuffed.'

The paperwork, authorisations and agreements for the logistics of a pre-planned operation, all took time. Detailed risk assessment, and a working strategy addressing the risks associated with the suspect, were required. The arrest would be led by Sergeant Mike Blake and DC Wilkie Connor. All personnel on the ground would require protective clothing. Charley knew that the destination was out of the public eye, so the decision was taken that the arrest could go ahead without it being general knowledge: not having to co-ordinate involvement without outside parties made security for the operation tighter.

Charley looked extremely tired and her eyes were hazy when the meetings were finally over, the arrest packages completed and the participants briefed. It was late into the night when she finished the notifications to those she needed to make aware. She sat behind her desk, alone in her office, with only her desk lamp for light. The others long gone, she cleared her desk in order to enjoy the takeaway she'd ordered. She was in no mood for company. The meal tasted as good as it smelled. She would have sworn it was home cooked, if only her taste buds could remember what that was like. When she'd finished, she leaned back in her chair, her fingers idly playing with a string of paper clips she'd hooked together. All was quiet and still. Resting back in her chair, she closed her eyes.

She hadn't realised that she had fallen asleep until her watch alarm woke her. Mike was standing at the door before she was fully awake; he looked tense as he gestured to her that it was time to go. She didn't stop to speak to those in the office; they knew the drill. As she ran down the steps to take the last minute briefing downstairs in the Void, she was fully aware that the team would already be anxiously waiting, eager to get on with the task in hand. She took a quick check of the station clock which told her time was indeed of the essence.

'Game on,' Wilkie said the moment he clapped eyes on her, his face brimming with excitement. She could feel the adrenalin galloping through her veins as she stepped up onto a box Ricky-Lee had dragged towards her. The Void, where the police cars, motorbikes and vans were kept, was a huge chamber. She stood up on her makeshift platform, in front of one hundred officers, and her voice bounced off the walls, enabling all to hear her instructions.

Winnie watched the fleet of operational vehicles disappear out of the compound from different levels in the police building. There were no blue flashing lights, no urgency about them, just a unified convoy on a tactical pursuit. With a big sigh she pulled a duster from beneath her apron strings. 'God be with you,' she said, before commencing the polishing of the windowsill in Charley's office.

Through the windscreen, Charley saw that Gibson Horticultural's two huge iron gates were open, which suggested to her that someone might already be there. She drove the car at a crawl, wincing at every noise the vehicle made and that might alert Solomon Myers to their presence. Her car crunched to a stop and then there was silence.

Charley adjusted her rear-view mirror to see a unit park up at the entrance, confirming to her that nothing could enter or leave without her permission. She waited for the radio to announce the arrival of DC Wilkie Connor and his team, travelling on foot through the woods towards the only other possible exit, the rear of the polytunnel. Once they were in position, the signal was given for the officers to alight from the vehicles, each with a job to do. As quietly as they could, designated officers headed towards the reception shed; others followed her and DS Mike Blake to the area where they had last seen Solomon working.

The noise of a radio blaring out suggested Solomon Myers was currently in the polytunnel, just as anticipated. Soft-footed, they honed in on the source of the sound of running water and a yard brush sweeping the concrete floor.

Wilkie and his team could now be seen walking towards them from the rear of the tunnel. Neither Solomon nor Mr Gibson were anywhere to be seen. However, there was a ten-foot-high stack of blue plastic barrels which formed a square at the centre of the tunnel and there was no mistaking that someone was working behind them. Charley pointed to the barrels and Wilkie pointed to the opposite end, but before they could initiate the surprise move, the barrel wall suddenly came tumbling down and the officers could do nothing more than run for cover. The police-dog handler held Bruno on a short leash.

'Do you want me to let him go?' he yelled. Such was the noise of the barrels being thrown in a frenzy that it muffled any response.

'Armed police, get down on the ground,' came the call.

Solomon made an attempt to flee in the direction of the woods.

'Armed police, get down on the ground!'

Still Solomon ignored them.

Bruno was on a short leash and his handler was having difficulty holding him back. Straining and barking, the dog was keen to do what he was trained for.

Solomon swung out his upper arm towards an officer who was near enough to grab at him and his colleague made use of his pepper spray as they struggled to clamp the handcuffs to one of Solomon's arms. Four officers were now about him, but each lost the fight for supremacy over the madman. The police dog was released and immediately attached himself to Myers. The pepper spray had failed to subdue him and he managed to attack the dog with a flailing leg, which the dog promptly bit into. As his head was gripped by another officer in a headlock, Solomon still had strength to lift the officer off the ground. His teeth were bared and an almighty howl came from deep within his body as he continued to fight with the strength of a bullock being taken to the floor for branding.

Charley shouted out, with authority. 'Solomon, calm down. You're being arrested on suspicion of murder whether you like it or not.'

But still he fought on, this time attacking the police-dog handler and rendering him unconscious. Without his handler being able to call the dog off for a second time, it bit into Solomon's arm. Another officer activated his Taser and warned Solomon, who continued to attack the dog. The Taser hit Solomon in the back and finally, to everyone's relief, he fell motionless to the ground.

Bruno went to lay his paw on the handler's back as he lay, face down and unmoving on the ground. There was blood on the dog's bared teeth. Once Solomon was down, leg restraints were quickly put to use to fasten his legs together and prevent him injuring himself or anyone else further. Once handcuffed, he was unceremoniously hoisted to his feet. Paramedics worked quickly and expertly attending to the prisoner's wounds, and it was decided he needed hospital treatment. The dog handler was taken away in an ambulance for tests, although he was now conscious again and able to speak to Charley before he left on a stretcher. Charley's sigh of relief was heartfelt. Never before had she feared for an officer's life when he was under her command.

'Well done, everyone,' she said. 'I'll see you back at the nick for the debrief.'

While the teams prepared for the next phase, Charley went over to where Wilkie Connor stood with Mr Gibson. The old man looked every inch his seventy-nine years. His pallor was grey, his skin clammy; he leaned heavily against the door frame. Charley reassured him, explaining what they had found at the recent murder scene and the necessity for Solomon's arrest. She told him what would happen to Solomon next.

'By 'eck lass, I'm in shock. I still can't believe he would do something like that, not murder, not Solomon. Could it be that it was an accident?'

Charley shook her head and took the mug of tea that Annie Glover offered her. They had taken the old man inside and were now sitting round the table in Mr Gibson's kitchen. 'It wasn't an accident that's for sure, it was a deliberate act. Just like the disposal of the bodies.'

'It doesn't make sense. Don't you see what I'm trying to tell you? He's not bright enough for premeditated murder. He wouldn't know how or what to do, unless somebody instructed him. He's like a robot. He does what he's told, nothing more ... And I should know – he's worked for me for long enough.' Mr Gibson was saddened. 'I hope your officer's all right – and the dog,' he said.

'Will you come down to the station and make a witness statement?'

'Whatever you need,' he said.

'We need Solomon Myers' record of employment and any other background information you can help us with, to be honest.'

'The vehicle?' Gibson said. 'Your sergeant, he said it would have to be taken away?'

'Yes, the pick-up truck will be going on a low loader to be put under intense scrutiny by Forensics.'

Mr Gibson stood and hobbled to an old tin cupboard that was fitted to the wall. He unlocked it. 'I've got spare keys. You don't need to go to the expense of a carrier.'

'That's extremely kind, Mr Gibson,' she said, 'but we need to ensure that nothing is lost in transit.'

He slumped back in his chair. 'Of course. I never thought. I guess you'll hope for something in the tread of the tyres and the undercarriage...'

'We can't afford to miss anything.'

'I understand. I wasn't trying to...'

'I know you weren't.'

'When will this be in the papers? I'm sorry to sound so cold, but the business...'

'At this moment in time there has been no need to share anything with the media, but it won't be long before word gets out. I will be updating the victims' next of kin on Solomon's arrest as soon as he has been processed down at the station, and there will be a subsequent press release.'

Solomon Myers didn't appear to be in any discomfort from his wounds. He arrived at the custody suite handcuffed to two officers.

His boots were scuffed and dusty, his bloodied trousers crumpled, the shirt he wore looked as if it hadn't been washed in an age. His face was the only thing about him that was clean, no doubt due to the fact it had been washed to alleviate the effects of the pepper spray.

The arresting officers emptied his pockets and placed the contents onto the custody suite counter in front of the uniformed sergeant.

Keys for the vehicle lay next to another, larger bunch, possibly from his workplace. A Yale and a mortice-lock key were attached to a metal keyring shaped like a house, which suggested they belonged to his home address. Finally, there was a black fold-over wallet, containing a single ten-pound note.

If looks could kill, then Solomon had just slaughtered everyone around him.

The custody sergeant spoke to Solomon and explained to him that if he behaved himself, the handcuffs would be removed. He offered him the chance to give him the name of a solicitor, so he could contact them to ask them to attend at the police station with a view to representing him. 'In the event you tell me you don't have a solicitor in mind, or that you don't want a solicitor, we will contact one for you. Do you understand?'

The prisoner's face was devoid of all emotion. His jowls hung down and his slack mouth was in a perpetual sneer, making him appear menacing. The blotches of red on his nose and cheeks made those surrounding him look ghostly white by comparison.

The sergeant continued. 'When you've been arrested on suspicion of murder, you need legal support.'

Solomon Myers offered no response.

'OK,' said the custody sergeant. 'Let's try again. What's your name?'

'Solomon.'

'Any middle names?'

'No.'

'Last name.'

'Myers.'

There was no rush for further details – at least he was responding – however, the sergeant soon began to realise that perhaps Myers didn't fully understand what was happening.

'I think we need to have him assessed to see if he needs a responsible adult alongside, don't you?'

Wilkie was in agreement.

'We'll wait until the duty solicitor arrives and discuss it further.'

The sergeant felt it safe to take off the handcuffs. Solomon looked from one officer to the other and instantly lifted his stiff, straight arms so they could be removed. He rubbed his wrists together and a slight smile turned to a broad grin, then a little titter to a laugh. Solomon threw his head back and laughed some more. The officers looked at each other, both at the ready to restrain him again should it be necessary. With their hands on his elbows, they led Solomon to the cells, and there removed his footwear and clothing. He was given the standard issue prisoner clothing to replace his own.

At first, as the door closed and locked behind Solomon, there was silence from within the cell. But when the officers walked away, they heard the soft, hicupping sobs of Solomon crying.

Charley was in the incident room being updated on the information that had been collated regarding the arrest. 'I'm more than aware that, due to his reluctance at being arrested, there was a delay in seizing his clothing, and therefore we may have lost vital evidence. But you never know. We may still get something that links him to our victims. We can only hope,' said Charley.

Charley was mindful of all the plates she had to keep spinning. The brief post-arrest briefing was structured, but arduous nevertheless. Logistically, the pick-up truck was the easiest to deal with as it was a straight lift onto the low loader and away, but the searches were more complicated and required careful consideration. The scene was being subjected to a systematic search: Charley wondered if there was within its boundaries a murder scene.

'We are in possession of the keys Solomon Myers had on his person when he was arrested. These include those for his home address, given to us as Flat 23, Red Brick House, Meltham; his workplace and the truck he's been using. The latter needs to go to the allocated teams at the scene. His clothing and footwear need to go to Forensics,' said Mike.

'We'll need soil samples from every location to see if there is a match with those identified by Forensics. Mr Gibson told us that Solomon was proactive with the jet wash. The machine is still *in situ*, so perhaps that's the place that holds the secrets, if there are any to find,' she said.

'It's as good a place to start as any,' said Wilkie. 'The concrete floor has certainly been scrubbed clean recently.'

'Although Myers might have washed things on the ground, the roof of the tunnel might have traces of blood, or other, splashing on it, which may possibly confirm our suspicions, Neal suggested earlier. He's got it in hand,' she said.

'And it's highly unlikely that he would be aware of the possibility that the roof may hold clues,' Mike said.

Annie's sudden attendance at Charley's side was unexpected. The young detective had just arrived back from Gibson's. 'I've just seen Danny Ray skulking about on the A62, at Peggy-in-the-Woods. He flagged my car down and asked me what was going on. I hate to say this, but do you think there's a grass amongst us? How come he knew we were there?'

Charley knew that Danny appeared to be able to smell a story a mile off, but her instinct told her this was different. 'What did you say to him?'

Annie held up crossed fingers and grimaced. 'I lied. I told him we'd got information that somebody had been cultivating cannabis.'

'Good, the last thing we want right now is the press there and more unhelpful headlines. Give him enough rope, as they say…'

Gibson's Horticultural was set back far enough from the main road to give them privacy, but if someone were to visit, there would be no denying the police activity. Why would Danny Ray be visiting, Charley wondered. Could it be that he had been following her? At least Annie had dispatched him for now, and if he made an attempt to follow her in, the static unit at the gates would stop him in his tracks.

A dedicated team had been despatched to Solomon Myers' flat and the good news for some, although not all, was that they didn't have to smash the door down. What would the flat reveal, wondered Charley as she headed over there. The realisation that Danny might be following her made her check, and then double check, her rear-view mirror repeatedly en route. His turning up at the scene of the first murder, then at the pub when she met with the pathologist after the second murder post-mortem and now near the scene of the arrest, was too much of a coincidence. With all her senses heightened, she would hopefully become aware if someone was following her.

The traffic was heavy through the town centre and her mind

wandered, driving on automatic pilot. She wondered if the officers going into Solomon Myers' flat would disturb anyone. There was no way of knowing if there would be anyone within. Gaining entry into a person's house was not as simple as it had been before health and safety became a priority. Where would the rules for health and safety stop? If you hadn't been on a course to learn how to gain entry through a door, you couldn't use the door ram! And the use of slash-proof gloves; a must! However had the Peelers managed in the past without the mountains of paperwork? Common sense, that's how it had worked, but because of the possibility of litigation all that had changed and, like everyone else, she was forced to conform.

The photographs were being taken by Neal Rylatt and his team of CSIs when she arrived, and the search had begun. It was busy, it was organised, it was teamwork. The smell of bleach wafted along the corridor and led her into an orderly kitchen. The dull, white background of the faded linoleum gave little contrast to the cream and brown. The cream cooker and fridge blended with the patterned floral wallpaper that she knew to have been popular in the eighties. A small toaster, a kettle and a microwave sat neatly on the melamine worktop. A wooden tree mug holder had four tea-stained mugs hanging from it. The microwave was old and tatty, but, like the rest of the appliances on show, it looked relatively clean. The bins were empty and contained new liners. The cupboards held a few bits of odd crockery and some food, mainly tins of soup and milk puddings.

The kitchen led onto a small, square lounge. A large screen television with a games console on the coffee table dominated the living space. Again, although the furniture was dated it was neat and tidy. Piled high between the wall and the TV was a variety of DVDs including children's animation and porn. She saw a suited and booted police officer taking a DVD out of the player and popping it in an evidence bag and felt compelled to ask him what it was that Solomon had been watching. But she stopped herself. This was no time for idle chit-chat. She had a job to do and so had he – and she could check it soon enough. Power leads trailed from behind the television set, possibly for a laptop. But, if that was so, where was the device? Another suited officer sat on the floor, bagging and tagging computer games that he had retrieved from a cabinet. Action, Adventure, Sci-fi ... She frowned. What else had she hoped to glean from his recreational activities? Paperwork relating to a mobile phone gave them a number, but as yet they hadn't found the device at his home address, or on his person when he was arrested.

A small anglepoise lamp sat on an occasional table next to a large alarm clock, within reaching distance of the settee. Was this where he slept, she asked herself? The answer came more quickly than she expected when, standing at the bedroom door, she saw the dishevelled room. It was in stark contrast to the orderliness of the other rooms: untidy and littered, not only with bits of clothing, but with upturned furniture, overturned drawers and loose-leaf papers strewn all over the double bed. The bed covers beneath, however, looked newly neat. It didn't add up.

Charley hadn't expected Solomon to be house-proud. Without a doubt, the bedroom was out of synch. Why?

Wilkie pointed out a packet of condoms, which lay alongside an empty glass vase on the windowsill. 'Durex. The same as those found at the scene of Stewart Johnson's body,' he said eagerly.

Charley's stomach flipped. 'You know they're ten a penny round here. Durex is a make found in every pub machine from here to Manchester.'

'What if we can prove they came from the same machine?' he asked eagerly. 'Bag it and tag it?'

Charley put her gloved hand to her brow. 'Of course, we bag it and tag it,' she said, a razor-sharp edge of anger and frustration in her voice. 'Find me a mobile,' she told the search team. 'I'm going back over to the search at Gibson's. From there I'm heading back to the incident room if you need me.'

Charley dropped her coverall and overshoes in an evidence bag at the door, where an officer was guarding the entrance. As she walked down the corridor, she rolled her shoulders and cracked her neck, another habit she had inherited from her dad, and that her mother had hated. She smiled at the memory of her scolding and wished she could hear her voice, angry or not, just one more time. She called the elevator and looking upwards watched the numbers counting down as the lift gravitated towards the basement. Inhaling deeply, she ran a hand over her face and proceeded to tap her foot on the tiled floor. A tall, thin woman was standing at the window that overlooked the car park, her back to Charley. Her elbows on the windowsill, she stared outwards, a cigarette perched between two stiff fingers, burning away without any help at all. Charley pressed the elevator button once more and, taking her eyes off the illuminated numbers, stuck her hand in her handbag where she busily rummaged for her car keys. The woman coughed once, twice and three times. She moved the cigarette away from her and the smoke floated in Charley's direction. 'Should you be doing that here?' Charley asked, looking around for a sign that would tell her otherwise.

The woman gave a low throaty groan and stood up. 'Probably not,' she said, looking over her shoulder.

As the redhead's eyes focused, their eyes met and a flash of recognition passed between them. Charley hastily turned away.

'Go on, tell me what's the weird bastard been up to?'

'Not sure yet,' said Charley, checking the situation of the elevator which remained at basement level.

There was a pause. The woman studied Charley. 'Actually, you just missed him. He left minutes before you arrived.'

She turned towards the woman. 'Really? You saw the man who lives in the flat here, today?'

The woman took one last puff, swallowed and squeezed the flame from the end of her cigarette. Throwing the butt to the floor, she rubbed it with the sole of her feather-topped slipper. 'Well, I didn't actually see him. But I heard him moving around and the door slam when he left. Bloody heavy doors, fire doors. Wish the walls were as thick! There's no mistaking when your neighbour's at home in this place.' Her eyes looked up to the ceiling.

'That's very helpful, thank you. Tell me, what makes you call him weird?' asked Charley.

The woman sniffed, pulled her hoodie sleeve over her hand and ran it under her nose. 'Let's put it this way. There's no mistaking the noises for a start. I hear them a lot in my line of work. I can even tell when they're faking it ... been there, done that, bought the T-shirt – even worn the fucking socks.'

Charley refused to be drawn in, but now knew the last time she had seen the woman: in the Bar Amsterdam.

'Does he go out a lot, the man who lives in the flat?' She tried to avoid eye contact.

'He's never in. Apart from during the night, that is.'

Certain as she could be that the young woman didn't recall where she had seen Charley previously, she put her hand out to shake hers. 'I'm Detective Inspector Charley Mann, Yorkshire CID. Would you mind speaking to one of my officers and telling them what you've just told me?'

The woman's mouth turned down at the corners. She nodded. 'Guess so. Do I know you from somewhere?' she said. 'You look familiar. My name's Sunny.'

'Have I locked you up?'

Sunny screwed her nose up. 'Yeah. Probably.'

Charley felt relieved. 'Are there any particular dates that you remember, when you'd have said he was behaving weird?'

Sunny pulled a face. 'I can ask Chastity, my friend, if she remembers the date – the night we were entertaining ... like you do.' Sunny winked an eye. 'His telly was on so loud the men were getting randy before we'd managed to drink the good stuff they'd brought with them and that'll never do.' Her smiled turned to a grimace. 'Then the screaming began ... The guys, they got a bit jittery. Chastity was so fucked-off she was going to call the police herself, but business is business. Then it stopped as suddenly as it had started. We didn't hear anything more.' Sunny leaned in towards Charley and her voice turned to a whisper. 'Can you get him thrown out of 'ere, then we might get someone normal. Y'know, like Brad Pitt.' Sunny's natural smile was infectious.

'Have you ever seen anyone else with him?' asked Charley.

She shook her head. 'No, never ... Told you he was fuckin' weird.'

A combination of several scenarios ran around each after the other in Charley's mind. Who else might have a key to his flat? If Mr Gibson said he was a loner, and so did his neighbour, maybe he had family that neither had met? Someone who looked after him, or looked out for him? There was one thing for certain, it was an impossibility that Solomon Myers had been at his flat at the time

Sunny had stated because, since he'd left for work that morning, he'd either been at work, at the hospital, or locked up.

So, who had?

CHAPTER 13

At Gibson's, the pre-planned search was well underway. Charley watched the suited and booted search team crawling over the sites identified to be of interest. Like ants on a mission – hurrying this way, scurrying that, searching, peering, poking, probing, scrutinising – all were eager to make the ultimate find that would secure the prosecution of the perpetrator of the crime. They came together now and then, pinching, pawing their finds. Were they valuable to the investigation or not was the burning question. Ultimately, that wasn't their decision to make. As SIO, it was Charley's. Bagged and tagged clothing or computer device: it would be a waiting game to see if any item was deemed worthy of further scrutiny by the forensic experts – and if the budget would allow it.

Charley spoke briefly to members of the search team. Then, secure in the knowledge that they were doing all they could, she headed back to the incident room where she was in a position to converse with them all via the airways, liaise when necessary with the powers that be and discuss the interview strategy for Solomon Myers. One way or another, today they would find out the extent of Solomon Myers' involvement in the murders.

The incident room had been informed by the custody suite sergeant that Myers had been interviewed by the on-call doctor and deemed fit to be detained and, on her return to Peel Street, Charley was told he was presently having a consultation with the duty solicitor.

Apart from a couple of the HOLMES team members tapping away at the keyboards, inputting data, the incident room was quiet, as it should have been. It meant the rest were out working at one location or another and, unless there was anything that needed immediate attention, the results of their labour would be discussed at the end-of-day team debrief. Charley felt her energy levels dipping and, in the absence of a canteen, she headed through the office towards the kitchenette with its promise of coffee and a biscuit if she was lucky. As she passed Wilkie's desk, she noticed a bottle of whisky on it, and not just any bottle of whisky, but a Glenmorangie eighteen-year-old single malt. A small card was attached.

Tattie Tate, headphones covering her ears and appearing to be all-consumed by the audio tape she was transcribing, spoke suddenly, much to Charley's surprise. 'Came this morning,' she said, nodding her head in the direction of Wilkie's desk without shifting her gaze from her computer screen. 'Her with the French accent from the front desk brought it up,' she continued.

It was no good replying as Tattie wouldn't hear her, so Charley bent and touched the card very lightly at its corner to enable her to read the writing thereon. 'Simply, thank you,' it said.

A mug of hot coffee in hand and a ginger biscuit in her mouth, Charley retraced her steps from the kitchenette back to her office. She was in a speculative mood. Was the expensive gift for services received from an officer in her incident room? Everything about it suggested to her it had been bought to make an impression from a very grateful source.

Ricky-Lee entered the room whistling cheerfully.

Tattie, taking her headphones off, immediately frowned. 'I hate whistling. My father always said it was a pastime for the lower classes.'

Charley turned her head in Ricky-Lee's direction and silently raised an eyebrow indicating the large, sturdy box on Wilkie's desk. He stopped and immediately changed his tune to a long, low whistle.

'What the hell did he do to deserve that?' he said. Opening the box, he took out a shapely, substantial glass bottle. 'A superb example of the aesthetic,' he said, knowledgeably.

Charley was impressed.

'I swear I could just about pound a nail into a two-by-four with this thing.'

Tattie sat back in her chair waiting for the document she had been typing to print out. 'I don't advise using that or any other whisky bottle as a carpentry tool,' she said.

'Even the stopper capping it off is class...' Ricky-Lee continued with total disregard of Tattie's remark.

Everything about the gift on DC Connor's desk troubled Charley, but it would be quite some time before she would see him to be able to address the issue. Evidence-gathering was a long and meticulous process and he was now at HQ garage with Gibson's truck, waiting to speak to the forensic advisor to see if they could take a look over it as a matter of urgency.

Sitting alone in her office, having informed the family liaison officers for both murders of Myers' arrest, to be passed on to the relevant parties, Charley found herself feeling somewhat deflated, distanced as she was from the hands-on searches. She hated this part of the job that the rank of detective inspector inflicted upon her, the part that meant she had to be at the hub, relying on information being fed to her, to keep her up to date.

She called Annie in and they immersed themselves in the planning of the strategy for the initial interview with Solomon Myers.

'I wish we had some information that would enable us to get into his ribs,' said Annie. No sooner had she finished the sentence than Charley's phone rang with information that would make for an extremely interesting forty-five-minute interview with the prisoner. In Solomon Myers' work locker they'd found a long, brown, matted wig and female clothing. The information from the search team at his home address told her they'd found a mobile phone down the back of the cushions on the settee. It wasn't charged so it wasn't known when it had last been used, but it was a start.

But the third piece of news was more than the interviewers could have hoped for. The film found in the DVD player included the murder of a transvestite.

Michael Parish, the duty solicitor representing Solomon Myers, was small and had an extremely long, thin neck. A studious-looking man in his thirties, he sat on a hard, plastic chair, his bony elbow on the interview room table. He held two fingers to his temple and in silence, head down, he read through the handwritten notes Charley assumed he had made during his time with the prisoner in his cell. Her eyes were drawn to the deep, pink vee on the bridge of Michael's nose and whilst she waited for Annie to set up for the recording of the interview, she wondered how it had got there, since he wore his glasses way down at the end of his nose now.

The detectives sat at the opposite side of the desk from the solicitor and his client, case files in front of them. Charley sieved through her file slowly and in silence before they began. Parish sat upright, his serious grey-green eyes raised to the ceiling, as he waited patiently, in the shadow of a nervous-looking Solomon Myers who was checking out the panic strip, the soundproofing and the video camera. Solomon looked bigger, more muscular than he had at his place of work, towering over the little man at his side.

Charley cleared her throat, snuggled her chair nearer to the table and commenced the interview by doing the necessary introductions for the recording. She read out the caution and told the men the reason for Solomon Myers' arrest.

'Do you live at Flat 23, Red Brick House, Meltham alone?' she asked the prisoner.

'Yes,' he said.

'Does anyone have access to the flat other than you?'

'No,' he replied.

'Are you sure?'

The prisoner frowned. 'I've just said no, haven't I?'

'Yes, but I don't think that's true, because one of your neighbours said that someone has been in your flat since your arrest, prior to us arriving to search the premises. How do you explain that?'

Solomon smirked. 'A robber?'

Charley glared at the giant of a man before her. 'I don't think you quite understand the seriousness of your situation, Solomon. You're under arrest for murder. So, let's start with the murder of a young black man by the name of Stewart Johnson, shall we? Do you know anyone of that name?'

The prisoner shook his head. 'No,' he said, followed by a sigh.

'His body was found at the bottom of Four Fields. I believe you know the area owing to the fact you planted lots of trees there recently?'

Head down, Solomon twiddled with his thumbs. 'Don't know him.'

'Can you explain how a condom found next to the body contained your DNA?'

His eyes flew upwards to meet hers. He looked from the SIO to Annie, then turned to his solicitor. He clenched his fists. 'No way. They've fit me up. I've seen it in films.'

'Explain to us how the condom got there?' Charley continued. She saw a flash of panic cross his face.

'How should I know!' Again, he turned to his solicitor. Beads of perspiration appeared on his top lip.

'I'd like to take a short break, while I speak to my client about the implications of the condom,' said Mr Parish.

When they returned, Solomon looked pale. His lips formed a straight line. His head hung down, his chin to his chest. All questions put to him were met with silence.

'For the purpose of the recording, the prisoner refuses to answer,' Charley said over and over again.

Annie tried to engage him in a conversation, but still he remained silent. All planned questions asked, he was returned to his cell.

'Bloody solicitor! It's obvious he told him not to talk to us.' Annie looked downcast.

Charley raised an eyebrow. 'Not right at the moment, Annie, but we will continue questioning him, we've a lot more to put to him yet.' Her eyes were bright. 'It would be easier if he spoke to us and gave us some explanation, I give you that, but we've got to accept that isn't going to happen. We'll prove what took place with hard evidence. After all, these days an interview is for nothing more than to allow the prisoner to give us their view on the matter. It's early days. In all honesty I didn't expect him to roll over and give us an admission, did you? In fact, it would have shocked me if he had, especially with a solicitor advising him.'

Charley was back in the incident room collating the day's events in readiness for the debrief. The information from the team at Solomon's workplace was forthcoming: soil samples had been taken which included some that had been washed away into a pile by the jet wash. Swabs had been taken from marks on the walls and the roof. The consensus from the experts was that if there was anything to find, they should have collected some traces of evidence, but Charley knew only time would tell.

The pick-up truck had been fingerprinted, according to Wilkie, and the rear swept into one sample bag. What they had found was traces of green netting which had snagged on the hinges of the rear tailgate. 'It's being checked as priority,' the DC said. 'I still can't believe anyone in their right mind would buy a monster of a truck like that for someone like Myers to use.'

From Solomon's flat, they had found several pieces of period women's clothing, condoms, DVDs and video cassettes and an uncharged mobile telephone. All these had been seized and labelled as exhibits. Someone would have the task of watching the DVDs and videos to make sure the content was what it said on the sleeve and determine if anything in them might be relevant and have some bearing on the case.

Ricky-Lee looked pleased with himself as he booked the exhibits into the property store. 'Who was the supplier of his netting, I wonder?' he said. Charley immediately wrote down the question, to raise for further investigation.

'I took a statement from Myers' neighbour, with regard to her hearing someone in the flat between the time of his arrest and the police search,' he said.

'Pity she didn't see anyone.'

'Indeed, but she's adamant that she heard someone moving round the flat, which might account for the missing electrical equipment and the state of the bedroom.'

'How do you know anything is missing?'

Ricky-Lee shrugged his shoulders. 'I suppose I don't know for sure … just gut instinct when you see leads plugged into live electrical sockets and nothing attached. The flat's now sealed and the locks on the doors have been changed.' There was a twinkle in his eye. 'Guess what, we also found the newspaper with your picture on it, on the front page.'

'No doubt a few hundred others got a copy of the same paper, so I'm not going to worry about that too much.'

Ricky-Lee raised an eyebrow. 'Just saying…'

With a suspect in custody, they needed to prioritise the exhibits. Automatically Charley looked up at the clock and adrenaline warmed her from the inside out. 'Jesus,' she said.

'Even he can't stop the custody clock ticking,' said Marty from the front office, who had delivered the afternoon mail. 'Where you at?' he asked.

'One interview over and another planned for later this evening,' Charley said, as she flicked through the post.

'Then I guess you'll be bedding him down for the night?'

Charley nodded. 'Yep, eight hours sleep if he wants it, three square meals a day and a nap whenever he wants one, too.'

Marty chuckled. 'Who says crime doesn't pay?'

Even at this early hour Charley knew it was likely that she would be seeking the Divisional Commander's sanction for a further twelve hours' detention. And if thirty-six hours wasn't sufficient time to obtain proof of the prisoner's involvement in the murders, sufficient to charge, a trip to the Magistrates' court would be necessary for the approval of a further thirty-six hours. At the most, Charley had three days to charge or release Myers from custody, and at each stage of seeking approval to grant her further time on the clock, she would have to show that all enquiries were being carried out diligently.

Charley was pleased with the efforts of the team. She couldn't have asked for more professionalism and she thanked them all for their sterling work at every opportunity.

Wilkie Connor was just about to leave the debrief with the others when Charley collared him.

'I need a word in your shell-like. My office, now,' she said, and he followed her into the DI's office. She shut the door behind him.

'Do you like working here, DC Connor? I thought we had an understanding?' Charley said, feeling suddenly weary. She slid behind her desk, sat down and arched her back in a stretch. Finding his face, she looked directly at him. He sat on the edge of the chair opposite her, trying to guess where this was going.

'I know what this is about. The whisky...' he said, in the hope of taking the sting out of her tail.

Her eyebrows were raised in question. 'Looks like payment for a good deed to me,' she said. 'So, tell me, what on earth could you have done to be worthy of such an expensive gift?'

Miserably, Wilkie shook his head. His eyes found hers and he looked hurt at the accusatory tone of her voice. 'I know how it looks,' he said. 'That's why I've already asked CSI to fingerprint it.' He lifted up his arms and showed her the palms of his hands. 'Your guess is as good as mine!'

She held his gaze, unflinching.

His voice went up an octave. 'Ask them! Everyone who knows me, knows I've got beer goggles.'

Charley looked at him with a satisfied expression. 'OK, calm down. I believe you.'

His shoulders dropped; he still looked pensive.

'But, if someone is trying to set up one of my team, I want to know who and I want to know why.'

The detective rubbed his temple with the pads of two fingers. 'You and me alike! Don't you think I've racked my brains? I can't think of anyone who would think I deserve...' He looked sheepish. '...who can afford...'

'Let's wait and see if CSI can come up with anything. I want an update on any developments. Do you hear?'

The muscle in Wilkie's jaw flinched. His eyes didn't leave Charley's face as he rose from his chair. Emphatically he nodded his head; hurriedly he retreated to the door. 'Deffo, boss. Deffo,' he said. 'And,' he turned and grinned. His hand remained on the door handle for a moment. 'I don't *like* working here; I *love* working here.'

Wilkie exited, closing the door quietly behind him. Charley sighed deeply. She rubbed her tired eyes and looked down at the neatly stacked pile of papers on her desk. The day job didn't stop just because she had two murder investigations to deal with. She put the first document she picked up on the non-urgent file, the second on the filing pile and a copy of the monthly stats document to enable HQ to see what she was doing in the bin. Slowly she lifted the next document, which was of great interest to her. This gave her, in writing, the expert's opinion on the soil samples found on both bodies and the information confirming their belief that they had been in the same place at some stage, which was just about all she had to connect the killings. She sighed again. There was a vast amount still missing from the jigsaw and she desperately needed more evidence to support her theory that Solomon Myers was involved in the murders.

She looked up at the clock. The second interview was to commence in half an hour. There was no evidence to suggest any sexual acts had taken place, and there was no evidence at this time that Solomon Myers knew either Stewart Johnson or Kylie Rogers. Let's face it, she didn't have any evidence to show he was the murderer, but she had enough not to allow him to walk free.

Twenty minutes later, Annie Glover walked with Charley to the interview room. She had been told that Solomon Myers was on his way up from the cell area. It was pitch black outside and the station was uncomfortably warm and quiet. This time when they sat opposite Solomon Myers and his solicitor Charley was in no doubt that the prisoner was acting on his brief's instruction to say nothing. 'No comment,' he said, in a rhythmical fashion as each question was put to him by the detectives.

Having been told he had cried when he had been placed in a cell earlier in the day, Charley was interested to see how he coped with spending a whole night in the confined space, with just a toilet, a plastic-covered, two-inch-thick foam mattress, a blanket and no privacy. Would it weaken his resolve?

CHAPTER 14

'According to a witness, a dark-haired lady in a long black worsted skirt, wearing a lace shawl about her shoulders and a bonnet on her head, and carrying a wicker basket, was seen apparently disappearing into the hedgerow off the Bradford Road just after Monday's accident,' DC Ricky Lee informed his audience at the end-of-day debrief.

Tittering and rolling their eyes, the staff in the office mumbled among themselves.

Ricky-Lee's voice rose above the noise. 'Was the driver distracted?'

The mumbling stopped and all heads turned towards the detective constable once more.

'More importantly, one of our own reported seeing a lady of the same description when he was exercising his dog that same afternoon. I was told she looked to be floating, her pace was so quick along the path. Again, his recollection of events was that she appeared suddenly, as if from nowhere, only to disappear again just as quickly. Knowing the ghost story pertaining to the area, he admitted to me he got the dog back into the van and fled quite sharpish.'

The drumming of Charley's car tyres on the dry asphalt road changed quite dramatically to the specific crunch of the gravel in the stable yard. She'd hardly slept as she tried to process all the information chasing round in her head.

'Cock-a-doodle doo.' She heard the resident rooster crow. At the quickening of her heartbeat, she switched off her headlights and grimaced, looking up at the farmhouse windows. Thankfully, she saw no lights turn on, so she pulled on her handbrake and turned off the engine. As always when she drove at dawn or dusk, she was extremely glad to arrive at her destination, because even though the sky might be bright, the road surface, pedestrians and other vehicles were shrouded in shadow. Maybe the light had played the same tricks on the witness who came forward after the accident on the Bradford Road and the officer who had been exercising his dog close by at Peggy-in-the-Woods. Both were adamant they'd seen the figure of a woman. Perhaps the 'woman' had been Solomon Myers in disguise? But how had he got down to the road without being seen in his dressing-up garb?

Charley got out of the car, stood with her back to the door and breathed in deeply, embracing the approaching dawn. All was calm and quiet. There were no human beings around, only equine friends to greet her. The dog had abandoned its kennel, it seemed, and the cats were nowhere to be seen. She smiled to herself. Oh no, she knew where they'd be: snuggled up on their owners' bed.

Wilson stood at the stable door, his head cocked, his ears twitching. There was a rustle of straw as he moved impatiently from side to side inside his stall. He blew out steaming air with a whoosh and his lips curled back to show his teeth in what appeared to Charley to be an attempt at a smile. She grinned back at him and, leaning forward, she put her nose to his over the stable door. His neigh when she unbolted it and let herself in was more of a snicker. Wilson greeted her playfully, nudging her person in search of a treat. He was rewarded with a mint. She heard the clock chime and brushed him aside to locate his tack in the darkened stable. With fingers trembling in her haste, she tore the saddle from the rack and took the bridle from its hook.

Finally, her feet were in the stirrups and, crouching low in the saddle, she urged Wilson on. He was alert to her indecisive mood. After trotting out of the stable yard, she gave the horse his head and he chose to lead her up the trail across the moorland to the north of Peggy-in-the-Woods. A cool wind laden with moisture blew down the unmade road, lifting the strands of the bay horse's mane and sighing through the tops of the trees. Once on top of the hill, Wilson put his nose high into the air, his mane fluttering, his tail raised. He broke into a ground-gathering canter. As one, they pounded across the springy turf; it seemed as though they were covering miles. They were going at a fair speed when they came across a dry-stone wall, but rather than panic, she loosened the reins and Wilson aimed for the rise in the turf and soared a foot over the wall. Charley was breathless but exhilarated as they slowed down to a trot. She gathered her reins and together they picked their way through a field full of boulders. Then, winding their way through the trees, she let Wilson stretch his head after the exertion. She could feel the heat from his sweating body. Giving the gelding a solid pat on the neck she leaned forward in the saddle to whisper into his ear. The wind was now behind them as they ambled down the soil path to the side of Gibson's solid perimeter fence. There was no doubt about it, Mr Gibson took security very seriously. Looking ahead from her elevated position, she could see that the path led down into a small coppice of trees. Beyond it, she could hear the sound of cars on the Bradford Road below.

Now on the level, she pulled Wilson to a halt. His front legs spread out to the sides. He leaned back. His ears tipped forward and stiffened, his nostrils flared; he'd been spooked by something and was just seconds away from bolting, she could feel it. He pawed the ground impatiently and she squeezed his flanks with her thighs. The animal obligingly walked on.

At the bottom of the path, she saw that the fence around the horticultural site sported high, spiked railings with barbed wire on top. Bewildered, she considered the cost of the security keeping the public out. There was a man-made dip in the earth that left a space between the fence and the woodland and the snicket appeared to lead around the corner. She jumped down from the horse and tied his reins loosely to a tree. Stroking his neck to soothe him, and willing him to be quiet, she braced herself and set off to investigate. Ducking under the low branches of a large oak she soon saw a door in the fence. It seemed to have no keyhole. Puzzled by this, she grabbed its handle and pulled. At first it seemed to be stuck fast, then she pulled harder and the door popped open, its hinges making no sound as it swung open. She stuck her head through the opening, to be confronted by a thick hedge with an opening wide enough for her walk into. She listened. Feeling for the miniature torchlight in her pocket, she turned it on and flashed the light into the distance. Something appeared before her. The shadows cast on the polytunnels walls were eerie.

At Wilson's neighing, she turned away and shut the door behind her. Keeping the flashlight on now to show the way, she saw steps cut into the hillside leading directly down to the main road. Was this the place where the witness had seen the woman 'disappear', she wondered?

Charley looked at her watch as she and Wilson clattered back noisily into the now inhabited stable yard. She pulled the panting gelding up at the entrance to the field. He snorted and dipped his head to smell Bwyan, his spotted Shetland friend, who lifted her nose to nuzzle his mouth. At eleven hands high she was the little to his large. The stable hand took Wilson's reins from her, rubbed him down and walked him to the field where she could hear him braying. She turned to see his ears pulled back as he galloped away. Bwyan followed until the gap between them increased too much and, sensing it, Wilson galloped back to her, bucking and rearing as he did so. As the two came together, Wilson lay down and rolled onto his back.

'Scratching his sweaty hide to get rid of the human odour?' suggested Kristine as she joined Charley, who was standing with one foot in her car and her head on her folded arms resting on top of the door. 'You're up early. Didn't you sleep last night?'

'As much as Solomon Myers, I hope,' she said with a sigh.

Kristine looked at her, puzzled.

'I'm hoping that he hated it so much in that cell that he'll want to talk to us today.' She gave her friend a straight-lipped smile. 'But you know as well as I do: in this job we can never assume anything.'

The incident room was buzzing. Having a prisoner in custody meant a collective feeling that a case could soon be broken. This wasn't always to be, of course, but for now the high felt good.

'To understand the buzz, you've just got to be involved, haven't you?' said Annie.

'Days, weeks and sometimes months of hard work might give us a resolution, and therefore an update for the family of the victims.' A pained expression crossed Charley's face. Not closure as people liked to think. The victims and their families were the ones that serve the life sentence.

The custody officer from the cells informed her that Myers had complained of feeling claustrophobic during the night, but the old-timer wasn't having any of it.

'A big, burly man like him acting like a church mouse. Pff! When I took him breakfast in this morning, his attitude seemed to have changed somewhat. I think you might find he's ready to talk.' He winked before turning to leave and Charley watched him saunter away, shoulders back, whistling a cheerful tune.

She felt a second flicker of optimism as the prisoner's mobile phone analysis report came in with the initial findings: two pictures – both murder victims' bodies *in situ*.

'I'm sending the images over on email for you to view,' CSI Supervisor Neal Rylatt said, as a loud ping notified Charley of incoming mail. 'And I want you to inspect them very closely.'

Slowly, she dropped the phone on its cradle; her eyes didn't leave the screen. Her fingers hovered over the keyboard and, as if in slow motion, with an unintentional intake of breath, she switched the first image – the close-up picture of the dead Kylie Rogers – to full screen, and did the same with the next image, Stewart's dead body.

'Calm down,' she said under her breath. 'Evidence, but still not proof that he was there.'

Charley scanned the first picture back and forth, comparing it with the scene as she remembered it in her mind's eye. Then she flicked to the second picture. Suddenly, she realised that something was not quite right in the first image and she flicked back to the picture of Kylie's body, only to see something alien poking out from under a clump of long green grass. Her heart leapt inside her chest. Were her eyes deceiving her? No, someone else was in the picture. Someone else had been there when the picture was taken; someone who was wearing brown brogue shoes.

Someone else was involved. But who?

Annie Glover walked into the office as Charley was searching her desk drawer for the Sherlock Holmes magnifying glass that had been bought for her on promotion. It had been intended as a joke, but it worked perfectly. Annie looked at her boss quizzically. 'You can zoom in, you know,' she said, as she walked round the desk to look over her shoulder.

'I know. I have done,' said Charley, screwing up her eyes. 'But ... Tell me, did CSI manage to lift any footmarks at the scene?'

'I don't know,' said Annie. 'Do you think the murderer is photographing his work for himself, or to show someone else?'

'Whatever, it's something for this morning's interview,' she said.

Heads down, the two set about planning their interview strategy.

'Firstly, we get confirmation that it is his mobile, and then we show him the pictures.'

'See if we get a comment?'

Charley nodded. 'Then we push the fact that the picture shows that someone else is present.'

'And we ask him who it is?'

'Exactly! A failure of many interviewers is that they don't ask direct questions.'

'Like, did you kill him?'

Charley nodded her head. Her eyes returned to the pictures. 'These images connect him to both murders.'

'He's got some explaining to do,' Annie frowned, 'but will he answer, or will his solicitor stop him from speaking out?'

Charley shrugged her shoulders. 'We can only ask the questions for now and hope that his mobile data tells us more.'

'It'll be interesting to see who he's been communicating with…'

'It will, but what bothers me is that the phone just happened to be down the back of the settee where it would obviously be found quite easily … And where is his laptop?'

'If he had a laptop.'

'The leads are there.'

'You think someone has been meddling with the investigation?'

'If they have, they're one step ahead of us.'

Annie's look was one of surprise. 'Maybe the shoe in the picture belongs to the person who was heard in Solomon's flat.'

Charley's phone rang. She picked up. It was Connie. 'The local paper has a headline that concerns me.'

Charley frowned. 'Go on.'

'"Local man arrested for recent murders" – it's causing me loads of grief amongst the rest of the media who are demanding to know if it's true. How'd Danny Ray know about the arrest?'

'I've no idea. I've not spoken to anyone nor, as far as I know, has any of the team. But you can confirm to them that a twenty-seven-year-old local man has been arrested in connection with the murders, if that helps.'

'And, I guess, no further comment at this time which is normal protocol when a suspect is in custody?'

Charley knew she could only keep things quiet for so long, but how dare that bastard run with the story? There was no doubt in her mind he had decided he would be a thorn in her side by ignoring protocol. Was he wanting a reaction from her? She banged the palms of her hands flat on the table and Annie jumped.

'Enough,' she said under her breath – she wouldn't be sidetracked by him; she had work to do and Solomon Myers' custody clock was ticking – 'I have a briefing to do before the interview.'

With positive findings to put to him, the interview with Solomon would be interesting. Charley had decided that she would go back into the interview with DC Annie Glover to see if being in his presence gave her any gut feelings about him. After this, she would watch any further interviews onscreen through direct video link, where she could study his body language without any distractions.

The briefing was a positive start to the day. All enquiries were focused on Solomon Myers. The anticipation in the room was tangible. Did they have the killer in the traps?

'Michael! Good to see you again,' said Charley, in a cheery voice. Their meeting, prior to Myers' joining them in the interview room, was expected. With a limp hand, Myers' solicitor reciprocated with the briefest of handshakes. He swung his briefcase up onto the desk and let his fingers explore the inner pocket of his suit jacket, producing his pen before he took the jacket off and sat down. He took out his notebook, found a clean page and began to write. He didn't look up when Charley spoke to him.

'For your information,' she continued, 'I will be asking for a twelve-hour extension in custody, via the Divisional Commander, and if we still need more time, I will be going before the Magistrates to extend his detention in custody for the further maximum thirty-six.'

'And I'll appear for my client at the Magistrates. We will,' he emphasised, 'be asking for bail.' His eyes found hers and he smiled.

Charley raised her eyebrows. 'Good luck with that one,' she said.

The look in her eyes wiped the smile off his face. 'I don't rely on luck, Detective Inspector,' he snapped.

'But I rely on the courts of justice to be prudent, knowing that after the seventy-two hours I am granted by law to interview your client, I will be ready to charge,' she said, her voice lowered to a whisper, 'or release.'

Once again in a cell-area interview room, dwarfing Parish at his side, Solomon Myers was relaxed, or so it seemed. The solicitor had been informed of the findings on Myers' mobile phone and the clothing, and he had already spoken with his client about the disclosure. All that was left to do, after the caution and identification of those present for voice recognition on the tape, was for the detectives to remind Myers that he was under arrest for the two separate murders, before the interview commenced.

'Solomon, as you are aware, we have your DNA from a condom found at the scene of the murder of Stewart Johnson and we have also now recovered, from behind the cushions on the settee in the lounge of your flat, a mobile phone. This mobile is presently under examination by our technical team. We already know there are two photographs on that phone.' From beneath the file in front of her Charley produced paper copies of the two photographs showing the bodies of the two murdered people, and a picture of the mobile phone. Exhibit CM1 was a picture showing Kylie Rogers hanging from a tree by her feet. Pointing to it, Charley asked, 'Did you take this picture?'

Solomon Myers' eyes were red-rimmed and his hair badly needed a brush. 'No comment,' he said.

Charley produced the second picture. 'I am now showing the

prisoner Exhibit CM2 which is a picture of a mobile phone. Is this yours?'

His eyes glanced at the picture and then back at her. He shrugged his shoulders.

'Solomon Myers is shrugging his shoulders. Could you please answer the questions and speak out for the purpose of the tape?'

The prisoner cleared his throat. 'No comment.'

Charley showed him the third picture depicting Stewart's dead body. 'I am now showing the prisoner Exhibit CM3. Did you take this photograph?'

Again, he looked up at the CCTV camera. 'No comment,' he said, before returning his gaze to her. 'Carry on.'

'Thank you,' Charley replied, without a trace of sarcasm.

Myers rhythmically tapped the table.

'The pictures, the DNA, all suggest that you are responsible for both of these brutal murders. Did you kill them at your place of work and then take them to where they were found?' Charley fired across the table.

Myers smiled, turned to his solicitor, and then nodded his head. 'Same answer. No comment.'

'Did you do the murders by yourself, or was there someone else with you?'

Myers drew a long breath, exhaled and then continued. 'No comment.'

'Was there a reason for hanging Kylie's body where it was found?'

'No comment.'

Charley pushed the picture showing Kylie's body *in situ* across the table. The image sat directly in front of Solomon. He didn't look at it until he was asked to do so.

'Take a closer look. You see, this picture brings me to a pretty inescapable conclusion, that you didn't commit these murders alone. Tell me who was with you?'

Myers gazed at the detectives across the table, silently, for several seconds.

'Solomon?'

'No comment.' He whispered at first, and then added loudly, 'for the purpose of the recording device.'

'I want you to look in the bottom left-hand corner. There was someone standing with you when you took this picture. How do you respond to that?'

Myers flinched. He turned to his solicitor and frowned.

Without lifting his head from the notes he was making, the solicitor crossed his legs and hunched in his chair, before looking over his glasses at Charley, his mouth fallen open like the hinged jaw of a ventriloquist's dummy. It was apparent to her that he had not scrutinised the photograph and seen what she'd seen. He turned to his client and looked at him questioningly.

Hurriedly, Charley continued to push the line of questioning which had obviously touched a nerve. Leaning forward across the table, she lowered her voice. 'Someone make a mistake?' she asked, raising one eyebrow.

Myers sat up, cleared his throat and shuffled back in his seat, as far away from her as his chair would allow. 'I don't know what you're talking about.' He scoffed.

An answer! Charley felt a surge of adrenaline run through her veins. She carried on. 'By taking this picture, you've implicated someone else, haven't you? Are you just the brawn?' Her eyes narrowed. 'If so, who's the brains?'

Solomon was clearly becoming agitated. He turned to his solicitor with a questioning look in his eyes. His solicitor remained silent.

Charley's voice became gentle and sympathetic, but firm. 'We will find the other person, but at this moment in time this interview is to give you an opportunity to tell us what's been going on and with whom.'

Myers shook his head slowly from side to side. 'No comment, no comment, no comment, no comment! What don't you understand about that?'

From the file in front of her Charley slowly slid out a picture of the women's period clothing. 'Are these yours?' she asked.

'No comment,' he said.

'It's your prerogative, Solomon. I think we get the message,' – she stopped, picked up the papers in front of her and shuffled them into a neat pile – 'but perhaps you should think about your position. No one is worth that sort of loyalty. Let's face it, you're in here being questioned about two murders. And the other person? Well, they're at home, sleeping in a nice comfy bed and just getting on with their life.'

Charley didn't wait for a response, but terminated the interview. She walked back to the incident room with Annie with a spring in her step.

'Do you think we'll be ready to charge him, even if we aren't granted the full seventy-two hours in police custody?'

'It'll not be for the want of trying.'

'It's so obvious: he's not clever enough to set up a dump site to look like the scene of the crime, is he?'

'No, definitely not. He's someone's puppet, that I am sure of. The good thing is he's going nowhere for now. He can wriggle as much as he wants, but he's in the net. We have to keep on digging though. I'm going in to the debrief to tell everyone that we need one hundred and ten per cent, no distractions. We need the evidence to put him and his accomplice behind bars.'

Annie sniggered.

'What?' said Charley.

'I guess a little help from the Hobgoblin wouldn't go amiss? Maybe we should all put a jug of milk out tonight?'

The two women were laughing as they entered the incident room to be met by a wall of shocked faces.

'Wilkie's been involved in an accident. He's in an ambulance, on his way to the hospital. It's not looking good,' said Mike.

'Has someone been in touch with his wife? Does he have a wife?'

Mike Blake and Ricky-Lee exchanged glances. 'He has. She's wheelchair-bound. She's totally reliant on him,' said Mike. 'I thought you knew.' His head down he followed her into her office. 'But then, why should you?'

Charley collected her car keys from her desk drawer. 'Children?'

Mike shook his head. 'No, there's no other family. He's devoted to Fran.'

'He is?'

'Yes, he is. All his spare time, and spare money, is spent on looking after her: doctors, homeopathic treatment, magical gold rings warranted to cure rheumatism in quick time – the lot.'

'And what else don't I know about him?' She didn't know why she felt shocked, but she did.

'Oh, he does most of the housework, the washing, keeps a nice garden, a dozen hens and a hutch with rabbits – he bakes a nice cake.'

'I had no idea…'

'No, he keeps his personal life pretty much to himself.'

Charley rushed into her office to grab her jacket. There was a message from Wilkie on her desk. 'I think we might have found us the perpetrator of Eddie's murder,' it said.

She shuffled into her jacket. 'I'll be at the hospital if anyone needs me,' and with that she was out of the door. 'Inform Roper,' she called over her shoulder.

CHAPTER 15

Charley put her hands on her head and sighed. She wound down the car window, much in need of fresh air, and for a moment closed her eyes, letting her head fall backwards on the headrest. She turned her face to feel the cool breeze and composed herself. Sitting in the line of traffic, she waited for the lights to change. The north-easterly wind that had blown her hair away from her face appeared to have picked up suddenly, rocking the tall trees. She saw a lady lose her hat and a small child chased it into the road. Charley held her breath until he was safely back on the pavement. A group of school girls from the private school, clad in dresses and skirts, held on to their hats. It all seemed surreal. Whatever her initial thoughts about Wilkie had been, they had changed after their discussion. She had thought she had the measure of Detective Constable Connor, but how wrong could she have been? And could he really have found the culprit who'd flown the drone in the restricted airspace that they believed had spooked her beloved Eddie to his death?

The quickness of her step caused her shoes to make tiny, sharp squeaking sounds on the tiled floor in the hospital's entrance hall. Swiftly, she turned a corner. The corridor ahead was long, straight and narrow. The sun shone brightly through the sealed half-wall of windows, which made it feel extra-warm and very humid. En route she took off her coat, rolled up her sleeves and undid a few buttons of her shirt, as a variety of trolleys clanked along past her, some with people on board, others carrying magazines, beverages, sweets and biscuits. There were voices talking on mobile phones, some hushed, others shouting, even laughing. She looked upwards to read sign after sign, went past ward after ward and traipsed along corridor after corridor, until finally, right at the end, some closed double doors awaited her and through them she found the nurses' station.

In contrast to the noisy corridor, the sounds emanating from the ward as she stood waiting for a staff member to appear were soothing. The gentle bleep, bleep of monitors, the quiet scrape of nurses' shoes and the muted voices lulled her into a more relaxed state.

'What can I do for you?' asked a cheerful, loud, friendly voice.

Charley jumped and turned towards the voice, instinctively offering her hand towards the man dressed in nurse's garb. 'Detective Inspector Charley Ma–' Their eyes locked. He looked blank for just a second, but then his shoulders hunched and his jaw tightened. '*Mon ange?*' he said. Immediately he questioned the words and his gaze dropped away from her. Charley's racing heart juddered. How could she ever forget those striking green eyes?

'Ruby?' she whispered so low that no one else would hear.

Ruby sat and focused on the computer. 'An update on Wilkie Connor, I presume?'

'It is, isn't it?'

Ruby's shoulders dropped. He leaned forward, a flush to his face, rolled his eyes and groaned. 'Awkward,' he said, showing a dimple in his cheek. 'Funnily enough, it's usually Rubin that gets "clocked", not the other way round.'

'And, of course, I don't make a habit of visiting...' Charley said with a shake of her head.

''Course you don't,' the nurse said with a quick smile. 'Look, I'm hardly likely to tell anyone if you don't.'

Charley's relief was palpable. 'It goes without saying...'

'Now, let's start again, shall we? I'm Nurse Rubin and I guess you're wanting to know how your Detective Constable Wilkie Connor is faring?' His animated facial expressions turned into the familiar professional mask. He raised his eyebrows and his voice was hushed. He looked about them before edging closer. 'Just between you and me?'

Her eyes didn't leave Rubin's face and she nodded.

'He's been taken to ICU, presently breathing with the aid of a ventilator, in an induced coma.'

'Will he make it?'

'The next few hours are critical.'

'Can I see him?'

Rubin shook his head and grimaced. 'I'm sorry, only his closest family are allowed in right now.'

Charley's face fell. 'It's just that I feel so responsible...' she said, her voice cracking.

'Tell you what. Give me your number and I'll let you know as soon as he can have visitors – and, I'll keep you updated on his progress.'

Charley sucked in a breath and gave him a smile. 'Thanks, that's very kind.'

On her journey back to the police station she was able to update Mike and he her. Charley wanted to know who Wilkie had been going to meet when he had been struck by a car.

'A call came into the incident room this morning. He was on his way to see an anonymous informant who stated they had information about the murders.'

'Why was he alone?'

'The caller insisted on it.'

'Who took the call?'

'Tattie did and all we know is that it was a male who made the call from a call box.'

'And we're in the process of...'

'Yes, yes, trying to get a location for that call.' The line was silent for a moment or two. 'I discussed it with him before he left. We talked about me going with him, but we're chasing the custody clock with Myers and Wilkie didn't seem to see going alone as a problem. In fact, he was more than happy; he doesn't get a lot of time out. He often uses times like that to pop in and check on Fran, so I didn't question it.'

'Please don't beat yourself up. Let's face it, it could have been the two of you in hospital if you'd gone together. Accidents do happen.'

'But that's just it, the traffic lads are suggesting it may not have been an accident.'

Charley's eyes were fixed upon the car in front. She listened intently. It was raining, but only gently. Her mood was tranquil, or was it just that she was emotionally drained?

'The car that hit Wilkie apparently mounted the pavement. There is no CCTV at the location and, as it was at the caller's request that they met there, it does seem highly suspicious don't you think?'

'No speed cameras, mobile units or ANPR? God forbid!' She looked up to the sky from where the dispersing moisture fell. It was dove-grey.

'We've got that line of enquiry already covered,' he said.

'Witnesses?'

'It appears not. Or, none that have come forward yet.'

There was silence.

'What're you thinking?' he said.

'I'm thinking he has a bottle of whisky delivered and then this … Can you think of anyone who might have it in for him?'

Charley could hear the smile in his voice. 'He's a gobshite. Everyone knows he's a gobshite, but he's got a good heart,' he said. 'I don't know anyone who would do this to him, no.'

'Then could it be that someone is trying to silence him, or divert our attention away from the investigation?'

'Could be, but it's a bit over the top to mow someone down just to try and take our eye off the ball, don't you think?'

'Oh, I don't know. If you've already committed murder once or twice, then maybe the collateral damage is done … I'll be with you in ten. I can't do any more at the hospital. They won't let me see him … and I assume his wife is with him.'

'Do you think we need to get a uniform on guard outside the ICU department, for his protection. If it was a deliberate act, then whoever it is that's trying to get to him might try again.'

'Good point, I'll have a word with uniform when I get back to the nick.' There was silence. 'Oh, and Mike,' she said.

'Yes, boss?'

'Get t'kettle on, will you. I'm parched.'

The pavements and roadway were darkened by the wetness, but the leaves on the trees glistened and the grass on the verges somehow seemed greener. A flash of sudden emotion brought a tear to Charley's eye. Although she would put the perpetrator before the court – and she had never been more determined to catch her man, the person who had done this to Wilkie – she knew she would be handing it to others to determine the sentence, no matter if it hadn't been a deliberate act by the person responsible, who may have been using their mobile phone, drunk or on drugs at the time of the incident. A car was no different to a loaded weapon in her eyes. She swallowed hard to get rid of the lump in her throat. At a recent meeting she had suggested that offenders' cars should be seized immediately, along with the mobile phones they'd been using – and they shouldn't get them back either. The idea hadn't gone down well, but something needed to be done to reduce road fatalities and why shouldn't the offender pay?

The car in front turned right at the traffic lights and she turned left. The action broke her reverie. If it was the case that Wilkie Connor being knocked down had been a deliberate act, then she had an attempted murder on one of her officers to investigate, as well as the two existing murders. They couldn't speak to the DC yet, but the anonymous phone call was a starting point. If the public telephone box where the phone call had been made could be traced, maybe there was also a chance it was covered by CCTV. Her spirits rose at the thought and, having parked her car, she made her way to the incident room feeling more focused. She noticed the rain had ceased and that a soft, blurred light seemed to be spreading over the back yard of the police station. She raced up the steps to the incident room two at a time.

There was a mug of hot coffee waiting on her desk, along with a plate of biscuits. The team were eager to hear her news of Wilkie Connor and they too had news. 'Myers has been to the Magistrates' Court and remanded to the cells for a maximum of a further seventy-two hours in custody. In the end, Michael Parish made no objections to our request,' said Annie.

Charley's eyes fixed on the young DC. 'I want the photograph that includes the image of the shoe blown up to A4 size. We must keep this information close to our chest. If the person doesn't realise their footwear has been captured in a picture, then they won't be intent on destroying the shoes. This could be their downfall.'

Ricky-Lee sat in the background, his eyes on the computer screen. He was in deep conversation with someone on the telephone, his elbow on the table, his hand to his brow. 'A large number of the films that Solomon had in his possession depicted brutal rape scenes, strangulation,' he told Charley when he'd put the phone down. 'There are scenes of people being hung by their feet.'

'Do you think this is where the idea to hang Kylie came from?' asked Annie.

Charley shrugged her shoulders. 'Do we know where the films were purchased? If he bought them, he would have needed a method of payment. Do we know if he has a bank account? He didn't have any bank cards on his person when he was arrested.'

'We didn't find any at his flat, just a lone ten-pound note in his wallet. No credit cards, no bank statements. But that doesn't prove anything.'

'Maybe Mr Gibson could help us? He pays his wages.' Annie raised her eyebrows at the others.

'Make asking him a priority. Myers' financial profile could help us.'

Annie was scanning through images that had been located on the films, depicting the scenes he may have used as inspiration for the murders. Charley saw her put her elbows on the desk and her head in her heads. She put a hand on her shoulder. 'If it's getting too much, I can always get someone to take over.'

Annie turned, 'No, it's OK. But tell me something. How long will I do this job before I begin to understand?'

'Understand what?'

'Understand how anyone in their right mind could be excited by this sort of thing?'

Charley afforded herself a smile as she sat. 'Never! When you think you've seen it all, but there doesn't appear to be an explanation for a murder, my experience tells me it's usually sexually motivated. Sex offenders are not normal. Sex offenders are excited by, and do things, that a normal person wouldn't even contemplate, and that's what makes them so dangerous, because not even in our wildest nightmares could we ever imagine what extremes they will go to for their gratification.'

Annie looked momentarily relieved.

'All any of us can do is deal with the facts and see what transpires; that's my approach.'

'My cousin, she says she's seen it all. She's a nurse. She works in casualty. I thought she'd made up the stories she told me until now...'

Charley shook her head. 'Ah, the "accidents" that occur with perverse sexual activities! Yeah, I've taken a few to casualty myself.'

'Do you think Solomon fits into this category?'

'I don't know. Maybe. Or maybe there is someone else telling him what to do and how to do it.'

'Why?'

Charley shrugged her shoulders.

'Do you think the victims are chosen at random?'

'Who the hell knows? I wish I knew how and why.'

Heads turned as the door of the incident room slammed behind Mike.

'Boss, Danny Ray's been asking to have more info on the hit-and-run involving a police officer and Connie's chasing you too, about the same thing,' he said, his eyes on Charley as he walked in her direction.

Charley put the palms of her hands on the desk and raised herself slowly from the chair. 'I'll talk to Connie, then she can speak with the media.' Her eyes looked from Annie's face up to the ceiling. 'How is it that bad news always travels more quickly than the good, eh?' she said.

Annie gave her a half-smile and continued with the job in hand. Mike followed the DI into her office.

'We need to open a HOLMES account for the attempted murder of Wilkie. Any news on the origin of the whisky, or our anonymous caller?'

Mike shook his head. His face was grave. 'No.'

'Do you know if the fingerprint bureau checked the thank-you card that came with the whisky? And, if so, did they get a hit?'

Mike shrugged his shoulders. 'Don't know.'

'Ask. If not, I want them to make it their priority. I'll have to go and update the Divisional Commander. I'm sure he already thinks I'm a Jonah. God knows what he'll think now that one of his officers has been mowed down.' She looked out into the office. 'Solomon Myers needs interviewing; I want Annie and Ricky-Lee to do this one and I'll observe. Can you organise that for me?'

There was no need for her to seek the Divisional Commander Brian Roper out, as it happened, because, as if saying his name could conjure him up, he appeared at her office door.

Mike nodded at him as he left and Roper walked in and closed the door behind him.

'If Mohammed won't come to the mountain, Inspector,' he said, raising an eyebrow. He sat down facing her, his expression one of concern. 'I'm upset and extremely annoyed that one of my officers has been targeted. I'd like to front the media on this one, if you don't mind?'

Charley nodded. 'Sir.'

'I've made arrangements to go and see him as soon as I can. He's still unconscious, I understand?'

Again, Charley nodded her head. 'He is, as far as I'm aware.'

'I've also arranged a press conference.'

'Thank you,' she said, sincerely. 'That will enable me to get on with the investigation.'

'Your thoughts, Inspector?'

'I think DC Connor was set up. Someone telephoned the incident room anonymously suggesting they had information and expressing a wish to meet with him alone. Prior to that he'd received a bottle of whisky with a thank-you card attached. Again, we don't know who that was from and neither did he.'

Roper scowled. 'Connected to the murders do you think?'

'I'd like to think they were separate incidents, but the connection to the incident room and the timing makes me think otherwise.'

'Tell me,' he said, leaning in, 'how are you doing with the pillock in the cells?'

'Typically "no comment" at the moment, sir. They're just about to start another interview with him. What we are confident about is that someone else is involved, but as yet we don't know who that is.' Charley took a deep breath. 'But we'll find them, I'm confident of that.'

Roper stood. 'I'll leave you to it.' There was a flash of teasing in his eyes. 'I need to work on my speech. Maybe even a quick haircut before the cameras arrive?'

Charley was left shaking her head. How did that man's mind work? It was all about him, his image; nothing had changed. But her heart felt somewhat lighter. The weight of the police rank that Roper held alone would give the appeal some credence. It was her hope that someone would come forward with information about the offender and the vehicle they had been driving at the time.

The screen on her desk showed Charley that Myers' solicitor Michael Parish, and Solomon Myers himself, had entered the interview room. She turned up the volume. Slouched in the chair, from beneath drooping, sly eyelids Solomon looked across the table at the officers. His opening reply to the first question was what they had become accustomed to – no comment – but subsequently his answer was a wall of silence. The officers were not distracted. Systematically they went through the previously discussed line of questions, which gave Solomon Myers every opportunity to respond. In this, the fourth interview, the prisoner appeared more controlled, more confident. Was this due to the fact there'd been a change in the interviewers, with the boss out of the picture – or so he might think? His gaze was fixed on the wall beyond Annie and Ricky-Lee. His expression gave little away. Inwardly, Charley wondered if the solicitor's advice had calmed his state of mind, or was this façade just an act and was he still conspiring, but in secret? Charley had specifically asked the interviewing team to end the interview by asking Myers if he knew Detective Wilkie Connor and she was eager to hear his reply. Why, when there was no comment, did she feel so deflated? What did she expect from him, a confession? For him to start talking now? Michael Parish nodded at Solomon, as if in approval of his conduct throughout the interview. Myers smiled back. Was this the stance of someone who realised his freedom was possible if he only trusted his brief?

The stupid smirk Myers gave to the camera as he stood to be taken back to the cells was not a welcome one. He was telling the police nothing. But, bizarrely, what did dawn on Charley as she watched the interview back, was that Mr Gibson could not only help them with Myers' financial background, but might also be able to tell them who Solomon's landlord was and whether he shared the flat with anyone. Why hadn't that occurred to her before?

Charley placed the phone on its cradle. She had listened to what the representative of the Crown Prosecution Service had said. She understood that they didn't want her to charge Myers with murder. After all, all she had at this moment in time was circumstantial evidence which didn't prove he'd committed the murders. But what it did show her was that he'd been present at the murder scene. And now enquiries were in progress.

A wave of excitement went around the incident room at debrief. The anonymous phone call to the incident room was found to have come from the motorway service station at Hartshead and a unit had been sent to seal off the area. CSI had been booked to attend and the CCTV by the telephone kiosks was known to be in working order. They had an exact time at which the call had been made, because it had been logged. These two vital snippets of information together meant they might also be able to identify the vehicle which the caller had used to get to the service station.

Believing herself to be alone in the car park when she left that night, Charley looked up at the stars in the night sky. 'Thank you, God,' she said, slowly exhaling.

'Put out a jug of milk for the Hob last night, did you?' said Annie, with a grin as wide as her face would allow.

Charley looked around for her colleague. When she found her doing much the same thing, she laughed out loud. 'No. Why?'

'Good job I did then,' said Annie, with a wink.

CHAPTER 16

Charley watched the TV interview held by the Divisional Commander.

Standing on the steps of the police station he looked very smart and indeed he sported the new haircut he had threatened to have for the occasion. Assembled were local and national media. 'The pursuit of the person or persons responsible for knocking down my officer will be relentless,' Roper declared, his face determined. 'I appeal to the public for their help in finding the driver and the vehicle involved,' he said.

A muffled shout could be heard in the background, from one of the media personnel present, Charley suspected. The camera scanned the line-up for the offender before stopping at Danny Ray. 'Do you think that this incident could be connected to the unsolved murders of the two young people in our town recently?' Danny was a head higher than most and with his hair being blown about wildly by the wind it was hard for the person with the camera not to notice him. The journalist waited patiently for a reply to his question, unblinking, goading. Staring at the screen, Charley could see that he was pressing his lips together, the muscle twitching along his jawline.

Brian Roper's dark eyes fixed on him with a strange, flaring look, but the expression on Danny's face as the camera moved between them remained unchanged and unreadable.

'We have no motive for this apparently deliberate attack. The officer concerned remains stable on a life-support machine at this moment in time.' Roper dipped his head. 'Thank you. There will be no more questions,' he said, turning his back on the camera. Shoulders back, head held high, he walked back into the station as if being dangled by a puppet master from a set of strings.

Intelligence arriving in the incident room bubbled like a hot spring throughout the rest of the day and Charley harnessed it all ready for the team debrief. The incident room was buzzing when Mike and Charley walked in, and chatter gave way to silence the minute they sat down at the front. It appeared most of those assembled were drinking coffee from Costa, judging by the number of discarded plastic containers littering the desk tops. It also looked like a sandwich run had recently been completed. Charley noted the updates on the incident boards. She made eye contact with each person in the room as she asked if they had an update for those present. The anticipation was palpable.

There was no change in Wilkie's condition, said the liaison officer for the hospital, and Charley reminded them they all needed to be alert.

'Whether the attempt on Wilkie's life is connected to the recent murders or not, it is without doubt that he was targeted whilst working on the enquiries, so we all need to be aware of our personal safety.'

When it was Ricky-Lee and Annie's turn, they told those assembled that Solomon Myers was continuing to make no comment to questions put to him, although his cocky attitude had wilted as the interview had progressed. They'd had the impression he was doing as he had been told, whether that was from fear of repercussions from a co-conspirator, or instruction from his solicitor, they didn't know. What was known now was that Mr Gibson did pay Myers' salary monthly into a bank account in his name and the details had been passed to the financial investigation unit who were treating the enquiry as urgent.

'With regard to the landlord of his rented property, that's been traced to a letting agency and arrangements are in hand to speak to the manager tomorrow morning about the details,' said Mike. 'Fingerprints have told us they have not only Solomon's marks on the mobile phone, but also a partial mark that is not his. It is not good enough for a search of the database, but what they can tell me is that it belongs to a male. The phone is currently at the Mass Spectroscopy Unit, so I am hoping that they may be able to tell us more later.'

'The enquiry at Hartshead motorway service station is still ongoing; the kiosks have been fingerprinted by CSI and the receivers swabbed. The CCTV tapes have been seized and reviewed, but unfortunately the only image we have at that time is of someone's feet,' said Annie.

'Do we have a picture?'

There was a nodding of the head. 'Yes, boss.'

'And is the person in the photo wearing brown brogue shoes?' Charley held her breath, her tired eyes pleading for a reply.

'Yes, boss, and the team are comparing images,' said Ricky-Lee.

'Urgently, I hope. This may be it – the thing that connects Wilkie's attacker to the murders.' She moved on. 'CSI update, Neal; give me some good news.'

'Depends what you want to hear…' Neal's eyes were heavy.

'I want to hear that the netting recovered from the tailgate is a positive match with the netting used on Kylie Rogers.'

'The marks lifted from inside the cab were all glove marks. The soil sample enquiry is still ongoing. However,' he nodded his head, 'the netting is a positive match.'

Charley shook her head, but smiled at him. His old eyes appeared to light up. There was mischief in the old dog yet. She pointed towards Tattie. 'Go on, share the update you've got from the intelligence unit, Tattie,' she said.

Tattie had a serious face. 'They've resurrected an old case in which a woman was viciously raped and left for dead on the moorland at Scammonden. She had been exercising her dog at the time and didn't see her attacker, but woke up in hospital having sustained severe head injuries.'

Charley scowled. 'Why are we only being told about it now? Are they suggesting that it might be connected?'

'Apparently, the cold case review team have just got the news of a low copy DNA profile from a previous scene sample. The technology at Forensics at the time wasn't able to do this, but with technology continuously evolving, they have found this hit on the National Database.'

'Has Solomon Myers' DNA been checked against it?'

'The whole file has been attached to the database. Jean Weetwood was lucky to survive.'

'Do they know what weapon caused the head injury?'

'No.'

At the end of the day, Charley shut her desk drawer, turned the key in the lock, sat back in her chair and looked around. Through the Venetian blinds on the window to the outside world she could see nothing but darkness. The half-window in the door that led to the incident room was dimly grey. Slight movements now and then told her a skeleton staff were still working, but the silence was like a bubble blown from a pipe. It swelled, it floated into the air and then it burst. Quickly, she reached out to her desk lamp, put her finger on the switch and illuminated the room. She unlocked her drawer and pulled out a notepad and pen. There were so many questions yet to be answered. She drew a line down the centre of the page. 'Positive' she wrote at the top of column one, before adding: '1. They knew roughly where the murders had taken place. 2. The victims were transported to the dump site using the seized pick-up truck. 3. The seized piece of netting from Gibson's Horticultural was confirmed as being the same as the netting used to cover Kylie's body, and Charley had an offender in custody.'

Her pen hovered over the paper. She put her elbow on the desk and ran a splayed hand over her head. She pondered, sat back in her chair and raised her eyes to the darkened ceiling. The missing link was the second person. And the motive. She wrote 'Motive' in the second column; without it the case would not be solved. Experience told her that if there wasn't a clear motive then the likelihood was that there would be some sexual connotation. The jigsaw wasn't complete, although things were coming together.

Charley frowned. The other person appeared to be trying to confuse things, but, if so, why? Were they showing off their knowledge of the investigation process? And if so, why would they attack Wilkie? Had her DC rumbled the perpetrator without knowing it? Or knowing it, but not sharing that knowledge with the rest of the team? Was he, for some inexplicable reason, unable to, or felt he couldn't share it? Was it a timing issue, or was he being bribed; but why and how? What could the perpetrator have over Wilkie?

She dragged her heavy, tired body from behind the desk. For a moment she could see the faces of the victims with their wide, staring eyes … and then Wilkie's face loomed at her through the darkness. She gave her head a shake, although she wasn't conscious of doing it and, going quickly to the door, she got out of the room and shut the door after her. She leant against it. The racing of her heart had passed, leaving her feeling exhausted. She felt like she was going to sink to the floor, but she wouldn't allow herself to; she stiffened her knees. The humming of the computers in the now vacant, dimly lit incident room was somewhat comforting. It was warm and she felt somehow safe within these walls. She walked through the room to the kitchen and found herself staring at the jar of coffee. She seized it, unscrewed the cap, took a cup from the shelf and spooned the coffee powder into it. She filled the kettle from the sink, turning the tap on full and letting it splash over the surround.

You can do it. Hold it together. They're depending on you, she told herself. And, with a deliberate calmness she set about collecting the discarded Costa cups and putting them in a bin-bag along with the empty milk cartons and fizzy pop bottles, wiping the sugar that had spilt over the kitchen tops.

'Just when you think you've got a breakthrough. Then the camera turns out to have been offset and you only see feet,' said a voice from the doorway. It was Ricky-Lee.

She turned. She couldn't help but raise a smile. 'Not in this case though. It's a godsend.'

'You really think so?'

'I know so, I'm sure that they're the same as those in the picture on Myers' phone.'

Ricky-Lee's eyes were wide. 'Or is that wishful thinking on your part? We'll need expert analysis to confirm.'

'Sure, but I've got this gut feeling…' she said, fist to her stomach.

'Wilkie's would-be killer really would have put his foot in it then, wouldn't he?'

The next morning, before briefing, Annie was sitting with the team trawling through CCTV footage. Mike was on the telephone and Charley was photocopying. Mike walked towards her, a solemn look upon his face.

'Solomon Myers' DNA isn't a match for the Jean Weetwood attack,' he said.

Charley's disappointment was like a lead weight dropping into the pit of her stomach, but she would not show it. 'Look at the positive. Every new sample that comes onto the database will now be checked,' she said.

'Boss, over here,' came a sudden cry from Annie. 'We've got a sighting of Myers in Bar Amsterdam the night before Stewart Johnson's body was found.' When Charley did not appear at her side imminently, she looked up and across to see she hadn't moved.

'Boss?' She called again. 'He wasn't there long, but it's definitely him,' Annie said excitedly when Charley finally arrived and looked over her shoulder at the screen.

Charley leaned heavily with one hand on the desk and the other on the back of Annie's chair. 'Run it again,' she said, her heart beating frantically in her chest, her mind trapped between worlds. She looked at Annie, frightened she might hear the beating, so loud was it to her ears. Sunny and her platinum-haired friend sat at the bar talking to the bartender. 'And again,' Charley said. Satisfied the camera hadn't picked up her seat at the bar, she could now concentrate on the job in hand. 'We will need expert analysis and confirmation it's him. Get it,' she said, almost too quickly.

'Stewart Johnson isn't there ... Not that we can see, anyhow.' Annie sounded disappointed.

'I didn't expect him to be. After all, he was sleeping rough on the town centre streets at the time, wasn't he?' The rush of adrenaline that had raced through her body moments before made her heart race, her breathing deepen and the delicate blonde hairs on her forearms stand on end.

Annie's eyes narrowed. 'Yeah, and who'd notice if someone who's sleeping rough goes missing? Do you think that's why he was targeted? I guess the usual assumption when someone on the streets goes missing is that they have moved on, or been locked up.'

'Exactly,' said Charley, her voice rising an octave. 'We now know Solomon was out and about and in town though. Have we got any further sightings of him that night?' she said, searching the screen. 'Do we know if he met anyone, talked to anyone?'

Annie shook her head, looking slightly oddly at Charley's flushed cheeks. 'Not according to the viewing team. He appeared to be alone. He didn't mingle with the crowds. In some respects, he looks like he's bemused, as if he has somehow been transported to an alien time, and place. That, for me, is what made him stand out.'

There were still hours of footage to review. Charley returned to her office and Annie to her task.

An hour later Myers was having his last interview with Ricky-Lee and Annie. Charley clicked on the video link. She listened and watched whilst at the same time reading and signing off completed enquiries from the pile on her desk.

As before, Myers was making no comment. As the officers wrapped up the interview, Charley picked up the phone to speak to the Crown Prosecution Service. The prisoner had had every opportunity to speak up if he had wished to do so.

The lead case worker at CPS was a Mr Joseph Seagull. Charley was fully prepared for all-out war at any suggestion that Solomon Myers should be charged with anything less than two counts of murder and be placed back before the courts for a remand in custody. The foundation for the success of the remand was based on the fact they were confident one other person was still outstanding.

'Court tomorrow morning, I presume, Inspector?' said Mr Seagull.

'Yes,' replied Charley.

'Good. Will you be there to liaise if there are any matters that arise?'

There was a knock at her door and Tattie walked in, her face serious. Were those tears Charley saw in her eyes?

'Yes,' she said in reply to Mr Seagull. She smiled at Tattie who stuck a Post-it note in front of her and left abruptly, closing the door quietly behind her.

'See you, then,' she heard him say as she put the phone down.

Charley read the note: *Hospital requesting you ring them in respect of Wilkie.'*

For a moment her heart seemed to sink even further. She picked up the phone and dialled.

CHAPTER 17

Detective Ricky-Lee Lewis was the one to charge Solomon Myers with the murder of Kylie Rose Rogers and Stewart Johnson.

'What was his reply?' asked Charley.

'Would you be surprised if I told you it was, "no comment"?'

Charley shook her head.

'But you might be surprised to know that as he was led away to the cells he was crying.'

'And yet he still won't tell us who his co-conspirator is?'

It was Ricky-Lee's turn to shake his head.

Charley's brow was furrowed. 'Why, I wonder?'

Ricky-Lee shrugged his shoulders. 'He'll be appearing before Huddersfield Magistrates tomorrow morning. I've liaised with Connie at the press office and she's doing the necessary release to the media.'

Charley's phone rang and she picked up instantly, recognising Rubin's number. Ricky-Lee left the room.

'We'll be removing the ventilator tomorrow morning,' Rubin said.

Her mood immediately lifted. 'His vital signs are improving?'

'The swelling to Mr Connor's brain has reduced. That's all I can tell you at the moment.'

His voice had neither a negative nor positive tone to it and the phone call left Charley feeling slightly anxious. Her mobile phone beeped a message from the Divisional Commander. She found herself clenching her jaws tightly together when she read it: 'Just heard the news, keep me in the loop. I'm on the sixth hole at the moment.'

There was no time to overthink things and maybe that was a good thing. A remand file had to be done – despite what the public thought, the charging of an individual was only the start of the long, arduous task necessary to secure a conviction. A meeting with uniform supervision was required. It was highly likely that there would be a lot of public interest in Myers' appearance at court, as well as from the media.

In addition, she pondered, if the plan was to wake Wilkie up from his induced coma tomorrow morning, she didn't want him to be without support, so she needed to arrange a visiting rota for his colleagues, together with a reminder to Wilkie not to overdo it. Fran needed continued support and security at the hospital had to remain constant.

The next call that came into the office was from Neal Rylatt and was more than welcome. There was an unusual quickness in his delivery. 'I'm at Forensics. They tell me that the shoe seen in the picture at the graveyard and the one in the kiosk at Hartshead are an exact match.'

Charley was cautious. 'How's that?'

'Two of the holes on the brogue near the outer edge are split, forming one.'

Thoughtful, she put the phone down. 'Wow!' she exclaimed out loud.

'Wow?' said Annie, standing in the doorway, papers in her hand. 'Not a word I've heard you use before.' She moved further into the office.

'Sit down,' said Charley.

Without taking her eyes off Charley's face, Annie sat down on the edge of the chair in front of her desk. 'News? We know who the accomplice is?'

'Well, no, not exactly, but when we find his shoes we will.'

'Come again,' Annie said with a frown.

'The evidence I have just been given must be kept tight, only shared with the few.'

Charley finished her tasteless microwave dinner for one, put the washing machine on, poured herself a large glass of red wine and ran a bath, throwing in a lavender bomb that had been her Secret Santa Christmas present the previous year. She wondered what Wilkie Connor could have told her – and would hopefully still be able to tell her, when she could finally talk to him – about Eddie's death.

There was something about soaking in a bath that allowed you to totally relax. Peace and quiet at last, she thought: everything still. Her bed beckoned and she set her alarm clock for five forty-five: she would do the morning briefing before going to the Magistrates' Court.

Prior to the arrival of the team at the incident room, Charley read over the remand file for Myers. She was satisfied that all the evidence had been identified and that the reasons for the remand were clear. The CPS should have no concerns, but, of course, if they did, she would be there to answer any questions.

When DS Mike Blake arrived, they discussed the areas of the investigation they would highlight during the briefing. Mike was to remain in the incident room whilst Charley was at the court hearing.

The briefing was an overview of the events and findings thus far. 'I want to reinforce that any intelligence discussed about this investigation stays within this room. Whilst we have one person involved charged with two murders, another remains outstanding and just as responsible. Whoever that is, they are the one who has knowledge of the crime scenes that hasn't yet been released to the media, and that is how I want it to remain. Thank you for the good work so far, but this is no time to drop your guard; remember, there is work yet to do to secure the conviction of those involved.'

Briefing over, Charley headed for the Magistrates' Court in the knowledge that other plain clothes officers would be in attendance, scouring the room for something, anything and anyone, that might be of special interest to them, although they were unsure precisely what they were looking for. Their intention was to update the files and record faces for future investigation. Would Myers' partner-in-crime be amongst the crowd? This was a possibility that couldn't be overlooked and an opportunity that couldn't be missed by the investigators.

On the stroke of ten, Charley climbed the handful of stone steps to the court building. Inside, a dozen or more rose before her. Those wishing to attend the hearing filled the foyer and lined the stairs. Jostled along by the crowd and wheezing with exertion and apprehension, she reached the top of the stairs in record time. Offered the opportunity to go down several well-signposted corridors she was ultimately carried along on the wave of people turning left into a narrowing, chair-lined entrance lobby before they all came to an abrupt stop. The listing posted outside courtroom four read 'R v. Myers'.

Squashed between several sweaty bodies, she looked around at the assembled crowd. Some had heads raised high, looking quite ready for and capable of violent retribution; others chattered away in a frenzy of morbid excitement.

Emerging into the relative glare of the court, Charley stepped to one side, swiftly finding a viewing spot along the back wall of the room, from where she was aware that at the end of the hearing she'd be able to make a swift exit.

Head down, Myers still towered silently above his guardians. When he finally looked up, Charley saw his eyes protruding wildly as he glanced nervously around, scanning the packed room as if perhaps seeking an ally. His stares, to those who caught his gaze, appeared angry. There was a low muttering and whimpering from family and friends of the deceased who had arrived early and found a seat. There was shuffling as the crowd complied with the order to honour the entering magistrates. The courtroom fell as silent as a morgue when the three magistrates entered the room.

Forehead glistening with sweat, his fists clenched tightly, Myers waited, then remained standing when the audience sat. He stared straight ahead, as though permanently paralysed.

Charley took a moment to survey all around her. Standing a good foot taller than the rest, Danny Ray was easily identifiable amongst the rest of media, but he wasn't close enough to her to speak to, and she had no intention of hanging around after the hearing. Photographers and camera crews were barred from entering the courtroom in the United Kingdom. 'Illegal since 1925 per code 41 of the Criminal Justice Act and the Contempt of Court Act,' she found herself regurgitating the information from her detective training days. It steadied her nerves.

Solomon Myers spoke only to confirm his name. The prosecutor stood, shuffled his papers, narrowed his eyes and proceeded to outline the facts of the case and the reasons for remand. Mr Michael Parish from Booth & Co, on behalf of Mr Myers, stated his client's denial of the charges against him, but assured the magistrates that he would co-operate fully with any restrictions they wished to place upon him, should they decide to grant bail.

The magistrates retired to chambers, but returned almost immediately. Myers was ordered to stand. The chair of the magistrates spoke.

'Our opinion is that this is a case which ought to be decided by a jury. You will be remanded in custody to face trial by the crown court.'

Solomon Myers smirked at the clean-cut, chiselled-faced magistrate before he was taken away. Amid the hustle and bustle that followed, Charley was out of the door and down the stairs posthaste.

From the courthouse she drove to the hospital to see if the medics would let her see Wilkie. The positive news that greeted her was that he was off the ventilator, breathing normally and they were expecting him to wake at any minute.

As if on cue, as she stood at the doorway of the sun-kissed room, Wilkie Connor's eyes flinched, flickered and finally opened. From the look on his face it seemed that the window he was looking at suddenly opened up a world of shimmering blue skies. Wilkie turned his head to look at the ceiling. He lifted a finger, then two. A slight tear trickled from his eye and down his broad nose, but when he opened his mouth to speak, there were no words. For a moment he looked puzzled, licked his dry lips, swallowed and tried again. Fran Connor tightly gripped the arms of her wheelchair. Leaning forward she spoke to him reassuringly. Her face flushed, her eyes bright and eager, she reached out and softly touched the crisp, white pillowcase, just in time to catch the tear that continued its journey down the side of her husband's face. Charley couldn't help feeling as if she was imposing on their moment, and was quite unprepared for a twinge of envy for the love between them.

She very quietly slipped back into the corridor. A young man was watching the scene through the tilted slats of the Venetian blind. Charley gave him a tired smile, followed by a long outward breath. 'Thank God,' she said.

'You believe in God, Detective Inspector Mann?' he said, with a nod of his head, and a pursing of lips. 'That's good!'

Charley frowned. 'Hey, what's that supposed to…?' she said to his retreating back as his white coat billowed out behind him. She caught up with him at the nurses' station, clipboard in one hand and coffee in the other. 'Come on, tell me. What did you mean by that?'

'All I'm saying is, if you do have a God, keep praying. He's a long way to go yet.'

Marty nodded at Charley as she hurried through the enquiry office. She pushed the door open harder than she intended and let it slam behind her. The drunk who was sleeping it off on the bench lifted his head, scowled and lay down again on grubby hands that were clasped together, as if in prayer. Marty chuckled.

'It's true what your dad used to say, you could wake the dead.' She twisted her mouth in a smile. 'I wish. I'd give my right arm to see my folks again.'

'I know you would,' he said kindly.

DS Mike Blake was sitting at his desk in the incident room when she walked in, his shirt sleeves rolled up to the elbows, the knot of his tie pulled down a couple of inches.

'How's Wilkie?' he asked.

'He's awake.' Charley was quick to reply. 'Any information on the person in Myers' flat, or who owns it? Because I get the feeling there's someone out there who is quite happy for Myers to take the rap.'

'I agree. Myers might have the physical strength, but, like we've said before, I don't think he has either the knowledge or the intelligence to commit the crime alone. Someone has tried to confuse us from the very start by throwing everything into the mix. Could it really be a serving cop? Much as it goes against the grain to say it, it has to be, doesn't it?'

Frown lines wrinkled Charley's forehead; her gaze fixed on the detective sergeant. 'Well, whoever it is, Mike, we'll find them. He might be trying to wrongfoot us, but the shoes he's wearing might just be his downfall. What worries me is that they might end up being disposed of before we get to him and it's about all we have…'

Charley flicked the lights on in her office. A square, yellow Post-it note from Connie was stuck to the computer. It said, 'Danny Ray wants to speak to you regarding DC Wilkie Connor. He's asking for your help to do a human-interest story which, he suggests, may bring any reluctant witnesses forward.'

Charley squared her shoulders, screwed the note up and aimed it at the bin.

Connie stood in the doorway. 'Steady on!' she said, sliding into a chair opposite her. 'Are you going to meet with him?'

Charley nodded. 'Tell him I'll do it.'

Connie smiled. 'Good.'

'But only in the company of Detective Sergeant Mike Blake and in an interview room at the station,' she said.

An hour later, Danny Ray was at the front desk. Mike went ahead to greet him and escort him into the adjoining room.

Charley braced herself, her palms sweating. She would hear him out, listen to this idea of his and, if what he suggested might help the investigation, she would gush over his plans as much as any other and lay on the charm as thick as his use of aftershave.

When she walked into the interview room, Danny smiled at her a little too brightly. Had he thought she would refuse? Her greeting was a non-committal nod. She was glad to see from his fidgeting that he appeared to be as uncomfortable as she felt. Hesitantly he half-stood and leaned in to take her hand and her stomach knotted up. Mike remained seated, apparently not seeing the awkwardness.

The journalist and the detective sergeant seemed to be comfortable with each other. Danny picked up his coffee cup and took a sip. It was black; she'd remembered it was how he liked it – black and sweet. His notepad and pen lay between them on the table. Formalities over, Danny shuffled in his seat, blinked and she knew he was about to go into the dark side, just like all reporters do when they smell the blood in the water otherwise known as 'the story'.

'You do know,' he paused for effect, 'Wilkie Connor is in serious debt, don't you? And I don't mean for a couple of hundred pounds,' he said.

It was Mike's turn to shuffle in his seat, looking at Danny as if he no longer found the journalist likeable.

Charley said nothing, so Danny continued. 'We think we know someone, don't we? I know I do it all the time. Then they do something out of the ordinary and we're surprised. It's very naïve.' Danny's eyes moved from one detective to the other and settled on Charley. 'You know as well as I do that there are many sides to a

person, and people interpret the actions of others in different ways…'
His eyes bore into hers as he paused again, then turned to Mike. His
voice remained flat. 'I'm not saying he deserved what he got, but some
folk, when upset, are not forgiving. I thought it might help to get
some facts, just in case…'

Charley's lips formed a straight, narrow line and she stood up like
a military officer ready to march. 'I don't know what you're trying to
insinuate, but I have no desire to discuss my detective constable's
private life.' A quick glance at her watch produced a grimace. 'If that's
all you want to talk about, then you're wasting your time and ours.'

Danny raised his hand in an apology. 'I'm sorry. What can you tell
me about Wilkie Connor's condition?'

Charley sat back down. 'I can tell you he's been taken off his
ventilator and he's breathing on his own, but nothing else is assured
at this moment in time.'

The journalist sat perfectly still. 'Have you been able to talk to
him?' he asked, as he prepared to write the answer in his book.

'He was only taken off the ventilator today and, as far as I know,
he hasn't spoken to anyone yet.'

His pen hovered above the paper. 'Any update you can share on
the offending vehicle or driver?'

'No,' said Mike. Danny's eyes looked up to meet Mike's. 'But what
we do know is that it was a deliberate act,' said the detective sergeant.

Danny's eyebrows rose. 'You do? And I can say that?'

Mike nodded.

'Let me assure you, he wouldn't be telling you that if it wasn't the
case,' said Charley.

Danny's eyes narrowed and his lips thinned, one corner of his
mouth curling up into a smile. 'Thanks. It's a big ask I know, but do

you have a picture of Wilkie that you can give me? One that his family are happy for me to use? Or even better, could we get one of him in his hospital bed?'

Mike looked sideways to Charley for a response. When none was forthcoming, the journalist continued, his voice hopeful, appealing. 'That sort of picture always gets a good response from our readers. They pull at the heartstrings.'

Hearing the cliché come out of his mouth, and seeing the detective inspector's reaction, Danny looked a little embarrassed. 'Obviously, it would be a tasteful picture of him in his hospital bed...' he added.

Mike's brow was furrowed. 'We don't have a picture that has been approved by the family.'

Charley shook her head. 'No. And, personally, I don't think taking a photograph of him looking vulnerable in a hospital bed would be appropriate. When he is able to speak to us, we will ask him if it is something he would like to do for you. The decision will be his. I'll ask Connie to let you know if that's the case.'

'I just thought...' When Danny saw Charley clench her fist, he stopped. 'I understand,' he said eventually, unsmiling and with a nod of his head. But then, with renewed vigour, and adopting a different tone of voice, he continued. 'Can you tell me anything about the officer's background?'

Charley went doggedly on, speaking through gritted teeth. 'I believe Connie has already sent this out on a press release?'

Danny's chin dropped to his chest and he shook his head. 'I've got all the regular stuff.' He looked up and pulled a face. 'No more titbits for the local rag?'

Charley shook her head unbelievingly and Mike followed her lead, his face serious.

'OK, then. Moving on,' Danny said as, head down, he checked his notes. He was sweating and Charley felt a quiet satisfaction at how distressed he looked. 'Any motives to suggest that this was a reprisal attack?'

'We are keeping an open mind and all available resources are currently making enquiries into his attempted murder.' Charley stood, a tight-lipped smile on her face. 'And if you'll excuse us now, we have to get back. As you can appreciate, we have a lot of work to do.'

Mike stood and shook Danny's hand. Charley was away out of the door. When Mike joined her, she was speaking to Marty in the front office. 'There's something about that man,' Mike said, as his eyes followed Danny's exit from the building.

Marty nodded his head. 'I guess he's just got a job to do, like us. I've met worse.'

'I don't know about that,' Charley said.

The two officers watched her quick exit with raised eyebrows.

Within the hour, a distressed PC Susan Vine, who had been put on hospital watch, was on the phone to Charley. As she spoke, Susan carried on watching the newcomer, as one of the staff gestured him to sit in a chair beside the desk while he waited to be seen. He stretched his long legs in front of him, chatting amiably to the nurse who'd supplied him with the chair.

'I'm really sorry to bother you, ma'am,' she said in a hushed voice, 'but a journalist by the name of Danny Ray is at the nurses' station making enquiries about Wilkie Connor's whereabouts, and he has informed them that you've given him permission to see him and take pictures?'

Charley felt parts of her body tingling. 'No one has my permission to take pictures of DC Connor without his permission. Do I make myself clear?'

'Yes, ma'am.'

'And Susan...'

'Yes, ma'am?'

'Would you do me a favour? When you get back to the office, come and see me.'

'I will, ma'am,' she said.

Charley was sitting with her office door open, looking at the telephone receiver in her hand, when Mike walked in. 'What an utter bastard,' she said, shaking her head in disbelief.

Mike ignored the expletives, but stood waiting in anticipation of an explanation.

'That prize pillock has only gone to the hospital and told the staff that I said he could take pictures of Wilkie! Luckily the police officer on security wasn't naïve enough to allow him to without asking me first.'

A glimpse of a smile crossed his face. 'You can't blame him for trying.'

'Can't I?' she said, angrily. 'We tell him nothing from now on, do you understand? And I'll have a word with Connie.' Charley's nose flared at the nostrils. The thought of Danny sitting at the nurses' station, chatting them up and looking like butter wouldn't melt, made her stomach churn. That cool, polished exterior hid a squirming wormfest of nastiness that could be unleashed at a moment's notice.

Mike looked at her in exasperation. 'What did you once tell me? Don't let things get personal: it blurs your vision?'

Danny Ray confidently approached PC Vine, who continued to sit, as ordered, in the chair outside Wilkie Connor's room. She stood to block his entrance. He looked into her expressionless eyes, a self-assured smile forming on his lips, as he spoke confidently to the young woman.

'OK, darling. I'm here to take the pictures. You'll have seen me before. I'm from the *Chronicle*, you don't need to worry your pretty little head about anything,' he said in a determined voice. 'I've cleared it with Detective Inspector Charley Mann and the staff over there,' he said, looking over his shoulder at the nurse he'd been speaking to, who was now engaged with a patient. 'I promised her it won't take a minute.' His voiced lowered to a hushed tone as he tried to peer nonchalantly round her into the darkened hospital room.

'Actually, it won't take any time at all,' she said, taking a step forward. She had taken him unawares and he stumbled backwards. Susan suppressed a smile. 'Because you're going nowhere near the officer.'

'Come on, stop messing. Your boss, she's an old friend of mine. I'm writing a story about your mate in there.' He raised his eyes to the ceiling. 'For God's sake, love. I'm trying to do something nice here to help you guys! Let me in, will you?'

'No one has permission to take photographs. I heard you talking to the nurse and I checked with DI Mann.' Susan's face was devoid of emotion.

His eyes glazed over and narrowed, his face turned pale. The corridor that had been busy not two minutes ago was now empty. A shiver ran down Susan's back.

'You're going to regret this. You've no idea who you're dealing with. I'm Danny Ray,' he declared.

Shoulders back, heart pounding against her ribcage, Susan returned his stare. 'I hope you're not threatening me, sir?' She looked down towards her belt and put her hand on her pepper spray. 'I haven't used this yet – this week, that is.'

'Oh, I don't make idle threats,' he said, his words riding on a throaty laugh. 'I'll be seeing you.' He turned and headed for the exit. Susan let out a sigh of relief, but, as Danny reached the door, he turned and took her photograph.

Perplexed, but knowing that there was nothing she could do about it, she sat back down. She wasn't about to leave her post to go after him and if that was what he'd been hoping for, then he would be sadly mistaken. She pondered his veiled threat, but she had dealt with stronger, younger, far more violent men on a weekend in the town when alcohol was in and brains out. They thought that because she was female, she wouldn't be able to do much to protect herself. How wrong were they? Susan smiled to herself. A black belt in karate, quick on the baton and, if it was necessary, always happy to use her pepper spray, one thing Susan Vine was known for was not backing off. What a slime ball that reporter was! What was his name, Danny Ray? That wasn't hard to remember, but in any case, she would make a note of it in her pocket book for future reference.

The woman at the nurses' station headed towards her with a cup of tea. 'He loves himself, doesn't he? A charmer if ever I saw one,' she said.

Susan smiled politely, took the cup and saucer from her and thanked her. 'Just what I needed,' she said. 'A nice cuppa char, as my ma used to say. They come in all shapes and sizes: wolves in sheep's clothing,' she continued.

The nurse frowned. 'They do.'

'And just so you're aware, Danny Ray isn't allowed to go anywhere near the patient for an interview, picture or anything else,' said Susan.

'Thanks for the heads up,' said the nurse. 'I'll let the others know. He tried to get one of the young ones to make him a coffee, as if we have nothing better to do.' She sniggered. 'He wasn't happy when she told him there's a cafe on the ground floor.'

CHAPTER 18

Charley had arranged with her deputy SIO on the enquiries, DS Mike Blake, that she would be finishing early. It would mean he'd have to take the afternoon debrief.

'A night on the tiles?' asked Ricky-Lee. For a fleeting moment there appeared to be a knowing behind his eyes.

'Can I come too?' asked Annie, flopping dramatically onto folded arms on her desk. 'It's ages since I got wasted.'

There was a softening, gentle touch about the wafting fingers of the evening breeze. Charley let herself into the busy stable yard and was greeted with the sight of Wilson at his stable door. Ears pointed forward, lips pulled back, he nibbled at Charley's pocket as she opened the door and let herself in. 'Fancy a hack?' she asked as she ran her fingers through his mane.

'As long as he can call at the Old Moor Cock for a crafty sweet cider!' interjected a voice from the yard, one that she knew well.

'I'm sure that can be arranged, can't it mate?' she said, as she forced the bit between his teeth. 'And they've got tables outside, enabling me, the little short arse with a giant horse, to get back in the saddle for him to carry me home.'

'As if! You've the longest legs I know.' Kristine's smile turned into a titter. 'Amuses the locals no end when he drinks his pint, smacks his lips together and looks towards the bar as if to say, "I could do with another!"'

'Good job you're not still in the job, mate,' Charley said fondly as she fastened the straps of Wilson's halter. 'It'd be a problem getting you through Huddersfield town centre with all them pubs en-route to the town ground on match days.'

Kristine came with them through the stable yard, with Bwyan on a leash. They stopped at the gate. 'Won't be long now before you're back in this saddle,' said Charley.

'I can't wait. And I can't wait to be back at work on the case of the little bastard who caused our Eddie to lose his life.'

Wilson pawed the ground and lifted his head, eager to be off.

Kristine slapped Wilson on the rear. He never flinched. 'This boy, thank the Lord, is bomb-proof, in fact you two make a good pair. I know you never give up and that's why I was so glad when I knew you were coming back to help me. We will find the one who flew that drone that fateful day...'

A sadness crossed Kristine's face and Charley didn't miss the stray tear her friend wiped swiftly away from her cheek.

Her own throat clogged. A lump rose and she swallowed it down. She opened her mouth to tell Kristine about the note that Wilkie had left for her, but the last thing she wanted was to get her friend's hopes up, when she didn't even know if Wilkie would pull through, let alone be able to remember his proclamation that he had information about Eddie's death.

Just then a gust of wind whistled through the barn, carrying bits of hay and straw, twigs and leaves across the yard. A nickering sound emerged from Bwyan's quivering lips and Kristine put the palm of her hand to his nose to soothe him. Wilson threw his head up and snorted. The women looked up at the sky as thunder rumbled in the distance. Kristine shrugged her shoulders; it was still blue. Charley took the opportunity of the distraction to change the subject. 'Do you know Wilkie Connor, the detective that got knocked down?'

Kristine raised her eyebrows. 'You're not...'

'No! Nothing like that,' Charley was quick to respond. Her grin dropped instantly from her lips. 'I gave him a right bollocking just before it happened and now I feel terrible. In fact...' Charley looked sheepish. 'I gave him a "dead man's lift", slammed him against my office wall and threatened to punch his lights out.'

'You did what?' Kristine extracted a tissue from her pocket and wiped away the tears of laughter.

'It's not funny.'

'No, it's not funny, but what is funny is that underneath that cool, calm exterior you haven't changed a bit from the spunky young girl that used to give the lads a run for their money and yet put out a jug of milk for the Hob if she needed a bit of luck on her side.'

Colour rose in Charley's cheeks. She gathered the reins in her hands.

'You don't? Tell me you don't still reward the Hob?' Kristine watched them ride away, a smile on her face. It was good to have her friend back. Turning Bywan's head, she ambled down the field towards the water's edge where a flock of ducks took off with the next loud rumble, their feet trailing as they skimmed across the lake.

It was eight o'clock when Charley arrived at the incident room the next day, revitalised and feeling more positive than she had done in a while.

PC Susan Vine was waiting in her office, sipping a coffee. She had one of those faces that naturally showed no emotion. When Charley walked in, she stood up. 'I'm sorry to disturb you, ma'am, but you told me to call in and make myself known, and as I had to bring in some exhibits, I thought I might as well...'

'Please. Have a seat. Any more news on Wilkie this morning?'

'They're monitoring his levels of responsiveness: eye opening, verbal response, motor response. Apparently,' she paused, 'he's showing signs of having to relearn the simplest of everyday tasks which we take for granted, like how to eat, use the bathroom, brush his teeth, put on his shoes. The worst part is that he's not talking. Not to his wife, the doctors, the nurses...'

'Is he allowed visitors yet?'

Susan's lip curled up at one side. 'Yes, ma'am, he is. Brief visits only. I think they're hoping that one of us might entice him to speak.' She looked thoughtful. 'Danny Ray, the journalist who tried to get in to see him, he said he was a friend of yours?'

'He's no friend of mine. But as far as you're concerned, honesty, integrity and never accepting what is said as gospel, however plausible the person telling you, are the signs of a good cop. I'm impressed. I'll be sending a Minute Sheet to your inspector and if you ever fancy a secondment to see how you'd fare in CID, just let me know.'

Putting in a call to Nurse Rubin, she arranged a visit to see the man himself.

'Do you mind if I come with you, boss?' requested Mike.

An hour later the two of them had the first glimpse of Wilkie, sitting up in a chair, facing the window, his back to the door. His wife saw them looking and beckoned them in. Charley gently opened the door and left it open behind her. Fran Connor's pale face looked towards her. Dark circles surrounded her sunken eyes. 'I wondered when you lot'd make an appearance,' she said, sniffling into a handkerchief. 'Maybe you can get him to speak. He won't talk to me, but then, what's new?' she said irritably.

Rubin went down on his haunches and held her swollen hand tightly. For a moment he looked at her with deep compassion. 'I'm sure he would if he could.' He stood directly. 'Tell you what,' he said, taking hold of the handles of her wheelchair. 'Let's go for a nice hot chocolate with cream and marshmallows, shall we, and leave these lot to talk shop?' At the door, Rubin navigated her wheelchair's passage expertly. He took a deep breath and gave Charley a knowing smile.

Mrs Connor looked suspiciously at the brown paper bag in Mike's hand.

'Grapes,' he said, opening it and offering her the fruit.

'He doesn't like grapes,' she said, throwing a nod in Wilkie's direction.

'Hey, don't you be telling them that, they'll eat them and there'll be none left for us two,' said Rubin.

Mrs Connor sniggered conspiratorially.

Alone in the room with Wilkie, Charley and Mike looked from him to each other, not sure what to do or say, so instead they sat on the bed opposite the patient. Both were startled to see Wilkie lift his head to look at them the minute the others had gone. The look, a quick frown of eagerness and fear, his eyes open wide. He opened his mouth as if to speak, but no words were forthcoming. And then his face changed. It clouded over with a kind of brittle sullenness. He sat very still staring at Mike for a moment. A flash of recognition sparked the raising of his lips at one corner when he looked up at Charley – then suddenly there was nothing but blankness in his eyes. It was as though many emotions moved within him, but not one of them could reach the surface and find an outlet. Or perhaps the emotions neutralised each other. His head jerked upwards. One hand, the right one, opened and closed its fingers with a slow, spasmodic jerkiness. The two were hopeful, but, instead of the communication they'd hoped for, his face took on a helpless frozen look and he turned once more to stare out of the window.

'Please let me know if there is any change, will you?' Mike asked Rubin when they left, pushing his contact details into the nurse's hand.

'I promise you,' Rubin said, slipping the card into his top pocket and fastening the button to hold it secure.

Back at the incident room Charley had a message to contact the Divisional Commander and decided to telephone him from her office, rather than put herself within arm's reach.

'Just to keep you in the loop, Inspector, I've got our local reporter coming to see me tomorrow. He's after an update on how the investigation into Detective Connor's accident is going. Have you something against Danny Ray? He tells me that you aren't being co-operative?'

'I can't think why he would say that, sir. Myself and Detective Sergeant Blake have met with him.' There was silence at the other end of the line, so Charley continued. 'As it happens, we've also just returned from the hospital and although Wilkie Connor is now conscious and able to sit up in a chair, he is neither communicating with, nor recognising, even his nearest and dearest. As you can imagine, he has an awfully long way to go before he is fit to be interviewed by anyone, or to have his photograph taken, as Danny

Ray requested. I said no. Maybe that's what he means by being unco-operative? But I'm sure you can understand that the last thing I want is for the person responsible for his accident to be gloating over some photograph in the local rag.' She could feel her blood pressure rising and she had to make a tremendous effort to keep a lid on her temper.

'Yes, of course,' Roper stuttered. 'I see where you're coming from. Maybe if I tell Danny that I'll arrange to go and visit the detective in a couple of days' time, when he's better, and then he can have a picture with me, too. That might suffice.' He sounded pleased with the compromise he had come up with and paused.

Charley didn't speak.

'Maybe you'd like to join us both in my office at about two p.m.?'

Charley took a deep breath. 'That's very kind of you, and I'd like nothing better than to join you, but you know, I'm certain I have something already arranged.' Charley shuffled a few papers on her desk. 'Ah, yes, a strategy meeting with CSI regarding another batch of exhibits for forensic. Sadly, I'll have to take a rain check on the tea and biscuits, sir.'

'Ah, not to worry. Anything on the investigation side I can share with him?' he said, with more than a little hope in his voice.

'No, sorry. Nothing, as yet. We are still appealing for anyone with information to contact us, though. The vehicle involved in hitting Wilkie must have some bodywork damage. Maybe he could appeal for information?'

There was a pause and Charley could hear Roper muttering to himself. 'I've made a note. Right, I'll ask my secretary to get hold of our press photographer to arrange a meet at the hospital as and when the detective is feeling better.'

'The detective's name is Wilkie Connor,' she muttered between gritted teeth as she put the phone down. It rang instantly. She picked up. 'Charley Mann,' she snapped.

A hushed voice came over the line. So hushed, she could barely hear the man on the other end of the phone. 'It's Rubin. I promised I'd let you know if anything changed. He's had a seizure. He's on his way to theatre. I'll update you as soon as I can.' There was a click and the phone went dead.

Charley, elbows on the desk, put her head in her hands.

Annie knocked on the office door holding two cups of coffee and with a file tucked under her arm. 'Can I come in?' she asked. 'You look all in.'

'Wilkie's in theatre.'

'The phone call?'

Charley nodded her head.

'Do you think he's going to be OK?'

With a shrug of her shoulders, Charley reached out for the file. 'Incomplete enquiries,' she stated. 'Best to keep busy. Spending time worrying is not going to help him, or us.'

Annie slumped down on a chair. 'Yes, sure,' was all she could muster.

Charley picked up a marker and a dry wipe board from her desk. 'We'll go through this together, shall we?'

An hour later, papers, along with half-drunk mugs of coffee, had joined the dry-wipe board on the desk. The plan had been to distract themselves by trawling through enquiries for which they had no answers as yet and listing them in some sort of order. But it hadn't worked, there were too many … it was messy.

Charley wiped the board clean and proceeded instead to write down the outstanding tasks that she considered to be a priority.

Firstly, identify and interview the landlord of Solomon Myers' flat. Update: Rental management on holiday. To do: Arrange to see and get relevant information. 'It may tell us something or nothing, but it needs doing quickly,' said Charley.

Next, she wrote: statement from Mr Gibson needs revisiting now Solomon Myers has been charged, either to see if he recalls anything else, or has anything he would like to share now Solomon is to remain in custody.

Then: 'I want you to get me a pair of brown brogues identical to those shown on the CCTV footage and pictured on Solomon's mobile phone images.'

Silently, Annie made notes.

'Solomon Myers definitely didn't have a pair in his flat?'

Annie shook her head. 'The style to me suggests an older man, but I don't want to make assumptions.'

Together they revisited questions they had asked themselves and others and reviewed the answers they'd received, clearing the ground beneath their feet. If someone was trying to wrongfoot them, it seemed sensible to constantly ensure that they were on firm ground.

CHAPTER 19

In the middle of the night, Charley woke suddenly, the covers above and below her soaked in sweat. She must have been dreaming. Throwing open the window, she leaned against the wooden frame, drawing in long, what she hoped were calming, breaths. They were certainly deep; so deep she soon felt light-headed, which didn't help to stop her mind from racing. Torturous fears of failure had been chasing round in her head for hours. She dropped to her knees and hung out of the window, gripping the windowsill hard, her knuckles turning white as she stared down into the street below.

When she caught herself trying to calculate how many metres it was to the ground, and the possibility of a serious injury, if not sudden death, if she lunged forward, she reached up, pulled the window shut, locked it and threw the key down. She didn't want to be in pain; she didn't want to die. What the hell was she thinking? That was just it; she wasn't thinking, not rationally anyway. Normally when she was anxious, she'd go out for a ride, but this was far beyond normal and the feeling of anxiety was starting to scare her. The intensity of emotion, the extremity of the agitation, the feeling that she could gladly walk out and never come back ... that wasn't her usual thinking – she was a fighter. Was she going insane? She whirled around and threw herself on her bed, punching the pillows until all the fight had drained from her body.

Over a breakfast of toast and coffee, she reflected on the previous night. The window key was lying in front of the bedroom door, which puzzled her; all she could recall was the night sweat and waking with the words of the detective's mantra going round and round her head: 'Clear the ground from beneath your feet,' she whispered.

She frowned and bit into her cold toast, caked with butter and orange marmalade, relishing the bitter-sweet spread on her tongue. Brushing the crumbs from her fingers on her pyjama bottoms, she stood, opened the back door into the yard and picked the jug up from the step. She sniffed the contents. It hadn't gone sour; it was a good sign. Hob was happy! She smiled at herself, ran crumb-covered fingers through her hair and headed up the stairs two at a time to take a shower.

Eight o'clock was not a good time to drive into town, Charley decided. The queues were long and her journey into work slow, but, on the positive side, it gave her plenty of quality time to think. Whose name was the most reccurring in the investigation? Whose name was niggling at the back of her mind, on the tip of her tongue? She had to smile. Usually when she asked herself the question it was a prolific criminal, but this time it was Danny Ray. Her smile turned to a sneer as she passed the *Chronicle* newspaper building. 'The thorn in my side,' she said.

Charley breathed in deeply through her nose. Feeling uneasy and slightly warm, she touched the electric button on the car door to lower the window several inches, and breathed out through her mouth. The unmistakable din and clamour of town life instantly filled the air. Immediately she closed the window and tried to relax, settling back again in the quiet interior of the car. The traffic in front crawled forward and as she drove through the town she absent-mindedly gazed at the passing waves of humanity as she slowly navigated the busy streets.

'Danny bloody Ray.' Then, as if a bolt of lightning had surged through her veins, a thought struck her. How would she deal with her nemesis if he was the perpetrator? If *he* was involved in the flying of the drone that had killed the horse for his own ends – for the information he might glean from the device for the newspaper? If he was the one being held in the cells for the murders? He was part of the ground beneath her feet: he was a man, he hadn't been eliminated and she knew he was capable of committing a crime. It wasn't considered a crime in Roper's eyes though, was it? Not even when she had told her boss that the reason for the bruise on her face was that her boyfriend had assaulted her, wielding a knife. Instead, he'd questioned *her* actions, not his. Roper's accusing tone was loud in her ears. 'Are you certain it was a knife?'

She had been. She had recognised the penknife Danny's grandfather had left to him. He had used the blade many times on their expeditions growing up to prepare fires and food he caught, cut bandages or rope, make tools and even as a signal mirror. They had used it as a hammer, screwdriver, even a spade, in the fields and the woods and on the moors...

'Were you *trying* to make him jealous?'

Charley had strenuously denied Roper's accusations.

'If not, then why did you lie to him about where you were going?' Roper said. 'Any red-blooded male would be enraged if he caught his girlfriend lying to him – especially when she was at the pub with another man.'

'Not just any other man, I was with Richard, my work partner, as you well know. We were at Bill's retirement do.'

She wondered briefly what Roper would say, or do, if he knew that the person about whom she had confided was in fact the journalist he wanted to meet for tea and biscuits with her?

To Danny Ray, she had to admit, death was just another natural process, like eating, drinking, having a bowel movement. He'd grown up on a working farm, like her. Her mind continued to pursue her theory. He could be violent: she had been surprised – shocked – to see that characteristic in him even as a child, she recalled, when he'd held her down on the ground by both wrists. It was in play, but he'd had a certain look in his eyes ... When they were teenagers, she'd thought it was cute that he was jealous of others with whom she spent time. 'He just loves me!' she would say to Kristine who voiced her concerns about his behaviour. 'He's trying to control you,' Kristine would reply. He liked to be in control, but had he the ability to murder a human being?

'Oh, for God's sake,' she berated herself audibly. 'Stop it! Get a grip!' She dealt with facts – hard and fast evidence, nothing else.

Reaching the station at last, she parked and got out of the car. With her hand gripping the metal of the car door, she felt her body tremble ever so slightly as she prevented any emotion from manifesting on her face. She made her way into the bowels of the police station and, as she did so, heard the words of her predecessors whisper in her ear: 'Everyone is a suspect until proven otherwise.'

Her decision was made. She would put Danny under the microscope, and because of his sham likeability factor and, more importantly, his friendliness with several officers, including the Divisional Commander, she wouldn't be sharing this line of enquiry with anyone else.

Charley went straight to her computer. She put the pile of papers pertaining to the murder investigation, together with the morning's briefing notes, next to the monitor. After making only a few keystrokes she took her first sip of coffee. Already lukewarm, and bitter, she screwed up her nose. No one in the office actually made coffee like Wilkie Connor. Logging in, she scowled at the computer's slow progress. So many passwords, so many screens to plough through. Her pulse raced and her palms went moist as she tapped in Danny Ray's name. Her trawl of his social media sites was enlightening. He was a journalist of long standing at the *Chronicle*, that much she knew. He had recently undertaken a master's degree in Criminology – she hadn't known that. She made notes. Her search widened. A host of articles he had posted online were listed; one in particular caught her eye: 'Serial Killers' had been his chosen subject at university.

'It's about time you showed up,' she said, as Ricky Lee passed her a small white bag and rolled into the chair opposite her.

'What d'you mean? I've done a day's work already!' he protested.

'Where've you been?' she asked, unwrapping the paper napkin surrounding the roll. 'You missed the briefing.' The smell of bacon wafting up her nostrils provoked memories of the farm, of home, of her dad. Digging her teeth into the soft white teacake, she relished the sweet, salty taste of the meat on her lips.

'I've been to the *Chronicle* with Connie.'

Charley's heart leapt and then did a series of cartwheels. 'Why?'

'Why what?'

'Why've you been to the *Chronicle*?'

'Danny Ray's article…'

Charley sucked in a deep breath.

'He's actually quite an interesting chap – better for knowing, that's for sure. It must be you that antagonises him.'

Her mouth full, Charley scowled.

'He reckons he could pull off the perfect murder. And you know what? I think he may be right.'

A shiver rippled down her spine. 'Does he now?'

Ricky-Lee nodded and his grin spread from ear to ear. 'In theory, of course.'

'Of course'.

Charley glanced longingly out of the door at her colleagues outside, but she knew that no matter what, she couldn't share her thoughts and feelings – not again; not ever again. This was for her to deal with, and her alone. They'd think she was weak, insane even, just as Roper had. She'd seen enough psychos for one lifetime, and she had to get to the bottom of this one. Tears leaked reluctantly from her eyes. She had trusted Danny – and her Inspector, who she'd thought would advise her, not tell her to get a grip; what had she expected if she went about messing with her boyfriend's head…? Now, it felt as if she was the only one who still recalled the days and nights after that night in the pub car park.

Those assembled were attentive to her every word. 'I believe that our outstanding perpetrator will have made a mistake along the way,' she said. 'It's our job to find that mistake. Bear with me ... We know where our victims were murdered. We know how they were transported. What I have difficulty understanding is why our murderers didn't bury them in the woods, or on the moorland near the nursery, where I believe they could have remained undiscovered for years. The only thing that I can think of is that someone has set out to confuse and mislead us, while at the same time setting up Solomon Myers for the fall.

'We have pictures on Solomon Myers' mobile phone, which we found at his home address. That mobile has not been used for anything else. This says to me that if they didn't need a mobile phone for communication, then they were in touch by other means. In the second murder enquiry, the condom was left intentionally. Once again, this was a deliberate act to confuse and mislead, again setting up Solomon to connect him to the murder should the police be successful in the investigation. Two things the second person could not predict, or didn't think of, was that the soil samples would connect the murders and that his shoe would be in the photograph. The hit-and-run of Wilkie was another distraction we could have done without. Was this a deliberate act to try and slow down the investigation, or derail it? It was another calculated risk to lure the officer to a quiet location. Solomon couldn't be blamed for this one. So, what was he thinking? We'd arrested Solomon, which no doubt he would have expected at some stage, but did he expect it so soon, before he had done with Solomon as his stooge? Or was he going to see him off too?'

Charley's telephone rang and it distracted her. She rolled her eyes, 'I must take this call,' she said, as she stepped to the side.

'Inspector. Divisional Commander here,' she heard from the other end, 'Mr Ray's visit has been delayed until two-thirty this afternoon. Is there any chance at all you could make an appearance for a short time after all? It would be greatly appreciated.'

'Sorry! I don't have the time.' Her dismissal sounded final to her ears.

There was silence at the other end of the line for a moment or two. 'Maybe I need to remind you...' Roper said, in a hushed tone '... that it's always good to keep the media focused and on side – especially with Mr Ray, our local reporter.' He sighed. 'And, isn't it about time you put your feelings for your old flame to rest?'

Charley was shocked. He knew! He *knew* ... How did he know about her and Danny Ray? He had never said, before now. How did he know? Did he realise what he had just done? Had he dropped this on her now, intentionally, because she was unwilling to conform, or was it a mistake on his part? There was only one person who could have told Roper about Danny's history with Charley – and that was Danny Ray himself. She had to think quickly.

'I understand perfectly well what you're saying, sir. But even I can't be in two places at once. Maybe, if you're seeing him, you could have a word in his ear for me, though. Police Constable Susan Vine – you know Susan, one of your own officers – was approached by him the other day at the hospital and she tells me she felt threatened by his behaviour after she told him that he couldn't see, talk to or take a picture of Wilkie Connor. And he blatantly lied to her and the hospital staff when he told them he had my permission to do all of the above.'

Roper's voice was monotone. 'And did he get in to see him?'

'No, but that's not the point.'

His scoff was gruff. 'No harm done, then. I can't see your problem.

We've all tried to pull a fast one at one time or another have we not? Maybe if you pushed a little harder, we wouldn't be having this conversation; the job would be sewn up.'

'I'm sorry, sir. I don't agree. I don't know about you, but I need to be able to trust our local media to work with me, not against me.'

Roper sighed. 'Well, if I get the opportunity, I'll mention it,' he said.

Just at that moment the phone on the desk next to her rang. She turned, searching for someone nearby who could answer it. Charley paid no attention to Mike's conversation, but the raising of his finger caught her eye and instead she ended her phone call to the Chief Superintendent abruptly.

'What is it?' she said eagerly.

Mike's eyes were unusually bright. 'Guess who Gibson's did a job for recently?'

Charley frowned. 'Who?'

'Danny Ray.'

'And?'

'And, therefore, he must surely know Solomon?'

Charley frowned. 'And yet, to my knowledge, he's never let on.'

'In passing, Mr Gibson also told me that Danny Ray promised him free publicity for a knock-down quote, which he never honoured. But the positive for Solomon was that he got a flat rental out of it ... and guess who his landlord is?'

Her eyes narrowed. 'Danny Ray?'

'The one and only. Confirmed just now by the estate agent who rents it out on his behalf.'

'But that doesn't make Danny a suspect, it just means he's not being up-front, and I guess there's nothing we can do about that?'

'Why would he withhold information like that if he had nothing to hide?' Mike said. 'A well-educated journalist, with a degree in criminology. Could he be our puppeteer?'

Charley felt her heart leap – somebody else was making the connection which made Danny Ray fair game. 'Let's get Ricky-Lee and Annie in my office for a meeting. I don't want Danny Ray to have the slightest inkling that we are looking at him. He's in the station this afternoon meeting up with the Divisional Commander, talking about Wilkie's hit-and-run and I'm invited. I declined, but maybe we could use his time here productively – I have an idea how we can move the investigation forward, but, for now, I want you to find out everything you can about Danny Ray, down to the last time he had a spot on his arse. Let's get the team in and start digging. And keep it tight.'

CHAPTER 20

'Ricky-Lee, I want a statement from Mr Gibson, and I want it made clear to him that he doesn't speak to anyone regarding its content. That includes Danny Ray. Annie, I want copies of the rental agreement from the estate agency acting as managers for the property where Solomon Myers lives. That will have Danny's signature on it. I also need them to be told that they must not inform him, or anyone else, of this request.'

Charley was building evidence. Was there a connection between Danny and Kylie Rogers? Was there a connection between him and Stewart Johnson?

'Mike, get the CCTV team to see if he appeared on any of the seized footage.'

She racked her brain. Did he wear brown shoes? All the times she had been in the journalist's company and yet she couldn't recall the make or colour of his footwear. Why couldn't she? She berated herself. Call herself a detective! Charley picked up the phone. 'Marty, are the CCTV cameras covering the enquiry desk up and running today?' His affirmative confirmation made her smile.

Her next point of call was the Divisional Commander's secretary, Becky. Her old school chum wouldn't let her down. Becky was preparing the afternoon tea tray when Charley caught up with her in the kitchenette used specifically for the command team. She found her staring at a packet of tea. She seized it, ripped it open, plucked the canister from the shelf and emptied the tea into it before she noticed Charley, then smiled.

'What can I do for you, or are you just loitering?'

'Actually, there is something,' whispered Charley, sidling up to her friend.

Becky frowned. 'That sounds ominous. What is it?' She filled the kettle at the sink, wiped the spout with a cloth and plugged it in before turning round to face Charley.

'I need you to play detective.'

'Detective?' faltered Becky, in a voice louder than intended. 'I don't like the sound of that.'

Charley put her finger to her lips. 'Shhh ... please. I need your help on this murder enquiry. I wouldn't ask if it wasn't absolutely necessary.'

The tension in Becky's arms made the china cup she'd retrieved from the cupboard quiver in its saucer. With a flash of panic crossing her face she placed it down on the tray as delicately as if it were a newborn baby. 'If I broke his personal cup, he'd have a blue fit!' she told Charley.

With deliberate calmness Charley continued, 'Remember we used to played Harriet the Spy when we were kids? This is no different, I promise.' The simile sounded juvenile even to her own ears, but Charley was desperate.

Becky continued to prepare the tea tray. Head down, she shook it feverishly. 'I'm sorry. Whatever it is, I can't. Mr Roper would know instinctively ... he knows me too well...'

A sudden crash and clatter outside in the corridor got their attention. Becky put her hand to her mouth. 'Do you think he heard?' she whispered. Immediately her face paled and her hands trembled. 'Oh, my Lord.'

Charley held out her hand, palm up, to her friend and listened. In the tiny room there was an absolute silence – a shocked, bewildered silence.

Suddenly, they heard subdued giggling. 'She might not be able to help you, but I will,' said Winnie, head peeping round the doorjamb. She tittered as she walked further into the room. 'Her face,' she said, pointing at Becky. 'I thought you were going to pee yourself.'

Becky turned towards the door. 'I'll leave you two to scheme. But count me out.'

Charley blocked her path. 'Just one thing…'

Becky's eyes stared past her into the distance.

'…after his meeting with Danny Ray, could you please put the tray, just as they leave it, here on this work surface? You don't need to do anything else…' She turned to Winnie and with an arm around her shoulder steered her out of the kitchenette and down to Winnie's 'office'. 'We need to talk,' she said.

'So, this man,' said Winnie, with one of her all-knowing looks, 'I guess he was the reason you left?'

Charley nodded. 'Partly…'

'Why? I've known you since … what, forever? It's not like you to run away, even from your mother's slipper.'

Charley put her head down. 'How do you know about that?'

Winnie shook her head. 'It's only a turn of phrase,' she said sheepishly.

'This was a bit different,' Charley said, rubbing the palm of her hand with her thumb. 'I was a stubborn, cheeky little mare.'

'You can't kid me … I know that look … You fell in love and he was spoken for, right?'

Charley slowly shook her head.

Seeing the expression on the younger woman's face Winnie's tone softened. 'So, he was aggressive? Violent? And you reported it, I suppose? I guess you know the drill better than most…'

'I told Roper – Roper was my boss at the time – but, because he's Roper, he wasn't interested in taking a domestic incident any further and that was that!'

'And that's why you left?'

'Not altogether. I was given promotion at the boards and then immediately seconded to London.'

Winnie clasped her hand warmly.

'And now, you're back to face the music!'

'Exactly!' Charley sighed.

'Do you have more empathy with victims after what happened?'

'Without a doubt!'

'So, why do this now?'

'Because at first I thought I might be vilifying Danny Ray because of what he had done to me – that I was desperate to find something to hang on him – but now I realise that Danny Ray might actually have gone a step further this time and be involved in the murder of two people.'

Winnie lowered her voice. 'So, what is it you want me to do?'

'We have an opportunity to get his prints and DNA without his knowledge.'

'And today's planned afternoon meeting could provide you with both?'

'Yes. The cup and saucer he uses will be taken away on the tray by

Becky after the meeting, as I requested. I want you to bring the tray to me in my office where we can bag and tag it without Danny Ray's, or Roper's, knowledge.'

'How will we know whose is whose?'

'Mr Roper apparently has his own personal bone-china cup and saucer so there is no chance of a slip-up.' Charley stood at the door, her hand on the handle. 'By the way, if you see Danny Ray, could you take a look at the colour of his shoes?' She was thoughtful. 'Even better, get a picture on your mobile.'

Winnie looked puzzled. She shrugged her shoulders when no further explanation from Charley was forthcoming. 'OK. Will do.'

Charley's attention was so fixed on the clock face in her office that afternoon that when the telephone rang, it made her jump. Feeling her heartbeat quicken she picked it up. 'Detective Inspector Charley Mann,' she said abruptly.

'Prison Liaison at Armley, Officer Tommy Newton. The intelligence report I have in front of me, in respect of one of our inmates, Solomon Myers, states that you are the person in charge of his case with regards to the charges of murder he's facing. Is that correct?'

'Yes, that is correct. I hope you're ringing me to tell me he wants to confess all.' Her attempt at humour was lost on him. There was a long, uncomfortable silence.

'No, sorry. The reason for the call is that he has just attempted to murder his cell mate by strangulation.'

Charley sat up in her chair. 'Attempted? He didn't succeed?'

'Luckily, a landing guard witnessed the attack and was able to intervene quickly. Myers was restrained and the victim has been hospitalised.'

'Will he survive?'

'Detective Sergeant Trueman, who is the officer dealing at our end, tells me that the hospital staff are confident he will.'

'Thank you.'

Another silence. 'We are also hearing on the grapevine that there's a price on Myers' head.'

'Really? I don't suppose you have any idea who wants him dead?'

'No, but I don't think we need worry about that for now as he's in isolation.'

Charley replaced the receiver and walked directly into the incident room to inform the team. She ensured enquiries were raised to liaise with the prison and collate all the information which would ultimately be merged with his present offences and, finally, recorded the fact that DS Trueman from Wakefield was the investigating officer.

Shortly before Divisional Commander Roper's meeting with Danny, Charley's strategy meeting with Neal Rylatt commenced. The CSI supervisor ran over the items that had been sent for forensic examination and what still remained bagged and tagged in the exhibit store.

'What's the budget looking like?' she asked.

The ever-cautious Neal shook his head. 'It's gone.'

'Later today, I want a specific item sent to Forensics.'

Neal nodded his head.

'Urgent,' said Charley.

'Who's gonna pay?'

'It'll be paid, don't worry.'

When her phone rang, she had difficulty hearing the voice on the end of the line.

'The journalist is wearing black, slip-on dress shoes, over and out,' said Winnie.

Neal Rylatt's eyes watched Charley with curiosity. No doubt the withholding of information intrigued him. She fancied he was rather amused at her way of working, but there was no anxious flicker, only trust.

'Thank you. Just let me know when the exhibits are ready.'

'Signing off for now,' said Winnie.

Charley couldn't help but smile, which didn't go unnoticed by Annie who had just walked over to offer her a fax printout. 'You heard the news?' she said, offering the pages, which Charley took and placed on her desk before her.

'News? What news?'

'Wilkie has spoken his first words.'

Charley's eyes lit up. 'Can we go see him do you know?'

'I don't know, but I can ask.'

Alone once more, Charley picked up a pen, played with it, put it down again. Then she pushed her chair back, crossed her legs and examined her fingernails. They still bore slight remnants of bright red nail varnish. She found it hard to settle, thoughts of Danny and the colour of his shoes swirling around her head. Why had today's preferred footwear been so important to her? It made her question if she had been letting her personal feelings about the journalist cloud her decisions.

She shook her head to clear her thoughts. Evidence told her he was linked in some way to the perpetrator of the murders. He was Myers' landlord: fact – something Danny hadn't been forthcoming about in his contact with the police. Eyes narrowed, she scrutinised the pictures of the victim's faces stuck to her noticeboard. Once she had Danny's prints she would have them checked against those lifted from the flat. Her heart soared momentarily at the thought, then plummeted. Sharp as he was, he'd have a valid excuse for the presence of his fingerprints; as landlord he was required to do maintenance work. As managers of the rental, the estate agent would be able to verify that.

Charley put her fingertips together and gazed thoughtfully at the document on the desk. The fax from the prison suggested that Solomon Myers' attempted murder of his cell mate had almost been successful.

'It took six prison officers to restrain prisoner Myers, a whole wing of trained staff to get him to release his victim, who was on the floor with his trousers round his knees.'

Charley drew her breath and held it before reading on. Myers hadn't denied attacking his cell mate, but denied any intent to kill him, which was in total contradiction to what the victim said. Turning the pages, she read on. The victim's statement revealed more.

'We'd been watching *Lord of the Rings* on TV and we got into a discussion about elves. He said, "We have a ghost in the woods where I work. She's famous." Obviously, I know that can't be true, so I said, "Are you having a laugh? There's no such thing as ghosts." His immediate response to that was, "Shut that fucking cell door!" I knew he wanted a fight, so I said, "OK." When I turned around after shutting the door, he ran at me and put his hands round my throat. Then he proceeded to throttle me and punch me for a while whilst shouting, "You're wrong!" He was beating the shit out of me and I don't remember anything else but waking up in the hospital wing. My head was a bit busted up. I also had bruises around my throat, but I saw it as a victory because I hadn't backed down. I knew I was right and he'd had to resort to violence because he couldn't think of a proper argument.'

Charley's mind turned to who Solomon's next cell mate might be. Contrary to popular belief, inmates were not celled up with the same person for their entire time inside. Prisoners could share with up to twenty different people throughout the course of a short-to-medium-length sentence: convicts were regularly moved to other jails, or were taken to attend court appearances, leaving empty beds to be filled. She shuddered. Sharing a tiny living space with someone you knew without the option to leave, never mind a stranger, was definitely her idea of hell.

Eager to read what the intended course of action for Myers was, she speed read to the end, to the note from Bill Trueman.

'Once we have the full statement from the victim, we'll give Myers another interview. Then we'll charge him and ultimately merge our file with yours, if you and CPS are in agreement.'

Charley considered the likelihood of Myers' brief asking for separate trials, unless he pleaded guilty. Her snigger was audible. 'I can dream, can't I?' she muttered.

Winnie stared hard at the CID office door, willing it to remain closed as she walked with trepidation towards Charley, carrying the tray and its precious items. For Roper to have followed her would not be good. Winnie's round cheeks were blushing red and her top lip held a hint of perspiration.

'In here,' Charley said, hurrying her into her office. Her entrance made Charley's heart start to pound.

Once the tray was laid on her desk, Winnie stood to one side, her clasped hands unusually fidgety. 'Becky said Danny actually handled them both. Sir Galahad, as he likes to think himself, apparently put them back on the tray for her – the reason, she was certain, was that he'd seen her hands shaking.'

'That's fine, she needn't worry. We'll have Roper's prints for elimination purposes. Neal Rylatt will need to take your fingerprints,' she advised Winnie as she carefully picked up the items with a gloved hand and bagged them. 'And Becky's too. He's on his way. He'll also need a statement from you both and I'll need to,' she signed the exhibit label, 'sign this, as I'm the one who's bagged them.'

'Becky's usually in her office until five, she never leaves a moment before,' said Winnie, standing proud.

'You did good,' Charley said, beaming. 'And the best bit is we've done it without his knowledge, so, if he is guilty of anything, he'll not think there's a need to get rid of anything that might implicate him – such as his shoes.'

Winnie's eyes were as excited as a child's. 'Working with you gives me so much joy. Being with you is just like being with your dad all over again, he was such fun.'

'Dad?'

Winnie looked a little flustered.

'I didn't know you knew Dad so well.'

CHAPTER 21

Morris Flanagan had a reputation as a hard nut – and rightly so. At thirty-six years of age, he was in prison for kidnapping drug dealers and taking hammers to their kneecaps. His hobbies included smoking crystal meth and shooting up heroin. He had a padlock in a sock and had threatened previous cell mates, saying he could smash them with it while they were sleeping and kill them whenever he wanted. 'But I'm no grass,' he said when questioned about the assault.

'He's got bruises on his throat, petechiae erupting on face, body and upper extremities and his eyes are congested. He's a bloody mess, truth be known; must be in extreme pain, not that he'd admit it. Sounds awful, but it would be so much easier if he'd died,' said Trueman, in his telephone conversation with her when he resumed his evening shift at the prison.

'Either way, one thing is for sure: Solomon will be looking at a long sentence.'

The quickness with which the colour had drained from Winnie's face, and the sudden dizzy spell that meant she'd needed to sit down, had worried Charley. She hated that she couldn't be the one to take her home, but she needed to be in the office when Neal arrived so she could hand over the exhibits. Annie reassured her, on her return, telling her boss that she'd left Winnie settled in front of her TV with a nice cup of tea and a couple of Rich Tea biscuits, and had been told 'not to fuss'. Charley vowed to visit as soon as she could.

'She's been like a mother to me – to us all here … She never married, no family. She doesn't need to work,' she told Annie. 'I keep forgetting she is as old as my parents would have been had they still been alive, yet she's still running around after us lot.'

The latest newspaper article, already live on the internet, was sent to the incident room from the press office the next morning. It was interesting, as was the note attached from Connie. 'I don't know if you've seen this, but it mentions Danny Ray's meeting with Divisional Commander Roper. It's not a bad human-interest story, but the ending leaves a lot to be desired.'

Charley was pleased to see that the piece was minus a picture of the injured DC.

'"What confidence does it give us, the general public, if no matter what resources they throw at finding the perpetrator, the police still can't find the person who mowed down one of their own?"' she read out. 'Twat! Well, maybe now Roper will see what an untrustworthy person he is, and have a word in his editor's ear,' said Charley.

'I wouldn't hold your breath. I've just seen the pictures of last night's dinner at the golf club showing him and Roper together,' said Connie.

'Danny plays golf?'

'Danny Ray's the Chairman!'

Since Myers had been arrested and charged, no more bodies had been discovered, but there had been the attempt on Wilkie's life. A fifty per cent success rate on the murder investigations was not good enough for Charley, even if the Divisional Commander was satisfied enough to be calling back the staff he had loaned to the incident room. 'If the muscle of the team has gone, what is the likelihood of the brains striking again?' he'd said, having called her in to his office.

'I'm not willing to take that chance, sir. Are you?' asked Charley. 'We need every last piece of the jigsaw in place to get the Is dotted and the Ts crossed in the prosecution file.'

'The brains behind the operation have beaten you. Why can't you accept that? The money's gone, the budget's spent; you've had your fun trying to catch the culprit, but now I want you to start to scale down the enquiry.'

Charley spluttered, confused, before bursting into laughter. When Roper's face remained emotionless, she shook her head in disbelief. She stood up as if to leave, then changed her mind. Leaning forward she put her palms down on his desk and looked him squarely in the eye.

'You really don't give a shit, do you? Not about the job, not about the victims – not even about the officer under your command who's lying injured in a hospital bed. You only care about one thing: your blasted budgets!' She watched him recoil as far away from her as was possible in his big, comfortable leather chair. Then, much to her surprise, he suddenly stood up and, leaning over her, he crooked his forefinger under her chin and grasped it tightly.

'I said, leave it! Do you hear me?'

She drew back, alarmed.

'Leave it? Leave what? Leave the murderer to get away with it? Not bloody likely!'

Her cheeks flame red, Charley spun on her heel and stormed out of the office, slamming the door behind her. She hurried down the stairs, almost ran through the incident room and, closing her office door behind her, dropped shakily into the chair behind her desk before letting out a shuddering sigh.

'What on earth had just happened in Roper's office? She had been insubordinate, but he had seriously overstepped the mark, and for what reason? This was more than just concern over his budgets.'

Her eyes turned to the hard-working group beyond her door and her heart sank. She'd let the team down. How was she going to break the news to them?

The door opened and Annie walked in, bearing a welcome pot of steaming coffee. 'You look like you could do with this,' she said.

Charley raised her head and smiled wanly as Annie approached the desk. 'Why? Is there a double brandy in it?' she asked, reaching out for the mug.

Annie's smile faded as she became aware of the seriousness of Charley's expression. 'That bad?'

Charley nodded and leant back in her chair. She covered her face with her hands and let out a mighty groan. 'Roper has instructed me to scale it down,' she said.

Annie bit down on her lower lip, her forehead wrinkled. 'Really?'

'Really.'

'And there's nothing we can do about it?'

'Not unless we can come up with something to up the ante.'

'You mean like new lines of enquiry?'

Charley nodded. 'That'd do for starters.'

A spark of light glimmered in the younger woman's eyes. 'Well,' she began eagerly, perching on the edge of the chair opposite Charley, 'then you might be pleased to hear that we've had a call into the incident room from a Mrs Sykes who, after reading Danny Ray's article, thinks she might be able to help us with our enquiries.'

'Go on.' Charley sat forward.

'Apparently, she'd been travelling on the road, on her way to a funeral, at approximately the same time that Wilkie got knocked down that day. She recalls a grey Golf being driven at speed in the opposite direction. And she also remembers seeing a man of Wilkie's description standing on the kerb by the telephone box that she had passed moments earlier.'

Annie paused for a moment. 'I must confess, the fact that Mrs Sykes said the man was smartly dressed almost threw me,' the young detective allowed herself a little chuckle. 'Bet that's the first time anyone has ever said Wilkie looked smart...' she paused again and appeared to be weighing up the odds '...but then again, I guess he was wearing a suit. It made her wonder if he was going to the funeral too, because she questioned whether she might know him. All good for us!'

Charley could feel her heart racing. 'Anything else she could tell us?' she asked, taking a sip of coffee.

'She remembered at the time she had her window open; she'd been feeling warm and a little flustered as she'd been rushing around, taking the grandchildren to school and calling at the doctors for her father's prescription. She says she distinctly heard a loud thud, like a clap of thunder, but didn't think anything more of it at the time, as getting to the funeral was uppermost in her mind. Apparently, she hates being late for anything.'

Charley raised an eyebrow.

'So, Danny might have done us a favour by writing the article,'

Annie said, 'because it wasn't until she saw his derogatory comment regarding the police, and she said she was so very grateful for our help when she was recently burgled, that the memory came to her.'

'I guess a unit has been dispatched to see her and to obtain a full statement?'

'On their way.'

Two hours later, Charley was reading Mrs Sykes's statement which was accompanied by a brief report from DC Nicky McDonnell, attending.

'Mrs Sykes is adamant about the type of car she saw. She owns a VW Polo and last month she visited the garage where the salesman tried to get her to upgrade to a Golf, even insisting she sat inside one. Hence her confidence in her ability to identify the vehicle concerned.

'She will testify to there being only one male driver present in the vehicle, who was not a young boy racer – her words. All she could tell me about the speed of the vehicle was that it was going fast and the roar of the engine gave her the impression that the driver was accelerating at the time it passed.

'Her timeline is very specific as she was on her way to attend a funeral, had dropped the grandchildren off and had been to the doctors. The latter two can be verified by CCTV.'

At the mention of the grey Golf, Charley's mind veered off in another direction. As far as she was aware, Danny Ray didn't drive a Golf; she felt a flutter of panic. She must stop being blinkered, immediately. She picked up the phone and spoke to Connie, passing her the details she'd been given so she could put them out to the media with further appeals to see if anyone could add to this new information.

The warm croissant on the cardboard tray and the now cooling latte were forgotten when Wilkie Connor's accident file was handed to her. The team had kept up the roster for visiting their colleague, but, as yet, he was still unable to recall what had happened on that fateful day, or offer any information as to the person who had knocked him down and subsequently left him for dead. Nor did he recall any of the information he had promised in his note to her, regarding the death of her beloved horse, Eddie.

She plucked the pictures out of the folder one by one. His injuries at the time had been photographed and documented and, as she read the statement of the officer first at the scene, it turned her stomach – not just because of the terrible injuries sustained, but because she was reading about one of her own officers, and the accident had been recorded by someone who knew the detective well. She revisited the images and her mind mulled over the crime scene from the point of view of the officers when they first arrived there. So intense was her concentration – her prayer that something would be glaringly obvious, even though she'd looked at them a hundred times before – that she was only vaguely aware of someone hovering in her office doorway and of a thin muttering of voices.

Connie broke her reverie when she entered the office and sat opposite her. 'Wilkie Connors' accident file?'

Charley nodded and pointed to a picture. 'This illustrates how the incident looked to the attending officers at the time. If there had been any witnesses to the accident, these show the scene from where they would have seen it.'

'The witnesses' point of view is taken to enhance the credibility of witness recall when testifying, in some cases years later, presumably?'

'Yes. And because the scene may change in the intervening weeks, months or years. People forget overall details, as much as they think the images are imprinted on their minds. Photos show the placement of any vehicles, the trees in their current stage of foliage and the approximate lighting and can contribute later to a more accurate recounting of the incident as it happened.'

'And human memory is elastic; it changes as other factors influence it,' said Connie.

'Absolutely, so filming the scene of a crime incident can be a very valuable tool in the investigation as well, as it defines the Force's response.'

Connie scoffed. 'In my experience, it can also hurt your case in court should mistakes be made inadvertently while completing the recording.'

'That's true. Investigators and administrators are quick to suggest, though, or even order an officer who has just been through a significant violent event, that he or she re-enacts the steps leading to the Force response.'

'No way,' Connie looked horrified.

Charley drew back from her with a scowl. 'Yes, but in my experience it's almost impossible to portray the dynamics of the incident accurately via an informal walk-through of the events soon after they happened, much less weeks or months later.'

Laid out in front of them were the pictures of Wilkie's head injuries and the severe bruising.

'He was very lucky,' said Connie.

'He certainly was. I need to start looking at his home security for when he is released. In fact, I need to have a word with the Divisional Commander to see how he sees that happening.'

'Really? Why?'

'Why what? Do you mean why do I think Roper will offer anything useful towards my predicament, or why does Wilkie need security?'

'Need security,' Connie said, concerned.

'A serious attempt was made on his life. Who's to say they won't try again?'

'Hmm…' she said, thoughtful. 'Well, if it's Roper you want, I'd save your legs. He's holding the monthly divisional management meeting this afternoon and I must say the buffet lunch that's just been delivered looks fit for a king!' And, with that, Connie bade Charley farewell and left her alone.

The talk of food made Charley look at the croissant and, picking it up between finger and thumb, she considered it closely. The butter had congealed. Her stomach grumbled as if her brain had somehow told it that it was empty. With no chance of a gap in her day to get out for a sandwich, she closed her eyes, took a bite and, shivering slightly, gulped down the remainder of the cold latte. She swallowed hard, crumpled the empty paper cup in her hand, took a deep breath and tossed the remainder of the pastry in the bin.

She turned her mind back to the enquiry. DNA had been lifted from the teacup that Danny Ray had used in the meeting, together with fingerprints. Nothing ventured, nothing gained and the rest was in the hands of the relevant departments examining both. For now, there was nothing she could do but wait.

Mike Blake greeted her to discuss the health of the database in respect of the ongoing investigations. Ultimately, the murder file would be created using statements and reports. She was eager to ensure they were up to speed with recording, and retaining the ability to reveal under data protection regulations, issues for disclosure.

Absolutely everything would be revealed to the defence unless it might jeopardise someone's life, but the reason for non-disclosure had to be recorded and the trial judge made aware.

The meeting was also about workloads, outstanding matters that still needed a resolution and by how much the expenditure was over budget at that point in time.

The volume of work the computers held, and the ability for them to cross-reference quickly, was still an enigma to her and she wondered how they'd coped in the past with just a card system. Charley had done her policy logs. Her personal reports were always completed, even when she was exhausted from what would most likely have been a twelve-hour or longer work day. They would be her bible in the days, weeks, months and perhaps years ahead when she was tasked with the job of giving evidence as the person in charge of the murder investigations. They recorded why she had decided, or why not, to pursue a particular line of enquiry. She flicked through the pages, each one timed and dated with her signature. They formed an overview of the structure and strategy of the investigations completed at the time, or as soon as possible thereafter.

The audit over, she felt a little happier with the state of affairs. She would, however, be even happier with the second offender in custody. She returned to her office and sat down behind her desk. After a moment or two, she was pleased to see DC Ricky-Lee walk in with a warm drink in hand.

'There you are, boss,' he said.

Charley eyed him suspiciously. 'Where else would I be?' She nodded her head towards the drinking vessel in his grasp and smiled. 'Your appraisal due or something?'

The detective smiled sheepishly. 'No,' he laughed. 'Tattie was just on her way in with it, but I was on my way to find you so I intercepted. Forensics rang while you were with Mike. Apparently, they couldn't get hold of you. They've had a hit on the DNA database with regards to the stranger rape on a Jean Weetwood. Could you ring them as a matter of urgency?'

'Jean Weetwood? In West Yorkshire?' For a moment, Charley was speechless. 'That's great news,' she heard herself saying. Her stomach flipped.

Ricky-Lee, chatted on regardless. 'Of course, they'll send the necessary formal report through, but I thought you'd like to know immediately who the match was for the DNA hit.'

'You thought right,' Charley said.

CHAPTER 22

Charley sat for a moment alone, quietly absorbing the information she had just received. Damn that man! Damn Danny Ray! Damn him for putting someone else through trauma – and damn her for not taking him to court, because if she had, then she might have saved this poor woman her ordeal. If a sample of blood was taken from every child born and went onto a database, and anyone entering the country had to give a DNA sample that was also subsequently put on to the same database, then there would be very few cold case enquiries to be investigated. Criminals would be identified instantly, and the immediate knock-on effect would not only save the country money, and police time, but also, more importantly, save lives as a direct consequence. And then there was the small problem of it being a breach of human rights...

Tattie walked past her office door. Charley shouted for her to come in.

'Tell Mike, Ricky-Lee and Annie I want them urgently for a meeting, please.'

A few minutes later, behind closed doors, Charley shared with her colleagues the recent update from Forensics. 'We have a hit on the DNA database. It's a cold case: the stranger rape of Jean Weetwood. It's confirmed. Her attacker was Danny Ray.'

Charley looked into their eyes, one by one. Annie was unbelieving, shocked, she thought she saw a tear. There was a pause. The three looked at her expectantly.

'I had the cup that he handled at his meeting with the Divisional Commander sent off for DNA examination and fingerprinting. This is a direct result of those samples.'

Charley knew she had been lucky, but she hadn't realised just how lucky until now...

Ricky-Lee whistled through the gap in his teeth. 'What a bastard,' he said.

The others remained silent.

'I still want the information we have on Danny Ray kept tight. We know he is – or should I say was – Solomon Myers' landlord. We now know what he is capable of. There is no doubt he left Jean Weetwood for dead. What I want to know now is, is he our missing link in the recent murders? He has a degree in criminology, so the wrongfooting at the scenes could be right up his street. I've yet to speak to the fingerprint section, but, in the meantime, I want you to research and record everything we can possibly find out about him. His daily routine, his present address, the vehicles he has use of ... We'll reconvene in an hour and discuss our strategy to arrest him and the subsequent searches that will be necessary.

'Once he's locked up, then the work will begin. We may yet need to do some surveillance because, when we go for him, I don't want anything left to chance.' There was fire in her eyes, and in her belly. A fire she'd never thought possible. 'OK, let's do it.'

The level of adrenaline racing through her body had just risen ten-fold. They had evidence to arrest and charge for the Jean Weetwood enquiry, which would give them some breathing space to wait for further results if they hadn't yet got the necessary evidence to connect Danny Ray to the murders.

Charley felt an almighty surge of euphoria. At last, the journalist was going to get what was coming to him; and the nice thing for her was, he didn't have a clue they were on to him, thanks to Roper, who she was also going to keep in the dark lest he feel obliged to make enquiries of his own with Danny – as he no doubt had the last time she had put her trust in him.

She savoured the feeling, even started to fantasise over how the arrest would be conducted. Should she invite him into the police station on the pretence that she wanted to see him? He would come in to the station willingly and she could have him arrested on site. A press release was imminent. The murder investigation had hit a wall with no new evidence to share and with one person in custody pending trial. Any SIO would be looking for something to bring the case back to the front pages, in the hope of catching another believed to be involved. She shook her head and dismissed the thought. Nah. It wasn't public enough – behind closed doors with no paparazzi? That would be too good for him. She wanted him to be scorned, forcibly dragged out of his bed. She raised her eyebrows – or out of his car, much more appropriate in her mind. The greatest gift of all was that the decision would ultimately be hers.

Charley paced the floor waiting for the fingerprint department to come back to her. She berated herself for having been so easily persuaded by Roper not to pursue a conviction for the aggression Danny Ray had shown towards her. Letting her confused emotions and embarrassment get in the way of speaking out had led to Danny Ray being free to rape Jean Weetwood.

She had been young in service at the time, with a natural desire to fit in and be accepted on his shift of all-male officers. Had her naivety clouded her judgement?

She was well aware from Marty's teaching in the early days that bad cops didn't fear rejection by other bad cops; they were afraid of good cops.

'The slope of wrongdoing is steep and slippery, and it is important not to step onto it at all,' Marty had said to her and Kristine.

She'd learned that Roper tolerated wrongful conduct by officers. He involved newcomers in soliciting bribes from pub landlords, bar owners and restaurants on their beat – money, cigarettes, drinks in exchange for turning a blind eye. He, in turn, turned a blind eye to his officers drinking on the job, sleeping on duty in secret places, accepting sexual favours from prostitutes, knowingly using too much force on suspects, filing false reports. She would never partake in any of it and he hadn't liked her for not conforming; he was used to getting his own way.

Her thoughts roamed as she waited for the reply from the fingerprint department. She'd asked them to check Danny Ray's marks against those found on the thank-you card delivered with the whisky to Wilkie in the incident room, as well as against the marks lifted from Solomon Myers' flat.

Could the journalist really be the mastermind behind the recent murders? Had he been at the first murder scene, waiting for her to arrive? He had been under her feet as an aggressor, but was he a killer? What was the saying: keep your friends close and your enemies even closer. Is that what he had been doing by courting Commander Roper? Should she tell Roper? Should she put her trust in him again? Her thoughts sent a multitude of ideas and feelings reeling through her brain, all evaporating under a cloud of trepidation. Or was he already aware of Danny Ray's indiscretions and was Roper the person who was trying to fit in to his world and be accepted? She shook her head. No, no, no ... surely not ... please, no.

Despite the restlessness of her mind, Charley felt riveted to the spot as she waited, her body tense. Drumming her fingers on the desk, she returned her attention to the well-thumbed copies of the Jean Weetwood file. It wrote of a brutal attack, a stranger rape where the young woman had been left for dead. Charley considered herself lucky to be alive, but to think another woman had suffered at the hands of that man made her heart sink. Beads of perspiration appeared on her brow; palpitations hammered in her chest. She read through the file once, before skimming through it yet again, hoping against hope to find the missing piece of the puzzle. She just hoped she wasn't being blinded by her own desperation.

She had hoped for good news from the fingerprint department, but when news came it was not what she wanted, or expected. The only full print of Danny's found at the flat was from a plug. Her heart skipped a beat at the news. 'But that's moveable. It doesn't necessarily put him at the flat,' she said. 'I need to prove he was actually inside the flat.'

'We've lifted a partial mark from the inside of the mobile phone cover.' There was a pause. 'Hmm ... But I guess that doesn't put him where you'd like him either?'

Charley shook her head. 'They're good enough for court purposes though, the fingerprints?' She sounded desperate even to her own ears.

'Yes, yes. They're good enough for court purposes.'

'And the thank-you card?' she asked, hopefully.

Neal sounded defeated. 'Again, we have partial prints, though you can be assured they are his.'

That revelation brought a heavy weight to the pit of Charley's stomach. 'Damn,' she said through clenched teeth. She put the phone down and questions chased each other around in her head. She'd failed dramatically, diverting the police enquiries into all manner of irrelevant paths along the way to satisfy her desire for revenge.

How did the pieces fit in the puzzle? The prints on the inside of the mobile phone cover where photos of the victims were stored were most definitely a bonus. It had been found in Solomon's house – and maybe it was Solomon's, maybe it wasn't – but why would Danny Ray's fingerprints be on it? Had he supplied him with the device?

On the day they'd arrested Solomon Myers, the journalist had had time to go to the flat. Had he known of the arrest? Was the gift of whisky planted to distract them? An assumption, but was it him who'd tried to kill Wilkie? Did he think the detective suspected somehow that he was involved, if so, of what?

When the team returned, she updated them with the fingerprint news from HQ before asking for their findings. They had Danny's home address, a property known as The Starlings, on Union Road in Slaithwaite, where it was believed that he lived alone. They had confirmed a private mobile phone number, on which Charley immediately wanted enquiries to find out who he had been ringing and texting, along with a cell site analysis around the times of the murders.

'His car, boss – not his work vehicle – would you believe it's a grey VW Golf?' Annie chipped in with the result of her enquiries. 'And now we have the registered number.'

'Get on to an ANPR operator and research the number urgently,' Charley said. 'I want a meeting in half an hour to discuss the arrest strategy.'

'You have a plan?'

'Yes – to make it as painful and public as possible for Danny Ray!'

Annie's eyebrows rose. 'Is it imminent?'

'I can't risk anyone else being attacked, or word getting out so, yes, it needs to happen sooner rather than later. Even though I think he's probably more the brains than the brawn behind these recent murders, what we now know is that he is capable of so much more than we had previously been able to prove.'

Half an hour later, Charley stood in front of the team for the briefing. Sergeant Jack Cooke, who would be receiving the prisoner in the custody suite, had been invited. Fail to plan, plan to fail: her mantra – with everyone and anyone who was likely to come into contact with him in the room, there were to be no surprises. Head held high, back straight, she delivered her strategy with a confidence and determination that she hadn't allowed herself for a long while. She reeled off her requirements to a team who hung on every word.

'I want a uniform arrest team with protective gear. We will follow in once the suspect has been restrained and removed. I want POLSA search teams on standby to move in with me to the inside of the property, but I also want them to search the outside. From today I want surveillance on the house, with CROP men buried in the grounds, if it is deemed necessary. I want Danny Ray located and a mobile unit to follow his every move. Once we're ready, the decision to strike will be made, his car seized and taken away under cover on a low loader. His place of work needs searching: his office, his desk, his locker. I want no stone unturned. I am hopeful that, as this is our local newspaper, we will get total co-operation from its editor, but I'm not taking any chances so a warrant will be obtained immediately.'

Charley walked back to her office leaving the officers busy with their personal tasks, which would ensure her instructions were adhered to, to the letter. Annie followed her.

'What's next,' she asked eagerly.

Tears welled up in Charley's eyes. 'I just want justice so badly,' she said, turning to the young officer.

Annie looked at her quizzically, 'You OK?'

Charley cringed inwardly. The guilt was all hers. If only she'd had the courage to do what she so often asked of others: to tell the police all they knew … If only her boss had not brushed her off, but had acted on the revelations. She knew that the fallout from her decisions would be on her conscience for the remainder of her days. She just hoped that, this time, her decisions were untainted by impulse or desperation.

Her mood spiralling, she turned to her computer. Her smile was forced as she focused on the screen. 'I'm fine. But I've decided to call Danny and invite him in to see me tomorrow in regard to answering his comments in his recent article. If he answers, then we'll have him on our radar via cell site analysis.'

As she gazed past Annie and into the incident room, she could see that most of the team sat behind their desks, either gazing at their computer terminals or talking on their telephones, seeking updates or agreements to their requests.

Her eyes back on Annie as she put her phone to her ear, she listened to the ringing. His mobile went to voicemail, so she left a message suggesting a meeting late the following morning, at a station convenient to him. If he wasn't on their radar by then, at least she knew he'd be coming in.

Annie briefly raised her eyebrows at her.

A few minutes later, Charley's phone chirped to life. Her mouth went dry and her heartbeat increased. Immediately, she recognised her sergeant's voice, and a wave of disappointment flashed through her.

'Ray's vehicle had been flagged up on ANPR as an interest sighting,' he said. 'Have you been informed by HQ yet regarding the name they have designated for the operation?'

'No,' Charley said, the briefest sigh of disappointment in her breath. It took her a moment to regain her composure as she listened to his words regarding the setting up of the command room from where the operation was to be co-ordinated.

'Thank goodness Roper's left the office,' said Annie.

'Left?' replied Charley. Suddenly, she felt more optimistic. 'Really?'

'I was talking to Becky. Apparently, he's going straight from some meeting or other for a golfing trip while his office is being refurbished.'

The smile in Charley's eyes didn't go unnoticed.

'So there is a God,' she said.

'Ah ... I get your drift. He won't be able to argue the cost of the overtime until it's over?'

Charley faltered 'Yes, of course ... absolutely!'

'And – bonus –' her eyes twinkled, 'that nice, new, young uniformed chief inspector will be in the command room,' she said, beaming. Charley smiled at the young woman as, fist in the air, Annie pulled an invisible cord. 'Kerching!'

More than two hours passed. The teams were sorted and observations were in place.

The observation team reported back. The Starlings was a large, old, semi-detached house with a lean-to vinery, newly planted. It was surrounded by a walled garden with remnants of whitewash on the south side where a glass house had once stood. The garage door was ancient, dried out and rotten in parts. It was pretty obvious from a quick inspection that no vehicle could possibly be kept inside and, with no car on the driveway, it was also obvious that Danny was out and about in his own vehicle.

Because of the information that had come to light on the rape, he was deemed to be a threat to the public and, as it was the police's job to protect the public, it was imperative that they locate and neutralise that threat with an arrest as soon as physically possible. But, with Is to dot and Ts to cross, and with paperwork needing to be duly signed by the correct level of command, a warrant put in place and the threat of the custody clock ticking once they had done so, Charley was more than aware that timing was crucial every step of the way.

The sound of a text being received on her mobile encouraged her to take a look at the screen. Danny had accepted her offer to meet at the station and suggested eleven a.m. the following day. Directly, she picked up the phone. 'Can you locate this mobile?' she asked the cell site team.

A motorcyclist was the quickest surveillance unit to despatch in the attempt to locate Danny Ray. His car was parked at Blackroyd Foot, Crosland Moor, but on arrival the motorcyclist confirmed that he was nowhere to be seen.

A dedicated channel was opened up to speak over the airways and the next voice Charley heard was that of the motorcyclist. 'Do you want me to stay with the car?'

'Yes, please. We have no further instruction other than to keep him under observation,' came the immediate reply from the control room operator.

No further news was forthcoming for some time and Charley began to feel more and more discouraged and emotionally drained the longer she sat at her desk waiting for news. She went through the case file with a fine-toothed comb. She could not afford any doubt, slip-ups, or unforeseen ramifications further down the line, not with a journalist of long standing on the local newspaper being involved. With one suspect in the traps, and one of their own publicly vilified, both the local and national newspapers would have a field day at her expense.

'Target seen walking out of a cul-de-sac to his vehicle.' The news over the airways made her sit up straight. She listened intently as the motorcyclist gave his commentary. From his observation point, he could see Danny sitting in his vehicle. He noted a young woman he knew to be a police officer walk from a house and get into her car, under Danny's watchful eye. His voice faltered. Charley held her breath. 'Who is she, Andy?' she asked, tapping her fingers on the wood veneer. Danny then appeared to follow the police officer's car at a distance in his own vehicle and the motorcyclist, Andy Day, stayed on their tail. When the police officer's car turned into the police station yard, Danny did a U-turn and the waiting team were on his tail, to the Bradford Road.

Unaware of the attention she had been getting, Susan Vine contacted the control room, signing on for duty.

Danny Ray didn't go back to his home address, but headed for the woods over the hill and to the stables. The team could see there was a light on inside the house there, but the stable yard was in relative darkness.

If there was a light on inside the farm house, was Kristine inside, Charley wondered? Her fists clenched. If she asked the team to approach him now, she could risk the operation's successful conclusion. But could she be putting her friend's life in danger by allowing him his head?

The surveillance team reported eyeball on the door. No attempt on

Danny's part was made to knock. Was he watching Kristine? And if so, why? Some twenty minutes later the grey Golf moved off, unaware of the follow. Charley gave a sigh of relief. It was nine p.m. when he was reported to have arrived home. He drove his vehicle onto the driveway and went inside his house alone.

The decision was made that, unless Danny Ray was called out on a job, he had more than likely worked his hours and wasn't expected to go out again that night. However, his house remained under constant observation. Whilst inside alone, he was no threat to anyone. At midnight, the teams were stood down until four a.m., so they could strike by means of forced entry at four-thirty a.m. Although stood down, a contingent remained in the police station, putting their heads down for a few hours of fitful sleep; going home was not an option taken by many.

Charley was prepared for her stay in her office. She was close to completing her first murder investigation as the SIO, but she was aware it wasn't over yet. How could she have been so naïve as to think that, if he had assaulted her – someone he had known all his life, his childhood girlfriend – he would stop there? How many other people had he attacked before and after? The unknown answer didn't bear thinking about. Was she really such a bad judge of character, or had he been hoodwinking her all her life? How many people could she have saved from trauma by his hand? She couldn't dwell on that now. All she could think about was making sure she had all the evidence she needed to put him behind bars for good.

Charley sank back in her chair and shut her eyes. Tomorrow was going to be a very long day. She looked around her dishevelled office and remembered her promise to go and see Winnie. It was too late now, but she'd go as soon as she could.

CHAPTER 23

Even though Charley's office door was ajar, the room had become unbelievably hot. She was irritated. How were officers supposed to remain focused and wide awake on a night shift when the working environment was akin to a Turkish steam room? It was three in the morning as she looked at herself in the mirror. Her face was pale and drawn and although her trousers hadn't creased, her shirt was highly crumpled – not surprising, since she'd tossed and turned all night. She stretched out her aching limbs, splashed cold water on her face and ladled water in the palm of her hand to reach the back of her neck, slick with oily sweat. After blotting her skin with paper towels, she sprayed deodorant under her arms and brushed her teeth.

Ricky-Lee spoke with a throaty rasp in his voice when he popped his head around Charley's office door. 'The Obs team have confirmed Danny is still in the house, ma'am.'

'He'd better be, or it'll be a question of which one of the surveillance team will be driving a Panda car by the end of the day,' she called to the retreating figure heading for the water dispenser.

The kettle could be heard boiling and the smell of coffee and warm, buttered toast was in the air when she walked back into the incident room. Ricky-Lee had tried his utmost to hide his bloodshot eyes and mask the smell of stale alcohol from her with mouthwash and aftershave.

'Did you manage to catch a few hours' sleep?' Charley asked Annie as together they watched the DC chucking painkillers down his throat. He saw them looking at him. His head tilted slightly and a near-smile curved his lips.

'Not really,' Annie said, turning to Charley. 'I seem to have spent the whole night with a coffee cup in my hand and my eyes latched on to that dial,' she said, angling her head at the office clock. 'Do you think he's going to be OK?' Annie nodded towards Ricky-Lee.

'He'll have two choices,' Charley said with a forced smile.

'But ... he looks shot...'

'He'll learn not to try to keep up with the Surveillance team,' she said, elbowing Annie as she saw members of the team arrive with bacon sandwiches. They wafted the food under Ricky-Lee's nose and, observing his obvious green gills, followed by his objection to the smell of the food, they goaded him further. Eventually, he covered his mouth and ran for the door. Judging by their jeers there was no doubt he hadn't heard the last of it.

It was four a.m. as she headed to the briefing to ensure everyone knew their role in the forthcoming arrest – and the reasons for it. The adrenalin in the room was tangible. The team were ready.

There were four cars in the convoy. With her hand on top of the passenger door Annie closed her eyes and made the sign of the cross across her chest before getting in the vehicle.

Charley felt her own heart pounding. 'I didn't know you were particularly religious,' she said in conversation as she rolled the car forward.

'I'm not,' Annie scowled. 'I left that shit behind me when I left school. I had religion shoved down my throat every day. Priests and nuns telling us how to live a good, honest life. Every day there was one guilt trip or another to send us down, while we prayed for forgiveness. I was regularly told I would go to hell if I didn't change my ways. I wouldn't have bothered if I'd been one of the bad kids, but I wasn't. I learnt to keep my head down and clear my plate because "There were children starving in Biafra".'

Charley's eyebrows were raised. A glance across at her young colleague showed her wringing her clasped hands.

Annie sighed heavily. 'And then there was the hypocrisy of the whole thing. The priests telling us what to do and what not to do and all the time they were abusing their power and touching up my brother and his classmates. He was a good kid – he never got over what they did to him...'

Charley heard Annie's voice crack, but her eyes were focused on the road ahead.

'I'm sorry,' she said. This was not the time nor place to continue.

Those whose job it was to batter down the door went to work. The front-line officers in protective clothing stormed in, followed by Charley and her team, all wearing stab-proof vests. Lights were switched on. Shouts of 'Police!' went up from several different sources, but the overriding noise was of boots running up the stairs, while downstairs officers veered off into the rooms to search them. The clamour was enough to awaken even the deepest of sleepers. Charley's heart was racing with anticipation.

In a first-floor bedroom, they found Danny Ray. White-faced and clearly shocked he had barely managed to raise himself on an elbow before a couple of uniformed officers, followed by the detectives, had surrounded him. Before he could say anything, Charley stepped forward. There was a flicker of recognition on his startled face.

'Danny Ray, you are being arrested for the attempted murder and rape of Jean Weetwood and the attempted murder of Detective Constable Wilkie Connor.'

No sooner had she begun to recite the caution than suddenly, from under his pillow, Danny produced a piece of wood formed into a handmade truncheon, which he swung at her. She sidestepped the mediaeval-looking weapon and instinctively, with a powerful right fist, hit him in the face with such force that he fell back on the bed and a moment later looked as though he didn't know what day it was. Charley removed the weapon from his open hand. It was incredibly heavy and her belief was that it was somehow filled with lead. 'Bag and tag,' she said, to a startled young uniformed officer. 'Arrest him. Dress him, and cuff him,' she said to another. Dragged from his bed, nude, Danny was forced to dress in front of them. Charley turned her head away.

Dumbfounded, the journalist obeyed instructions. He was motionless as the cops handcuffed him.

Furious, her heart still racing, Charley turned on her heels. 'Let's go,' she said to Annie.

'Does it hurt?' the younger woman said, grimacing at the red knuckles on Charley's right hand. 'Remind me never to upset you. Ouch!' she grimaced at the sight.

'Yeah, but it was worth it,' Charley whispered out of the corner of her mouth.

'I thought for a moment he was trying to hit you with a bloody vibrator!' Annie gave a nervous titter, which Charley found infectious, and a few heads turned.

A search of the house soon revealed Danny Ray's personal incident room, with maps and pictures of victims and crime scenes, including recces for locations. Four groups of pictures to the top left-hand corner were enough to make Charley's heart skip a beat: PC Susan Vine, an aerial map of the area where she lived, internal pictures of her house; a picture of Kristine, an aerial picture of the farm, Peel Street, the police headquarters and surrounding grounds; pictures of Charley riding Wilson and last, but not least, a picture of Ruby at the club.

'Look at all this,' Annie said.

'Let's keep digging,' Charley said with a nod of her head at the search team. 'Find me a pair of brown brogues, will you? Please God, don't let him have got rid of them,' she pleaded. 'We'll have a full debrief in the incident room at noon. That should give you time for one of you to be able to update me at least, even if you haven't finished searching.'

Outside, Charley stopped and took a long deep breath of cool morning air. Focusing on the garden gates ahead she saw they had been taped off and two uniformed officers stood guarding the entrance, one of whom she recognised as Susan Vine. The sight of the officer triggered her to move forward. A statement would be required from her as to Danny Ray's threats at the hospital.

'Don't you have a home to go to?' Charley asked the policewoman. Susan looked tired; her eyes were reddened.

'As soon as I'm relieved, believe me, I'm off to my bed, ma'am,' she said. 'It's been a long night.'

The update from the team who had gone directly to the newspaper offices where Danny Ray worked was positive, the editor herself shocked by the news and fully co-operative.

Could the day get any better Charley wondered? And then she got the news that Wilkie was being released from hospital, although he still couldn't speak for long periods or hold a pen. That would come in time, she was told, and she hoped that when it did he would be able to communicate the information about Eddie's death.

Visibly shaken, a handcuffed Danny Ray was helped out of the police car when it pulled up in the station yard. He was ushered into the custody suite, where he entered as a remand prisoner who had been arrested for, but not yet charged with, the attempted murder and rape of Jean Weetwood and the attempted murder of Detective Constable Wilkie Connor.

The custody suite sat at the heart of the police station. The only access to the area was by someone inside opening the door. Sergeant Jack Cooke's lip turned up at the corner in a lazy grin as, at his command, Charley was allowed access to the suite. Sergeant Cooke was a short, thick-set, bright-eyed man with a large, bulbous, purple nose and an expression that was both droll and complacent. He sat behind the custody desk, perched on a buffet, his eyes focused on the computer screen in front of him. Shouts and thuds could be heard from the cell area.

'He's not a happy bunny,' Jack said, nonchalantly. His eyes still didn't leave the screen. Charley went to stand at the other side of the desk. Tilting his head, Jack narrowed his eyes and waited. Another three bangs and an angry roar. 'He wants to make an official complaint about his wrongful arrest and is presently insisting I get Divisional Commander Roper in.'

'You'll have a job on; he's golfing.'

He closed his eyes slowly and nodded briefly. 'I know.'

'Have you got him in a paper suit?'

Jack turned to face her this time and nodded again. 'And he's being monitored, as per your instruction.

'Suicide's far too good for him. Has he been seen by a doctor yet? We need him deemed fit for interview.'

'The doc?' The CCTV screen was secured on the wall to his right and he looked up at it. 'Aye, she's here now,' he said. Charley could see the figure of a young Asian woman carrying a black bag, being escorted by Marty from the front desk down the steps leading to the cells. Once at the door, the two could be seen chatting and laughing. The officer requested access and Jack responded by pressing another large green button to his left. The officers waited for the doctor to appear.

'By the way, mi'laddo tells me he'll be going home once he's seen Roper. According to him, Roper's a good friend.'

Charley looked quizzical. 'I think "good friend" might be stretching it a bit. Anyway, I think whatever relationship they may have had in the past will just have come to an abrupt end, don't you?'

At the closing of the door behind the doctor, Jack raised his chin. 'Hello, Dr Ande,' he said, seeing the doc in the holding chamber. Jack released the steel-barred gate and she walked towards them. 'How bloody lovely to see you.' He made a flamboyant open-handed gesture to introduce the two ladies. 'Doc, this is Detective Inspector Charley Mann, the person in charge of the murder enquiries.'

Secretly, Charley surveyed the prisoner as he gave his fingerprints and DNA, her heart still unbelieving, her head knowing otherwise.

The offence he'd been charged with was deemed a holding charge, which enabled the police to place him before the court for a remand to police cells so he could be interviewed about other matters: these being the two murders.

'He doesn't want the duty solicitor. Apparently, he has another friend who's been called to the Bar! And, flummoxed or not, he remembered the guy's phone number.' Jack showed Charley the barrister's details.

She studied them for a moment, then shook her head. 'No, I don't think I know Donald, do you?'

Charley returned to the office to discuss the forthcoming interview strategy with the elected officers. Assumed to be off the cuff, but actually well-rehearsed and polished, interview questions were considered and agreed. After questioning him regarding the attack on Jean Weetwood, they could charge him with murder, and attempted murder, when the evidence was irrefutable.

For some reason, Charley's debris-strewn desk distressed her – it was usually kept orderly by another. It was lit by a harsh fluorescent striplight, whose artificial glare reflecting off the office windows showed how dark it was outside. The atmosphere in the room was one of quiet satisfaction: at times she had thought there was more chance of her understanding the off-side rule in football than solving the case.

Snippets of conversation drifted into her office from the incident room, but most of it was drowned out by the endless fevered chatter of a team wound up by the success of their enquiry and the buzzing of the telephones. Most of the team sat at their desks, transfixed by their screens: the HOLMES team updating, the remainder either writing up reports, updating the dry-wipe boards or conducting telephone conversations with others, in the hope that they would lead to the solid conviction of the perpetrators.

She wanted justice for the two murdered victims and their families so badly, as well as for Jean Weetwood; but also, perhaps selfishly, she wanted it for herself.

Still deep in thought, she sat behind her desk, where the paperwork overflowed to such an extent that documents threatened to fall onto the floor. Feeling the onset of a headache, she brushed the articles aside to open her desk drawer and search for paracetamol. Popping two pills from the foil wrap, she placed them into her mouth and swallowed them down with the dregs of a cup containing cold coffee. It had skinned over; her throat lurched and stomach heaved, but with an effort she managed to keep the pills down, though her face reddened and her eyes filled with salty tears in the process.

They say you didn't know what you had until it was gone and it was true; she missed Winnie and vowed to go and see her at the next opportunity. Winnie had always been there to clean up her mess, even taking her clothes to be washed or cleaned if she'd left them around when she was in uniform. She brought her team homemade cakes and soups. Mother hen, she was. Now it was time to pay her back in her hour of need.

Charley would have loved to be with the team rooting through things and finding the evidence to put Danny Ray where he belonged. A satisfied smile crossed her face. There was going to be a vast number of exhibits; the team would be seizing all his clothing on her instruction.

'I'll find those brogues if it's the last thing I do,' she muttered under her breath. Popping her head around the exhibits room door, she was expectant that the empty wooden-slatted shelves would be full of packages and parcels very soon – every item would be revealed to the defence whether it was used or not, that was the process; although the defence didn't have to reveal their evidence beforehand, which she still thought gave them an unfair advantage in court.

There was a vast amount of work to be done, but, no matter what it took, she didn't want Danny Ray seeing the light of day again. The young, innocent boy she had once played kick-a-can on the street with, the teenager she'd partnered at the school disco, the boyfriend with whom she had once thought there was a future ... Roper had been right on one thing: if Danny hadn't startled her that night, she would have floored him – and Danny Ray had known it.

Her thoughts were broken when Divisional Commander Brian Roper walked into her office.

'Sir! I thought you were...'

'Golfing? I was.'

Her haste to rise from behind her desk caused a pile of papers to fly to the floor.

'Oh, for goodness sake,' he said, as she scrabbled around his feet to retrieve them.

Charley hesitated and looked up to see his scowl.

'You really are pathetic, do you know that?' Roper hissed. 'Does the Chief know yet?'

She shook her head, trying to clear the commotion within.

'Leave it with me,' he said. Huffing and puffing, he left the room.

CHAPTER 24

Charley was at her office window, looking out over the yard.

'You OK?' asked Annie, coming in. Without waiting for an answer, she sat down, screwed up her face and gently slid off one shoe. Kneading a big toe, she continued. 'Can you begin to imagine having to turn your shoes upside down and inside out to let the water pour out at the end of the day?' she asked, shaking her head in disgust. 'I know, I know, it sounds absurd, but back in the day the broguing on a pair of wing tips wasn't just for show it was a necessity.' She looked quizzically at Charley and carried on. 'Brogues weren't meant for the boardroom; they were specifically designed for the bog, first worn by English and Irish countrymen who had to slog around their soggy farms all day. But you'll probably know all this coming from a farming family.'

Charley appeared distant. 'They don't have complete holes now, only abbreviated, decorative dots that give the shoes personality,' she said flatly.

'You sure you're OK, you look rather er … odd.'

The briefing room was packed. The clock struck twelve. The attendees fell silent the moment Charley stood up. As she was about to speak, she became aware of the door opening at the back of the room and the shuffling of feet as those standing in front moved to allow someone through. The crowd made a pathway and she realised that it was the Divisional Commander, who unceremoniously pushed his way to the front. With a nod of his head to those assembled, and an uncompromising look at Charley, he sat down uncomfortably close beside her.

Though bewildered to see him at the briefing, she found herself surprisingly unaffected by his presence, so focused was she on the job in hand. Maybe that was a good thing.

Firstly, she thanked everyone for their efforts, thus far. 'For those of you who don't know, Mr Danny Ray was arrested at his home this morning, as planned. Thanks to your sterling work, all went to plan. He was alone and still in his bed when the team forced entry. Presently, he is complaining about his wrongful arrest and has refused the duty solicitor, expressing a desire to use a friend of his, who is a barrister. Mr Ray had the details readily available and therefore the barrister has been contacted.'

She could feel Roper's eyes upon her and deliberately omitted to give the barrister's name in case he knew him. Was that the reason he was here? To find out what they knew? To pass on information to his friend?

'Mr Ray will be interviewed later today regarding a cold case where we have DNA evidence connecting him to the crime. This was, for those who are unaware, a violent attack on a lady called Jean Weetwood, who was out walking her dog on the same moorland as Kylie was found. Ms Weetwood was subjected to a violent rape and apparently left for dead. The strategy will be to interview him first about this historical crime. Once he has had the opportunity to comment, he will be charged. This charge will be used to have him remanded to our cells for three days. He will then be interviewed about the murders and attempted murder of one of our own. After this morning's searches, let's hope we have more evidence to help secure his convictions.

'Before I open the meeting and go around the room to see what you have for us, I want you all to know that our colleague and friend Wilkie Connor is leaving hospital today. His recovery is likely to be a slow one, I am told. For those unaware, he was diagnosed as having suffered a serious brain injury from the impact of the car and, as most of you already know, he has spent time in the intensive care unit where he was taken directly after the accident. He is now having to re-learn how to eat, use the bathroom, brush his teeth, put on his shoes – all the things we take for granted...' Her voice wavered. 'When he woke out of the coma, he couldn't talk. He's starting from scratch. We will do everything we can to continue to support him and his wife, Fran.' She took a look sideways to see the Divisional Commander looking straight ahead with a blank expression. She took this as an indication that he didn't want to add anything. 'OK, so, down to business!' Charley looked around the room to find the face of the custody sergeant. 'Anything?'

'I am reliably informed that Mr Ray's barrister will be joining us at about eleven a.m. Danny Ray is under constant supervision. As advised, our officers are not speaking to him, but we are recording anything he says. At the moment, however, he remains silent.'

'The team that went to his place of work, DC McDonnell, Nicky, anything?' asked Charley.

'Firstly, can I just say that the staff at the newspaper appear to be in total shock. However, they are co-operating fully. There was nothing in his desk drawer other than what I would consider the normal office equipment that we all use on a daily basis. However, we have seized his desk diary, which we're hoping may show us where he was on the dates of the incidents, or indeed what he might have written in the diary to justify being out of the office. And ma'am, I've been assured by the editor that they don't condone the use of drones to obtain information.'

Next up was the team that had the job of recovering Danny's vehicle and the search of his garage.

'Vehicle recovered, boss, to the undercover garage at HQ, where a full examination is underway. In the passenger well we discovered a piece of piping and some gaffer tape. And there was a camera drone in his garage. I'll update you as and when we have any more for you.'

Sergeant Fennell was representing the POLSA search team. 'The team is still at the house, boss. As you saw for yourself, Mr Ray had his own mini incident room. Photographs on the wall are being removed in two halves, on boards, just as they were *in situ*, so they can be brought into the incident room and displayed as was.'

Charley's eyes lit up. 'Great idea!'

Sergeant Fennell continued, to a captivated audience. 'There is a mass of clothing to be recovered. Over two hundred exhibits have been seized so far, including tools. But I don't want to steal your detective's thunder...' The sergeant scanned the room and his eyes fell on Mike Blake.

'Mike?' Charley asked, a hint of curiosity in her tone.

'Photographed *in situ*, boss, beneath an old wax coat which is bagged, tagged and in our possession, but, I thought you would like to see these in person.' He held up two labelled plastic bags. In one was a left shoe and in the other a right one. 'Pretty sure these are the brown brogues, boss.'

Charley could hardly contain her excitement. 'Get them off to Forensics immediately for confirmation they're the ones in the pictures.'

Mike looked hesitant.

'Are you done?' she asked, giving a sideways glance at Roper – surely he might want to pat his officer on the back, even if he had no kind words for her.

'Yes, yes, but if I could have a word afterwards, ma'am, that'd be great.'

Charley tipped her head in his direction, puzzled that after that one, glorious revelation Mike should have turned shy.

When the briefing was over, Divisional Commander Roper was the first to leave, with nothing more than a slight nod of the head. There was no 'well done team' and she felt aggrieved on behalf of her team. Purposefully, she went to the door and thanked each individual as they left. With work still to do to keep Danny Ray off the streets, the next briefing was planned for six p.m.

Mike Blake was the last to leave. He shut the door before turning to her, his face serious.

'Danny Ray's computer was still on when I was waiting for the POLSA team to go in to search. I think you should know Roper's email address was on his contact list.'

'Is that all? I wouldn't have thought that unusual since they play golf at the same golf club.'

Mike stopped her. 'No, listen, before you say anything else … He's in a group with whom Danny Ray shares indecent images.'

Charley was taken aback and tried to think fast. 'That doesn't necessarily prove that Roper looks at them – and if he hasn't forwarded them on, then there is no offence.' Why was she defending him? 'We will need to seize Roper's computer, though.'

Sergeant Blake, Ricky-Lee and Annie Glover worked diligently. Mike and Ricky-Lee would soon commence the first interview and Annie would join Charley to watch it via the video link in her office. The family liaison officers would now be required to update the families of the victims, including those of Jean Weetwood.

'Make sure Wilkie is aware of what's happening,' Charley said. 'I want him to feel part of the arrest.'

At one p.m., Sergeant Mike Blake and Detective Ricky-Lee Lewis entered the interview room. On the video link, Charley and Annie could see the featureless room. It had no natural light; it was plain, uncluttered and business-like. The prisoner, dressed in a light blue, cotton, one-piece prisoner-issue suit, sat with his back to the officers. Charley and Annie could see clearly that he was dishevelled and unshaven. Before the tape started, he was asked to turn around to face the interviewing officers, but, instead, he settled himself in his chair next to the robust figure of his brief, Mr Thompson, with a straight back, his feet flat to the floor and hands clasped on his lap. His head faced forward, eyes staring at the blank wall, as if he intended to take that stance for the duration of the forty-five-minute tape. The officers sat behind a grey-topped wooden table. Mr Thompson showed the officers – immaculately dressed in suits, collars and ties – his open palms as he shrugged his shoulders.

'I can't make my client turn around, just as much as you can't make him turn around. It would be classed as assault,' Mr Thompson said.

Ricky-Lee pressed the buttons to start the recording and little lights glowed in response.

'For the purpose of the digital recorder,' Sergeant Blake pulled up a pristine cuff from under his pristine suit jacket sleeve and checked his watch. 'It is 13.09 and I am Detective Sergeant Mike Blake of Peel Street CID.'

'And I am Detective Constable Lewis,' said Ricky-Lee who sat alongside him, jacket abandoned on the back of his chair.

'You do not have to say anything, but it may harm your defence, if you do not mention, when questioned, something which you later rely on in court. Anything you do say may be given in evidence. For the purpose of the digital recorder, please give us your name,' he said, looking towards Mr Thompson and to the back of Danny.

They all knew that Danny Ray could hear the officers as they went about asking their questions and putting the evidence before him, giving him every opportunity to respond should he wish to do so. For forty-five minutes the two detectives worked through the questions about the savage attack on Jean Weetwood. Danny made no response to any of the questions, even when they dropped in that his DNA matched that of the rapist. Donald Thompson concentrated on what was being said and constantly made notes. At the end of the interview, the prisoner was returned to his cell and arrangements were made for the barrister to be available for the second interview which would take place at five p.m.

Charley took a deep breath and turned towards a thoughtful-looking Annie. 'This may be all he does for every interview.'

'You've got to hand it to the detectives of yesteryear. Can you imagine what it was like having to record everything in contemporaneous notes, as well as trying to talk to the prisoner?'

Charley nodded. 'Every question asked, every answer given … They had to write bloody quickly!'

'I wonder what life was really like for a copper, pre-PACE. Making sure the prisoner admitted the offence was the most important thing.'

Annie chuckled. 'I've heard there were some interesting interview techniques available.'

'Like threatening a prisoner with the arrest of his wife or taking his kids into care if he didn't cough up to the job? Deemed good interviewing that, by the likes of Roper, putting the offender under intense pressure. "Don't worry about bending the rules, you are acting in the interest of justice," he once told me.'

'Blimey. Really? I was thinking it was all further back in the dim distant past,' the young officer said.

'I'll never forget it … He didn't agree with the fact that we could no longer interview a drunken prisoner, because often they'd admit to anything when under the influence. Since the introduction of PACE, if a prisoner hasn't slept, then they must be allowed a reasonable time to sleep, some would suggest as much as eight hours.'

'I guess keeping a prisoner awake until they coughed was a good ploy, especially during a night.'

Charley agreed. 'Anyone who has experienced sleep deprivation to the extent where your spirit is wearied to death, your legs are unsteady and your one sole desire is to sleep, knows that not even hunger and thirst are comparable. And no one used to ask for legal representation in those days. Or if they did, the news soon flew around the station that they must have done something serious!' Charley chuckled.

'Of course! Otherwise, why would they want a solicitor? The legal aid bill must have gone through the bloody roof post PACE!'

'It did. At one point, legal aid cost almost as much per year as the total funding for over forty police forces in England and Wales.'

'I guess it was the first time the detainee was actually given detailed advice about it.'

At that point, Ricky-Lee stomped into the room, followed by

Mike, and the women's heads turned his way as he flopped into a chair.

'The arrogance of the bloody man! We gave him every opportunity to respond.'

'I think reality has actually hit home, don't you? When we spoke to him about the DNA hit, I noticed an instant change in his stance,' said Mike.

'He knows he's fucked,' said Ricky-Lee. 'It'll be interesting to see what he does when he's faced with the evidence for further charges.'

'Like you said before, boss, he knows the system,' said Annie. 'He's attended crime scenes, major incident court trials. He's got a degree in criminology. He thinks he's an expert. Maybe, just maybe, he thought he was capable of the perfect murder, wrongfooting us with his messing around at the scenes.'

Charley was thoughtful. 'Or maybe he got complacent. Got to a point where he thought he was untouchable because someone had his back?'

Mike gave her a knowing look.

'What worries me is what he's got away with previously. The people who didn't come forward, dared not come forward; it's those that I feel sorry for. The ones who don't have enough faith in the system to report the crime,' said Annie. 'Let's face it, he didn't start out as a full-on murderer, did he? He's got to be a prime suspect for assault, perhaps flashing, before it got to rape and murder.'

Charley felt sick to her stomach. The only other person who knew about his attack on her was Roper and now, with Mike's recent revelation, the past felt like a time bomb ready to explode. But what would Roper have to gain? There must be a reason why Roper hadn't reported Danny sending him indecent images? Did Danny have him over a barrel like Roper had so many others under his command? Solomon Myers hadn't welched on Danny Ray; Danny Ray was at the moment keeping quiet about Roper…

Charley could hear the others talking in the background. She cringed and closed her eyes.

'Vigilance and patience allow us to take advantage of the perpetrator's mistakes. The truth will out,' said Ricky-Lee. 'We'll gain the evidence needed to convict him for all the others and maybe, just maybe, once this is out, some of the others – if there are any others, of course – will trust in us and come forward.'

The others didn't appear to notice Charley's inner struggle as Ricky-Lee continued, 'I don't think he'll respond in the second interview either, though. I think he's actually enjoying the ride now. Gloating over his ability to somehow outmanoeuvre the police and continue to operate under our noses.'

'Yeah, well he might have won a few battles, but he sure as hell hasn't won the war,' said Annie. 'He's met his match in Detective Inspector Charley Mann.'

There was a rap at the door and Tattie entered. 'Mr Ray's desk diary, ma'am,' she said. 'Apparently, although we've drawn a blank with the investigation in relation to Wilkie Connor, he made an entry regarding interviewing a homeless person called Stewart Johnson on the day before he was murdered.'

At the end of the second interview with an unresponsive Danny Ray, and a debrief that yielded no further information or results from Forensics, Charley decided that the night would be best spent in her own bed. Exhaustion was threatening to close her system down as the adrenaline started to subside. Tomorrow was another day.

CHAPTER 25

Despite the bone-deep exhaustion, Charley tossed and turned in her bed, sleeping fitfully. Inspector Roper's voice haunted her; she, the young police officer under his command. Annie Glover's eyes searched hers for more than Charley had told her, her voice gentle, hard to hear against the high-pitched bark of Commander Roper, the angry despot. 'I'll wait to hear from you,' she heard Danny Ray telling Roper in a sinister way. She sat bolt upright in bed. 'I can't sleep! I can't breathe. I've got to get help. I didn't do anything!'

Seven a.m. was late for her to wake. She showered, grabbed a slice of toast and was on her way, her hair tied back but still soaking from the shower.

The incident room was bustling with an industrious team that didn't appear to have slept at all. She opened her office door to see the coffee cups from the previous day still lined up on her desk. She ran a finger over her windowsill and a layer of dust stuck to it. Dead flies had already collected in its corners.

'Tattie?' she called. 'Is there any news of Winnie?'

Tattie shrugged her shoulders. 'No! Not that I know of, anyhow. I'll have a word with Personnel and find out when she'll be back.'

'I keep meaning to go see her, but time is just running away,' Charley said.

Before she had managed to take her coat off and sit down, Mike Blake came into her office and closed the door. She turned to see a look of shock on his face.

'I've just had a call from Fran,' he said. 'Wilkie's perked up a bit more...'

The colour had drained out of Charley's face, she'd feared the worst at the mention of Fran's name. She breathed out in relief.

'Apparently,' went on Mike, 'Wilkie says Danny Ray lured him to a meeting to tell him he knew who the flyer of the drone that led Eddie to his death was. Roper told him he had found out that the drone was one of our own...'

'The drone found in Danny Ray's garage is a police one?'

'He said so, yes.'

There was one thing Charley knew for sure: an admission from those concerned would never be forthcoming, even if it was true.

Danny Ray was at court for remand so they didn't need to concern themselves about him: he was going nowhere and rumour had it that his barrister wasn't making a bail shout on this appearance.

The morning briefing couldn't have been more positive. The evidence trail was of paramount importance and it was imperative they proved every fact beyond doubt, but things were falling into place. The search of Danny Ray's car had revealed damage to the front nearside and fibres had been removed from the edge of the front headlamp and bonnet. These were still being checked against the clothing seized from Wilkie Connor after the accident. Soil removed from the car mats had proved to be a positive match against those found on the bodies, thus putting Danny on site at Gibson's Horticultural. Under the passenger seat, they'd found a used condom containing DNA linked to Solomon Myers, suggesting his relationship with Solomon was sexual.

Charley wondered if he was like any addict, where the craving didn't subside with everyday involvement, so he was always left needing something more. Was murder the ultimate answer to satisfying an insatiable sexual appetite? Again, she asked herself how she had not seen the monster in him.

The case against Danny Ray was building at great pace. He was interviewed about recent events in the order they'd occurred. First, the murder and hanging of Kylie Rogers.

He would neither answer any questions nor look at the interviewing officers. Ricky-Lee threatened to forcibly turn him around, but was advised strongly against the action by Danny's barrister.

'If you do that, there will be, without doubt, an allegation forthcoming of assault by Mr Ray,' said Donald Thompson in warning.

Undeterred, the interviewing officers moved on to question Danny about the murder of Stewart Johnson. But nothing changed in his demeanour. The hit-and-run in respect of DC Wilkie Connor was also met with silence. Mike and Ricky-Lee questioned Danny Ray tirelessly. They asked if the photographs on his wall were those of intended victims, and the aerial photos taken by the drone in his garage, but they received nothing back in response.

There was one question that Charley would have liked him to answer, but, as with the rest: 'Are the brown brogues yours?' was met with a wall of silence.

The pair of interviewers unloaded all the evidence they had in order to give him an opportunity to respond, but he steadfastly refused.

'Charge him with all offences and we'll take him back to court to be remanded in custody until trial,' said Charley.

She collaborated with Prison Liaison to ensure that Solomon Myers and Danny Ray didn't meet within the system. She was told it was unlikely in any case, as Solomon Myers would remain in solitary.

Danny's barrister applied for bail at court, stating that his client would be pleading not guilty. Bail was refused.

'When all the evidence is laid out before him, he may well change his mind, or there again he may want his last stand to be in a courtroom.'

He had tried to wrong-foot the investigation, and with all his experience had expected to succeed, but he had tripped himself up on more than one occasion. He'd underestimated Charley Mann, just as he had done once before. Her biggest regret was that she hadn't stepped up to the mark back then and put her faith in her wider police family. It was fruitless to go back to that now. However, she would ensure he'd never again be able to hurt anyone in the way he had hurt her and his other victims.

The media were already in a frenzy and Danny Ray's trial would no doubt make national news. Over the next few days, weeks and months Charley knew the prosecution file would continue to build; there would be no loose ends, she would make sure of that. All enquiries would be concluded in a timely manner and everything would be disclosed to the defence. The paper file would probably be as tall as her when it was complete, but it would be well worth the effort to see him sent down for good. It would probably be a year before the Crown Court trial, but she knew this would pass quickly and, in the meantime, she, DI Charley Mann, would have to deal with many more crimes.

The Old Moor Cock was where the team, already drunk on success, planned to meet for a drink. Just as she was leaving, PC Susan Vine joined her in the incident room. For a moment she was taken aback to see her own photograph on the boards that Danny Ray had created.

'Gosh, you never know who you're dealing with do you?' she said.

'No, you don't, so remember: never assume anything and you won't go far wrong. If things don't feel right, or look right, there's probably a "rabbit off", as my dad used to say,' said Charley. 'Gut feeling people like to call it, don't they? But me, I just think it's down to natural instinct and being observant.'

Just then, Ricky-Lee burst into the incident room and whipped his jacket from behind his chair. 'They've already started a tab in your name, boss,' he shouted. His smile was infectious. He stopped and turned back at the door. 'You coming, Sue?' He winked at Charley. 'I think I'm in there,' he mock whispered.

She could hear the sound of laughter from where she stood in the pub car park, where the assault had happened so many years ago. But her feeling of triumph was not to last long. Chilled by the voice of someone coming up behind her, she had to force herself to turn. Eyes as dark as midnight stared back at her.

'You've been asking about Winnie, I understand?' said Roper. 'She's asking for you.'

'Me?'

'Yes, you,' he said.

'Tell me,' she said. 'The drone that killed Eddie. Was it really one of ours?'

Roper looked shocked. 'Was the drone one of ours? That's too far-fetched even for you,' he said. 'And, by the way, if you're thinking of reporting me for the indecent images, there is no crime to answer, I didn't pass them on. And, for your information, I've handed in my ticket today. So my pension is secure.'

Charley tapped on the door and waited. She knocked again, louder, like a quick double rap on a drum. There was still no reply. She put the key in the lock and reached for the door handle. Darkened by years of use, the door opened easily. There was no sound from inside the house. She entered cautiously and smelt perfume. Blue Grass, the perfume her dad had always bought for her mother.

In the small hallway, she found herself transported to another time, another place, her childhood home. Straight ahead she saw the stairs and she instinctively knew the hall to her right led to the lounge. Stepping onto the threadbare carpet, she peered around the half-closed door. The room was lit dimly by a table lamp, complete with a fringed shade, which shed just enough light for her to make out the room's furnishings. There were pictures on the bureau, she picked one up. The sight of her dad's young, smiling face, large as life, stared back at her. His image and the perfume overwhelmed her and she reached for a chair to sit for a moment. On a side table, she saw another framed picture and she picked it up. It was of a young couple: Jack and Winnie in each other's arms. They could have been no more than teenagers. The sight made her gasp. She touched her dad's face and a surge of love rippled through her.

Elbow on the chair arm, Charley rested her chin on her hand, trying to sort out what was happening. She had never seen this picture before. Why did Winnie have a picture of the young Jack Mann and why were they together? Her eyes scanned the room, unbelievably similar to the one of her childhood, even down to the snub-armed easy chair, covered in a scarlet velvet darkened by age, which had been her father's favourite at home.

Hearing a faint thud upstairs, she walked quietly back into the hallway and looked up the staircase to see what she thought was a shadow crossing the landing. Charley opened her mouth to shout, 'Hey, Winnie', but the words stuck in her throat.

Reaching the top of the stairs she saw that the streetlight that shone from the outside through the small landing window may well have played tricks: all was quiet and still. Winnie's flowered apron was draped over the bannister along with her outdoor coat, a scarf and a felt hat. Charley didn't try to rationalise her snooping, but let herself into the bedroom, where the old lady lay on her back, bed covers neatly tucking her in, safe and sound. Her head was slightly raised on an embroidered pillow, her thinning white hair coiled in pinned curls around her face. Her soft pink lips were slightly open and her expression was peaceful.

As she could have predicted, Winnie's bedroom was neat and tidy. Only a dressing table set sat on her table, a brush and a mirror, together with Winnie's signature red lipstick. She noticed a shiny edge of paper protruding from the pages of the book on the bedside table: a dog-eared photograph. Curious, Charley pulled it out. It caught her completely by surprise: Jack with Charley, a babe in arms, he laughing into the camera's eye.

Why hadn't Winnie shared their close relationship with her? Had she feared that Charley would pepper her with questions until she'd revealed something that she didn't want to tell? Charley slipped the photograph back inside the book. She had seen more than Winnie had wanted her to see – and the more she knew, the less she understood.

Charley leant her back against the slats of the bedside chair, realising that the woman whom she had known for so much of her life, who had been like a second mother to her, might have plenty of reason to hate her father. Yet, she had obviously loved him enough to let him go…

Long shadows crept across the room, and Winnie slept on. Charley knew she would stay with her as long as was needed. There was no point in waking her. There would be plenty of time to talk when she was stronger. For now, she watched her sleep.

'We did it, Winnie. We got a result,' she whispered into the darkness. 'And Roper's not all he seemed, but I guess you suspected that too. I hope the new Commander will stay for a while and not just want to make sweeping changes then move on. Just like in life, we need some stability at Peel Street.'

THE END

ACKNOWLEDGEMENTS

Our special thanks to our publisher Rebecca Lloyd and everyone at The Dome Press for their hard work and their commitment to making this DI Charley Mann novel the best it can possibly be. To our literary agent David H. Headley at DHH Literary Agency, who 'found us', continues to support us, believes in us as writers and is as passionate about our storytelling and about finding us the right editor as we are about writing the stories. To David's PA Emily Glenister – always on the end of the phone with a cheery voice and the boss's ear. And, last but not least, to talented designer Jem Butcher for making our book look so good!

Thank you to Pamela McNulty, Sarah Dodsworth and Kristine Wilson for your support and contributions, and to our ancestors for sharing with us the fascinating legends, folklore, superstitions and rituals associated with Yorkshire folk and our truly magical home county!